8-2021

DATE DUE

		PRINTED IN U.S.A.

Hayner PLD/Large Print
Overdues .10/day. Max fine cost of
item. Lost or damaged item: additional
$5 service charge.

WHAT COULD BE SAVED

What Could Be Saved

Liese O'Halloran Schwarz

THORNDIKE PRESS
A part of Gale, a Cengage Company

For Marghi Barone Fauss
and
in memory of my parents,
Jacquie and Paul

Wherever I am
I am what is missing.
— MARK STRAND,
"KEEPING THINGS WHOLE"

Bad seven times, good seven times.
— THAI PROVERB

Wherever I am
I am what is missing.
— MARK STRAND,
"KEEPING THINGS WHOLE"

Bad seven times, good seven times.
— THAI PROVERB

PART 1

PART 1

CHAPTER ONE

2019

"Caught in the act," said Sullivan, appearing at the top of the studio stairs. He stood there for a moment, slightly out of breath from the four-story climb.

"Not quite," said Laura. She was in the little kitchen area, working the color from her hands using a rag dipped in mineral spirits; her cleaned brushes lay in an exhausted regiment across the counter.

Sullivan's nose wrinkled. "All this technology and you can't open a window?" he said. "I'm going to find you dead in here one of these days."

"Where's your business sense?" she said dryly as he crossed to the glass panel set into the wall. "My untimely demise would definitely drive prices up." Although how untimely would it be, really? Fifty-four was young enough for people to murmur *so young* but not mean it, old enough for youthful sins to have caught up.

He tapped at the controls. A muted growl came from the back wall as motorized shades

11

began to descend over the windows there. They stopped and reversed. The side lights blinked on and then off again, then the overhead lights on and off. Finally, a click overhead and a whir, and two of the high slanted skylights began to move. Sullivan stood with his head back, watching them lift away from the ceiling. A damp spring air blew in.

"It is a good smell, though," he said, taking his hand down from the control panel. "Means you've been working." He crossed the room to stand in front of the easel. "Another ghost, I see." His voice maddeningly neutral.

Sullivan had been excited about the Ghost Pictures at the beginning. He'd given them a prime-time autumn opening in the New York space, had written lyrical catalog copy: *scraped canvases intrigue the viewer with muted, suggestive images, like the residue of a dream.* That had been four years ago.

"Why are you here?" It came out more abruptly than she'd intended.

"Because you don't answer your phone," he said. "Or email. Or texts." He bent close to scrutinize a section of the painting. "Someone called the gallery trying to reach you."

"I think my phone is downstairs." Finding a clean place on the solvent-wet rag, working it into the webbed crotch between two fingers, she nodded to the landline squatting on the counter. "You could have called me on that."

He shrugged. "It gave me an excuse to check on you."

That was what it had come to. Sullivan was six years younger than she was; at one point, he'd wanted to sleep with her and she'd considered it — he was funny and smart and good-looking, and she'd been feeling raggedy after Adam and wanting a boost — but had decided against it on principles of *don't shit where you eat.* Since then, apparently, Laura had edged over an invisible hill: now Sullivan was checking on her as though she were his elderly aunt.

"Also I promised Kelsey," he added. "She's the one who took the telephone calls."

"Oho," Laura said. Kelsey, the Washington gallery's new front-desk girl. Mid-twenties, very pretty, her manner toward Laura infused with that millennial you-go-girl faux heartiness reserved for the elderly or otherwise pathetic. *It's been a world wind in here,* Kelsey had told Laura when they met. Laura, indulging an evil impulse, had gotten the girl to repeat herself and Kelsey had obliged, speaking more slowly. There again was the space between the syllables, the unmistakable thud of the extra *D:* Kelsey was saying *world wind* — or possibly *whirled wind.* She was at least twenty years younger than Sullivan, but no one would blink if the two of them began an affair. Perhaps they already had.

"Apparently you've ignored *three* emails," said Sullivan. He had his phone out now, was tapping and swiping through screens. "The caller was very upset." Laura imagined Kelsey's whimper: *He yelled at me, he was awful.* "Here." He held out the phone. "Something about your brother. You don't have a brother, right?"

Laura stared at him, then put down the rag and reached to take the phone, ignoring his wince at her still-painty hand. She read the brief message through once, twice; then holding it up before her, eyes on the screen, she walked over to the landline, took up the receiver, and dialed.

"Listen to this email," she said when Beatrice answered. She cradled the receiver between ear and neck and read aloud.

I believe I have found your brother Philip. Are you Laura Preston born on 25 March 1965 to Robert and Genevieve Preston? If so, please reply. If you are not the correct Laura Preston, I am sorry for deranging you. Thank you. Claude Bossert

When she finished, Bea was silent.

"It has my birthday in it," said Laura in an arguing voice. Across the room, Sullivan was looking at her, eyebrows raised. She turned her back on him. "Did Mum ever give out that information?"

"Who knows," said Bea, her words surfing down through the phone on a sigh. "Probably." Her voice held the weary reflexive accommodation of the elder sibling, always an aggrieved shadow of *They left me alone to look after you when I was ten years old* in it. As if the servants hadn't been there too. "Just delete it."

"But why would it come *now,*" said Laura.

The squeak of the terrace door latch, the rattle as it shut: she turned to see that Sullivan had gone outside and was standing at the railing looking down over Woodley Park.

"Did you mention him in the *Post* profile?" said Bea.

"No," Laura said.

"Maybe someone did a deep dive on Google," said Bea. "Everything lives forever on the internet." Voice taut: "You're not thinking of responding to it."

"It didn't ask for money," said Laura.

"The next one will," said Bea.

"Well, they could *ask,* but that doesn't mean I would *give.* One reply email, asking for details — what could that hurt?" Laura heard the bargaining tone in her own voice with irritation. How did an older sister keep the power to shrink you back to childhood? One minute on the phone with Beatrice reduced Laura to the tagalong little sister she had once been, whining *Play with me.*

"I thought we were done with all this," said Bea. "It was the only silver lining about Mum."

"I'm not an idiot." That truculent baby sister again, lower lip stuck out. Laura strove to make her voice neutral. "The first demand for money, and I'd be out."

"Why engage at all?" said Bea. "What would be the point?"

She was so much like their mother, swift and breathtakingly confident in her assessments, dismissing whatever she deemed unworthy of her attention, capably taking charge of the rest. Like their mother *had been,* Laura corrected herself.

A long pause. Morning was leavening the sky outside the windows of her aerie, the knotted spires of the Gothic cathedral pushing up from the skyline. She'd been smart or lucky or both, to add this level to the narrow brick town house back when this was a modest middle-class neighborhood. No way she'd be able to get a permit to do it now.

"Are you going to see Mum today?" asked Bea, her voice turned brisk, as if moving to the next item on a checklist. "I can't get over there. There's a thing at the boys' school." A *thing.* A tennis tournament, or diving championship, or academic awards ceremony: it could be any of those. Beatrice's twins were multiply, almost preternaturally gifted. You'd never know it from Beatrice, though: trophies stayed out of sight in the boys' bedrooms, and she didn't boast about their accomplishments. It seemed like humility, but Laura knew it was actually the most rarefied form of pride. Of course Bea's children were extraordinary; proof wasn't necessary.

"I was planning to have lunch over there —" said Laura. What day was it? She looked at Sullivan's phone, which by now had flicked to the lock screen: Tuesday. "Tomorrow." Thank goodness; she hadn't missed Tuesday dinner. Edward hated when she missed.

"If you do, make sure to check on the garden. Noi says the gardener's been slacking off."

"I will," said Laura. Wondering, what would she look for? Weeds? "But Bea, if it is him," she said. "What if it is."

"It isn't," said her sister. "It never is."

"You hungry?" said Sullivan, coming back inside and finding Laura cleaning his phone off with the mineral-spirit rag. "Come on. I'll treat you to breakfast."

"I was going to take a walk," said Laura. "I haven't been out of this house in three days."

She held his phone out; he took it between two fingers, waving it gingerly in the air to speed the evaporation of solvent.

"Do you want to talk about that whole

17

thing?" He inclined his head toward the land-line.

"Nope," Laura said.

He followed her down the stairs, through the kitchen to the back door she held open for him, stood below her on the long exterior flight of concrete steps while she locked up.

"I'll send the guys for the painting in —" he said.

"Two weeks," she said. It would be varnished by then and dry, ready for transport. At the moment of completion it had been vital, almost like a living part of her; now it was a husk, inanimate, taking up space in her studio. Wampum, to trade for groceries.

Sullivan's car waited in the parking space beside the weedy oblong that was far too small to be called a backyard. He hesitated beside it, keys in hand.

"The new painting," he said. "It's not really new, is it."

His eyes were manganese blue well-diluted, maybe a little viridian mixed in, a rim of indigo. During the last twenty years she had looked into these eyes as often as any others, even Edward's, even her sister's or mother's. A sad statement: her gallery owner might be her closest friend.

"I'm not done with the series," she said. "Or it's not done with me."

"It's just —" he said, and stopped himself.

"What?" she said.

18

"It's starting to feel like a gimmick." In a jokey tone to soften that, he added, "Not to mention a waste of a lot of perfectly good paint."

"Kawara's *Today* series went on for decades."

"Time was part of that concept," he said. He did not add, *And you are not Kawara.* He pressed the fob in his hand and the car double-chirped; he opened the driver's door. "Come on. Let's talk over breakfast. This new place in Tenley does great avocado toast. Also French toast. All the toasts."

"They sell, right?" she said, not moving. "So why do you care?"

He sighed, looked away from her, down the alley. Then back. "I'm going to have to put someone else into the slot I was holding for you in New York."

"Fine," she said, turning away.

"Laura," he called as she took long strides up the one-way alley, past the garbage and recycling bins paired tidily behind each house. As she came out of the alley onto Cathedral Avenue, she heard his car start up behind her and drive away.

This part of Washington was beautifully walkable; Laura hadn't owned a car in years. The neighborhood had evolved since she'd moved there, the teachers and midlevel professionals dying or downsizing, the rich young moving in. The old sidewalks that had been humped and broken over the roots of midcentury maples were jackhammered up and the trees themselves replaced; now concrete flowed in smooth pram-friendly ribbons beside compact and fruitless ginkgoes. Laura reached Connecticut Avenue and turned left, toward what had once been a strip of secondhand shops and bars and a battered Safeway. It was now a decorous array of pastel-painted boutiques, a vegan bakery, a gourmet supermarket. Tucked in the middle was a tiny ultra-hip coffee shop, where Laura joined the line that snaked patiently away from the counter.

She carried her shade-grown, fair-trade decaf latte past a rank of gleaming smartbikes toward the zoo. On a weekday morning with school still in session, crowds would be thin and she'd be able to walk for nearly two miles, taking the long outside loop all the way to the end, swinging around the Kids' Farm and coming back through Amazonia. She paused for a *don't walk* light beside the corner kiosk that was, as always, neatly colorblocked with notices for local events, items for sale, music lessons. She admired the dedication of the invisible someone who managed this small piece of the world, taking down the past-date advertisements and stapling new ones into place.

A mild misting rain had started by the time

she reached the zoo. She discarded the coffee cup into a bin and set off, hands balled in her pockets. The long walk after finishing a painting was usually something she enjoyed: it drove the fumes from her sinuses and stretched out her tight muscles. It also allowed her to savor a curious and temporary aftereffect that made her vision sharper and colors almost surreal, her brain still painting after her body had stopped. But today she found herself brooding, annoyed. By Beatrice's dismissiveness, by Sullivan's bland intrusion, his *gimmick.* With that word he had turned Laura to face what she'd been resolutely trying to ignore.

Down the years, she had known other artists who were suffering from block; she had sympathized, of course, but not really understood. Her mental knock on wood, an internal *There but for the grace of God* had been reflexive and insincere. How smug she'd been, how certain that her own engine of inspiration would never fail.

Yet it had. Or at least, it had downshifted. Laura still turned out paintings regularly — too regularly. Too comfortably. Making art had once felt exhilarating and terrifying, like combustion or freefall, like peeling herself open. It had felt dangerous and important. Had youth been the necessary ingredient there, or naiveté?

She passed a zoo worker, huddled into his

windbreaker. He shot Laura a concerned look and she saw herself through his eyes: a middle-aged woman in jeans and T-shirt and scrubby ponytail, rambling alone past the Small Mammal House in the rain, without an umbrella or even a jacket. She had to laugh: this was what counted as iconoclasm now.

Gimmick. She rolled the word around like a bitter pill. With trepidation, and not a little panic. But also, she realized, gratitude. No one else would have said it. Sullivan's investment in her work wasn't solely financial. He'd been the one to discover her, back when he was a gallery assistant, had stuck by her through the long, slow rise; he was willing to say the hard thing to her now. It was part of the reason why Laura had also stuck with him all these years, spurning the lures dangled by fancier venues. She knew better than most: truth was hard to come by.

When she let herself into Edward's house that evening, the air smelled heavenly. She followed the scent back to the kitchen and found Edward there, at the stove.

"We're at T minus seven minutes," he said with a smile, replacing a lid on a saucepan. When she went to the cutlery drawer, he said, "Table's already set. Just relax."

He poured a glass of wine, nudged it across the counter toward her. The first sip spread across her palate and rolled a rich vapor up into her nasal passages. She watched him plate: a fish fillet laid onto a pallet of ivory grains, a clutch of brussels sprouts nestled beside, a sauce drizzled over the lot.

In the dining room, there were fresh flowers on the table; silverware winked under the chandelier.

"It's a new recipe," said Edward as they sat down. "The sauce has a secret ingredient."

A fancy table for no occasion. A new recipe with a secret ingredient. The conclusion was inescapable: something was bothering Edward. The nature of his work was often confidential, and sometimes when wrestling with a dilemma he could not discuss he'd become terse and preoccupied, a tortoise with his head pulled into his shell. A very productive tortoise: a lot of house projects got accomplished during these periods.

No amount of coaxing would draw Tortoise Edward out before he was ready, so without resentment Laura carried on a largely one-sided dinner conversation, commenting on the fish (quite good), trying and failing to guess the secret ingredient (white pepper).

"Oh," she remembered when they were nearly done eating. "Sully brought over the weirdest email this morning." She told Edward about it, and also what Bea had said.

"How did Sullivan get the email if it was

sent to you?" asked Edward, forking up a bite of fish.

"It was sent to my gallery email," she said. "It's set up so that if my inbox reaches one hundred unread items, he gets an alert. He's like an overflow valve." To Edward's amused headshake, she added, "Bea was in fine form. Totally dismissive."

"She's right, though, isn't she?" he said. "After all this time. It's not really possible."

"It's not *im*possible," she said. "He was never found."

The words opened up a well inside her. That was what it was like — like having a well inside you with no bottom. Things dropped in and fell forever.

Edward was looking at her closely.

"Was there something in particular about this email?" he asked.

"Just a feeling." Although as she said it, she realized that the feeling she'd had that morning had faded significantly; what she felt now was mainly defiance against her sister. "Also this Claude person is persistent — he telephoned the gallery when I didn't respond to the emails."

"He will stop, though, if you don't respond," said Edward. "Right? Sullivan will handle it." There was a tinge there of condescension, as though Sullivan were her trusty Saint Bernard. But then, a minute before, Laura had likened him to an engine part.

24

"I guess I'm curious," she said. "I mean, what would the angle be?"

"Money," Edward said baldly.

"I'm sure you're right."

His eyebrows asked for him: *But?*

"But — my mother wouldn't ignore it." There it was; that was the kernel of the matter. She scraped her knife through the sauce on her plate and watched the line fill in, hearing her mother's admonition across the decades: *Don't play with your food.* "I know I should delete the email and forget about it. But she wouldn't." She looked up at Edward. "What do you think?"

He didn't respond immediately, frowning down at his plate as though scrutinizing the remnants of his dinner. Laura knew his legal mind was ratcheting and processing, choosing language that would convey his meaning as precisely as possible. Others might cheerlead *Go for it* or *Listen to your heart,* with a gushing, easy volubility that had all the depth of a social media Like, but for Edward, delivering an opinion was a commitment.

"I think that you're under no obligation to chase this particular wild goose," he said. "Even if your mother would choose to chase it." A gentle smile as he took up his water glass. "And even if your sister wouldn't."

A lawyerly way to say *Make up your own mind.* Laura laid her silverware across her empty plate, wondering whether Edward's work problem had been knotty enough to have inspired dessert.

Edward put his water glass down, cleared his throat. "Martin asked me today if my girlfriend would be attending the partner dinner on Saturday."

"I haven't forgotten," Laura said.

"My *girlfriend,*" repeated Edward. "That word. At my age. It sounds so . . . flighty."

Flighty he was not. Edward lived by Flaubert's philosophy, *Be regular and orderly in your life, so that you may be violent and original in your work.* Edward's original violence required an alarm at 5:40 a.m. each weekday, ablutions and breakfast and on the road by a quarter to seven, carrying the same steel travel coffee cup that had been brought home and washed out and left on the drainboard the night before. Why waste precious thought choosing a cup every morning? After reliable purveyors of shirts, socks, and underwear had been found, why seek others? *Serial killer closet,* Sullivan had commented after Laura described the row of identical button-downs and slacks to him, back when she and Edward were new.

"Martin could just use my name," Laura said. "He's known me for six years." She added, "You know he does this kind of thing to goad you."

"Maybe so," he said with a hint of surprise.

26

Although his career butted him up daily against politicians and other criminals, he never assumed the worst of people. "Still." He was fussing at his plate, brows knitted, scraping some pearls of quinoa together with the tip of his knife.

"What is it?" she said. Although suddenly she knew.

How could she have been so stupid? It wasn't a work problem that was preoccupying Edward. The flowers, the nicely set table, his nervousness. She knew. She knew, even though she'd had only one marriage proposal in her life before, and that was decades ago and totally different, Adam going down on one knee with a tiny box in his trembling hand, his voice fracturing with emotion.

"We're happy together," Edward said. His knife pushing, pushing the grains into a damp little hill. He shot a glance up at her. "I mean, *I'm* happy."

"We're happy," she said.

"And it has been six years." He laid the knife down and put his hand out to capture hers. "At our age, it's not a big jump. It's not like skydiving." A smile fluttered at the corners of his mouth. "More like stepping down from a curb."

She looked down at her fingers trapped in his. Paint rimed one of her fingernails, Sap Green that had stubbornly prevailed against the mineral spirits, the long shower, the scrubbing with a nailbrush. Rough, dry, big-knuckled, these were not the hands of a bride.

"Why can't we just continue as we are?" she said.

It was terrible to watch the hope drain from Edward's face, see it replaced by disappointment and hurt. What was wrong with her, blurting it out like that? Perhaps the long, solitary hours in the studio these many years had eroded her social skills. Or simply too much wine with dinner.

"We're happy as we are," she said, squeezing his hand. "As you said. We're happy."

He gripped back briefly, then pulled his fingers from hers and took the napkin from his lap, put it onto the table.

"Maybe Shelby was right," he said with a tight, rueful smile. "I should have had a ring." Shelby. So he'd talked to his daughter about this. "I told her you didn't wear jewelry on your hands because of the paint." He stood up, lifting his plate and reaching for hers, carrying both into the kitchen.

Laura could imagine Shelby, who was as forthright as Edward was reserved, telling him *Dad, don't be a dope, it doesn't matter about the paint, women are magpies, we like shiny things.* Shelby's mother, Edward's wife, Elaine, was dead for years yet still part of the world in her vibrant, good-hearted daughter, as well as other ways: the stained-glass panel across the top of Edward's kitchen window that glowed a jewel pattern onto the floor in the light of morning, the layout of the garden beds. Elaine had made Edward a good home. Which he had cherished, and which now he was offering to Laura. She and Edward spent most nights together in this house. Wasn't he simply suggesting the natural next step?

She followed him into the kitchen, where he was scraping the plates into the step-bin.

"I don't need a ring," she said to his back. "I don't need the piece of paper either." After all, the ring and the paper had meant nothing to Adam. She'd learned recently that he'd married again, to a woman barely thirty. Laura hadn't known whether to laugh or cry when she had the realization that on that long-ago day when Adam was down on one knee stammering his eternal devotion to Laura, his future second wife was two years away from being born.

"Do you realize that you never call me just to check in?" said Edward. He let the bin lid drop, set the plates in the sink. "Just to ask how I am doing?"

"Do you want me to do that?" She'd liked that they weren't like other couples, relentlessly checking with each other all the time. She'd also liked, she realized, the Tuesday-Thursday-Saturday template of their dates, the element of spontaneity it granted to the rest of the week. Seeing him always felt like a choice happily made.

"When you disappear into your work, it sometimes feels like I disappear for you too." He turned on the tap, pulled the spray nozzle out of the end of the faucet, and directed it over the dishes. "It isn't just paper," he said. Raising his voice a little above the sound of the water. "And it's not what the paper means. It's what the *absence* of the paper means."

"It means nothing," she said. She put her arms around him, laid her head against his back. "It means that we're happy without it." She felt his shoulder blade moving under her face as he reached forward to turn off the tap.

"I want us to be married," he said, his voice thrumming against her cheek. He turned in her arms and looked down at her. "I know it's old-fashioned. I'm old-fashioned."

"Not that old-fashioned," she said, smiling up at him. "Not like take-your-name old-fashioned." Her voice teasing. She hadn't even taken Adam's surname, and back then she hadn't yet sold a painting.

"I wouldn't ask that," Edward said.

His voice held a wistfulness that surprised her; the flood of rage she felt hearing it surprised her more. His emphasis on *ask* felt like an assault. He wanted to swallow her identity up into his? She took a step back, out of his arms.

"I want us to live in the same house," he

30

continued earnestly, oblivious to her reaction. "You could keep your house, of course, for the studio, and stay there whenever you wanted."

"Thank you," she said, unable to stop the sarcasm that shot out of her like a slim angry knife.

He blinked, perceiving her animosity. "I didn't mean it that way," he said. He turned, opened the dishwasher, began slotting the rinsed items into it. "I don't want to change much. I just want us to be official." Dropping the cutlery into the basket in separate tiny jolts. "I don't want my obituary to include the words *longtime companion.*"

Obituary. "Is this about Geoff?" One of Edward's friends had unexpectedly dropped dead the month before; he'd been a couple of years younger than Edward.

"Not entirely. But his death has made me think about what I want." He corrected himself, "What I need."

"This feels less like a proposal than an ultimatum," she said.

"I did this all wrong," he said, vexed. "Shelby is going to kill me."

"Edward's asked me to marry him," Laura told her mother the next day, at the house in the quiet neighborhood in Northwest Washington now known as Forest Hills. It hadn't been called that when she grew up there. It

31

hadn't been called anything. When the Metro had come in the 1980s, spreading across the area like a crack in a windshield, existing neighborhoods like Cleveland Park and Friendship Heights and Foggy Bottom became Metro stops, and then steadily, like a catalyzed reaction, the rest of the city coagulated into boundaried shapes with names. Real-estate agents had accelerated the process, seizing upon posh-sounding monikers like Crestwood and Berkley and validating their use, and sometime while Laura was in college, or sometime after that, the trapezoid between Connecticut Avenue and Rock Creek became Forest Hills.

Laura and Genevieve were sitting out on the screened porch, overlooking the side garden. The azalea was at peak, making its blaze against the far wall, and bees toiled among the near flowerbeds. Laura watched a tall coneflower swaying just outside the screen, a bumblebee hugging the yellow-gumdrop center and scrambling pollen against its belly. The property was a marvel in spring. As a child, Laura had been unimpressed by her first American winter — cold and snow had seemed part and parcel of the unwelcoming strangeness of the return — but spring had been a magnificent surprise, the dead land resurrecting in a way she had never seen. It was a reliable annual miracle. Everywhere she looked now, things were budding and blooming. From here, she couldn't see any lassitude on the part of the gardener. Goddamn Beatrice anyway.

"How wonderful," said Genevieve. "Have you set a date?" Was it cruel, having this conversation? Her mother wouldn't remember it tomorrow. "There's a narrow window, of course, if you want to have it outside."

"We're not outside-wedding people," said Laura. Of course, they might not be wedding people at all. They'd agreed last night to shelve the subject, *put a pin in it* as Edward had said; they'd both pretended that everything was all right. But it wasn't all right.

"Good for you," said Genevieve. "All the bugs, and everyone's heels sinking into the grass." Her face became thoughtful. "The InterContinental has a generator. They do book up fast in the rainy season, though."

"We don't have to worry about a generator. Or the rainy season." To the uncertainty that flitted across her mother's face, she said, "We're in Washington." And the old Siam InterContinental had been demolished decades ago, she didn't add.

"Well, that's convenient," said Genevieve.

She doesn't lay down new memory, the neurologist had explained to the daughters at the time of diagnosis four years before. He'd added with an apologetic air that he couldn't be more specific about what type of dementia it was. It didn't behave exactly like Alz-

33

heimer's, which kept long-term memory intact well into the process, nor like Pick's disease, which came with characteristic MRI findings, nor Lewy body dementia with accompanying Parkinsonian traits. Laura hadn't known that there were so many eponymous ways to be senile.

The damage wasn't limited to Genevieve's frontal lobes (the doctor pointed to the pinched tops of the walnut-looking brain on the MRI, then moved his hand in a loose claw around his forehead); it was more scattershot. The result was a stunning erasure, great swaths of memory taken and occasionally, unpredictably restored, like an electrical short buzzing on and off. Which meant that Genevieve's social behavior was fundamentally preserved, and casual conversation with her could often seem quite normal. Probably that had helped to delay the diagnosis, said the neurologist.

He'd brought Beatrice and Laura into his office to discuss his findings. She was *where?* he'd said, frowning down at the referral letter from the primary doctor. After hearing the details, he'd maintained an air of slight reproach, clearly feeling that the daughters had been wickedly irresponsible to let their elderly mother travel so far from home. As if anyone could have stopped her. *It doesn't matter what it's called,* Bea had said. *Is there any treatment?* The doctor's expression had answered before he opened his mouth to reply.

"I don't know if I want to get married," Laura said now.

"Why not?" asked Genevieve. Simply curious. No undercurrent of *At your age, it's astonishing that anyone is asking.* This unlayered, gentle inquiry was so unlike Genevieve in her prime that Laura felt pierced anew by loss. She was reminded of what Edward had said: it's what the *absence* means.

"I don't know," Laura said. "He's sweet to me, and we're very companionable. It's hard to think of my life without him." For that seemed to be the alternative. She and Edward had retreated from the cliff edge, had turned their backs on it, but now they knew it was there. "Still. I panic when I think about it." There it was again, that threatened feeling of being swallowed, of being ingested and made null. She hadn't felt that when Adam proposed — but when she looked back, she could see how juiceless and rote that decision had been, how she and Adam had been simply doing the expected, following some heteronormative pathway laid down over centuries, like a pheromone track for an unthinking column of ants, *love and marriage and baby carriage.*

"Is there a spark?" said Genevieve. "You

35

know what I mean." She raised her eyebrows, those two delicate paintbrush strokes above her still-brilliant blue eyes. "Are you compatible physically?"

"That part of things is quite good, actually," said Laura, feeling prudish and uncomfortable. Never in her long life had Genevieve alluded to sex in Laura's presence.

"Well then," said Genevieve, leaning back again, flapping a hand. "That's not everything, but it is important." She lifted her iced tea glass and pursed her mouth at the straw, but an exhaled breath made it slide around the curve of the rim and she didn't quite capture it.

Laura leaned forward, caught the straw and held it steady between two fingers. Genevieve laughed, as if Laura had done something inexplicable and amusing.

"Have some iced tea," prompted Laura.

Genevieve sipped obediently. "I think that's gone off," she said, releasing the straw with a moue.

Laura took the glass from her and put it onto the table. There was nothing wrong with the tea; her own tasted fine. *Their taste buds can change,* the doctor had said. *They'll like things very sweet or very salty; they might dislike things that they've always enjoyed.* So what's left of the self, wondered Laura, after personality traits and memory and personal preferences have all been taken away? When does one stop being the same person?

Genevieve hadn't yet transformed in some ways Laura and Bea had been warned to expect: no combativeness or paranoia or incontinence. At this stage, she most resembled a forgetful Girl Scout: polite, cheerful, and resilient, folding new facts into an invented narrative and then forgetting the whole thing, letting it go like someone dropping a package into a stream. Not for the first time, Laura wondered if loving this softer Genevieve as much as she did constituted a betrayal of the mother who'd raised her.

"Bea and I are in disagreement about something," Laura said. Another freedom of conversation with Genevieve 2.0: non sequitur was totally acceptable. "I'm nearly at the point of eeny-meeny-miney-moe."

"Catch a tiger by the toe," said Genevieve.

"Exactly," said Laura. "I know what Bea would do. And I know what you would do." The old Genevieve, she meant; who knew about the new one? "I'm trying to figure out what I should do."

Genevieve took the iced tea glass from the little table beside her.

"Well, what's the downside?" she said with the glass halfway raised, and when Laura didn't answer right away she lowered it and explained, enunciating carefully as though to a foreigner. "Consider the worst possible outcome, and the degree of risk you're willing to bear that it will come to pass. Doing that will often make a difficult decision quite easy." She raised the glass again, nimbly caught and held the straw between two fingers, took a long pull of tea.

The lucidity was startling and sudden. Was it just a bit of the past, hiccuping up whole into Genevieve's consciousness like a tangled knot of kelp rising to the surface of the ocean? Or had the shorting circuits made a true connection — was Laura actually conversing with the old Genevieve?

"That's a good way to think about it," Laura said, cautious, as if trying not to frighten off a bird that was hopping toward her hand. "There isn't really a downside."

"There you are, then," said Genevieve in that same crisp voice. She took another sip of the tea and grimaced. "That's gone off, we'll need to tell someone." She looked around, as though for a waitress. The old Genevieve, glimpsed so briefly, was gone again. In a hotel lounge, perhaps. There had been so many hotel and airport lounges in her history, so many club sandwiches and iced teas.

But she'd been with Laura for a moment, she had. And the electric joy, now ebbing, that had surged through Laura told her that she'd been wrong before, totally wrong. She didn't love the new Genevieve more; how could she have thought that? And she knew what the old Genevieve would want, of course she did. Blinking away tears, she took her phone from her pocket.

"What are you doing, dear?" asked Genevieve. She had never had a habit of saying *dear.* It was probably what the speech therapist called a prop word, being deployed in this case to obscure the fact that she wasn't sure of Laura's name.

"Nothing," said Laura. She tapped in a short message, waited for the *whoosh* of the email going out, and then put her phone down and stood, taking up her mother's glass. "I'll get some lemonade instead, shall I?"

Coming back through the center hall carrying the lemonade, she paused outside her mother's sitting room. An uninterrupted monologue came from upstairs: Noi on the telephone, giving someone lengthy instructions. Laura set the glass onto the marble table in the hall and went into the sitting room, walked around the desk to pull open the bottom drawer. It still held the sturdy manila envelopes Genevieve used instead of file folders. Laura had that habit too now, standing the envelopes on their ends, putting them in strict alphabetical order. Edward had been delighted by Laura's desk drawers. She flipped through the envelopes. Maybe it wouldn't be there. But it was, standing among the others, inscribed with the single word: *Philip.* Laura hesitated, then took it out and closed the drawer. She slipped the envelope into her messenger bag, which was slouching in the entry hall, then retrieved the lemonade and took it to her mother.

The reply to Laura's email came the next evening. It said nothing about money.

Thank you for responding. He was living here in Bangkok with my father, who died last month. I'm writing for him, as I believe that he has not used email before. I am hoping you can help with the next step. I am settling up the house.

Has not used email before? That seemed frankly insane. Even Genevieve had used email until her diagnosis. *Hoping you can help* sounded vaguely scammy-solicitous. Laura was regretting the impulsive decision to answer the email. She looked at the digital clock at the top of her laptop screen. Six-fifteen p.m. here meant five-fifteen a.m. in Bangkok. Apparently Claude was an early riser.

Do you have Skype? she typed into a reply email. *Can we video call?*

If this was a fraudster in an internet cafe in Côte d'Ivoire or Bangladesh or Ukraine, video would be out of the question. Laura would get an excuse saying the computer's

40

camera was broken, or the connection too slow.

My Skype name is Claude4142 came the answer.

A couple of minutes later the bouncy ringtones sounded, and then the video blinked to life on Laura's screen, showing a glowing white sweep of forehead and a pixelating eyebrow. The head retreated and the image coalesced into a sixtyish gamine with a chin-length haircut and red lipstick.

"Allô," she said, frowning at what must be the location of Laura's face on her screen, her eyes looking down instead of directly into the camera. "Miss Preston? Laura?" Her accent sounded French.

"Yes," said Laura, resisting the urge to shout. "Um, Claude?"

"Yes," said the woman. With a pitch of her head back and forth, as if shrugging off an accolade, she added, "Claudette."

In the old days, such an exchange would have taken weeks, onionskin envelopes borne by airplanes crossing above the clouds, perhaps an enormously expensive telephone call, the dialogue overlapping and echoing. Not anymore. In this miracle age everyone was connected all the time, as though by a Möbius strip of electrons flowing unbroken around the earth, and it had taken only a few moments to bring the two of them face-to-face, the video a bit fitful but the sound

41

perfectly clear.

Claudette was waving to someone off-screen. *"Moment,"* she said to Laura, and moved out of view as a shape loomed into the frame to replace her. A slender man, wearing what looked like muslin pajamas, like the garb of a hospital patient or an inmate. Was his head *shaved*? He walked slowly, irregularly forward — was he limping? — coming closer and closer until Laura was looking at his midsection. *"Elle est là,"* said Claudette's off-screen voice, and the man backed away again. The picture froze for a second, a line of static fizzling across the screen, and then abruptly his face was very close.

"Lolo?" he said. The image went transiently Cubist, patching itself with blocky pixels, then juddered into perfect clarity. His mouth was puckered with concentration; his brown eyes looked into hers. She could see her own face reflected, tiny pale ovals twinned in the black of his pupils. "Is that you?"

CHAPTER TWO

"Didn't you ask him *any* questions?" asked Edward, following Laura as she took the overnight bag out of her guest room closet and carried it into her bedroom. "You didn't ask him *anything* about where he's been all this time?"

"The connection was terrible," she said, scooping clothing from bureau drawers. "Clear for less than a minute before the call dropped." It seemed that all Laura had been able to say as the video sputtered and froze was *Oh my God,* and then when the call failed and would not reconnect, *Stay there, stay there,* the way you'd shout to a friend who was leaning over the upper floor in an indoor mall waving to you as you ran to the escalator. *Stay there, I'm coming.* "It's lucky my passport is still good." It had almost expired, slumbering in a drawer.

"And you think it was him?" he said. "What did he say to prove that it was him?"

"He didn't have to say anything." She laid

T-shirts and underwear onto the bed, tumbled an armful of socks beside them.

"Just stop," said Edward, putting his hands on hers. "Stop for a minute."

He sat on the bed and after a moment she sat with him, among the soft piles of clothing.

"You realize that this is crazy," said Edward intently.

"Not if it's him," she said.

"You know that's not likely," he said. "You know that the odds are very, very much against it." He was still holding her hands in his; he squeezed them. "Take a breath and just think for a minute. What did you see — or what did he say — that made you think it was him?"

She hated being told to *take a breath,* like a child, like a hysterical woman. Much less being told to *think.* It wasn't like Edward to condescend in that way, but naturally he was very alarmed, having arrived to pick her up for Thursday dinner-and-movie and found her packing.

"How do you explain how you recognize your brother?" she said.

"Well," he said. Extremely reasonable. "I grew up with my brother. I saw him every day of my life from the age of three until I went off to college. I've seen him regularly since then. That's how I recognize him. I wouldn't necessarily recognize someone

44

whom I hadn't seen since childhood."

"You might if it was your brother," she said.

He tried again. "Was there something specific about the man you saw? His features, his voice?"

She groped around in her memory to find whatever had surged up in her when looking into the man's eyes on the screen, but it was like reaching into a fog; what she grasped at dissipated and swirled away.

"He looked like Daddy," she said, finally. "His face looked like Daddy's." She frowned. "He's bald, though." Her father had always had a good head of hair. But if this man were Philip, he was older now than Robert ever got to be; maybe, given time, Robert would have lost his hair too. "Or his head could be shaved. It was hard to tell. He was tall like Daddy." At least, he'd been a lot taller than Claudette.

"What else?" said Edward. "What did he sound like? How did he seem?"

"He seemed — amused. Not silly. More like wry." She didn't add that his voice hadn't sounded quite American. There had been something about the vowels. Laura herself had apparently had an accent when they came back to the States; teasing from her new schoolmates had made her aware of it. "Like he was thinking of a private joke. Not laughing *at* anyone. Not really even smiling. Just — calmly amused."

"Okay," said Edward. With energy, as though she'd handed him a tool that he could use to pick a stubborn lock. "Not frantic, or frightened, or overcome with emotion?" She shook her head. "So — not much like a person who'd been abducted and held prisoner. Not like a person who's seeing his sister for the first time since he was eight."

"Maybe he's got Stockholm syndrome." She had a thought. "Or maybe he has what Mum has. Maybe he doesn't even know where he is."

"How well do you remember your brother?" asked Edward. "You were very young."

"I was seven," she said. An actual lifetime ago, and also yesterday. "We were close." But had they really been, or was that something she had been told for so long that it had taken the place of memory?

"Try something for me," he said. "Close your eyes and try to picture him as a child."

She closed her eyes and looked at the brown darkness inside her lids. After half a minute or so during which she banished a dozen stray thoughts, there he was, Philip, a little blond boy standing beside the open door of a car. His face was screwed up, his eyes squinted as though he was looking into the sun or bracing himself for a blow. Where had that image come from?

"Tell me about him." Edward's voice was soft. "Keep your eyes closed and look at him."

46

"He had blond hair," she said. "Almost white. We both did then." Keeping her eyes closed, feeling a bit foolish and stagey, the way she'd felt during the hypnosis sessions she'd done in her thirties in order to quit smoking. "He was small for his age. People always asked if we were twins." She smiled. "He'd get very offended by that; he was fifteen months older." The boy in her mind's eye looked nervously defiant. How unfair, to make one shutter-click moment in a person's life represent that whole person. As she was thinking that, she remembered her hands being enfolded, similar to the way Edward was holding them now, and an earnest voice: *I'll teach you.*

"He was kind," she said, her voice breaking a bit, tears brimming behind her closed lids. "He was a good brother."

"Okay," Edward said. "So what you remember is a small, blond, kind boy." She nodded. "And today you spoke with a tall, bald, wryly amused middle-aged man, for less than a minute on a bad Skype connection."

She opened her eyes. Was this what Edward did as a prosecutor, did he use a witness's own words to break her, selecting among them and repeating them back, nibbling away at certainty and fostering doubt? She pulled her hands from his.

"I knew the man on the video," she said. "I knew him."

47

"Maybe you wanted to," said Edward gently.

"Maybe. I don't know," she said. "But what I do know is that if Mum were able —" Her voice buckled in her throat; with effort, she made the next words firm. "She would go. So I am going."

She stood up, put the bag onto the bed, pulled the zipper to open it, then rolled a T-shirt into a cylinder of cloth and tucked it inside.

Edward said, "Is any part of this you running away from — what we talked about?"

"Edward, no. It's not about that." She pushed some sock balls into the deep corners of the bag. "I know this isn't rational. But that's just it — it's not rational. It's how I feel." Five narrow rolls of underwear; she considered and added another pair. A dictum of Genevieve's: you never, ever regretted extra underwear.

"Have you actually booked a flight?" He looked relieved when she shook her head. "If you can wait a couple of weeks, I'll go with you," he said.

"No," she said, then tried to soften it by adding, "I'm not sure how long it will take." Edward's schedule was too tight to insert a hairpin, the way he liked it. No room there for an open-ended, spontaneous overseas trip.

"You remember that NPR segment about internet hoaxes," he said as she rolled up two pairs of loose cotton trousers and laid them beside the soft bricks of underwear. "We both said how nuts it was, that that man flew to Africa after a few emails." The man had been robbed and beaten, left for dead; the report had speculated about other victims who hadn't survived to tell their stories.

"I honestly don't think Claudette is running a lonely-hearts fleecing operation," Laura said. She doubled a brassiere, cup nestled into cup, slid it into a chink of space.

"There are other kinds of scams," said Edward. Then, "What did Bea say? Why isn't she going with you?"

"Bea has thirty thousand things on her schedule this week alone," said Laura evasively. A pair of jeans, a light sweater for the sure-to-be-air-conditioned hotel. The little bag was nearly full.

"You could take Noi. To translate."

"Noi has a life, she can't just drop everything," said Laura. "I think I'll be able to get along in English. Bangkok is a major city." She spoke with an authority she didn't feel. She hadn't been to Bangkok as an adult; she didn't know anything more about what it was like now than a person who'd never been there at all.

Into one side pocket of the bag went the transparent plastic baggie of travel-size, TSA-friendly toiletries, a bottle of ibuprofen in case of migraine, antacid for gastric reflux, antihistamine for allergy, prescription thyroid pills. If it took a village to raise a child, it took a pharmacy to support someone over fifty.

"I am begging you," said Edward. "Please step back from this for a minute." Frustration and concern radiated from him. "What's your plan for after you get there?"

"I'll bring him back." She zipped the bag shut.

"What if he doesn't have a current passport?"

"I'll get him one," she said. "I have Mum's papers." From the top of the bureau she retrieved the manila envelope that she'd smuggled out of the Tudor after lunch with her mother. She slid it into the large flat external pocket of the bag, all by itself, where it would be safe if any of the liquids leaked in flight. She stood back, considered. Had she forgotten anything?

"That won't be enough," Edward said. "Are you listening? Look at me." His brow was wrinkled, his eyes intense. "Those papers demonstrate that there was once a boy named Philip Preston. They won't prove that the middle-aged man living in that house is that same boy."

"The embassy will help," said Laura. As Edward opened his mouth to respond, she said, "Stop. I'll figure things out when I get there."

50

He followed as she carried the bag downstairs. In the foyer, she turned to face him.

"I know you don't want me to go," she said. "I understand that. But I'm a grown-ass woman." She'd heard this phrase in movies and podcasts, but hadn't ever spoken it before. After hearing herself say it, she decided she probably wouldn't again. "I really am fully capable of making decisions." If he were her husband, if they were legally bound, would she be obligated to defer to his feelings? Was that part of what was included in *making it official*? "That's my brother. I'm going to go get him. You need to stop trying to stop me."

"I'm not trying to be overbearing," Edward said. "I'm concerned, Laura. I'm concerned the way anyone who loves you would be concerned. And if you're so sure about this, why haven't you told your sister?" He was guessing; Laura's face told him he was right. "Why not make another video call? This time with Beatrice. She's older; she has to remember him better than you do."

"She wouldn't agree to that. She didn't even want me to answer the email."

"Just ask her," said Edward. "Please."

Laura set down the bag and took her phone from her pocket.

I think it might actually be Philip, she typed. Call me.

She sent that to Bea, then typed another

message and sent a second text bubble to nestle on the screen below it:

I don't want to do this without you.

"Thank you," Edward said, relieved. "Please promise you'll wait to hear back from her before doing anything —" He put his arms around her and buried the next word, whatever it was going to be, in her hair. *Rash. Stupid.* Or possibly, if she gave him the benefit of the doubt, just *more.*

While waiting for Bea to respond, Laura and Edward stayed in for dinner and streamed a movie, as if it were any ordinary evening. Not totally ordinary, as they never did these things at Laura's house, where the refrigerator was typically empty and the creature comforts sparse. Edward didn't suggest they go back to his, though; he studied the options on the food delivery app on her phone and gamely folded himself onto the sofa in her office to watch the movie on the monitor swiveled around on her desk. It all had a somewhat concessional feeling, as if Edward was trying to demonstrate that he could be flexible, that merging their lives would not be a one-way effort. Or perhaps he was simply being practical, keeping an eye on Laura so she didn't go to the airport.

As they dished out vindaloo and saag and divided up the samosas, the brittle dialogue between them eventually loosened into real conversation. The movie was good and by the closing titles, with her phone silent and forgotten on the armrest and Edward yawning beside her, the tingling excitement that had been like champagne in Laura's arteries after the Skype call had dissipated. The whole episode seemed foolish now, like the vaporous logic of a fever dream considered in the light of day. The rush-packed bag in the front hall was frankly daffy. No wonder Edward had been so upset.

"I can stay," Edward said as he stood up and stretched, his anxious glance at the clock undermining his words.

"No, it's okay," she said. "You don't have any stuff here. You'd have to get up so early."

He put his arms around her, his forehead against hers.

"Promise you won't fly away in the middle of the night," he said.

"I promise," she said.

Their kiss good night almost ignited into something, but with effort Laura pulled back, patted him on the chest with her flattened hands, *There, enough,* and pushed him out of the door to his car.

Wandering back through the house turning off lights, she paused in the living room, where she'd left her laptop open. The browser homepage was a search window; its cursor blinked at her.

She'd read an article once about anonymous aggregated search data, how people often typed full sentences into Google, questions about personal dilemmas, as if beseeching an oracle. *How can I tell if he's cheating* and *What if it's cancer.*

She sat, took the computer onto her lap, and typed into the search box *Should I go to Bangkok.* In just a few clicks she found herself down an internet rabbit hole, in a discussion forum for frequent long-haul air travelers. It was amazing how much that specialized community found to discuss and quarrel about, in message threads cryptic with acronyms and inside jokes. *Update: the new 767 widebodies have a seat pitch of 30 degrees, unbearable. AVOID.* When Laura's phone buzzed, she put it to her ear with one hand, the other still tapping the down-arrow key to scroll.

"Don't want to do *what* without me?" came into her ear.

"Thanks for responding so quickly."

"We were having a no-screens night," said Bea. "I checked my phone before bed, and got this — what is this?"

"Just what it said."

"You think it's Philip. What, that email from the other day? Based on what?" Bea's voice was accusing but late-night low, although her children were not sleeping infants anymore but teenagers, probably online-gaming with headsets on, upstairs in her suburban mansion.

"A video call," Laura said. She was being obnoxiously curt, she knew it. She'd planned to explain everything carefully and clearly and without emotional overlay, but Bea's attitude had put her back up. Some grooves of siblinghood were cut so deep that no measure of good intentions could jump the needle free.

"You responded to the email." A barely suppressed sigh.

"He called me Lolo." Laura switched to a travel search engine window in her browser, typed in IAD, then BKK. "No one else has ever called me Lolo except family." She scrolled down, checking boxes to limit the search. "Also, his eyes."

"Lolo is in your email address," Bea said. "What about his eyes?" Then, her voice sharp, "Are you *texting*?"

Laura stopped pressing keys. "No."

"Tell me about the video call, please." A clipped imperative.

Laura described it: how Claude, the writer of the email, had turned out to be not a man but a brisk Frenchwoman; how the person who was supposed to be Philip was tall and bald and how although the connection was poor and extremely brief, she'd had a very good look at his face.

"What did you say to him?" asked Bea.

55

"What did he say?"

"I asked him 'How are you?' and he said 'All right.' " She heard his voice again, that odd, not quite American pronunciation. "And then the call failed and wouldn't reconnect."

"Did he —" But Bea cut herself off. It was too big, there were too many questions. "I can't believe you did that."

"We could video-call him together. You and me," said Laura.

"You *know* it can't be him. It's ridiculous."

"Tell me that after you see him for yourself," said Laura.

A pause.

"I'm not sure how much that would help," said Bea.

"What do you mean?"

"I'm not sure I would recognize him," she said. "I barely remember him."

"How is that possible?" said Laura, indignant. Beatrice had been *twelve.*

"I feel bad enough about it," snapped Bea. "It's hard now to sort out what I remember and what I was told," she added in a softer voice. "You know, all those fundraisers." The ones Laura hadn't been allowed to help with. "Maybe we should talk to Uncle Todd."

"He didn't even know Philip," said Laura, trying to keep the eye roll out of her voice. She'd always found Bea's hero worship of Uncle Todd annoying. He wasn't their uncle, wasn't even a friend of the family. He was a

Company man who had appeared in the wake of their father's death like a benefit issued along with the pension payments. After the funeral he'd been a recurrent presence, attending school graduations and sending along cards at birthdays and Christmas signed *Fondly.* Laura didn't even know who'd named him Uncle — probably Bea. While Genevieve had always been politely indifferent to him and Laura had tolerated him, for some reason Bea treated him almost like a stepfather.

"He might be able to do a background check on that Claude person," Bea was saying. "I hate to waste his time on something like this, though."

"Mum wouldn't think it was a waste of time," said Laura. "She would have replied to the email right away. She would have flown to Bangkok by now."

"*Would have* means nothing," said Bea. "All we have is *is.*" A sigh. "Hold on while I look at my calendar." Some muffled noises as she took the phone from her ear. Her voice returned, sounding farther away, obviously in speakerphone mode. "You picked the worst time to pull this."

Laura's hands crept back to her keyboard, pressed keys quietly. Her sister's doubt had chased her own away; she felt the tingling in her blood again.

"I can do a video call tomorrow," said Bea, as if granting a great favor.

Laura scrolled down the list of outgoing flights and clicked to select IAD to NRT leaving very early Saturday morning, connecting NRT to BKK and arriving midafternoon local time on Sunday.

"Hello?" said Bea. "Can you arrange it for tomorrow night? You have to come here." Of course Laura would have to go there; Bea had never been to Laura's house. There was always a good reason not to — the traffic; the children; it made the most sense to meet at the Tudor instead, where they could also see Mum — but still the fact remained that after arguing vociferously against the expenditure for the renovations to Laura's house, Bea had never seen the final product.

"I'll send an email to Claude right now," Laura said, clicking BOOK RESERVATION.

She and Bea made the video call together the next evening from Bea's Northern Virginia home, in the bay-windowed nook on the ground floor that Bea used as an office, with her sixteen-year-old twins hovering curiously in the background. Clem wasn't there, and Laura didn't inquire. One didn't ask where Clem was, just as one had never asked about Daddy.

"Hey, guys, what's the latest brainmelt?" said Laura to the nephews, while Skype was starting up. "Still *Fortnite*?"

"*Fortnite* is for babies," said Dustin.

"Not necessarily babies," said Dean, hastening to gentle his brother's statement. "Just — not serious gamers."

"It's all about loot crates," said Dustin with derision. "Not really about skill."

She didn't see enough of these boys; they were growing into men in between her visits, stuttering from eager rambunctious youngsters to awkward adolescents to near-adults with the wispy beginnings of facial hair. Dustin had given her a hug when she'd come in, and her nose had come to his shoulder.

"Hey, what are you two doing home on a Friday night?" Laura asked.

"Final exams next week," said Dean. She'd gotten a smile but no hug from Dean, who was shyer and more solemn than his brother. Laura had never had trouble telling the twins apart.

"What's a loot crate?" said Laura.

"Focus," said Bea sharply, as the Skype ringing tones began. "Boys, give us some privacy, please." They complied good-naturedly, no curdle of rebellion on their identical faces, returning to the adjacent great room, where they'd been lounging when Laura had arrived.

Claudette answered as before, saying "He is just coming" without explaining the delay, or where he was coming from. The connection was again poor, and the conversation as a result was halting. Bea asked questions Laura

59

hadn't thought to: How had Claudette become involved, how long had Philip been living there?

"My father died last month," said Claudette. She didn't pause to allow the offering of condolences. "I came to settle his affairs and found this house full of people." Her arched eyebrows invited them to join in her surprise. "I sorted the others, and now your brother is the only one left in the house." Her tone was hard to read — did she mean *in the house* like vermin, or like a stowaway, or like a prisoner? The video froze, and her next sentence began in its middle. "— he gave me your names, and I used Google."

That explained why she'd contacted Laura. Bea had been married and using her husband's name since before there was an internet, and while Genevieve had had a significant internet presence at one time, at this point it was vestigial. She was a smiling figurehead on the Foundation's website, a reverent mention on its About page; there wouldn't be current contact information for her online.

"Here he is," said Claudette. She turned the computer a little bit, toward a bank of windows; the screen went bright white, and the figure that lurched into the frame appeared first as a tall dark column wrapped in a flare of light. The column sat down in front of the computer, blocking the sun, and the picture adjusted, slowly congealing into the same gaunt man in mental-hospital pajamas whom Laura had seen during the previous call. Laura stared at his eyes, trying to see what she'd seen before.

"Don't cry," said the man who might be Philip.

I'm not crying, Laura almost said, but Bea spoke first.

"I'm not crying," said Bea. Her eyebrows were lowered and her features were drawn together; for a moment she was thirteen again, fierce in that way she'd been at the new American school, wielding a field hockey stick with vicious accuracy, making the varsity team on her first try. "Is that you? Philip?"

"How are you, Beatrice?" said the man. "Queen Bea."

"Where have you been?" Her voice was a flickering flame between anger and disbelief.

"Mostly here," he said, a patch of static flitting across the image. "Where have you been?" It had the cadence of a routine politeness: *Very well, and how are you?*

"You know what I mean," she said.

There was a ghost of a smile on the man's face. "You're not sure it's me," he said.

"It's been a very long time," said Bea.

"You look the same," said Philip.

"I don't, actually," said Bea. "And you don't either. If it's you."

"If it's me," said the man.

61

There was a pause, the two eyeing each other across the continents.

Then Bea leaned closer to the screen. "What was the color of your Easter basket ribbon?" she asked, rapping the words out, delivering the question like a gunshot.

In the wake of her surprise, Laura thought: *Clever Bea. Clever, clever Bea.* The answer had kicked through her own mind immediately.

They'd had the same baskets every year, heavy with treasure, gold-wrapped chocolate coins and slippery American jellybeans suspended in nests of ribboned green cellophane. Larger items rested on top of the faux grass, wooden Swiss-made toys or metal Chinese-made toys, a sparkling hard-sugar egg *not for eating* with a peephole in its side and a pastoral scene within. And always, leaning against each basket handle, presiding over the hoard like a solid-chocolate emperor, the rabbit. In a clear crackling bag stamped with the logo of a Belgian chocolatier in Washington, somehow transported across the world without melting. The children never questioned that Easter-morning magic, scrambling around the house in a rare episode of sanctioned chaos, each hunting for his or her specific basket. The floppy satin bow tied onto Laura's basket was pale yellow. Bea's ribbon was light blue. Philip's was a pastel green.

It was such a good question. Who else would know the answer but a Preston child? Robert was gone, and Genevieve was as good as gone.

"*B* for Bossy," said Philip, still with that almost-smile.

"We called you that," Laura murmured to Bea. "Philip and I. We called you Bea for Bossy, behind your back." She just now saw the pun in it — that Bea was a homonym for the letter *B.* She felt a stab: they'd been so young.

"What color was your ribbon?" Bea pressed Philip, ignoring Laura.

He could have forgotten, thought Laura. Couldn't he? He could have forgotten the ribbon. He could have forgotten the Easter baskets themselves. Perhaps Laura and Bea remembered the details so well only because the tradition had persisted for them until they were well into their teens, the same baskets and the same bows. If Laura had been eight the last time she'd seen her basket, she might not now remember anything about it at all.

The camera jerked around, the video pixelating and then settling on Claudette's scornful face. "You're asking him to remember a *ribbon*?" she demanded. "Ask a better question." She shoved the camera back into its former position, so that Philip's face was centered again. Off-screen, Claude's voice continued: "The name of your school. The dog's name."

"We didn't have a dog," said Bea and Philip in unison.

"Voilà." Claude, off-screen, triumphant.

Bea put a hand in front of her mouth to shield it from the camera, whispered to Laura. "The school was Pattaya?"

Laura shook her head no. If Bea could confuse the name of their school, Patana, with the Thai beach resort Pattaya that they'd visited as a family, then Philip forgetting an Easter basket ribbon seemed utterly reasonable.

"This is ridiculous," said Bea. She took her hand down from her mouth and spoke to the man on-screen in a challenging voice. "If you are Philip, why would you wait so long? Why wouldn't you have contacted us long before now?"

Because he's been a prisoner, thought Laura. *Because he's been in a cult.*

The camera turned again, the room wheeling by. "He is not well," Claudette said as the tumbling granules of video melted into each other and resolved into her face. Her expression was severe. "I have been trying to reach you for weeks. You can't do this by telephone. You need to come here."

The video window closed with a *ping* and a dialogue box appeared: *Rate this call!*

"Whoa," said Dustin from the other room. "She hung up on you, dude."

"That in itself tells me all I need to know," said Bea, pushing her chair back from the desk and standing.

"Come on," said Laura, reaching for the mouse and clicking Reconnect, getting an error message. Had she and her sister been looking at the same screen? "You really don't think that was Philip?" she said. "He looked just like Daddy."

"He didn't," said Bea. But she was shaken, Laura could tell.

"He called you Queen Bea."

"People in college called me that," said Bea. She left the room, and Laura heard a long rush from the kitchen tap, then the beeps of the coffeemaker being programmed for the next morning's brew. "One more hour, then bedtime," she called to the boys.

Laura abandoned her attempts to reconnect the call, got up from the chair, and went into the kitchen.

"Bea," she said.

Her sister was shaking coffee from a bag into the filter section of the coffeemaker. "Dammit," she said, holding the bag upright, looking at it. "This is decaf." She put the bag down and braced her hands on the counter, head bowed. "You don't know," she said. "You have no idea."

Laura didn't say what she was thinking: *I would know, if I'd ever been included.*

"All those years," said Bea. "All the false

leads. And that hope. That hope every time."
She turned her head toward Laura. Those
blue lamps of eyes, so like their mother's. "I
can't do it again."

"Okay," said Laura. "Okay."

Bea turned her head back. She stayed there
for several seconds, leaning against the
counter, looking down at the veined stone.
Then she nodded and straightened up, went
to the freezer, took out a different bag of coffee.

Laura opened the ride-sharing app on her
phone as she walked toward the great room,
where her nephews sat on perpendicular sofas
with their laptops, papers and textbooks surrounding them like a debris field. They
looked up at her approach.

She held up her phone, where a tiny car
icon was navigating a corner. "Christina my
driver is eight minutes away," she said. "Good
luck on your exams."

"Was it him?" the twins chorused.

"No," called Bea from the kitchen, as Laura
said, "Maybe."

When she let herself into her house, there
was the packed bag, docile and waiting. She
hadn't canceled the reservation yet; the flight
would leave in the morning. She remembered
her sister's face, that mask of pain. Then the
man on the screen came into Laura's mind,
his unreadable expression, the quiet *If it's me.*

Maybe Bea couldn't do it, but that didn't mean Laura couldn't. She lifted the bag. It weighed so little; it contained everything she needed. Her heart felt light, purposeful.

CHAPTER THREE

She'd booked business class on a Japanese airline for the first leg: fourteen hours from Dulles to Narita, a window seat in a cabin filled with businessmen. It was a luxurious journey, an orchid trembling in the bathroom vase and an omnipresent flight attendant, who appeared at Laura's elbow to offer something — a cloudy nonalcoholic citrus cocktail, an eye mask, a snack — approximately every forty minutes. The meal deemed dinner without regard to a clock was complicated and many-coursed, a tiny thing followed by a slightly less tiny thing followed by marinated eel and cucumber on a scoop of steamed rice. Laura hadn't thought she was hungry, but she ate and ate. She slept for a while, woke into a darkness scattered with small patches of light: no-smoking signs, fasten-seat-belt signs, call buttons. The engines hummed under her; the cabin air that had been sweet at first had grown stale. Outside the window was a wrinkled lightless land mass that the seat-back monitor told her was Alaska.

She retrieved the bag from under the seat in front of her and unzipped the outside pocket, extracted the manila envelope that she'd retrieved from her mother's desk drawer. She punched on the reading light above her and put a fingertip to the inked whorl of the capital *P.* Genevieve's handwriting had always been beautiful.

The envelope wasn't very full. Back then, childhoods were largely recorded in memory: school portraits once a year, clusters of snapshots at birthdays or on holidays. No selfies, no burst-clicked digital images that could be inspected on the spot and deleted, reposed and recaptured as many times as needed to achieve perfection. How blindly Laura's cohort had fumbled through their lives, pointing their cameras and hoping, the developed film coming back weeks later with so many dud images, blurry or underexposed, eyes closed or mouth open or hair blowing across a face.

Philip's existence, as attested to by the contents of the envelope, amounted to a thin sheaf of paper: a couple of snapshots, an accordioned yellow vaccination card gone fuzzy at the folds, some newspaper clippings, and the records from his birth in 1963, in Pennsylvania of all places.

Genevieve had told Laura that story, one

snowy day in the Tudor when Laura was about twelve. She'd come downstairs to find her mother seated with hands in her lap, staring out the sitting-room wall of windows at the blur of fast-falling white. It was such a rare sight, Genevieve doing nothing. Not on her way in or out of a room or the front door, not packing or unpacking or talking into a telephone while ticking items on a list. As Laura hesitated in the doorway, her mother spoke without looking over.

"Philip was born on a day like this," said Genevieve.

Laura had gone into the room and sat down to listen to the rest. Every detail stayed with her forever after, as vivid as if she'd been there: Genevieve and Robert, driving home from New England two weeks before Christmas, a light snowfall tumbling against the windshield, the baby who would turn out to be Philip due in a month and toddler Bea asleep in the back seat. The snow thickened, and Robert adjusted the wipers. He was leaning forward to scrub the fog from the inside of the glass with the side of his hand when his wife's sharp cry pierced the quiet.

Genevieve's story included the cry, not its provocation. She made no mention of pain, certainly did not hint at water breaking or other nether-region events. Urgency was conveyed by other details: the snow waxing into a blizzard, the windshield whiting out.

The lighted letters HOSPITAL appearing in the sky above the roadway like the star above Bethlehem and Robert fishtailing the car onto the exit ramp, following the sign until they reached the hospital beneath it, careening through undulating drifts in the empty parking lot right up to the building. Robert getting out of the car almost before it had stopped and running around to open Genevieve's side, helping her out. The two of them struggling together toward the entrance, pulling the door open to see the bored staff looking up from their cups of coffee.

The narrative made a jump cut then, from nurses whisking Genevieve into a wheelchair to a soft-focus Philip tucked into a blue receiving blanket, ten rosy toes at one end and a puff of startled-looking white-blond hair at the other. Babies of that era appeared in a cloud of mystery, not mucus. At this point in the story, Genevieve exclaimed, "He looked just like a little Dutchman!" and added with a low laugh, "At first, Robert thought they must have given us the wrong baby." *Robert,* not *your father.* Laura knew then that her mother wasn't telling the story specifically to Laura — she was merely telling it.

A long silence had followed. Laura was caught in a blend of emotions, pinned by fascination yet made uncomfortable by the intimacy that hadn't clearly been intended to

71

include her. A thousand questions crowded into her head; she felt too awkward to voice them before Genevieve spoke again.

"Snow always makes me think of him."

It was said almost apologetically. She smiled at Laura and got up, left the room with those words still in the air. Even at twelve, Laura perceived the lie in them, and for the first time understood: her mother was always thinking of him.

The two photographs in the envelope had both been taken not long before Philip had disappeared. One was a color school portrait from that spring; he was wearing the sea-green sweater with the crest, and his hair was slicked down and parted above his gapped smile, two front teeth peeking their triplicate points from his gums. The other photo was a black-and-white snapshot captured at a Fourth of July picnic, judging from the striped bunting just visible in one upper corner. The photo had been enlarged and then cropped to show Philip in three-quarters view, standing with one arm up, his elbow crooked and his finger pointing (at what?). The photograph demonstrated his height in comparison to a nearby table, possibly why it had been chosen.

Laura examined the rest of the items from the envelope. The birth certificate, embossed with the seal of Pennsylvania. A card with a yellowed saw-tooth of Scotch tape along its top edge that had probably been affixed to his newborn crib: it featured a jaunty cartoon stork with a cigar in his beak leering beside spaces for name, sex, length, and birth weight. The canary-colored vaccination record had scribbled, impatient-looking initials and dates in the cells beside *typhoid, yellow fever, polio.* Clippings from the *Bangkok Post* and *International Herald Tribune,* wearing through at the creases from having been unfolded and refolded many times. The last item was a brittle ivory onionskin sheet with a set of tiny inked footprints on it, one slightly ahead of the other. As though Philip were going somewhere on the day he was born, already disappearing and leaving tracks so they could follow.

CHAPTER FOUR

1972

The driver had been with the Prestons two full years, and in that time his service had been exemplary. He had never been involved in a collision of any significance; he employed the horn only when necessary; and he was always where he was asked to be, at the time he was asked to be there: idling outside Phloenchit Market or the PX or the salon or the tennis club, parked in the shade outside riding or ballet or piano lessons, crawling the white Mercedes up Soi Navin to collect the children after school. He was utterly dependable, staunch as the name Mrs. Preston had given him: Fred. But despite that blotchless record, one midsummer Tuesday he went home and never came back, and the next morning there was a different man in his place, polishing one of the twin sedans that stood in the driveway.

The Preston children were accustomed to unexpected adjustments in the household staff; they understood not to inquire. Doing so would elicit only a nonanswer from their mother, *Let's not dwell on unpleasantness.* Consequently, none of the children asked after staunch, dependable Fred once he was gone. They may not have given him another thought. Certainly none of them ever suspected that they themselves had been instrumental in his disappearance.

It had been Laura who had run to their mother on that Tuesday, on the balls of her bare feet across the blazing driveway and over the warm grass, up the three steps to the side terrace. The ground level on that side of the house lacked a proper wall; instead, a long screen of interlocked panels was drawn open each dawn and pulled back into place at dusk. Laura ran through that wide opening, through the ground floor, and up the front staircase.

Genevieve was at her desk in the alcove off the master bedroom, flipping through her glass box of gilt-edged address cards, drawing up the guest list for that weekend's dinner party.

"What is it?" Genevieve asked without looking up when her younger daughter appeared in the periphery of her vision. She had her fingertip on a card, in the process of making a decision. One couple was a colossal bore, but the other had a wife with the tedious habit of requesting plain soda water at parties instead of alcohol, and who — much more annoyingly — was always seemingly on

75

the point of explaining why.

"Mum," said Laura.

Genevieve was *Mum* to the children. Not her choice. She would have been *Mama* like her own mother; she'd called herself that, but her children had instead chosen to mimic their English father, who was always saying *Mind your mum* and *Look, here's Mummy.*

Genevieve looked up to see her younger daughter standing on one leg like a stork, scrubbing the top of her other foot against her calf, her mouth slightly open.

"What is it?" Genevieve said again. Adding the slightest edge to each word, a change imperceptible to a casual listener but not to one of her children.

Laura hesitated. Not too late to turn back, to say *Mai pen rai* and run away. Perhaps dropping a quick curtsy before she did: things from Home, like curtsies, were often helpful to ward off her mother's irritation. Laura, who remembered nothing else of any other place, was nonetheless keenly aware that this place was not Home. At Home, the water came drinkable from the tap, and things were *civilized,* which Laura construed to mean snakeless. Snakes were a constant concern. Earlier that week there had been one in the garden, dropping inquisitively from a low tree branch in a complicated pattern like dark lace. Beatrice had cried to the gardener, who snared it with a long, loop-ended pole and chopped it into two pieces on the grass, the children watching from the safety of the side terrace as the wedge-shaped head whipped back and forth, biting at the air.

Her mother dipped her pen into the inkwell, having made her choice — she'd exclude the couple with the tiresome wife. Asia was no place for teetotalers.

"Fred's locked the car, and won't let me and Bea in," Laura finally said.

"And what do you need to get in *for*?" Genevieve said, inscribing the names on her list.

"But he's let Philip, and he won't let us," Laura said. Her mother had picked out the flaw immediately: there was nothing to get into the car *for*. "It's not fair."

"What have I told you about bothering the servants?" asked Genevieve, never pausing in the perfect upstroke of an *R*.

"He likes Philip more than us," Laura said, dropping her head, looking down at her dirty feet. Knowing that she'd failed; she'd said the wrong thing, in entirely the wrong way. She awaited the corrections that surely were coming: *Stand up straight. For heaven's sakes, don't whine.*

Instead, Genevieve raised her head, her brows drawing together, and replaced the pen in its inkwell. She pushed her chair back, got up, and went to the window.

Laura held her breath, hoping that the

scene outside was as it had been when she'd left it: the fat man laughing inside the car, Beatrice running round and round it knocking at the windows, and Philip making faces from the front passenger seat, having locked all of the doors.

Genevieve stood for a moment looking down through the glass, her expression changing and hardening.

"I'm coming down," she said.

Laura hadn't really expected her mother to validate her outrage. Somewhat cowed by what she had instigated, she followed down the hall, down the stairs, across the warm tile of the foyer, where her mother didn't even stop for a hat; she pulled open the front door and strode outside bareheaded. Genevieve stood on the step with a hand raised to shield her eyes; at the sight of her, the movement of the three figures in and around the car ceased.

"He won't let us in!" cried Beatrice, and Laura thought, frightened and triumphant, *She knows that, dummy, I told her — I brought her here.*

"Fred, unlock the doors," said Genevieve.

Although she had not raised her voice, although the car windows were rolled up tight and the air-conditioning roared behind the glass, the driver heard her and obeyed. He pulled up the lock on his own door, reached across Philip and did the same for the passenger door as well, then snapped off the

78

engine and got out of the car.

"Philip," said their mother. "Come out of the car."

Philip hesitated. Laura could see him turning his head and considering, looking away from his mother and toward the man who was now standing on the asphalt straightening his suit jacket. Philip turned his head again toward the house and the tall woman standing before it, and his defiance wavered and broke. He pulled up the door handle and pushed the door open, sliding out of the car to stand on the driveway, an uncertain, blinking figure in a white singlet and navy shorts.

But the scolding that all of the children expected did not come. Their mother kept her eyes on the driver as she spoke.

"Children," she said. "Go and ask Annie if your suits are ready."

They ran off immediately, toward the porch side rail where their bathing suits were drying, guarded by Choy, the second house servant, until the requisite hour after breakfast had passed. Choy, who was also Annie. Daeng, the Number One, was also Harriet; Noi, the Number Three, was Sarah; Kai, the gardener, was Stephen. Before them had been Ruth, Nancy, Mimi, and George, as well as a stream of forgotten others who hadn't lasted long enough to earn what the children's mother called a *more manageable* name.

They snatched their suits from the rail as

they ran into the house, Philip shouting "Mum says it's all right!" over his shoulder to a protesting Choy, and thundered up the steps to the second floor. Bea, who had recently become private about some things, went into the bathroom to change. In the girls' bedroom, Laura and Philip scrambled into their bathing suits without speaking.

"She's wrong — it hasn't been an hour yet," Laura said, finally, ingratiatingly.

"Tattletale," replied Philip, pinching her arm with fingers still cool from the air-conditioned car interior.

She rubbed the place, accepting the punishment. That he had spoken at all was a kind of truce. The nastiness between them was settled, and soon would be forgotten. Philip never held a grudge for long.

The children didn't hear the rest, not the tight-lipped exchange that followed immediately between their mother and the driver, nor the conversation between the parents hours later, after the children had been put to bed.

"What kind of person, Robert?" Genevieve said with distaste. "What kind of person locks himself into a car with an eight-year-old boy?"

There was a pause, then "I'm sure it was nothing like that," said her husband comprehendingly and dismissively, lighting a cigarette and looking with meaning at his empty

80

coffee cup.

Genevieve lifted the coffeepot and filled first his cup, and then her own.

"Good old Fred," Robert said, smoke parping out with the syllables. "How could you say such a thing about him?" He sipped at his coffee, then took up the morning newspaper that had waited for him all day. At home, newspapers opened with a snapping noise, but here the humidity made their pages soft and they wafted lazily out of their creases. "Oh, before I forget," he said, the cigarette clamped between his lips as he unfolded the paper and smoothed it out. "Can we squeeze Maxwell Dawson in this weekend?"

Had he been looking, he would have seen that Genevieve's expression registered, if not exactly surprise (for the expression of surprise had been bred out of her by generations of poised forebears), then its restrained cousin.

"He'll be an odd man, I'm afraid," added Robert, leaning the paper against the coffeepot and taking the cigarette from his mouth, tapping ashes from its end into the brass ashtray on the table. Three pairs of taps, as always, evenly spaced. *Tap-tap, tap-tap, tap-tap.* Genevieve knew the action would have to be complete before he resumed speaking. "His wife's stayed behind in the States."

Maxwell Dawson. A man Genevieve had heard of but had never met. He was Robert's boss's boss, ultimately in charge of the dam that Robert's firm was endlessly designing but apparently never actually building in the north of Thailand. Maxwell Dawson would trump that soft-shelled person, Robert's immediate superior, whom Genevieve had to meet twice before she could reliably recognize him, whose gray eyes never settled down on anything and whose conversation, murmured and vague, never supplied any information. *How long does it take to build a dam?* she'd asked him once, as point-blank as she could bring herself to be, only to win the meaningless reply, *Well, there are so many factors.* And then, when her fixed gaze with raised eyebrows forced more speech: *And always complications.* It was no surprise that such a person could find himself relegated to the obscurity of Southeast Asia for so long.

By now, everyone else the Prestons had come overseas with had gone home. Robert could have (*should* have) inquired about repatriation after the first year, demanded it after the second. That he hadn't done so was beyond exasperating, but after thirteen years of marriage, Genevieve had to accept that the husband she'd chosen was himself rather soft-shelled. He was a tall man and handsome, with an athlete's poise and a good-natured, confident air. At home, it might never have been necessary to face his more disappointing qualities. There, his mild temperament might have counted as a virtue, sparing Genevieve many of the trials that other wives reported. No fits of peevishness or violence, no migraines to be cosseted, no dramatic confrontations about expenditures. At home, Robert's little habits — the tapping, the fussbudgeting microadjustments of cutlery on either side of the plate before he could begin eating — might have been her worst complaint about him. Here, his complacency blotted out everything else. Complacency here was a terrible flaw.

Apparently sensing something in his wife's silence, Robert looked up.

"If this weekend won't work, it's not important," he said. "We can have him another time. He'll be here all summer."

"No, it's all right," said Genevieve. "I'll adjust the guest list." No hint of *You could have told me before now, I worked on that list all morning.*

"As long as it's no trouble," he said. "No need to fuss." He lifted the newspaper and opened it wide, flaring the headline BOMBING RESUMES IN HAIPHONG, folded it back to follow an article to an inside page.

No need to fuss. A sit-down dinner for twenty. Husbands understood nothing.

She'd discard the list and start again, compose a roster entirely of Robert's colleagues. Such a dull assembly! But she couldn't simply mix Maxwell Dawson in with the planned group, which included an ambassador. Maxwell Dawson would need to be the guest of honor. *Maxwell Dawson:* the name had started a little efflorescence of hope in Genevieve's mind. Maxwell Dawson oversaw a great many people — he might not realize how long one specific family had been in Asia. Perhaps he just needed to be reminded that it was well past time for the Prestons to go home.

Home. The things Genevieve had taken for granted: the clean floors and walls, the unsticky air, the pure water rushing from the tap. The changes of season — delicate springs, piles of crisp autumn leaves, properly cold Christmases. Snow! Philip and Laura probably didn't remember ever having seen it.

The sojourn was to last only a year, four quick seasons away and then back to normal life, to the garden on the double lot wrapping around the house Genevieve loved, to the choral society where she sang mezzo soprano and the Arts Council, to whose board she'd been elected just before they'd left America. The council had been enthusiastic about what they called her adventure — Genevieve had thought of it that way then too — and proposed a slideshow after her return, tentatively titled "My Year in Siam." She hadn't received a council newsletter in a very long time. Possibly the fault of international mail, but more likely her name had been expunged from the mailing list. As though she had died.

Genevieve spent one morning per week writing letters, at a drawerless teak desk pushed under a small window in the master bedroom. While the geckos ran over the walls and the overhead fan lifted the corners of everything in a ruffling ocean shush, she would dip her pen into the deep inkwell that had belonged to her grandfather and summon the bright, game voice she used for correspondence:

Dear Sally, It's the rainy season again! The streets downtown have flooded so completely that locals are boating about; it's almost like Venice . . .

If Venice were boiling hot and its air thick with disease-bearing mosquitoes.

Dear Mother, Thank you for the hairbrushes. We saw a lovely exhibition of Thai dancing the other day. We must take you when you come . . .

Not that her mother would ever visit Thailand. She might have done so in other circumstances, perhaps as part of a round-the-world extravaganza, but to travel to Bangkok to visit her daughter who now appeared to be *living* there would be quite impossible. Genevieve imagined her mother telling her father across the dinner table, "It would only encourage them."

"I've sacked him, of course," Genevieve

85

said now, to the wall of newsprint.

"Who?" asked Robert, and then sighed in comprehension, bringing the newspaper down. "Was that necessary?" he asked. "We're getting a reputation. We've sacked an awful lot of servants."

"You mean I have. But Robert, really. I'm the one who has to live with them."

He regarded her through the rippling, rising smoke of his cigarette. Did he really see her? Three babies in five years and she'd looked eighteen after Laura, everyone had said so. Now she was thirty-three and dangerously close to looking it. Despite the sun cream; despite the wide-brimmed hats.

"Did you sack him completely?" Robert asked, his forehead creased and hopeful, as if there were a halfway measure.

No, Robert didn't see her. She knew she was partly to blame for that, so determined had she been to rise to the never-nagging, never-flagging examples of her mother and grandmother, who voiced no dissatisfaction in any circumstance, who always preached *make do* and *needs must*. Genevieve had withstood a monologue recently from a Swede at an embassy party, a minute description of an obscure sport. She'd been half listening, making the usual encouraging noises, when her attention was yanked fully to what he was miming: frenzied, focused sweeping. That was the sport, apparently:

silent, tactical sweeping of ice in front of a sliding stone, guiding its path while never touching it. To Genevieve, it had seemed an amazingly apt metaphor for her married life.

"It's all right," she said, taking up the coffeepot again, tilting a thin brown stream into Robert's cup. "Harriet has made arrangements for her son-in-law to come."

"All right," he said, mollified. "Good." He crushed out his cigarette, flicked his fingers free of moist bits of tobacco from its filterless end — *flick-flick, flick-flick, flick-flick* — brought the coffee cup to his lips and sipped, then returned it to its saucer and lifted the newspaper again. Smiling, his good humor restored. "Sack them all, if you want," he said. "We can always get more."

The new driver was there the next day, well before he was needed, smartly turned out in jacket and long pants, already perspiring in the early heat. Laura noticed him when she went outside after breakfast to skip rope, a strange man crouched where Fred should be, rubbing a cloth over the headlamp of her mother's car. He must have already cleaned her dad's car: yesterday the chrome had been foggy and the wheel wells encrusted with mud, but now the two cars were almost identical. Only the small crushed place on her dad's front fender identified it as his.

She began skipping, counting silently,

watching the new driver out of the corner of her eye. She had a private goal to skip one million times this summer, mostly because Bea had said she couldn't. She did it in lots, keeping track of the daily number, writing it down on a paper. One thousand thousands was one million. If a person did one million of anything, it had to mean something.

Twenty-two. The driver looked up at the slap of the rope. *Twenty-three, twenty-four.* He saw her looking at him, and smiled. She stopped skipping.

"Sawadee-kha," she said, letting the wooden handles drop onto the grass and stepping toward him, putting her hands in front of her face, palm to palm, and bobbing her head slightly. "I'm Laura."

He stood, still smiling, and returned her wai and her greeting, in masculine form, *"Sawadee-khrap,"* the white cloth hanging like a flag between his palms. He put a hand flat against his chest. "Somchit."

"Are you our new driver?" said Laura. He smiled, but didn't reply. "The cars look very nice." She shifted her weight from one foot to the other, watching her elongated, curved reflection in a shiny hubcap. "Perhaps you can take us to the toy shop today." They usually went on Tuesdays after their riding lesson, but this week their mother had needed the car for an errand and they hadn't gone.

In Laura's calculus, a toy shop visit was owing.

Somchit smiled and nodded.

"Not the one on Sukhumvit, the other one," she instructed. "With the ship in the window. Do you know that one?" He nodded again.

"He probably doesn't understand English," said Bea, coming up behind her. "Cheap bastard," she said to Somchit. He made another smiling wai. "See," said Beatrice. "You're an idiot," she told Somchit in a bright voice. His smile didn't change; Laura laughed.

Robert came out of the house carrying his briefcase, and the girls ran toward him. Somchit made a deep wai and Robert waved a kind of salute with his free hand, opening the door of the nearer Mercedes, getting in. "Daddy, may we please go to the toy shop?" cried the girls. Repeating the *please,* drawing the syllable out again and again into long girl-screeches. "Ask your mum," he said, as Genevieve came out and told the girls to Quiet Down. They turned their beseeching faces to her as Robert shut the door and started up his car.

"There's no time," Genevieve told the girls. "I have a luncheon at eleven and after that Philip has his lesson."

"We can go now, with the driver," said Bea.

"It's his first day," said Genevieve. "We

don't even know if he speaks English."

"He does," said Bea, her mendacity making Laura goggle at her. "We've been talking to him."

Noi, the Number Three servant, watched the girls teasing the new driver. She'd seen him before anyone else had that morning, when she opened the screen-wall of the house just after sunrise. He'd flashed her a wide white smile, and she'd been bewildered: Where was Fred? She hadn't returned the new man's smile, and under his eye she didn't sweep the terrace as she usually did, but left the broom propped there and went back into the house to help with breakfast. She'd avoided going outside again until ordered to do so by the Number One, who'd noticed the dirty terrace, strewn with blown petals from the twisting vines that crept across under the roofline.

Noi wasn't surprised to hear Beatrice lie to her mother. The farang children were gargantuan in size but immature in every other way, driven by wants like babies, always quarreling. As she bent to sweep the last of the petals into the dustpan, the movement caught Mrs. Preston's eye.

"Sarah," Mrs. Preston called. "Will you please go with the girls to the toy store?" As the girls shrieked with joy, she said, "I'll need the car in one hour." Her index finger went up for the emphatic repeat, "One hour only.

One hour, Sarah, say it back to me?"

Saying the words *One hour only, Madame* got Noi her first-ever ride in the Mercedes. The girls clambered into the back seat while the new driver opened the front passenger door for Noi. As the motor rumbled to life, Laura leaned out the window and called to Philip. After a minute or two of waiting, Bea said, "He's sulking about something, let's just go," and the driver pushed the stick in the middle of the car, brushing his knuckles against Noi's hip as he did, and then they were moving down the driveway, Kai running to open the gate.

While the girls punched each other in the back seat, Noi perched in the front, the inertial forces pulling her deeper into the cushion and then pushing her out of it, tipping her now toward the window, now toward the driver. Who, without taking his eyes from the road, put a hand to the dashboard and adjusted a louvered vent to blow a cool chemical breath in her direction. That felt nice, but she didn't acknowledge the kindness. She'd liked Fred, who'd treated her like a little sister. She was sorry Fred was gone.

CHAPTER FIVE

When Noi was eleven, her mother took the four daughters to the fortune-teller, whose house on stilts stood only a mile or so upriver from their own. The family was at a crisis point: the harvest had been poor, and the land tax would be coming due soon. Everyone had heard of the opportunities in the capital city; many families had sent a girl south to work. That seemed to be the answer. But how to choose which of the girls should go?

After the rice transplanting ended, Noi's mother collected money for the fortunes in a twist of her skirt, counting the coins several times before tying the knot. Fifty satang for each girl's fortune; it would have been twice that for boys. She poured a measure of rice onto a broad banana leaf and made it into a square package, tied it closed with a strip of the same fibrous leaf, and brought that along too.

In the prow, Noi's eldest sister, Pla,

paddled; in the stern, their mother. Sao, the second sister, held the rice bundle in her lap; she had been charged with watching over it, but she had her eye on the bank, waving at everyone they passed. Nok, the youngest sister, sat quiet, watching the long pleats of water raised by Pla's paddle. Noi sat near Sao and rested a hand lightly on the rice.

The fortune-teller was sweeping out her house when they arrived. She looked up as the family tied the boat to the ladder. As they rinsed their feet preparatory to climbing up, she made a vigorous scrape across the wood to send a line of dirt flying into the water. Then she stood the broom against the wall of the house and sat on the platform. The visitors knelt before her.

Noi's mother tugged at the knot in her skirt to retrieve the coins; the fortune-teller accepted them and politely put the rice bundle aside unopened. She beckoned to Pla, who came forward and put her hand out.

The old lady scrutinized Pla's hand and then her face, frowning in concentration, her jaws working as she chewed a betel nut, while the others waited in respectful silence. Noi could not tell what the woman was looking at; she had heard that fortune-tellers relied greatly on the shape of the ears. She wondered what her own ears looked like. She and Sao had each tried to describe the other's, drawing in the mud; they had pressed their heads together, ear to ear, feeling with their fingertips to compare their sizes, but with the rushing in Noi's head, the warm skin of Sao's ear had felt like her own.

The fortune-teller let Pla's hand go. "She is a fish," she told Noi's mother, who drew her breath in sharply in surprise: the girl's play-name meant just that. The woman went on. "A fish swimming wisely, far enough below the water's surface to avoid distress from the rain above, but close enough to dart up and snatch a hovering insect." The old woman smiled at Pla. "She has a cool heart. She will make a good marriage."

Even Noi could have predicted a good marriage for the beautiful Pla, and without having had to look at her sister's palm.

Sao was next; she went forward eagerly. She had been looking forward to the fortune-telling. The woman pulled the hand onto her knee, looked into it, and scowled. No clues from this one's nickname, which meant "young girl," expressing the parents' hope that she would be the youngest girl in the family — that all the children to follow would be boys.

"Stubborn," declared the fortune-teller. "A pebble at the bottom of the river; no matter how the water rushes over her, she does not move. She is lazy, not a good worker." She leaned, spat betel-nut juice over the side of the platform. "But she is a loyal friend," she added, as Sao backed away. Noi put her arm around her sister, but their mother removed it.

"Go on," said Noi's mother. "She is ready for you."

The woman inspected Noi's hand, pressing her thumbs against the fleshy part where the fingers joined, turning it on its side and drawing a forefinger over the braided tracks there.

"This one is a weed," pronounced the fortune-teller. "Growing up in the dry cracks of the road, where you would think nothing could grow. She is pretty, and hardy, but attracts little attention." She cackled. "Not a flower to place before the Buddha."

Noi retreated as her little sister crept forward and laid her trembling hand, palm up, on the old woman's knee. They all waited to hear the verdict. "Bird" would have been obvious — her play-name *Nok* had been given for her birdlike tininess and timidity. But that might have been too easy; anyone could see the bird in the girl. If Sao was a pebble, and Noi herself was a weed, probably their meek little sister was something even less substantial, a gnat or a tadpole.

But the old woman, after smoothing out Nok's hand and looking closely, broke into a beatific, betel-red smile. Nok, to the surprise of them all, was a lotus, serene in the moonlight, blooming on a pond in the garden of a king. Their mother looked at Nok with new respect: she'd had no idea.

That night, the family gathered to discuss the fortunes. There was no doubt that Nok and Pla were meant for marriage; but of the other two, which would be better to send away to the city to work? The pebble, who was lazy, would make a bad wife; but then she would also be a bad worker. The weed was pretty, but prettiness alone does not portend anything.

"She grows where you wouldn't expect anything could grow," mused one of the aunts. "That could mean she would be an economical wife, always able to stretch a meal."

"A pebble is smooth and round," said Noi's grandmother. "A pleasing shape for a wife." Sao was their grandmother's favorite among the girls.

"Stubbornness is a terrible trait in marriage," said an aunt.

"Stubborn can also mean steadfast," argued the grandmother.

"Ye-es," said their mother, in a considering voice. "The fortune-teller did say loyal."

"She doesn't budge," the grandmother reminded them. "Perhaps not someone who should be plucked from the riverbed and sent away."

In the end, it was one word — *dry* — that propelled Noi toward the city. The family's life depended on water. The rains brought

96

the beginning of the farming season, flooding the rice fields and making them ready for planting and also bringing fish, easily caught in the shallows. Everyone ate well during the wet season. When the hot season came, the water shrank away from the land and the difficult time began, the time of heat and hunger, of walking the water buffalo long distances each day to find a tiny fringe of grass. Water meant prosperity. A person who flourished in a dry place might even be bad luck, keeping away the rains. "If she is a weed in the dry road," reasoned Noi's mother, "then she should take the dryness with her." She noted that the weed had also been deemed hardy, so would adapt well to the change.

"Lucky," whispered Sao when she and Noi were lying side by side that night on their bed mat, the sleeping breaths of their family all around them. "Soon you'll be in the city, living in a brick house." The amulets around her neck slid on their chain with a tinkling sound as she turned onto her side. "You'll never have to plant rice again. You won't have to go to school anymore."

"I like school," said Noi. She vastly preferred school to field work and, despite the scant schedule of classes broken around the rhythm of farming, had learned to read and write a little.

"Tee says you'll take a long bus ride," said

Sao. Tee was the son of a neighbor, who had been to the city. "Hours and hours."

"I don't know if I want to go," whispered Noi.

"Mai pen rai," said Sao. "It's not so far. I'll come to visit, and we'll go to the king's palace." Her voice was full of longing. "We'll eat something from every cart." Tee had told them about the vendors along the streets, a hundred different choices in a mile.

"In the next life, maybe you will be a weed," said Noi.

"Then you'll have to be the pebble," said Sao, and the two fell asleep with smiles on their faces.

A cousin already living in Krung Thep, the city of angels, agreed to train Noi for service and place her with a household. Sao had been wrong about the brick house — there was a house made of white-painted stone, but Noi didn't live in it. The walls in her cousin's room were made of wood. In fact, the whole structure of the servants' quarters could have been plucked from the banks of the Suphan River as if by a giant wind, transported to the city and set down with a thump in the garden behind the white building where her cousin's farang employers lived.

Everything else was different in Krung Thep, or as Noi heard it called for the first time, Bangkok. Her cousin gave her clothing, things the cousin had outgrown, two long

98

dark skirts with zippers at their backs and two round-collared flat-buttoned white blouses slit at the hems. Noi had to be taught to pull the tab on the skirt's zipper to knit its teeth, and hook a piece of metal into a loop at the top. It seemed foolish effort, when the cotton panel of her *pha tung* could be wound around the waist and so easily knotted up between the knees when needed, for wet work. The farang skirts were heavy and the fabric slippery and dense; Noi mustn't try to knot them, her cousin cautioned her, or they would wrinkle. Madame didn't like clothes to be wrinkled.

Noi slept on a mat with her cousin and followed her around the farang house during the days, learning to clean the floors with a hard brush, to swab dust away from surfaces with a cloth, to polish silverware, to use the washing machine. The wringer with its cruel rollers threatened to squeeze fingers along with the garments; they used a stick to push the items through before clipping them up on a line to dry. Noi's cousin showed her a tall can that held wax for the low wooden tables; she pressed her forefinger down on the top and laughed when Noi jumped at the sudden expectoration. They cleaned every room every day, although the employers were childless and most of the rooms were unused. Noi cleaned the empty bedrooms carefully, fluffing the pillows on the small beds: *Come see, how soft and nice.* Still Madame's stomach stayed flat and those rooms stayed empty.

Noi worked for six months alongside her cousin, sleeping on the same mat, before getting her own job and moving across town to a similar wooden building at the double-lucky address 9 Soi Nine. She took the skirts and blouses with her, the black cloth slippers and her faded *pha tung.* The new madame, Mrs. Preston, gave Noi new skirts and blouses and slippers that were nearly identical to the ones she'd brought; Noi had never had so many articles of clothing at once. She'd also never slept alone before; her back felt cold without the warmth of her sister or cousin. The first night, she lay awake on her mat long after the traffic bleats had given way to a throaty chorus from the dark garden. There was no moon in the little window. After listening awhile, she could detect a low splashing under the voices of frogs and tokays. It was the sound of the khlong that flowed just a short distance away, beyond the garden wall. Hard to believe that it was the same water that ran beside her home in Suphan Buri province. Tee had explained how their river joined the Chao Phraya that ran all the way to the city, where it was dammed and divided into a network of slow-moving canals. The music of the water lulled Noi to sleep; she dreamed of flying high over the glittering brown threads of broken river, seeking the channel that would take her home.

Noi was in the habit of making an offering to the spirit house in the garden, putting a scoop of rice or a piece of fruit in the bowl inside, sometimes lighting a joss stick procured from a bicycle vendor. She always prayed for the health and prosperity of her family, and after a lonely month at 9 Soi Nine, she added an extra petition: for Sao somehow to join her in Krung Thep. Sao would have been delighted by everything that terrified Noi. She would laugh at scoldings instead of cowering, and would venture all over the city, jumping up and down on the paved roads to test their hardness, flirting with vendors to get things for free. Day after day, Noi made the heartfelt, impossible wish for the pebble to tumble toward the city.

Noi had been at 9 Soi Nine for about a year when a new Number One arrived, an older woman called Daeng; indeed her face was often red with anger. Suddenly Noi could do nothing right. No matter how careful her work, it seemed Daeng could always find a flaw. One morning when Noi was scrubbing out the family's dustbins at the road's edge in front of the tall gates, Daeng's voice came close behind her.

"Lazy country girl." The Number One grabbed the bin and looked into it, then twisted its mouth back toward Noi. "Look there — a black mark right at the bottom."

Noi looked, saw nothing but clean plastic. Daeng smirked, and Noi suddenly understood: Daeng wanted her to object. Insolence would be an excuse for firing. Daeng probably wanted to fill the Number Three position with a relative, as she had done already with the gardener and Number Two, going to Madame with reports of their poor work. Noi felt a stab of panic. Her family depended on her wages. Her oldest little brother was now studying at the local wat, and soon the yearly taxes on the family property would come due.

Noi took a deep breath and crawled on her knees into the bin. Surrounded by the echoing, smelly bin walls, water dripping from them onto her neck and back, she scrubbed at the nonexistent black mark until her arm ached. When she crawled out, Daeng was gone.

That night, Noi lay in her room with the sour-garbage smell of the bin still in her nose. She'd been reasonably happy with the job at 9 Soi Nine before Daeng had come. Now every day felt like a mountain she toiled up without ever reaching the top; every morning she was at the bottom again. Noi struggled to make her heart calm; self-pity was not *jai yen*. She closed her eyes and focused on the sound of the nearby khlong, its always-moving water.

Half dreaming, she heard a tinkling noise like amulets rattling along a neck chain, and automatically turned on her side, as she'd used to do at home to make room on the mat for her sister. She felt knees poke into the crook of her own, and then a hand came over her eyes. Awake now, Noi tried to turn back, but the hand slid away from her eyes and arms embraced her; she felt the round chin of her sister against the side of her neck.

You smell, said Sao.

It couldn't be Sao, of course; it must be her spirit, which should have been frightening but somehow was the opposite.

"P'Sao," Noi said, tears pricking her eyes. "I've missed you. I've wished for you to be here."

You think I'd let you come all this way alone? said Sao. *My Nong Noi?* The arms tightened around Noi. *Now go to sleep, stinky girl, or we'll both be tired tomorrow.*

"You're a spirit," said Noi. "How can a spirit be tired?"

She felt a pinch on her arm just above her wrist.

I'm a pebble spirit, said Sao. *Stubborn enough to be tired if I want to.*

Noi jolted awake at Choy's soft rap on her door. The window showed the light of early morning. Had it been a dream? She turned to look behind her. The mat's woven texture would accept no crease to betray a body's pressure, but when Noi slid her hand over it,

103

the surface did seem warm. She stretched, washed from the jug of bedside water, and dressed, going forth into the garden with a new purpose: to make the day rush by, so that night could unfold over the city and bring her sister again.

That night, when she was sliding into sleep, the rattle came again behind her.

Tell me what you did today.

"I washed the windows," said Noi. "I swept the roof."

What did you see when you were up there?

"I saw a traffic jam," said Noi, "and flower-seller boats all in a row on the khlong, and a man making a giant flower from pink sugar floss. I saw the tall point of the Dusit Thani hotel, and beyond that the golden tips of the Grand Palace where the Emerald Buddha lives."

Tell me what you ate, said Sao. *Don't leave anything out.*

"You are a very greedy spirit," said Noi, and then the two girls were giggling, Sao's face against Noi's back, Noi's mouth pressed into Sao's fingers to trap the sound and swallow it, so that it would not escape from between her lips and through the open window.

After a few weeks of Sao's visits, even Daeng was moved to comment on the improvement in the formerly useless country girl.

CHAPTER SIX

Philip had lain in bed all morning, dozing and waking, listening to the noises of the house — the distant clatter of breakfast, the girls shrieking in the driveway — and brooding over a question: Could he credibly fall ill in a rest-in-bed but not visit-the-doctor way, before two o'clock that afternoon?

He hadn't ever attempted the stunts of other boys, the thermometer held to the bedside lamp or the faked cough or sneeze. His mother would see through those in an instant. He had to be more subtle. He'd laid the groundwork by deliberately missing breakfast, to support a complaint of stomachache if he decided to use that. Although stomachache was not historically effective: *My stomach hurts* was typically met with the statement *Some fresh air and exercise will sort that out.*

He'd even sacrificed the trip to the toy store, not responding when Laura called his name. In the ensuing silence he'd drifted off to sleep again and a while later was awakened by the bedlam of the girls' return. After that, footsteps, unmistakably his mother's, rang across the floor below, followed by the percussion of the front door shutting. A rise of hope in his chest: Was it possible that Mum had forgotten, and taken the car out for the whole day? No, he thought, punching the hope down: it wasn't even lunchtime. Even if she was going to the salon, she'd send the driver back to collect Philip. She wouldn't forget.

"Madame say get up," said Noi, pushing open the door.

"I will," he said. He threw his covers off, baring his knees to the air-conditioning.

Noi left the door ajar; he could hear soft thumps and swishes of cleaning from his sisters' room.

Philip kept a mental list of Good Things to tick through when needed, and he reached for it now. He needed something to look forward to, to get him out of bed and through this terrible day.

Songkran, the spring holiday when you were allowed to throw water on anyone without getting into trouble, was well past for this year. *Fourth of July,* sparklers in the garden and fireworks at the embassy, also past. *Horseback riding* had happened just the day before and wouldn't happen again for another week. *Tooth fairy.* He turned on his side and pushed his hand under the pillow.

No surprises there; it had been a while since he'd lost a tooth. *Birthday* not until December, unimaginably far away. He would be back in school well before then. He tried to push that thought away, but too late: it was already soaking across the list of Good Things like a spreading blot of ink.

School.

It would start up again in two months, horribly different from last year, and also probably horribly the same. Different because Derek wouldn't be there; he had gone home to America. Perhaps he was even now riding one of the tractors about which he had boasted so much. Or perhaps he was asleep, or just getting into bed. Philip knew the time varied all around the globe; he had observed the calculations before telephone calls home, and remembered his father explaining when they flew here how most of a day had disappeared while they were in the air. It had something to do with the sun, and Philip had nodded as though he understood but was left with only the notion of a giant clock hovering above the clouds, its hands ratcheting endlessly backward.

Philip had told Derek one black day last term, *It's all right if you want to stop being friends too,* and Derek had told him not to be silly. He'd kept on eating lunch with Philip and choosing him for teams despite the groaning of the other boys. Because of Derek, school had been just barely tolerable.

Philip never knew why it had begun, but he remembered how. That last innocent morning replayed in his mind regularly, with painful clarity. Class hadn't yet started and boys were milling about in the aisles of desks when Jeremy Maitland, a boy Philip generally avoided, caught Philip's eye and smiled. *Philll-liiiip,* he said, in a high voice like a girl's. It happened in a coincident moment of conversational lull, and everyone heard; they all laughed. For the rest of that day, any word from Philip would start the mocking falsetto ricocheting all around. By afternoon, he had started to wonder if he really sounded like that, and the wondering was like a hand on his throat. When he got into the car at the end of the school day and spoke to his sisters, his unused voice scraped out, uncertain.

That had been just the beginning.

Of course Philip could hope that next term would also be different in nonhorrible ways. Maybe Jeremy would also have gone home. Also there were bound to be new boys in the class; perhaps one or two of them would be friendly. A part of Philip whispered: perhaps one of them might take his place as scapegoat. The thought streaked across his mind like a comet, dragging a long tail of shame.

More Good Things, quickly. He was closer to nine now than to eight; his riding instructor said he would soon be ready to canter; he had recently learned to somersault underwater. His father had promised to teach him to dive. His bicycle's training wheels had been taken off. His joy in that last was sharply circumscribed, though, as he wasn't permitted to ride unsupervised on the street and had to content himself with either loops in the driveway or pedaling up and down Soi Nine while a servant, usually Choy, waited for him outside the gate. Choy panicked if he got out of her sight and would call loudly for his return, making the passersby on the sidewalks laugh. So, not really very much of a Good Thing.

His weekly allowance had been raised to twenty-five cents — it now bought him one of the good comic books at the PX, or two candy bars with a bit left over. It got even more from street vendors: five ice creams or five packs of chewing gum, or ten of the little cardboard cubes the children had been buying earlier in the summer — not for the candy inside, tasteless transparent sugar beads that they threw at each other or dropped into the swimming pool to see what happened (nothing) — but for the plastic animal figure in each. Horses were the most desirable. Philip had amassed two horses, nine monkeys, five lions, three elephants, and something that looked like a bear before Beatrice decided the whole thing was silly and the craze abruptly stopped.

He could try measuring himself again. His mother hadn't yet found the pencil marks on the inside of his closet door. But he'd done that only yesterday — *why* had he done that yesterday, cheating himself of a possible Good Thing for today? He hadn't been able to wait, and anyway it hadn't turned out to be a Good Thing; the line had been exactly the same as the one from the week before. His father had said his own growth spurt had come late, and that when the time came Philip would probably shoot up like a weed.

Philip had overheard the games teacher telling his parents on Field Day that their son's coordination was quite good, and they might consider tennis lessons for the summer, or perhaps football, which would have the advantage of teaching team spirit. *It might help him fit in,* the teacher had added, dropping his voice a little bit for that sentence, and the three grownups had nodded at one another in a way that had made Philip feel queasy.

If only Philip had been put into tennis or football for the summer. If it hadn't been for Andrew Crawford, he would have been, and this summer wouldn't have been blighted, pocked with bad days, one a week, like a bright apple shot with secret wormholes.

Andrew Crawford was an only child. He had a playroom all to himself, his Tinkertoys his alone and all of them perfect, none of the wooden rods or wheels colored with markers or chewed by a baby sister. The half-built rocket ship Philip had seen at Andrew's birthday party would stay as it was until Andrew went back to it, in no danger of damage or deconstruction for someone else's project. For these reasons, Andrew was an object of Philip's envy even before the Friday last term when he'd gone into the boys' bathroom at the end of the day and re-emerged in a short white cotton robe tied with a white belt over loose white cotton trousers.

Andrew Crawford had begun judo lessons.

Even the older boys had gathered around to watch the demonstration, Andrew narrating as he flailed: *That was a throat chop — that one was right in the kidneys.* Next year, he reported, they'd be breaking boards and bricks with their feet. Philip went home that day and asked his mother if he could take judo lessons and learn to break things with his feet. The answer was an unqualified no.

Philip had never asked for anything twice; it wasn't in his experience that his parents' decisions might be flexible. But after several Fridays of Andrew in his judo outfit, Philip was beside himself. He knew that the Friday classes took place in the same mirror-walled studio near the PX where the girls took ballet on Mondays, and he made Laura get a brochure. He brought it out the next day at breakfast, to show his mother.

"You could collect me after shopping," he said.

"I don't shop on Friday afternoons," she said, putting her fingers on the brochure and sliding it toward herself. Of course not: Fridays were for the parties. He knew that.

"I want to take judo," said Laura through a mouthful of scrambled egg.

"Judo is for boys," said Bea. "We take ballet."

"I hate ballet," said Laura. "I love judo."

"How do you know?" said Bea.

"I know," said Laura.

"Be quiet, girls, and eat," said Genevieve. "The beginner judo schedule is very limited," she told Philip, frowning down at the brochure's gridded schedule. "Friday afternoons only."

"You could send me with the driver," said Philip.

"I need the driver Fridays," said his mother. "There's always so much to do last-minute." Again, the parties. Every week geared itself to them, grinding into motion on Monday and accelerating steadily toward the weekend. There would be a party at home on Friday and a party out on Saturday, sometimes the reverse. Sunday was the in-between day, when Genevieve had what their dad called "Mummy's lie-in" and took her morning coffee and toast in the parents' bedroom with the door closed, and the children were expected to play quietly.

"Daddy could get me."

"Daddy can't go all the way across town on Friday afternoon in traffic. I'm sorry," she said. "It just won't work out for the summer. Perhaps they'll have a different schedule in the fall."

"Andrew goes on Fridays," he said. "In the fall, it's still on Fridays."

"Perhaps you can go along with Andrew during the summer then? I'll call his mother."

"They won't be here," said Philip. Andrew's family was traveling for the summer. Andrew had complained about that in Philip's earshot, vowing to practice every day so he wouldn't *lose his skills.*

"Then you can go along with Andrew on Fridays after school begins again."

He didn't speak, his disappointment a fat bitter plum in his throat. Summer judo was critical in order to catch up to Andrew. Philip didn't think he could bear to be in the baby beginner class in the fall while Andrew was in another room breaking things with his feet.

"You could take dancing on Mondays," his mother said, in a teasing voice, still looking at the brochure. "It's a handy thing to know."

He wrinkled his nose, willing himself not to cry.

"I'm really very sorry, Pip," she said, lifting her hand and letting the brochure fall back into its trifold, laying her palm over the side of his face. His ear nestled into the warmth and his vision swam with tears, but she took her hand away and got up from the table. "Time for school. Chop-chop."

Each Friday after that nourished Philip's longing, each visit to the PX, where they'd pass the sign in the window that said JUDO BEGINNERS AND ADVANCED. He pleaded again with both of his parents; he swore never to ask for another thing, forsook all future birthday and Christmas presents and every bit of chocolate ever to come, if only he could enroll in judo. The mild initial negative was followed by I Said No, and then by the portentous We've Discussed This, Young Man. Philip pressed on into the bleak and scorching territory of Not Another Word, after which he subsided into a long sulk.

Then, one Wednesday afternoon in the last week of term, everything changed. The Preston children stood after school on the grass lawn playing a game of Beatrice's invention, which consisted of swinging their bookbags at each other and trying not to flinch. "Hold still," said Beatrice as Laura ducked out of the way, protesting "You've got something pointy in there." Philip bore the impact of the sharp-cornered books without a blink, which should have ended his turn, but the rules of the game were complicated. It seemed Bea's turn to be target would never

114

come. When it finally did and Laura was gripping the handles of her bag, preparing to swing, Beatrice called out, pointing, "The car's here. And look, there's Mum."

The silhouette of a back seat occupant was clearly visible in the white Mercedes inching toward them in the line of traffic.

"That means haircuts or the dentist," said Bea. "Or maybe we need shots," she added, with a wicked smile at Laura.

"None of the above," said their mother, when the door opened and Laura put the anxious question to her. Her voice was *I have a good surprise* light, the way it sometimes got near Christmas. "Philip and I have an errand. We'll drop you girls at home first."

"What's that?" asked Laura, climbing into the back seat after Philip, pointing at a large paper-wrapped package on the floor by her mother's feet. "Where are you going? Can I come?"

"She *said* just Philip," said Bea from the front seat.

"Yes, you can come," said their mother.

"So there," said Laura, kicking the back of Bea's seat.

"But you *may not,*" Genevieve finished. "And you had better stop that if you know what's good for you," she said, resting a hand on Laura's knee.

When the girls had been deposited at home, and the car was turned around to drive out through the gates again, his mother placed the bulky package across Philip's lap.

"Guess where we're going," she said as he pulled the paper apart and saw the folded white robe.

"Now?" he squealed. But it was Wednesday. Had she convinced them to change the schedule? How had he doubted her ability to accomplish it? "Oh, Mum," he said. "Thank you so much."

A full minute of bliss, before a cloud moved across the bright landscape of his joy. This might really mean no more presents for the rest of his life; wasn't that the promise he'd made? His parents had always been very clear about the importance of sticking to a bargain. Even if so, he decided, stroking the white fabric, it would absolutely be worth it. Imagine Andrew's surprise when they got back to school in the fall and Philip went into the bathroom to change into his own judo outfit. They might even be at the same level by that time, if Philip worked very hard. They could practice high kicks together, and set up bricks and break them *one-two-three,* in unison. And maybe he'd go to Andrew's house to play sometimes, and maybe Andrew would come to 9 Soi Nine and Philip could show him how to somersault underwater.

He looked up as they passed the big curved building of the cinema that showed American movies. Instead of turning right, the car went straight.

"We're going the wrong way," he said.

"That's what you think," said his mother, twinkling with the pleasure of her surprise. "There's more than one judo place in Bangkok."

The driver took them farther up the big road than Philip had ever been before, eventually turning into a smaller street. On this street, instead of flat-fronted, multicolored buildings all attached together, buildings were sparse and separate, their corrugated-tin roofs jutting far out; in the deep shadow under the eaves people were sitting at tables or squatting on the ground. An occasional palm tree fountained up from the dirt beside the road.

The car stopped beside a grassless lot. Far at the back was a small building; in the packed dirt of the lot were twenty or so barefoot, shirtless boys spaced neatly, facing the street. An old man, also shirtless, stood in front of them with his back to the street. As the car door opened and Mum got out, the boys went still. The old man turned to look, then started toward the car, and Philip felt a knell of alarm. There was something eerie about the way he walked, his body gliding forward without any up-and-down movement.

His mother knocked on the car window.

Fred, come out please. She knocked on Philip's window too and he cracked the door open, the heat punching in, and got out to stand beside his mother. He kept his head down while she explained in loud, precisely enunciated English — the first time her voice had seemed unpleasant to Philip — how her son was to have judo lessons on Wednesday afternoons, starting in a week's time, after the end of school. She spoke in bracketed clumps, a sentence or two and then a pause that the driver filled with Thai, then another sentence or two and pause.

Philip sneaked looks at the ranks of silent boys. They were staring at his mother, at how she towered over the judo master, in her wide-brimmed hat with black ovals of glass over her eyes. His mother kept talking; she didn't seem to perceive the unfriendliness rolling from the boys, or notice how the creases beside the old man's mouth deepened every time he flicked a glance down at Philip. Finally she stopped speaking and opened her purse.

A long pause, before the old man accepted the bills from her outstretched hand. He held up two fingers, growled out, *"Tuk wan phut bai song mong."* Two o'clock every Wednesday, translated Fred.

"Why in the world would they practice outdoors in the heat of the day?" his mother said as they got back into the car. "I'll have

118

Harriet boil two extra bottles of water and set them aside for you in the fridge. You'll need to take them with you, and drink them both."

"It's only Thai boys in the class," said Philip in a small voice.

His mother turned toward him, took her sunglasses off.

"Have you changed your mind?" she said. The hard blue of her eyes. "Tell me right now if you have. We'll go back and cancel."

Philip closed his eyes. Kicking in unison with Andrew. Fear and respect on Jeremy's face. He shook his head. "No. I want to take judo."

"All right," his mother said, settling back against the seat, the sunglasses folding in her hand with a *clack*. "You wouldn't know the boys in the other class either," she added, in a kinder voice. "You'll make friends."

The judo robe was a little big. "Room to grow," his mother said, pulling it straight on his shoulders and turning Philip to look at himself in the glass. Delighted by the sight, he put the mean-looking man and the coterie of unsmiling boys out of his mind, and spent some time tying and untying the white belt so that it looked just right, imagining how the yellow, the green, someday the cherished black would look in its place.

The first Wednesday lesson began with

stretches. Philip reached toward his toes, watching the others bend themselves easily double, foreheads against their knees. Then the instructor called a command and struck a pose, and all the boys copied it; Philip copied it too, putting his left foot forward and bending his knees, lifting his arms above him in a broken halo. The man and all of the boys stood there like that, unmoving. After just a minute or two, Philip's calves began to cramp; his arms shook. How could it be so difficult to stand still? How did this qualify as a judo lesson? He fixed his gaze on a dying bee nearby, its frantic wings rolling it in buzzing circles in the dirt. After some time, he heard snuffled giggling around him, and brought his eyes up to see that the instructor had rolled his weight forward onto his leading leg and lowered his arms. All the other boys had followed suit; Philip's were the only arms still in the air. Hot-faced, he adjusted his stance, and kept his eyes on the instructor after that.

There was a short break, during which the boys scattered and the judo master went into the small building, overhung with trees, at the back of the property. The patterned cloth bag that Daeng had packed with the water bottles was waiting where Philip had left it before the start of the lesson, but he couldn't bring himself to go to it, couldn't imagine taking out the bottles of boiled water and drinking them down while the others watched. He drifted instead toward a knot of boys that had collected in the shade under a tall banana tree beside the road. They were playing a game of some kind, looking at something on the ground and from time to time breaking into laughter. Philip stood on the fringes of the group, straining to peek between the slender tan backs, at the ready with a languageless smile if someone spoke to him. Prompted by a signal imperceptible to Philip, the boys all sprang up and streamed back to the practice area, where they arranged themselves in two facing lines. As Philip straggled uncertainly in their wake, he felt the master's hand on his shoulder pushing him to stand in one of the lines, across from a small glaring boy.

The master gave a short call, and everyone moved in unison, nineteen pairs of feet stomping into place on the ground, thirty-eight hands rising into position. Philip tried to copy the others' movements as the master counted *neung . . . song . . . saam . . . see . . .* The boys changed positions with each number. It was too fast, Philip couldn't keep up. Watching the boy to his left, Philip's head was turned that way when number five came, *ha!* with that upraised inflection — the way it had to sound, like a question, or it would mean something else — and there was a quick blur in the corner of his vision.

Breathless, staring up at the molten sun of afternoon, an ache deep in his center. Somewhere nearby, that bee was still buzzing. Then a blot came across the sun, resolved itself into the face of Philip's sparring partner, laughing. A dark pillar rose on Philip's other side and he turned his head that way, sharp bits in the dirt grinding against the back of his skull. The judo master. Now the laughing boy would be in trouble, for kicking Philip when he wasn't looking, when he was new and didn't even know what they were doing; it had been poor sportsmanship of the first order. Philip's eyes filled with tears in advance of the consolation and sympathy he expected.

"You get up," barked the master in English. And walked away.

Philip understood then that he had shamed himself. By allowing himself to be felled, or by not getting up quickly enough afterward, perhaps a hundred other ways. And even though a minute ago he had felt incapable of even raising his head, he got to his feet and stood there getting his breath back as the count began again. *Neung . . . song . . . saam,* and by *ha* Philip was on his back again. Over and over it happened, for the remainder of the lesson, Philip the only one on the ground, no further comment or intervention from the instructor.

When class ended, some of the boys ran to the side of the property to retrieve short pieces of board, and began industriously smoothing the dirt of the practice yard. The rest of them drifted away, up or down the street. No one spoke to Philip. He stood by the edge of the road listening to the *scrape-scrape* of the boards across the dirt while he drank both bottles of water down, dedicating every particle of his will to keeping the tears inside his eyes. When the Mercedes finally came, he saw to his relief that there was no one in the back seat. If his mother had been there, it would have been impossible not to weep. Philip climbed in and closed the door, saying nothing to Fred, who raised his eyebrows in the rearview mirror briefly before putting the car into motion again. Philip stared out the window, the air-conditioning chilling his scrapes and making them sting. He reached down to rub a bruise on his ankle and prepared himself for what he'd say when he got home. He'd tell his mother, *It's the wrong class.* He'd tell his father, *They don't play fair.*

Into his mind came his mother's reply, as clearly as if she were in the car with him. Hadn't he heard it often before? When the teenage son of another couple was tossed out of school for cheating: *He's made his bed,* with a dismissive headshake. The scandal reported in the newspaper, the businessmen imprisoned for embezzlement, which was

123

explained to Philip as a big word for stealing: *They've made their beds.*

You begged to learn Judo, she would say; *I moved heaven and earth.*

Philip's father's face, usually so convivial, would darken at Philip's whine of *not fair.* His father's childhood stories were typically hearty adventures in which he lost a shoe and carried on hiking anyway, or rowed a scull through freezing rain to victory. He'd once pulled up his trouser leg and showed Philip a bibliography of scars. Hearing Philip's description of the afternoon, he might well deliver one of his own customary admonitions. *Bear up,* or *Stiff upper lip.*

The two liters of water gurgled in Philip's stomach as he reached down with his other hand, to rub his other ankle in exactly the same way as he'd touched the injured one. He let the tears come, just for a private weak moment, remembering his mother's expression when she'd given him the robe, her eyes like stars, the dimples coming and going in her cheeks. He had forgotten that she could look like that.

If Philip complained to her about judo, especially after he'd agitated so long to be allowed to go, her face would harden into planes, her eyes into buttons of reproach. His father might try to be jolly and encouraging, but that would be a crackling shell of pretense folded around the truth that Philip had

124

recently come to suspect: *You're not the son I hoped for.*

Philip decided then. He'd made his bed and he'd lie in it, with his upper lip stiff as iron, stiff as stone. Stiff as the ground he had crashed into with such regularity all afternoon. Philip touched the sore spot on his breastbone with two fingers, and then quickly touched it exactly the same way with two fingers of his other hand. Then he put his hands on the seat beside him, one hand each side. He'd made the touching movements equally light and quick, keeping everything even; now he spread his fingers out on the leather seats of the car, adjusting their placement by millimeters, one and then the other. When he was satisfied that they were exactly the same, a peacefulness spread out inside him.

Peace enough to carry him home and through a brief charade of questions. *I drank both bottles,* to his mother. *The lesson went fine, it's hard but I'm catching on,* to his father. When the bruises blossomed he hid them, declaring to his parents that Noi no longer needed to bathe him, he was old enough to do it himself, and he took to keeping a shirt on until just before jumping into the swimming pool. Only Laura noticed and commented, and she didn't press the matter after he told her *mai pen rai* in a harsh big-brother voice he rarely used.

Every Wednesday lesson after had been the same: the stretching and slow-motion exercise like a nerve-racking preamble, the slow creaking climb of a tall roller coaster. The tip-top moment when the boys were paired up and Philip faced the glare of his sparring partner. Then the terrifying descent, the count *neung-song-saam-see-HA,* the attack somehow always catching Philip off guard: a foot hooked behind his knee to pull him down while he made a clumsy attempt at a kick, or the stamping foot against his chest that sent him flying backward.

He brought his beautiful judo robe home week after week smudged and filthy, and Choy clucked and took it straight to the laundry, where a prodigious amount of bleach brought it back to the color of snow. Donning the robe each Wednesday, Philip could smell the chlorine residue. In class, the garment blazed in the sun like a target and the smell rose in pungent waves that made his nose run; the boys laughed at the runnels of mucus above his upper lip. They took turns rubbing at their own noses and pretending they were crying.

They called him *Nitnoy,* a word he knew meant "little bit." *Nitnoy* rice, the cook would say, encouraging him to eat more dinner, *nitnoy* chicken. He was not Philip when he was at judo class. Not the only Preston boy,

126

named for both of his grandfathers, not the fastest runner in his class nor the best mathematics student, not the boy with remarkable coordination waiting for his growth spurt. He was not even *Philllliiiip*. He was Nitnoy, nitnoy. Nothing.

It was getting hot now. Noi had turned off the air conditioner in the girls' room that cooled Philip's room too through a cutout high up in the shared wall. He swung his legs out of bed, stood for a moment stretching his arms overhead in a yawn, then stumbled to the window and looked down. The driveway was empty. He could see Bea in the pool with Jane, the girl from next door. They'd probably forcibly excluded Laura, who was grimfacedly skipping rope in the driveway. Philip pressed his cheek against the window. From this squashed perspective, his little sister made a fuzzy moving shape at the edge of his vision. He knew she was counting. She always counted when she jumped, sometimes in English, sometimes in Thai. He always counted too, but usually not aloud, and not with any pleasure. And not only when he jumped rope; the counting went behind nearly everything. He turned his face and pressed the other side against the glass, held it there the same amount of time, to make things even.

And just at that moment, the Good Thing

Philip had been seeking came into his mind.

On some Wednesdays, the Mercedes that pulled up to the curb to collect him was his father's, with the damaged front fender and his dad at the wheel. Philip would get into the front seat and his father would say *How was class, break any bones this week,* and Philip would say *Fine* — he was always fine. As they got to the corner and were turning into the thick traffic of the bigger road, his father would say *Hungry?* and of course Philip was always that too, so they could go to the ice cream store.

Little more than an open-air box between a hairdresser and a shoe shop, the ice cream store had a spinning rack of magazines, a shelf of stacked cigarette packets, a coffin-size refrigerator case filled with bottles of Coke and Green Spot and Fanta, and the soft ice cream machine. Philip always chose vanilla and his father chose chocolate and vanilla mixed, and his father wouldn't object when Philip bit off the tip at the bottom of his cone and sucked the ice cream through.

They had an understanding: *Don't tell your mother.* His father didn't have to say it. It was in the way they canted themselves forward as they ate, to avoid drips on their clothing; it was in their ritual toilet afterward, before they got back into the car. His father would take two paper napkins from his pocket and give one to Philip. They'd solemnly wipe the stickiness from their lips and chins and fingers, and then Philip would run to discard the crumpled napkins in a bin. He always did that, even though the street had a long seam of rubbish at its edge. *Some people don't know any better,* his father said, *but we do.*

Ice Cream Wednesday was perhaps the best Good Thing of all. The front seat, the secret ice cream, but more than either of those things, the mostly speechless hour with his father when the Nitnoy part of Philip drained away. Not completely — he was still there inside Philip, loathsome and weak, deserving of torment — but he shrank as small as he ever got while Philip was in the front seat of his father's car, punching the buttons on the radio to find an American station, singing *Bye, bye, Miss American Pie* while his dad tapped out the beat on the steering wheel.

Ice Cream Wednesday wasn't a definitely-would-happen Good Thing, but might-happen was all Philip had, and it would have to be enough.

CHAPTER SEVEN

"First, let us welcome the new ladies to Thailand," said Genevieve.

Her audience, seated on the Duncans' re-arranged furniture, was a mix of familiar and unfamiliar faces. The three New Ladies, who had introduced themselves as Clara Pettis, Renee Martelli, and Julia Green, were seated together on a sofa; the flanking bentwood chairs held Irene Duncan and Joan Benderby and Alice Billings and Helen Malcolm, all of whom would be called Old Ladies if one were being consistent — but one was decidedly *not*. The term "veterans" had been ventured, but that had smacked of limblessness and foxholes, and was not taken up. So it was the New Ladies, and the Ladies. When new New Ladies came, as they did every year or so, old New Ladies would become just Ladies, and some of the oldest Ladies would return home.

"And gentleman," Genevieve added belatedly, looking at the lone man among them. He was seated on a hard chair that had been brought in from the dining room.

"I guess I'm an interloper," said the man, laughing. "I'm Henry Schultz. My wife is the, um, employee." He rose and came forward to offer his hand to Genevieve, and then continued it around the room. When everyone's hand had been shaken, he remained standing, like a schoolboy waiting to be quizzed.

"These meetings are really for the wives," said Genevieve. "Of course, you're welcome to be here, but I'm not sure you'll find it all that helpful."

"I told him it would be all right," said Irene, with a bit of anxiety. Genevieve had felt a rush of recognition upon meeting Irene when she'd arrived eighteen months before. She was like so many girls Genevieve had known at school, chipper and positive and can-do, an energetic seconder of motions, a born class secretary with no aspirations to be president.

"Oh, I think I will find it useful," said Henry Schultz. "I mean, I don't exactly do mending, but I'll be in charge of the household while we're here."

"We don't do mending either," said Joan Benderby. "We have people for that." Her face was flushed under her leaning tower of a bouffant; had she already been drinking? Her hairstyle was days old and she'd clearly been sleeping on it. Joan had been odd even before that disgrace with her son; afterward, she'd become a bit of a mess. In Genevieve's opinion, a weak mother made a weak child. Or perhaps it was the other way round — the difficult child weakened the mother. Chicken, egg. Genevieve gave Irene a meaningful look: perhaps it had been a mistake to include Joan, who was hardly a good example of how to cope in Asia. Irene gave a chastened nod: message received.

"That's a good place to begin," Genevieve said. Mr. Schultz took her meaning and sat back down. "How many of you had servants in the U.S.?"

Clara Pettis raised her hand. She looked like an overgrown child in her Peter Pan–collared blouse, hair scraped back and trapped by a headband. "I have a girl who comes in twice a week," she said. "Does that count?"

No, it does not, thought Genevieve.

"Any experience you have had will be helpful," she said. "However, no one would say that servants here are like servants at home." She smiled, and the Ladies broke into answering chuckles. "Servants here are absolutely critical to a well-functioning household. It's important to choose them well and train them properly. There are some pitfalls that you need to keep in mind."

Why had she said *pitfalls*? She normally used the word *principles*. She had a feeling of disconnection, a bizarre sense that if she closed her eyes and then opened them again,

132

she'd see a different group of women. Ladies long gone from Bangkok, current Ladies back when they were New. She closed her eyes and opened them like the shutter of a camera, saw the group looking back at her, quizzical frowns beginning on some of the faces.

Where was she? Oh, yes, pitfalls.

"You've probably already noticed how pleasant the Thai are, always smiling," she said. The New Ladies nodded; they had noticed. They had been here for a week already, staying at a hotel while their rental houses were readied. "They'll smile and speak softly in every circumstance. That's a lovely quality, of course" — her grandmother would definitely have approved — "but it means that you can't count on the usual cues of facial expression or tone of voice to tell you when something has gone wrong."

"A fire, a flood, a sewage backup filling your house, they'll still be smiling," said Irene. The New Ladies looked alarmed by the word *sewage.*

"And no matter what you ask them, *'Kha kha kha, Madame,'* " said Alice. Laughter among the Ladies; puzzlement among the New.

"That means yes," said Genevieve. "And also sometimes no."

"Kha kha kha, Madame," said Alice, encouraged by the laughter. "Would you like me to

cut your head off? *Kha kha kha, Madame.*"

All of the women were laughing now except Joan, who was inspecting her manicure, and Clara, who looked worried.

"It means yes *and* no?" asked Clara.

"It's impossible," cried Helen Malcolm, laughing.

"It is challenging," said Genevieve. "And what it means is that you have to remain attentive" — she had almost said *suspicious* — "and always double-check everything." She'd given this talk half a dozen times or more, and it was all true, good, useful information. Why, today, did it feel like propaganda?

"*Triple*-check," said Irene.

"Do any of them speak English?" asked Julia Green. She was a busty woman in a flowing green dress; her hair was long and loose. Add a crown of flowers, and she'd be a credible match for the subject of an art nouveau poster. Was this considered acceptable grooming in the U.S. these days? It seemed that each fresh wave of New Ladies was more unkempt than the wave before. Now one of them was a man. Another one, Renee Martelli, was wearing pants. The style called *capri* since Mary Tyler Moore had worn them on television a decade before, but which were really just the same old clam-diggers. In Genevieve's opinion, a more elegant name did not make them suitable for luncheon.

"Your Number One is the only one who

must speak English," said Genevieve. The New Ladies looked blank. "Your Number One is your head servant. She's the most important decision you will make in Thailand. She'll do the marketing and cooking and oversee the other servants. Once you've found a good Number One, half your work is done."

"And half your groceries are gone," said Joan, her voice overloud. The New Ladies exchanged glances.

"That happened to you," said Alice. "It doesn't happen to everyone."

"Tell me your servants don't feed every monk in Bangkok from your pantry," said Joan, still in that strident voice. "*And* waste good food in those spirit houses."

"Joan, *hush,*" said Irene, shooting her eyes at the doorway to communicate that her own servants might be in earshot.

"The spirit houses are for the spirits who were displaced by building on the land," said Helen. She had had a job in America, hadn't she? A teacher of some kind. "I think they're beautiful." Genevieve had never thought of them that way, but she had to admit that they could be, miniature stone temples on pillars, piled with flowers and offerings.

Joan was no longer paying attention, chewing at a cuticle.

"Feeding the monks and putting offerings in the spirit houses are important Thai

135

customs," said Genevieve. "It's best to look the other way. Monks and spirits don't eat much." Everyone smiled at that. "Plus, a good Number One is worth her weight in groceries. Once you have your Number One, she can help you find the rest of your staff — your Numbers Two and Three, and your driver and gardener."

"*Five* servants?" said Renee Martelli. Her frown accentuated her odd looks, her features already naturally crowded to the middle of her face. She would benefit from bangs, but her hair was pulled off her forehead and teased high above a shiny expanse of olive brow. She was looking less self-assured than she had when she'd arrived in her trousers, bearing a cellophane-wrapped plate of sticky, cobbled squares, like something at a bake sale. Irene had accepted it without a flicker of surprise, but while turning away to hand it off to her Number Three, had caught Genevieve's gaze and held it, a wordless communication.

"Once you've been here awhile, five servants won't seem nearly enough," Genevieve said.

"I've driven on the left before," said Henry Schultz. "I don't need a driver, do I?"

Genevieve didn't know what to make of him — didn't he have a job?

"Robert drives himself," she said. "But he doesn't enjoy it."

"Tuk-tuks are lifesavers," said Alice. "You do *not* want to walk anywhere, not even a couple of blocks. Too hot. Just flag one down and negotiate the price before getting in. One baht is reasonable for a short distance. That's five cents."

"Just be sure not to go where the tuk-tuk driver *wants* to take you. He'll drive you to a jewelry store or some tourist place and try to force you to buy things," said Helen.

"Tuk-tuks. Those motorcycle-cab things with the seats on the back?" asked Clara. "They look dangerous."

"They're perfectly safe," said Helen.

"Ha," said Joan. She took a cigarette box out of her purse and snapped it open.

As though that had been a signal, New Ladies began taking cigarette packets from their own purses and bending toward one another over the flames of lighters like tulips nodding in a rainstorm, the room filling with the lighter clicks and murmurs of *thank you.*

"No one tells you how it really is," said Joan. "None of this" — she waved her lit cigarette to indicate the gathering — "prepares you."

"I found these meetings very helpful," Irene said stiffly. She and Joan had been in the same batch of New Ladies.

Joan snorted. "Pioneer laundry and cooking. How to beat the heat." She coughed out a bitter laugh. "The servants do the laundry and cooking. And it's impossible to beat this heat. It's a hundred and three degrees outside right now at eleven thirty a.m., and this isn't even the hot season."

"What should we discuss, then?" said Genevieve. She heard the vibrato of anger in her own voice, quelled it for the next sentence. "What is it that we're leaving out, Joan?"

"This isn't the hot season?" whispered Clara.

"How about the poisonous water?" Joan said. "Dysentery streaming from every tap. How about incurable malaria, always one mosquito bite away? How about the rain? The rain!" She jerked her hand in a gesture of outrage, scattering cigarette ash. "It's biblical."

"There's nothing really to *do* about the rain," said Helen practically.

"It's not just the constant flooding," Joan said. "The rain brings the insects. And then the frogs come to eat the insects, which would actually be helpful, *except* that snakes come to eat the frogs, and worse snakes come to eat *those* snakes. Snakes are literally everywhere." She looked around at the other Ladies. "We had a snake come out of a toilet, remember that?"

None of the Ladies responded, but they all remembered that. It had been a nonvenomous variety of snake, and its fangs had merely grazed the thigh of Giles Benderby, but there had been a lot of talk afterward about how best to prevent such a thing from happening again. The decision had been reached: the toilet lid must always be kept down, and everyone must knock on the toilet lid and then look in carefully before sitting, every time. Even the smallest child was taught to do that.

The New Ladies were sliding alarmed eyes toward one another. Toilet snakes, malaria, dysentery. It was too much to tell them all at once. These meetings were intended to drip the truth onto the New Ladies, not deliver a choking flood. Irene was looking urgently at Genevieve. Genevieve knew she should speak, but sat as if mesmerized, her mind blank. How could she counter what Joan was saying? Every word of it was true.

"I once saw a tuk-tuk ride up onto the sidewalk," said Joan. "It pushed a crowd right into the khlong." She stabbed her cigarette toward Genevieve as if in accusation. "Those khlongs are basically streams of liquid garbage."

Immediately after making this statement, Joan gave a little scream and leapt up from her seat. It was inexplicable — was she possessed? — until Genevieve saw that the cigarette between Joan's fingers was no longer smoking: the burning end had fallen into her lap.

Henry Schultz was the first to move. He nimbly stepped on the ember where it had tumbled onto the floor, produced a square of handkerchief from his pocket and immersed it briefly in one of the carafes of ice water sweating on the nearby sideboard, then stepped to Joan's side and pressed the wet cloth to the smoking hole in the fabric over her upper thigh. Joan stood with the empty unburning paper tube still between the fingers of one upraised hand, looking down at the strange man's hand so close to her crotch. Genevieve felt an enormous desire to laugh.

Helen moved next, replacing Henry Schultz's hand on the handkerchief with her own and nudging Joan out of her frozen stance, crouch-walking along with her toward the room's exit. Their heels clicked down the hallway. A distant door opened, then closed.

"Joan's had a terrible time," Irene told the New Ladies.

"We shouldn't gossip," said Alice, her lowered voice warmly promising the opposite. The New Ladies angled their heads toward her. "Her son overdosed on heroin a few months ago."

It had been a horrible incident, the boy comatose in one of those rooms that were scattered around the seedier quarters of the city, his scared friends abandoning him there, leaving him to the mercy of strangers, one of

140

whom had taken him to the hospital.

"Did he die?" Clara quavered. She looked on the verge of tears.

"No, no," said Irene soothingly. "He was sent home to live with grandparents."

There was no appreciable change in the New Ladies' expressions, the word *heroin* still beating in the air.

"I've been here more than four years," Genevieve said. The crisp sentence pulled all of the women's attention to her. She watched it sink in: *four years.* "I've never seen a tuk-tuk on the sidewalk. No one I know has been bitten by a venomous snake, or contracted malaria." This was stretching the truth. "As for drugs, we all know that they are a problem with teenagers in the U.S. these days too." The New Ladies nodded. "It's a simple matter of discipline." The implication was clear: no *normal* teenager used heroin, no good mother let him.

"For every inconvenience to living in Bangkok, there is a solution," Genevieve continued. The words were coming easily now, automatically, as though from a mechanism inside her, a player piano plinking them out from a scroll. "To cope with the heat, install air-conditioning units in the bedrooms and good strong fans in the rest of the house and stay indoors during the hottest hours of the day, which are noon to four. Walk slowly, and get new clothing, everything sized just a little larger than you wear at home, so the fabric doesn't cling. You'll need several pairs of sandals to wear outdoors; save your closed shoes for air-conditioned events." She and Irene called this the *loose clothes, open toes* speech. "You can have an entire wardrobe handmade here for very little money. Think of it — as many new outfits as you want, and your husbands won't object to the expense." Relieved smiles were starting around the room, although to her own ears, her voice sounded like one of those demented television-commercial housewives: *Mmm, you can really taste the difference.* "And while it's true that tap water isn't safe to drink, bear in mind that you will *never* need to drink from the tap. Your servants will boil up a supply of water to keep in the refrigerator; you can have them put a small bottle into each bathroom for toothbrushing. As for malaria, having your garden sprayed twice a year will very effectively control the mosquitoes."

"Thus cutting down on the frogs, and thereby the snakes," said Henry Schultz.

"Exactly," said Genevieve. Everyone was smiling now. The spell was cast, the panic forgotten. "For you ladies — and gentleman — who would like some guidance about a practical weekly household schedule —" They nodded; they all would. "Let's start with Monday."

"Big Laundry Day," said Irene, her voice

142

suffused with relief: after a nasty detour, the program was back on established rails. She gestured to her Number Three, who had appeared in the doorway bearing an armful of pencils and writing tablets. "You might find it helpful to take notes."

They adjourned for luncheon, Irene's Numbers Two and Three lifting tea towels off the humps on the dining room table to reveal platters of sandwiches and cookies. Renee Martelli's sticky bars were there too, now stacked in an artful swirl around a design of cut fruit.

As the others went forward to take plates, Genevieve and Irene hung back.

"How are you?" asked Irene. In those words was an indictment of how badly the meeting had gone. She met Genevieve's eyes briefly, then lifted her hand. Across the room the Number Three moved, carrying a large pitcher of iced tea to fill Mrs. Green's empty glass.

"I think I'm starting a migraine," said Genevieve.

"I have some tablets," said Irene, her frown dissolving into sympathy.

"I took some earlier," lied Genevieve. She watched a circle of ladies crowding around Henry Schultz. As usual, any man in a group of women was attended and indulged as though he were a visiting prince. "Don't the

New Ladies all look impossibly young? Or is it that we're impossibly old?"

"You'll never look old," said Irene, matter-of-fact. She herself had what people called *strong features,* which was a nice way of saying a big nose. She wasn't unattractive, although her self-deprecation was constant, probably a consequence of never having been the prettiest girl in any room. She lowered her voice. "I'm glad I went with a dry menu. Considering." She darted her eyes to Joan, who was standing awkwardly by the sandwiches. She had returned from the restroom during the laundry discussion with Helen's headscarf tied around her waist, a creative solution to the problem of the burn hole in her dress.

"Probably best," agreed Genevieve, although she longed deeply for a cocktail. She sipped from her own glass; the tea had apparently still been warm when poured over the ice, as the liquid was tepid and the cubes were floating pellets. That servant needed to be retrained or, if it was a repeat infraction, let go.

"She should be ashamed of herself," said Irene, looking angrily at Joan. "Frightening them like that."

"It was lucky about that cigarette, though," said Genevieve. "That's all anyone will remember."

"The dam is a humanitarian effort," said

Irene, still on her own tangent. "It requires sacrifice on our part. So what? Imagine those poor villages, not having water."

"I don't have to imagine," said Genevieve. Water cutoffs were fairly common in Bangkok. She had begun to suspect that the dam project was a sham — a way to churn government money into the pockets of businessmen. Robert would never knowingly participate in fraud, but he might not even be aware of it. "Have you ever wondered," said Genevieve, "how does it take so many people, and such a long time, to build a single dam?"

"What has gotten into you?" said Irene.

"I had to fire my driver," said Genevieve. She abruptly felt near tears. "Fred."

"What did he do?" asked Irene. The soft concern in her voice was unbearable.

Genevieve shook her head. They were now on the fringes of a lively group: the women, carrying plates and glasses, had eddied back toward them.

"I tried to give a monk some money yesterday," Renee Martelli was saying. "And a total stranger *slapped my arm.*"

"A strange man slapped you?" exclaimed Clara.

"A woman," said Renee.

"Oh, dear," said Alice. "You couldn't have known, but it's a pretty big no-no to touch a monk."

"I was *giving him money.*"

"A woman mustn't touch a monk *or* anything the monk touches," said Helen in her teachery voice. "Not even the bowl in his hand. If you want to give something, wrap it in a piece of cloth and drop it in. If he's seated, you can drop it on his robe."

"So even the Buddha treats women as second-class citizens?" said Renee. "Enlightened, my foot."

The other New Ladies' lips primmed up; Genevieve was heartened to see it. From all reports, the women's lib nonsense that had been well underway when she'd left home was still raging there, but it seemed that most of these women hadn't been taken in. They might be young, disheveled, and naive, but they apparently had a firm grasp on their roles here: to support their husbands and care for their families in difficult circumstances. Genevieve felt chastened by their example. What *had* gotten into her?

"Make no mistake, ladies," Genevieve said, before remembering Henry Schultz, pressing on nonetheless. "Our husbands may be the ones who are officially employed here, but we are the ones who will make our time in Bangkok a success."

"But what does that mean?" said Clara in her plaintive treble. "How will we know we're successful?"

Before Genevieve could reply, Joan spoke, from her exile near the sandwich table.

"If you get out of here unscathed," she said. Her voice quiet, nothing like her previous rant. She spoke without looking at anyone in particular. "When you're on the airplane, buckled in, and your husband and children are with you, and everyone's healthy. When you're going home, and you're never coming back. That's when you'll know your time here has been a success."

In the ensuing silence, she lifted her glass toward her mouth, then noticed it was empty; the Number Three glided forward with the pitcher.

CHAPTER EIGHT

"A woman sits up," said Bardin, settling into the chair across from Robert. "In the middle of the night."

"Yes?" said Robert, looking up from his paperwork, trying to rearrange his face into lines of interest. No doubt this would be an off-color story. Bardin seemed the type. But then, Robert supposed, they were all the type, when it came down to it. There was so much else they couldn't say. Safe subjects played out fast: after generalities about weather, and distant sporting events, and the best places to get a curry or a cold beer or a handmade suit, only dirty jokes were left.

"She sits up with a little choking noise, waking her husband. Are you listening?" asked Bardin, leaning forward and tapping Robert's desk with two fingers. "Because this is a mystery."

"I'm listening," said Robert.

Bardin leaned back, took a cigarette box from his breast pocket, offered it to Robert, then shook one out for himself. They each lit up with their own lighters and sighed out separate lungfuls.

"She wakes up choking," Bardin said again, as the fan blades on the ceiling whipped the exhaled smoke into cirrus shapes, "and scrambles out of the bedclothes. Her husband wakes after hearing her fall. Maybe he thinks, with a clutch of fear, that her heart has given out. Maybe he thinks she got up to go to the bathroom and slipped. They are at that age when nocturnal bathroom trips are to be expected, and also slip-and-falls. Her husband calls to her. She doesn't answer. He sits up in bed and turns on the light."

"And what does he see?" asked Robert when Bardin didn't go on.

"He sees his wife, lying in a pool of bright red blood. He gets up and goes to her, and with some difficulty — the old joints aren't what they were — he kneels beside her. She is not breathing. The blood is running out of her mouth and onto the floor."

"And the mystery?" said Robert, since Bardin again seemed to have stopped.

"The mystery is what killed her."

A minute or so of silence, both of them smoking, Robert tapping his pencil against the papers on his desk. *Tap-tap, tap-tap, tap-tap.*

"Bleeding ulcer," he said. He'd had an alcoholic aunt who'd suffered that way.

"Wrong," said Bardin. He reached a long arm forward, deposited a few gray flakes from the end of his cigarette into the stamped brass ashtray on Robert's desk. "She was fit as a fiddle. Never hospitalized, apart from the deliveries of her three children. Never operated upon, not even for the children, who slid out easily as fish, hardly even bruising that tender doorway."

The phrase, so intimate and vulgar, made Robert wince; Bardin noticed, and smiled.

"She'd lived a quiet life," Bardin said. "Her biggest adventure had been her honeymoon in Italy forty years before. She ate carefully and looked after her teeth and walked briskly half an hour a day, weather permitting."

"She ought to have lived forever," said Robert.

Bardin leaned forward as if to tap his cigarette into the ashtray again. It wasn't necessary — the ash was short. Was he peeking at something on Robert's desk? Robert laid his crossed arms on the pile of paperwork.

"That last currency drop backfired on us in a spectacular way," said Bardin. He nodded toward the white sheaf under Robert's elbow. "Hope we're on to something better."

His voice was casual, as though they discussed work in this way all the time. They never had. Bardin had been hired on the year before; Robert wasn't even sure exactly what

150

he did, or how or whether their work over-lapped. To Robert, Bardin was only the mildly obnoxious redhead in the office next door. Or, more frequently, *not* in that office; its door remained closed, the pebbled glass panel dark, for long stretches at a time. When he was there, his presence could be rambunc-tious: Robert would hear him on the tele-phone, telling jokes too loudly, laughing longer than was seemly at his own punch lines. Other times, he'd be a silent apparition in the corridor after a late-morning arrival, pale under his freckles, shutting the door behind himself gingerly, as though a slam of the wood might burst his skull.

Another limey, the Boss had said, introduc-ing them when Bardin first came, but Robert had felt no kinship. There was something of the imposter about Bardin, his respectable accent almost parodic, as if veneered over a rougher tongue. Bardin hadn't seemed inter-ested in Robert either. The two of them had never had a conversation more probing than one might have with a fellow air traveler, courtesies elicited by forced temporary proximity. Even when lubricated by drink at one or another of the parties, their inter-changes were brief and pottered safely around superficialities.

For the most part, the men in the office worked on their own; there were few confer-ences or consultations. Robert's directives arrived in buff-colored envelopes that appeared at his office door periodically, carried by that bland-faced young secretary, Miss Harch. In due course, she'd return to collect the last one and deliver the next. Robert never even knew in which direction his completed work went: Down the hall and to the left, toward other men in the office? Or down the hall and to the right, toward the Boss's quiet room around the corner? He had tried to find out once, handing Miss Harch his envelope and then following her casually out of his office, on the pretext of getting a drink from the water cooler. He'd stood watching her go. Just before she reached the end of the corridor, Miss Harch had wheeled around and stood, one foot in front of the other, the pleats of her miniskirt flattening against the smooth forward thigh. She'd stood there, blinking slowly. He'd smiled a mask of innocence and lunged toward the water cooler, fumbling the conical paper cup from the dispenser with such nervous force that he mangled it. He filled it anyway and drank, under the eye of the blinking girl, water dripping from the damaged shape onto his toe. She had blinked him right back into his office, where he'd drained the paper cone, dropped it into the gray metal dustbin, and sat back down at his desk. After a few moments he'd heard her heels tapping away.

"So what was the answer?" Robert asked

Bardin. The heat was near his fingers; he stubbed out his cigarette. "What killed her?"

"No other theories?" Bardin looked disappointed at the quick end to his guessing game.

Robert shook his head.

"She had a tear in her thingummy, her aorta," Bardin said, miming a tube with a curled hand and knocking the fingertips against his chest. "The big artery that comes out of the heart."

"I thought you said she was healthy."

"Oh, she was, she was." Nodding vigorously, taking a last deep drag and then wisping out smoke with his words as he reached to the ashtray to crush out his cigarette. "She had no idea about the internal damage. It happened during a minor incident on the honeymoon railway tour of Italy — a short stop, not even a collision. It threw her husband to the floor of the car, but she braced her arms against her seat and managed to stay in place. Her husband wasn't injured; he dusted himself off and they carried on, not giving it another thought. What neither of them knew was that the incident had made a wee fissure in the bride's aortic artery. The cause was actually the action she'd taken, bracing herself." He cocked an eyebrow. "Our organs are fixed to one another in spots, did you know that? They don't simply float around separately inside us." Robert nodded, although he hadn't known that. "So when she braced herself, her body stayed in place but her internal organs continued to move forward, and her aorta tore away from the place where it was fixed to the structure behind it. It didn't tear all the way through, of course — that would have killed her almost instantly. The breach was in just the innermost layer."

Listening, Robert felt a slight nausea, discomfited by the notion of organs slamming about inside of a person. Short stops while driving in Bangkok were a daily occurrence.

"Over the ensuing years," Bardin continued, "while the newlywed couple settled down and had children, while those children grew up and married, during the matriarch's menopause and the patriarch's retirement, into their old age — all that time the blood was passing through that tiny fissure and down between the artery walls, ballooning them out. Each beat of her heart feeding the balloon." Bardin curled his hand again, twitched the fingers to make it pulsate. "Until one night, when she was a grandmother and he a grandfather and their main concern was keeping warm in winter, she got up to use the bathroom, and the balloon burst." Bardin opened his hand in a splay of long white digits.

Robert looked at it, then up to the vulpine smile. Was there ridicule there? Bardin was unmarried: What would he know about the constraints and surprises, the secrets and compromises, that went into a long marriage? The elderly couple in his story, probably invented but perhaps real, would have lived through their own crises and deep disappointments, their arguments spoken and unspoken. Bardin had boiled them down to caricatures, suspended them in a syrup of condescension. Perhaps only for the story, but even so it was inane. Robert himself had an ideal-appearing marriage. But beneath the surface was the desperate truth: he had married a woman he didn't deserve, had tangled her up in a lie and jammed them both into a corner from which he could see no escape. Bardin had no idea how that was.

"And the point of telling me this story?" Robert said.

"Can't you guess?"

"No." A cold, tired-of-playing-along syllable.

"Well," said Bardin, his jocularity undiminished. He furled his fingers back into a freckled fist, knocked that on the desk. "You think about it. I'm sure you'll figure it out."

Robert was still watching the place where Bardin's hand had been when the man had arisen and left the office, when he had disappeared humming down the hall.

Robert had been struggling all morning with

the latest envelope of materials; it had disgorged, among more typical items, a snapshot. Usually the photographs Robert got were official-looking head-on portraits in black and white. This photo was in color; the subject was out of focus and not fully facing the camera. To Western eyes all Vietnamese looked younger than their years, but this man looked absolutely just a boy in his casual collared striped shirt; his sidelong face was laughing. On the reverse side of the photograph, Robert had found light penciling in English letters: NGUYEN TRAN.

Robert often received materials without explicit instructions — he was allowed a certain artistic license in his work — but this seemed beyond the pale. He pondered it. The jolly, half-turned face, the Western clothing. Too carefree for a soldier. Not a sniper either — not the type to stare his enemy down through his rifle scope and mercilessly pick out their hearts or eyes. Too young to be a farmer rejoicing in new prosperity after having surrendered to the Southern Army; too old to make a heartwarming child-reunited-with-his-returned-soldier-father tale. Robert stared at the image until the answer came: He would make the boy an informant, a spy for the ARVN. The project would require an entire dossier, which meant a lot of intricate forgery; still, Robert felt pleased with his decision. He went to work on the supporting

156

documents for the photograph, telling himself that if the material didn't suit, it wouldn't be used. Someone higher up made those decisions.

When the doorknob turned again, Robert looked up. The blurred shape beyond the pebbled glass was too bulky for Miss Harch, and Robert framed a tart greeting for Bardin, something along the lines of *Haven't you any work to do?* But the words died on his lips when the shape instead became the Boss, easing himself around the door and closing it behind him, lowering himself into the chair Bardin had vacated not long before.

"The Tokyo Rose stuff was very good," said the Boss. "Just exactly what we were looking for." The script had been easy, a cry from the heart. "Gave me shivers." He reached out a hand and began idly to finger the neat stack of paperwork on the corner of Robert's desk, riffling the corners with his thumb. "I saw Bardin was in here."

"Yes," said Robert. A gust of relief within him as the Boss pulled his hand away from the papers. He left them unacceptably disordered, tiny triangles pointing in various directions, where before there had been a smooth-sided block of white.

"What did he have to say?" asked the Boss. Now he had taken up the framed photograph of Genevieve from the desk. Robert had wanted a different picture in that frame originally, a black-and-white image of her boating, a lock of hair blowing across her face, her even white teeth showing in a laugh. Genevieve had overruled him and selected the formal portrait.

"Nothing really," said Robert. Thinking about the old woman lying dead on her bedroom floor, blood running out of her mouth. How could he possibly explain that? "Small talk."

"He's alone here, you know, no family to anchor him," said the Boss. "Might be spending too much time in the field." So that was where Bardin took himself when he wasn't in the office. To the *field,* wherever that was, to do whatever one did there. "How are your children doing?" the Boss asked. "The little one must be seven by now?"

"Just turned in March," said Robert, surprised as he always was by the other man's genius for minutiae. "They're all fine."

"I got my invitation to your shindig this Friday. I'm looking forward to it," he said. "Your wife's parties are the best in Bangkok." He made an exaggerated *Oops* face. "Don't tell my wife I said that." Robert put a finger to his lips, playing along. "I haven't stopped thinking about that coconut shrimp thing she served last time."

"Oh yes, that was very good," said Robert. He had no recollection of a specific coconut shrimp dish.

The Boss put Genevieve's photograph back onto the desk.

"Did you happen to invite Bardin for Friday?" he asked.

It seemed no matter where this conversation turned, without fail it would veer back, licking steadily along like a brushfire in undergrowth until it reached its target: Bardin.

"I'm not sure," said Robert, and recognized the lengthening silence as a prompt. "We can add him, though."

"That would be, that would be just —" The Boss left the sentence unfinished. Nodding, he looked toward Robert but not at him, then veered his eyes away over the rest of the room: the file cabinet, the coatrack, the window. "We all need refocusing from time to time." While Robert wondered: Was the person who needed refocusing Bardin, or himself? "Well," the Boss said, rising out of the chair. "I'll let you get on with it." He waved in the direction of Robert's desk. He paused at the door, hand on the knob, head down as if he was brooding. When he looked up, his eyes lit on Robert and his eyebrows went up slightly, as if surprised to see him there; with a little smile he pulled the door open and left.

Robert took up the telephone and dialed.

"Would it be possible to add another to the

159

guest list for Friday?" he asked Genevieve.

A pause, and then "Of course," said Genevieve. "Who?"

"Bardin. I'll tell him to bring a date too, if that's all right."

"All right." There was another short pause. "Is there anything else? I'm just going out."

"Hair or fingernails or shopping?"

"Is that all you think I do," she said.

She wouldn't actually rush him off the phone, but her voice had a tautness to it, a smooth glassy quality that wouldn't permit conversation to get a handhold.

"Righty-o, won't keep you," he said.

They hung up before he could tell her, as he'd intended, that he hoped Friday's menu included a coconut shrimp dish of some kind. In the silence, he took up the stack of papers that the Boss had been thumbing through and held it vertically between his hands, tapping its bottom on the desk while smoothing the sides upward with his fingers. When it was a clean-edged brick he laid it down on the desk and opened a drawer, took out a folded soft cloth. He set about polishing the silver frame around Genevieve into smudgelessness again.

She was beautiful, really perfect. A wife for other men to envy. She had been right, the dignified portrait had been the appropriate choice; the other picture showed her in an unguarded moment, something only a husband should see.

CHAPTER NINE

During the cocktail hour before the dinner part of the party, the children — clean, sedate versions of their usual selves — were presented and allowed to mingle. Laura and Philip took themselves into a corner and ate crackers stolen from a tray while Bea lingered among the adults, chatting.

"Bea looks like a grownup," Laura whispered to Philip.

"No, she doesn't," he said, not looking. "Her socks are different."

It was true: Bea wore the same frilled little-girl white anklets as Laura, and the same patent-leather shoes with the single strap across the arch.

"What is this cheese stuff?" said Philip, sniffing at a cracker.

"She looks like Mum," said Laura, still watching Bea.

Philip scraped the suspicious matter from one cracker onto another, and ate the naked one. "Mum is beautiful," he said, chewing.

"Bea's got a monster face."

Laura laughed, although she knew it wasn't true. Laura and Philip both looked like their dad, brown-eyed and blond and knobby at the knees, with skin that tanned in the sun. Bea was a miniature Genevieve, dark hair and fair skin with deep blue eyes; she had to use special cream to prevent sunburn. Choy had done Bea's hair tonight, pulling it back with a velvet bow. Laura's own hair, which had a tendency to tangle, was kept short.

Across the room, Genevieve laughed a lovely long peal, putting a gloved hand to her neck, fingers splayed. As Laura watched, Beatrice mimicked her exactly, one dimpled hand flattened above her collar, her head cocked to one side.

I'll never look like that, thought Laura.

"That's a shiny lady," commented Philip with approval.

Laura looked. It was obvious whom he meant. The woman glowed near the center of the party room, as if drawing all the light there and focusing it: on her hair curved around her skull in a high glossy beehive, on her lips gleaming with pink lipstick, on her yellow silk dress. Her gloves were yellow too, and long, reaching up above her elbows. Her dress had little caps over the shoulders and a slit up one side of the skirt; the fabric was splashed with brilliant red flowers. Laura wondered if she could ever have such a dress.

Their mother's dressmaker seemed to make only ordinary clothes, in ordinary fabrics, with round flat buttons and zippers. No knot buttons or shiny flowered fabric or petals instead of proper sleeves. Laura didn't even consider the bright yellow gloves; she had a feeling they might be common.

When an hors d'oeuvres tray appeared, the lady in yellow turned from the redheaded man at her side and plucked a morsel from the decorative swirl. She held it with the tips of her gloved fingers and smiled at the Pettises, who were monopolizing the conversation in the little group, alternating sentences like a comedy team.

"They *promised* they'd return to collect us at five," Clara Pettis said.

"But at six there was still no sign of them," said her husband.

"There we were, in the wilds of Ayutthaya —"

"Night falling and no return transport in sight —"

"They didn't arrive until *seven fifteen.* Not one word of apology."

"Pretty standard," said Helen Malcolm. "Unfortunately."

"That's the Thai for you," said Joan Benderby. "Late for everything."

There was a little silence, during which all eyes went to, and quickly away from, the lady in the yellow dress. Joan colored. "I mean —" she began.

"She didn't mean anything by it," Mr. Benderby said.

"Oh, but you are quite right," the lady in yellow said. "The Thai have a horrible habit of tardiness. Of course, in their opinion it is no matter. For the Thai, everything is *sanuk, sanuk.*" She laughed. "You know — fun." The redheaded man beside her looked tense, and the rest of the group wore faint uncomfortable smiles. She looked around, puzzled. "Oh," she said, her face clearing. "You are worried that you might have offended me. Not at all." She took a sip from her glass. "I am not Thai. I am Vietnamese. We are very punctual."

The silence deepened for a moment, then exploded into bits of speech, each fragment highly pressured, like conversational shrapnel.

"Not *really,*" exclaimed Helen Malcolm.

From Mr. Benderby, "What is your home village? Do you —"

From Mr. Malcolm, "I'm sure you have some interesting —"

"Hi, look, there's Robert. We should say hello," said the lady's red-haired companion, taking her elbow to steer her away.

"Stay just a moment," Mr. Benderby said, laying a hand on the lady's forearm.

"We need to greet our host," said the redheaded man, keeping his own hand on his companion's other arm.

"He'll come over here," said Benderby.

The three of them stood like that, the slender girl flanked by the two men, all of them quite still, as though they were equally matched at a tug-of-war, with the girl as the rope.

This was how Genevieve came upon them. Had some tension in the air wafted across the party room and set her delicate social antennae trembling? Nothing about her face betrayed any consternation as she greeted them.

"How nice to see you again," she told the Benderbys and Pettises and Malcolms. Turning to the lady in yellow, "I don't believe we have properly met. What a lovely dress."

"Thank you," said the lady. Mr. Benderby dropped his hand from her arm. "I use Mr. Sip, on Rama IV."

"Well," said Genevieve. "So do I."

"Mrs. Preston," said the redheaded man. "Please let me present Miss Min Unpronounceable. Or is it Unpronounceable Min?"

"Mr. Bardin, really," said Genevieve, mock-frowning.

"Oh, Mrs. Preston," said Min. "It's much easier to forgive him his bad manners than to attempt to correct them."

"An eternal truth regarding men," said Genevieve. The women smiled at each other.

"Do you hear that, you're untrainable," said

166

Clara Pettis, delighted, slapping her hand against her husband's shirt front.

"Our family names can be challenging for Westerners," said Min. "It's simpler just to be Min."

"Well, then, I am Genevieve."

"We should have known you weren't Thai," Joan blurted out. "Your English is so good." The sudden silence made her look around the group. "What? It's *true.*"

"Blame it on the cocktails," said her husband with a practiced air of apology, plucking his wife's glass from her hand. "No more for you until you've had some dinner."

"Aren't you getting enough to eat?" asked Genevieve, looking about for a servant with a tray. "I'm afraid we've had oven troubles. You know how it is."

"Do I," said Clara Pettis, with feeling.

"I'm fine," said Joan. A flare of belligerence, before a light seemed to go out in her, and she dropped her eyes.

"My oven quit yesterday," said Clara, into the silence. "Right in the middle of a soufflé which took *hours* to make." She didn't specify whose hours exactly had been taken up by the preparation of the soufflé. "It was inedible. Like a cheese soup. The repairman said —"

"The dinner bell's about to go," said Bardin. "We haven't said two words to Robert yet." And the two moved off across the room, leaving Mrs. Pettis struggling on through her story, no one listening.

"— the wires were in such a snarl he wouldn't touch them for fear of electrocution —"

"Well, really," said Mr. Malcolm, watching Bardin and Min go.

Clara seemed to lose the thread of what she was saying, and abandoned her story.

"I think she *was* offended," said Mr. Benderby.

"To just walk away, right in the middle of a conversation," said Mr. Malcolm.

Nothing about Genevieve's expression betrayed that she might like to do the same.

"The bartender tonight seems to have a heavy hand," Genevieve told Joan. "I can't even finish mine. Why don't I get both of us something a little lighter?" She signaled across the room. As she did so, she caught sight of a man who had just arrived. He stood alone in a corner, examining the display of pottery on the shelves there.

"Sarah, please get Mrs. Benderby some ginger ale," Genevieve said when the Number Three was beside them. "Excuse me," she said to the group. "I must check on that tray of shrimp before everyone starves to death."

The shiny lady and the redheaded man were standing beside a large potted plant, having detached themselves from the other groups

168

in the party room. Philip, who was sitting behind the plant with his back against the wall, peered at them through the long fringes of leaf. He had dispatched Laura to find more provisions, but she had been waylaid en route by a conversation with a lady wearing pants, who bent way over and smiled ever more widely as she spoke, as though preparing to unhinge her jaws like a snake and swallow Laura whole. Philip had retreated behind the plant in hopes of avoiding a similar fate.

"You can't just say whatever you like," the redheaded man was telling the shiny lady.

"Why not?"

"Don't play dumb."

"You don't like dumb, big honey?" said the shiny lady, her features sliding into a greedy leer, her voice thickening into a pidgin. "Dumb, smart, you pay me same same." Then she laughed and her face transformed again, the fleeting ugliness vanished. The man looked away and caught a glimpse of Philip crouching behind the plant.

"Hallo, and who are you?" he said.

"Philip," said Philip.

"Of course," said Mr. Bardin. "I'd have known you anywhere. You have your father's eyebrows."

Philip was pleased by that. He liked that this man didn't bend his knees or make a big show of leaning forward to speak to him, as almost any other grownup would have done, and that he didn't comment on Philip's hiding place. He didn't laugh, or seem as if he was trying not to laugh. He spoke in an ordinary voice through the branches of the potted tree.

"Your hair is orange," observed Philip.

"Indeed," said the man, rubbing a hand over his head. "A family curse."

"Really?" said Philip. This sounded interesting.

"Every good family has one," said the man. "Doesn't yours?"

"They haven't told me yet," said Philip.

"Mr. Bardin, you are terrible," said the lady. To Philip she said, "He's only teasing."

Mr. Bardin stepped back a bit, made a sweeping bow. "Philip Preston, may I present —" and he said something like *MinWin*. It sounded like a joke name and Philip almost laughed but stopped himself in time.

"Hello," said Philip, getting up and coming around the plant. He made a wai, bringing his hands up high so that his thumbs touched the bridge of his nose. "It's very nice to meet you."

"*Sawadee-kha,*" said Min, making a smiling wai back. "It is nice to meet you too, Philip Preston. I take it" — she indicated the plant with a small bright flutter of her gloved fingers — "that you are not fond of parties."

"I hate them," said Philip with vigor. "The food is awful and the people are so boring.

They always want to talk to me about school."

"Unimaginative," said Bardin. "To be fair, though, school is what one mostly does at your age. Bear up, that won't be forever." He added, "And I promise that not all parties are like the ones your parents give."

"I wish Uncle Murray had come tonight," said Philip. "But they never invite anybody good to the *important* parties." He glowered at the crowd, then brought his eyes back to Bardin and Min, and flushed. "I didn't mean you."

"Of course not," said Mr. Bardin easily.

"What makes this party important?" asked Min.

"Some *guy* is coming," said Philip.

"Ah," said Mr. Bardin. "Well, think of it this way, Philip. Your parents are teaching you a valuable skill, forcing you to learn how to cope with dullards. The world is absolutely stuffed with them."

"Stop teasing him," said Min.

"Never more serious," said Mr. Bardin. And to Philip, "If you don't like to talk about school, what does interest you?"

Philip shrugged.

"What do you do during the summertime?" Min asked in her gentle voice.

"Swimming, and riding lessons, and judo," Philip said.

"Riding is very good for the posture," said Min. "Do you enjoy the judo?"

171

"No," Philip said. "It's the wrong class."

"What do you mean?" asked Bardin.

And in the shadow of the potted plant, to the accepting ears of strangers, the orange-haired man with the curse and the shiny lady, Philip divulged his secret. They listened without comment, all through.

"They call me Nitnoy," he whispered at the end.

"How horrible," said Min. She was frowning. "This is very unusual for Thai."

"Well," said Bardin, raising his glass to his lips. "Boys."

"Is this the place near Khlong Toey?" said Min. Philip nodded. She turned to Mr. Bardin and said something in a quick language that Philip didn't understand.

Mr. Bardin gave a low whistle. "Philip, you really are in the wrong class," he said. "Muay Thai boxing is not judo." He set his glass down on a little table beside the potted plant and took a cigarette box from the inside of his jacket. He opened it and offered it to Min, who shook her head. He then gravely offered it to Philip, who also shook his head, then he put it away.

"I can't tell my parents," said Philip. "They'd just say 'Stiff upper lip.'"

"Naturally," said Mr. Bardin, cocking open a square silver lighter. "Quite a dilemma." The hollows deepened in his face as he puffed the cigarette into life. He flipped the lighter closed, put it away. "You could sustain a small injury, I suppose. Sprain a finger, break a toe. Nothing too serious. Something just incapacitating enough to keep you out of class."

"He's teasing," said Min. "Don't listen to him, Philip."

"She's right about that," said Mr. Bardin. "You shouldn't ask advice of me. Philip, I am what your parents would call a scoundrel."

"You're not," said Philip earnestly. "I'm sure you're not."

"Thanks for the vote of confidence, old man." He hesitated for a moment as if considering something, then said, "That boy Andrew was lying, you know." He took a deep draft on his cigarette. "There aren't any high kicks or karate chopping in judo." He put his head back and released a long twisting cable of smoke. "Absolutely no breaking of things with the feet," he told the ceiling, then brought his head back down and looked into Philip's puzzled face. "Those antics at school were pure fiction."

"Why would he do that?" asked Philip.

"People lie for all kinds of reasons," said Mr. Bardin. "He was probably trying to impress the other boys." He smiled. "Or the girls." He took Min's arm. "Will you be joining us for dinner?" he asked Philip.

Philip shook his head. "We already ate."

Min put her hand out to him, and Philip

did what his father would do: put his hand up and took her gloved fingertips, letting them curl over his own fingers, trapping them lightly with his thumb and bending his head over them.

"It was lovely to meet you, Philip Preston," she said. She leaned toward him. For a frightened, ecstatic moment, Philip thought that she meant to kiss him. But she merely put her mouth close to his ear.

"Do not believe it," said Min, as the hairs on the back of his neck lifted from the warmth of her breath. "This man is the worst scoundrel you will ever know." Then she straightened up with a laugh, releasing Philip's fingers, and the two of them moved away.

The woman in the trousers in the middle of the party room smiled widely as she issued her edict: *Don't ever learn how to make coffee.*

Longing for escape, Laura looked across the room to the place where she'd left Philip, but he wasn't there.

"Mark my words," said the woman. There was a bit of lipstick on her teeth. "You'll find yourself in a group of men one day, and they'll ask you to make coffee."

There was Philip, behind a potted plant. Laura put her tongue out at him.

"It may seem like nothing," said the woman, speaking more loudly, jerking Laura's attention back. "But *if you do it,* it will diminish you. From that time on, you'll be thought of as a servant to the others. You'll be their subordinate; no one will listen to anything you say." She raised a finger. "If you know how to do something, it will be very difficult to refuse to do it if you are asked. That seems to be how we women are made." A rueful shake of her head. "And if you know how and you refuse, they'll be as affronted as if you slapped them. But if you *don't know how,* you lose nothing. It's not a skill they respect. They'll be annoyed in the moment, but it will force them to think about you differently." With a hint of wistfulness, "Maybe by the time you grow up, things will be different." Her brows lowered. "But I doubt it. Promise me right now that you will never learn how to make coffee."

Laura nodded, although the promise seemed unnecessary. Her mum never made coffee. If as a grownup Laura decided to drink coffee, she presumed that someone else would make it.

Maxwell Dawson was shorter than Genevieve had expected. His charcoal suit was flawless, no doubt custom made for his powerful build, and unwrinkled although he'd just gotten off an airplane — probably the hotel staff working their usual miracles. He had slipped into the Prestons' party room without fanfare and was standing in a corner alone, looking at the shelf of Sawankhalok pots Genevieve had procured for a song the month before.

"Mr. Dawson," she said as she approached him, the words emphatic enough to express strong welcome while not loud enough to draw the attention of anyone else in the room. "How was your flight? You must be exhausted. Let me get you a drink."

"They brought me one," he said, indicating the glass that was sweating condensation onto a nearby table. "Liquor doesn't mix well with jet lag, in my experience." He took up one of the blue-gray pots, palmed it in his blunt-fingered hand.

"The time change can be so disorienting," she said. "Perhaps a soft drink?" He shook his head no. "We have some shrimp coming out of the oven in a minute. Can I tempt you?"

"The famous Genevieve Preston," he told the pot.

"Excuse me?"

"Your reputation has preceded you," he said, removing the lid of the pot with a little grating noise.

"All good, I hope," she said without dimming her smile, although she was not at all certain of his meaning.

He said nothing, peering into the small well of darkness, while she felt a gathering anxiety — was a madman in charge of her family's future?

"When I was preparing to come over," he said, finally, replacing the lid and returning the pot to the shelf, taking up another, "at least three different people made a point of telling me not to miss one of your parties — *if* I was lucky enough to get an invitation." His voice lacked the light tones of flattery; it sounded almost as if he were scolding her.

"Of course you'd be invited," she said warmly. "You're the guest of honor." Squashing her frustration: How could she beguile a man who wouldn't even look at her? "And while I suspect that you're teasing me, it is lovely to think that they're talking about my parties back home."

"I didn't realize anyone actually considered DC home," he said. The pot he had in his hand now was Genevieve's favorite, a small unglazed globe with a beak and comb and tail pinched out on its surface to make a fat rooster. It was unprepossessing, but by far the most valuable piece in the display. "I thought the population there was fully imported, all lawyers and politicians."

"I was born there," said Genevieve. She hated the abbreviation *DC;* it sounded like a medical procedure. *Washington* was dignified, a hero's name.

"Such a European-looking city," he said. "And the cherry blossoms — spectacular."

"Oh, yes," agreed Genevieve. "Picturesque." Those damned cherry blossoms. She suspected that many who raved about them had never seen them. The festival was mistimed, scheduled too early in the spring; the Cherry Blossom Parade often marched down a chilly avenue flanked by tight-budded trees. The 1968 festival, the last one Genevieve had seen, had been unpleasantly windy, cool gusts ripping the petals from the boughs and swirling them around the parade marchers and watchers like angry snow.

"You've been in Bangkok, what, two years?" he asked.

"Just over four," said Genevieve, pleased that they were on the subject already.

He put his fingertip on the nipple of clay that had been pinched into being centuries ago to make the rooster's beak. Genevieve bit back the admonition that sprang to her lips: *Be careful with that.*

"I don't think anyone else from the project has been over here as long," he said. Only after the following pause had elapsed did Genevieve realize that she'd missed her cue, to say *You know, I think you're right,* with wide ingenuous eyes. "Blame your husband," he said. "He's too good at his job."

"If he were that good, the dam would already be built and we'd be home," she said, and immediately felt scalded: Why had she said *that*? He lifted his eyes to hers for the first time.

"Do you not like it here?" he asked.

His eyes were brown and heavily lashed, an oddly feminine detail on such an otherwise masculine man.

"It's so hot," she said lamely. She grasped for a narrative thread, found herself clutching at the Ladies' luncheon conversation. "And the Thai can be so confusing," she gabbled. "That whole *kha kha kha* thing they say. Why can't they simply say yes or no?"

"They like harmony," he said. "They don't want to tell you no."

"How do they even understand each other?"

"They understand each other," he said. "We don't understand them, that's all."

There was a pause, during which he scrutinized her face and then moved his eyes downward in a way that wasn't, Genevieve thought, quite nice. She knew she should say something, anything, to draw his attention up to her face again, but instead she felt herself preening a little, letting him look. In the cool of the party room it was possible to wear a fitted dress, and this one was particularly flattering.

"Heat is interesting," he said. "It affects different people different ways." The rooster pot fit into his palm like an apple; he rolled it between his hands as he spoke. She watched the little beak twist now clockwise, now counter-clockwise. "Some people get looser. Less *uptight,* as the current slang would put

179

it; have you heard that expression?" She shook her head. "Others become more callous. It's as if some personalities soften, while others bake to brick."

This was where she would normally inject a lubricating clump of syllables, *How interesting* or *Do go on.* But she said nothing, and he spoke again.

"A man I knew once had been living in West Africa for a year or so when I went to visit," he said in a storytelling tone. "I arrived at a moment of crisis: a young stray dog had dug under the wall of the storehouse and eaten a ham." They were now both watching his hands as they moved back and forth, the pot rolling between them. "This was a man who, when at home, pampered his Yorkshire terriers shamelessly; but on the other side of the world I watched him shoot a puppy in the head without a blink, before offering me lunch."

Genevieve imagined a Rudyard Kipling tableau, the dog whining and wagging, its tummy tight with stolen meat, the sahib in linen shirt and trousers staring coldly down, desert orange stretching away in all directions.

"It's always a problem sending a man to a hot climate," said Maxwell Dawson. "You never know what you'll get back." He tossed the pot into the air. *Say nothing,* she told herself, stifling her gasp, *say nothing.* He caught the pot, tossed it up again. "I wonder if that's also true of a woman. Are you the same person who left the States three years ago?"

"Of course I am," she said. Her eyes followed the five-hundred-year-old morsel of pottery. Up, down, up. She thought, *You know I said four.* The muscle of his arm swelled and pulled at the cloth of his upper sleeve; the white knobs of his knuckles flexed as his hand opened and closed.

"Are these pots valuable?" he asked.

She hesitated, on her lips *Heavens, I don't know, I just think they're pretty,* but something stopped her.

"Very," she said, two hard syllables.

He caught the pot with one hand and held it. Smiled. "Perhaps you could show me where you got them," he said, putting the rooster back onto the shelf, turning it so the little beak faced out into the room. "My wife rather fancies old bits of pottery."

His *wife.* Was she mistaken, then, about the undercurrents of their exchange?

He turned back toward Genevieve, the larger motion of his body hiding the smaller movement of his arm. He was very close to her now. He must have taken a step toward her; or had she moved toward him? His arm crossed the space between them and he curled the fingers of one hand, the one he'd used to toss and catch the little rooster, lightly around the swell of her forearm. At the touch, she felt a warm electrical jolt.

"There's a large outdoor market very near my hotel." His voice was still conversational, casual. "You must have to shop sometimes."

"My servants do most of it," she said. To her horror, her own voice was low, almost sultry.

"I'm at the Erawan. Room 510," he said. "Perhaps you might be shopping in that area next week. In the hot hours."

A movement then, out of the corner of Genevieve's eye. She turned to see the Number Three, Sarah. She was carrying a heavy tray and had clearly come to set it down on the low table by Genevieve, but something she had seen or heard had stopped her in her tracks. Under their double gaze, the girl backed away a couple of steps.

"What do you have there?" said Maxwell. Genevieve felt his grip on her arm dissolve. He beckoned to the servant; she approached and he leaned forward to examine the contents of the tray. He took up an hors d'oeuvre in its fluted paper, popped it into his mouth. "Mm," he said. "Mrs. Preston, would you like one?"

"Sarah, please take those somewhere else," said Genevieve. She could hear her own heartbeat coming through the words, making them waver. The girl looked up and their eyes met. "Go," said Genevieve.

The girl stumbled backward as if from a hissing snake, whirled around so fast her braid flew out behind her. She caught one foot on the fringe of the carpet that lay on the polished floor, and lost her balance.

"Another wild success," said Robert, as they were getting ready for bed that night. "Dawson himself told me that he found you charming, and the curry the best he's ever had in Thailand."

"That's good," Genevieve said, unpinning the fall from the back of her head. It was warm from lying against her skull; it felt like a sleeping mouse in her hand. She placed it on the dressing table and took up a comb, drew its long pointed handle just above her ear, isolating a lock of hair; she rolled it around to make a spiraling curl, reached for a hairpin.

"I know what you're thinking about," said her husband, bending to kiss the top of her head as he loosened his tie. Her fingers stilled, holding the curl and the pin, and her eyes went to his in the mirror. "That disaster with the hors d'oeuvres." He pulled the tie from his collar.

Just a tiny pause before she replied, "That carpet will never be the same." She drove the bobby pin in against her scalp, trapping the curl.

"Was it one of the good carpets?" Robert said, head tilted back, grimacing as he worked a collar button loose.

"No," she said. She pinned the curl on the other side and reached for the scarf that hung from the mirror, slung it around her neck and pulled it upward carefully, cradling the back of her hairstyle at the nape, then tied the points at the top of her forehead. She watched Robert's reflection bend each elbow in turn to undo first the left cuff, then the right, and drop the cuff links into the leather cup on the dresser. Then the long row of buttons on the stiff cotton front. Always the same sequence: collar, left cuff, right cuff, then shirtfront top to bottom.

"Mr. Dawson was interested in the Sawankhalok pieces," she said, dipping a washcloth in the jar of face cream and wiping it across first one cheek, then the other. "I thought I might take him around the little shops next week." She found a clean place on the cloth and wound it tight around her index finger, closed her eyes and worked her fingertip carefully across one eyelid to remove the color, hearing her mother's admonition, *Never mistreat the tissues around the eyes or in time they will take their revenge.*

Robert replied from the bathroom, his voice lost in the rush of the tap.

She twisted the cap off a jar of moisturizer and dove her fingertips in, captured a shoal

184

of cream that she smoothed upward in long strokes, collarbone to jawline, cheek to brow, slipping her hands around her neck. In the mirror, her husband emerged from the bathroom, trousers unzipped; in one motion he slid them and his undershorts down, then stepped away from the puddle of cloth. No man would ever stand naked in his socks again, she thought, if he ever once saw himself do it.

"Who was that girl Bardin brought?" he asked, taking his pajamas from the flat pile under his pillow, shaking out the top and putting his arms into the sleeves, left then right, then buttoning hem to neck, squinting with chin on chest to align the topmost button with its buttonhole.

"Min something. She's Vietnamese," said Genevieve. "Giles Benderby was pressing her for gruesome stories." She dipped her ring finger into the jar and patted cream against the soft places under her eyes.

Robert sat on the edge of the bed, peeled off the left sock and then the right, leaving them in dark balls on the floor, then swung his legs up onto the bed and lay back against the pillows.

Genevieve rubbed her hands together, driving the last of the cream into her skin, then screwed the top onto the jar and returned it to its place on the vanity.

"The Benderbys are altogether too coarse,"

she said. She went around to her side of the bed, turned the covers back, and got in beside her husband. Settling her head against the pillow, careful not to crush the hairstyle under the scarf or touch her anointed face to the linen, she reached with still-moist fingers to turn off the bedside lamp. "At home, I don't think that we'd know them."

The new driver might have become a dull figure, of no interest to Laura, if she had not spied him in the garden late that night of the party, near the servants' quarters at the back of the property. The wooden structure was strictly off-limits to everyone except the three house servants who slept there; the children accepted this, putting the Quarters into a category with other uninteresting grown-up things like cigar-smoking and olives, and jokes like the one about the polar bear, which Philip got spanked for listening to. Not even Kai, who went everywhere else in the garden and was responsible for the care of all of it, went into the Quarters. He didn't live there; both he and the driver arrived daily from their own homes somewhere in the city beyond the gates.

At first, Laura was not certain that it *was* Somchit; he should have gone home for the day long before then. Also, she'd never seen him dressed this way: no tie or jacket, just a short-sleeved shirt with the collar open. There was no reason for him to be slinking around the garden, or anywhere near the Quarters. He simply had no business being there.

Of course, neither did Laura have any business seeing him there; she was breaking rules by being out of bed so late. She pressed her forehead against the window glass, holding her breath so as not to fog the view, and watched the slim figure as it went down the path through the garden and disappeared into the darkness beside the gates. A moment later he emerged, now part of a complicated play of shadows. Half man, half wheeled, the apparition pulled open the gate and, just before slipping through, turned its face back toward the house.

Laura stood a bit longer at the window after he had gone. She found that she had risen to her toes in sympathetic stealth. Had it been Somchit? The whole episode, just moments past, seemed dreamlike. She turned to look at Beatrice, who lay soundlessly in her bed across the room. Laura crept back to her own bed, slipping in and forcing her toes right down to find the cool patch between the sheets.

It *had* been Somchit. The domed forehead, the cheekbones, the nose, the ink-black hair gleaming at the part — she'd seen them all clearly when the moonlit bicycle-beast had looked back toward the house, just before

slipping through the gate.
She wondered if she should tell.

PART 2

PART 2

CHAPTER TEN

2019

Suvarnabhumi airport was clean and modern, not much different from the ultra-high-tech and sparkling Narita, where Laura had spent a short layover. She followed the signs to the taxi stand with a blank feeling: nothing she saw, or smelled, or heard, sparked any recollection. She went through the glass exit doors into daylight and a heat sudden and stifling and close all around, as though she'd stepped into a giant mouth. The taxi driver read the address on the paper she gave him, then handed the paper back, turned on the meter, and pulled away from the curb.

They were soon on a highway, the traffic thick but moving well, the driver barely slowing at toll points as he rolled the window down to chuck the coins. It was a large roadway, four lanes in each direction; only the Thai characters on the green signs hanging over the road distinguished it from the Beltway that circled Washington.

She glanced down at the paper in her hand and realized it bore the address of Claudette's house. Laura had meant to give the taxi driver the other paper, the one with the hotel address. She considered telling him to change the destination, but decided against it. Apparently fate had intervened to send her directly to Philip.

From the map she'd studied on the plane, she knew this highway traveled north of the city and ran east-west, so Bangkok itself would be to the left of them. Laura kept her face turned to that window but she saw no skyline, nothing but scrubby industry, palm trees, houses. So much concrete. So many billboards. Where were the temples she remembered? Where was all the green? They took a hard left and traffic slowed to a crawl, the road narrowing to two lanes between a double array of diverse buildings: storefronts, two-story houses, apartment complexes with exterior staircases switchbacking up their sides, the open mouth of a car wash.

"You come to Bangkok before?" inquired the taxi driver.

"Not for a long time," said Laura.

"Oh, many change," said the man, nodding. He probably hadn't even been born when she'd lived there.

A break in the billboards revealed a stretch of horizon, a serration of tall buildings against a violet smudge of pollution, before the road crested up into the sky and plateaued at the new height. They were traveling in choked but steady traffic along the rooflines of buildings that crowded up on both sides of the concrete barriers when Laura saw, jammed between a billboard and a mirror-glassed office building, a red-tiled temple roof. Its ornate peaks and scrollwork passed mere yards from the taxi window, close enough almost to touch, then were gone.

They crossed over an expanse of brown water and the taxi peeled away down an exit, diving into the overpass shadow and emerging into a broad passageway without lane markers, traffic plaiting and unplaiting at high speed. After a few hair-raising minutes of that they were delivered into a narrow street with a topiaried median to the right, and on the left a line of open umbrellas like dirty canvas flowers. Abruptly there was a wall of cement outside Laura's window, and the road became shuddering dirt.

"Construction," said the driver, smiling into the rearview mirror, before turning into an alley. Sheet metal panels rose well above eye level on either side, making a channel barely wide enough for one car. There were no other cars and no pedestrians in sight.

Laura was suddenly aware that not a soul on earth had any idea where she was. *She* had no idea where she was, and she was a day's travel by air from anyone she knew. There was no protection against what might happen now, deep in this anonymous alley in this foreign place. She fumbled her phone from her pocket, turned it on.

It vibrated with text after text, alert boxes floating up on the screen in quick succession. Many of them from Edward. It was surprising that he had sent so many. He was used to her going incommunicado periodically while working; normally he'd send one or two texts and stop to wait for a reply. She flicked the alerts away and tapped in a text to Sullivan. I'm in Bangkok. Looking at the paper, she carefully copied the address of the house into a text and added, If I don't text you again in an hour, call the Bangkok police and give them this address.

No reply dots — of course not. It was barely six a.m. where he was.

The taxi stopped beside a high wall. The driver shut off the meter and turned on the dome light, announced the fare with a smile. She could still turn back, she thought numbly as she paid with her card. The driver popped the trunk and got out, returned with her bag in his hand. He stood beside her window, looking quizzically in at her. *Now or never,* she thought. She gathered herself, reached for the door handle.

And stepped out into the hot breath of her childhood. Potent and unmistakable, that tapestry of scent: flowers and sewage and cooking odors and things Laura couldn't name. She stood wavering, taking it in.

"You okay?" asked the taxi driver, setting her bag beside her.

"Yes," she said. "Thank you."

He made a wai and got back into the car. She went forward, carrying the bag toward a tall wooden gate. It bore shiny numerals that matched the house number on the paper, but she could see no button or call box. Puzzled, she looked to the right and left of the gate — nothing but smooth, featureless wall.

"Puuun." The syllable came from behind her.

She turned: the taxi driver was grinning from his window, making a pulling motion like a train conductor sounding his horn. She turned back and saw a hanging string, like the chain for a WC. She grasped it and pulled down, was rewarded by a tinkling sound from an invisible brace of bells.

"Right house?" called the taxi driver.

"I don't know," she said.

"Okay," he said, but he didn't start up the engine. They waited together. She was considering pulling the chain again when the gate cracked open and a Thai face peeked out.

"Hello, er, *sawadee-kha,*" Laura said. "I'm looking for Claudette?"

The opening in the gate widened; a short elderly man stood in the gap. He made a wai and stood back for her to go through.

"I wait for you five minute," the taxi driver called as the gate shut behind her.

Even in the gathering darkness, Laura could see that the property was magnificent, lawn sweeping around, long banks of shrubbery. A low stone wall surrounded a fishpond — she blinked and saw Choy sitting there, reaching out to the water with a hand loosely cupped around a ball of rice, two fingers extended to pluck the surface and summon the fish. Choy wasn't there, of course; there was no one sitting on the wall.

The man was climbing a set of steps that rose to a large framed wooden house; she followed, placing her feet carefully, some deep warning bell in her mind tolling *snake*. There were no lights on anywhere. The man paused outside the front door of the house to slip off his shoes and Laura did the same, leaving them in a line with the others there — just four pairs, she noticed — and then he led her inside. They went down a corridor that was lit only by the waning daylight coming through glass panes high in the walls, past a number of closed doors, before they arrived at a wide doorless opening. A far light glowed within, at the end of a very large room. From a distance it seemed to be a surreally suspended disk, like a hovering ball of lightning, but as Laura approached she could see that it was a 1970s-style floor lamp, a globe at the end of a curved silver arc, like an eyeball on a giant stalk. In the pool of incandescence it shed were four bentwood chairs, and in one of those sat a small woman, posture erect, holding a cellular phone at eye level.

"Miss Preston," she said, putting the phone down, standing up and coming forward, hand extended. "How was your flight?"

In person, Claudette's face was slightly too broad, the eyes too far apart, to be strictly pretty. She had a vivacity, though, that made her visually arresting, and she was pristinely groomed. She was tiny. Towering over her, Laura felt grubby and gross.

"Fine," said Laura, setting her bag down and enduring the brisk handshake. "Long."

"I'm sorry it's so dark in here," said Claudette. "No electricity in the house. We have had to improvise." She sat again, waved Laura to the chair opposite, spoke to the old man. "Kiet. Bring two bottled waters, please."

The room, scattered with shapes of furniture — carved low tables, a hinged screen — had the haphazard, unintentional look of a space that was just being moved into or out of. Laura supposed the *improvisation* was the long extension cord she could see snaking away from the base of the floor lamp and out of the pool of light. Toward a window, perhaps, and outside, to an electrical pole that Kiet or someone else had climbed in order to splice into the box there.

As if suspicious of Laura's interest in the room's furnishings, Claudette spoke sharply.

"My father didn't leave a will," she said.

"The house and everything in it now belong to me."

"Of course," said Laura. "Where is Philip?"

"Meditating," said Claudette, the word delivered with a strong flavor of restraint, as if she were suppressing an eye roll. "He meditates twice a day. They all did." Her air of vague disdain was familiar, from the Skype sessions. "The house was wired for electricity, but they did not use it. Over the years, the wires rotted or were eaten by mice." She shook her head. "Imagine, no air-conditioning in Bangkok." Reading something in Laura's expression, she added, "It wasn't a cult, if that's what you're thinking."

"I wasn't," lied Laura. But that had been the charitable option.

"It was more like a business cooperative," said Claudette. "They made things. Cloth, pottery, honey." She opened her purse and extracted a cigarette case. She allowed herself the eye roll this time, accompanied by a tiny headshake. "I had to relocate half a million bees." Tamping a cigarette against her thumbnail. "So. We must wait for the meditation to finish." She put the cigarette into her mouth and lit it.

"How long has my brother been living here?" said Laura. *My brother.* It felt so strange to say that.

"Decades," Claudette said. She pronounced it *dee-cades.* "According to him, he came here around 1980. Not long after my father left my mother and moved here." Her voice held a shadow of teenage pain. "When was the last time you spoke with him?"

No one that Laura knew smoked anymore. The burning tip, the smoke spiraling up, the acrid smell were mesmerizing.

"Philip has been missing since he was eight," she said.

Claudette stared at her. "Eight," she repeated, hissing smoke with the word. "Eight years old?"

"Yes," said Laura. "He disappeared in 1972."

In the stunned silence that followed, the servant appeared with the bottled waters. *Thank you,* murmured Laura in Thai as she took one, surprising herself. *Khob khun kha.* Where had those words come from?

"Well, my father had nothing to do with that," declared Claudette, twisting the cap off her bottle. "In 1972, my father was still living in Lausanne, with me and my mother." She put the bottle to her lips, took a swallow. "He was a professor of philosophy."

"Perhaps they met before they came to live in this house," said Laura. She strove to make her voice neutral, as if she were not accusing the dead father of kidnapping or pedophilia. Even if Claudette's father hadn't been the one who originally took him, Philip would still have been a minor, at least according to

U.S. law, until December 1981.

"Not possible," said Claudette. "My father lived with us until February of 1980." Her jaw was square, defensive. It was clear that February 1980 was her life's landmark, *when Papa left,* the way that August 1972 was the Preston family watershed. "He had never lived in Asia before. My mother thought it was temporary insanity, but it seems not." She took another drag on her cigarette. "Not temporary," she clarified.

In February 1980, Philip had been just sixteen. If he had come here to this house then, that still left eight blank years after his disappearance.

"What is your plan?" Claudette said. "Where will you take him?"

"Home," said Laura. "To the U.S."

"That will probably be difficult," said Claudette, in a not-my-problem tone. "He doesn't have a passport. No identification papers of any kind."

"I was thinking we could get a DNA test."

"Hm." A noncommittal sound. Claudette leaned forward to tap her ash into an ashtray on the low table between them. "We've had a doctor to visit," she said, non sequitur. "He said there is something chronic, possibly with the liver, and his heart is not strong. He prescribed some pills."

She leaned back again, and Laura saw her fatigue. In the midst of grief for her father, probably also coping with a lifetime's unresolved feelings of abandonment, Claudette had had to contend with all the mess left behind, a crowd of strangers (freeloaders, or cult members, or prisoners, whatever they had been), the half a million bees. Something perhaps like rehoming a litter of mongrel puppies one by one. Philip was the last.

They sat without speaking for a few minutes, Claudette apparently unbothered by the silence, smoking while Laura sipped from the tepid bottle of water.

"Here he is now," Claudette said.

Laura turned her head, and felt her heart seize at the sight of her dead father in the doorway.

"You two look very much alike," commented Claudette.

"It's the hair," he said. His smile acknowledged the weakness of the joke.

Laura stood up, went to him. His wai complicated her embrace at first, before he put his arms down. She looked up into his face, saw again her father adumbrated there, in the shape of the eye sockets, the long chin.

He seated himself on one of the chairs, and Laura sat opposite him.

"So," he said. "You turned out to be pretty." Dryly added, "Against all odds." Then he smiled, and the skin dented under his left eye, like a high, horizontal dimple. Their father had had that dimple. Laura had it too.

She tried to match his teasing tone. "You turned out to be tall. That's the real headline." Skirting around the gigantic question — where had he been, and in what circumstances, when that growth spurt had taken place?

She'd expected, without really planning it, to get the whole story immediately. *What happened that day you disappeared* and *Where have you been for forty-seven years?* But now that the moment was here, she found herself thwarted. Not just by the presence of onlookers — the servant in the corner, grim Claudette sipping from her bottle of water — but by a muffling shyness. As though Philip were a stranger.

"You're living in the States now?" he said.

Again, she noticed that he didn't sound completely American. Laura had worked hard to eradicate her own accent after they'd come back, mimicking her classmates, rounding her vowels and dulling her *T*s. Was Philip's voice the sound of her own youth, preserved as if in amber?

"Yes," she said. "We went back after — we moved back there."

He nodded. "And how are the rest of the Prestons?"

The rest of the Prestons, what an odd way to put it. Unnerved, aware of Claudette's gimlet eye, Laura became chatty.

"Well, Bea is exactly as you'd expect. As bossy as ever, running the world from her house in Northern Virginia. She has twin boys, you can't believe how handsome and smart they are. Her husband does something we're not allowed to ask about." She almost added *like Daddy,* but stopped herself. Partly from long habit — non–family members in earshot — and also because maybe Philip hadn't ever known. What had they understood about their father's work back in 1972? "Mum is doing well, very healthy." Too difficult to explain about the dementia now. "Noi helps with her, remember Noi?"

He nodded. "And Dad?" he said.

"He died." Her eyes instantly moist, thirtynine years a mere fingersnap to grief. "In 1980." Philip may have already been living here then, free to come and go. Or *had* he been free? And where had he been before that? Again, the question Laura's thoughts kept crashing against like a tide against a seawall: Why hadn't he contacted them sooner?

"I'm sorry to hear that." His tone kind but somewhat removed, as if he was sorry for *the rest of the Prestons,* for Laura and Beatrice and for their mother, for the untimely ending of a human life, but not as if he felt the loss personally.

"Philip," she said, leaning forward. *What*

happened to you? on her lips.

He shot his eyes sideways, toward Claudette. It was the first rapid movement he'd made, and the implication was clear: he didn't want to discuss anything in front of her.

So instead of speaking the question, Laura said, "We have to get you home, all right?" A thought struck her. "You do want to go back to America?"

"Well, he can't stay here," interjected Claudette. She'd lit another cigarette, and shot out a long skein of smoke between pursed lips. She turned her head, told Kiet, "Bring the little blue bag."

"I thought we'd sort this out over a day or two," said Laura, taken aback.

"You can sort it out at a hotel, yes?" said Claudette.

At that moment it all came together, muzzily overwhelming: the lack of sleep, the heat, the utter strangeness of the scene with the bald brother-stranger and the irritated Swiss woman, the orphaned furniture and the pool of light in which they all sat, the powerful but fragmentary nostalgia.

"May I use the bathroom?" she asked Claudette in a faint voice. Asking her permission instead of Philip's, although this had been Philip's home — his prison? — for *dee-cades.*

"Of course," said Claudette with a surprised

tone, as though she hadn't just made it clear that she intended to expel both of them from the property posthaste. She motioned to Kiet to show Laura the way. "Take a torch," she said, indicating a cluster of flashlights that stood on the table, flared heads down.

Laura slid the bathroom's pocket door closed — no lock, she noticed again — and balanced the flashlight on the sink, the basin muffling its glow, while she got out her phone. Six thirty p.m. was seven thirty a.m. there. Sunday, so Edward would be at home, having breakfast. She felt an abrupt longing to be there with him, fluffy scrambled eggs and buttered pumpernickel toast and hot milky coffee, the newspaper crossword cued up on the iPad. She would love to hear his voice — but she didn't want to hear his remonstrations. The person she most wanted to talk to, she realized, was Beatrice. Although what would she say to her? *Bea, I've come to Bangkok to get Philip and it's super weird and I wish you were here.* And more, her imagined monologue running down a surprising channel, *Why can't we ever be united on anything, we're sisters and Daddy's dead and who knows what Mum remembers, our childhood is gone apart from our memories of it and why are we always on opposite sides of some invisible line?* Even if she were disinhibited enough to say all that, she wouldn't get the first sentence out — by *Bangkok,* Bea's outraged questions would interrupt. And even if Bea listened, even if she were able to put aside her anger, what could she do to help, in this moment, from across the world? She recalled Bea leaning against the counter in her kitchen, her impassioned, defeated *I can't.*

Laura put away the phone. She had begun this on her own; she'd have to finish it.

Claudette called a car, and Laura and her long-lost brother left the compound together. Although the house had reportedly been his home for most of his life, Philip left it without looking back, slipping his feet into the largest of the paired sandals beside the front door and walking out. Kiet presented a small blue duffel — all of Philip's worldly possessions, apparently — and Laura slung its strap over her shoulder beside the strap of her own bag and followed Philip's limping form down the front steps and then the long path, toward the gate. Absurdly, she was still gripping the half-full water bottle, sloshing water against the cap with every step.

They rode into the heart of a positively futuristic-looking downtown, lighted skyscrapers rising all around them and an elevated rail running high alongside. Laura gave up looking for landmarks. She remembered grass, wooden buildings, temples. Of course things must have changed a lot in so many years, but how could *all* of it be gone?

From the U.S., she'd booked into a hotel whose name she was sure she had recognized; when the taxi drew up before a modern tower she knew it couldn't be the same building. They got out of the car and a bellman took their bags; Laura and Philip followed him into an extravagantly planted portico three stories tall, its ceiling a glassed dome of hovering twilight.

The doorman deposited the bags at the front desk and made a quick wai before heading back toward the hotel entrance. Laura gave her name and asked the clerk for a second room, if possible one adjacent to the one she'd reserved. The clerk shook his head — there were no other rooms available on the same floor.

"On a different floor, then," she said.

"I will look, madame." The word conjured up Genevieve so powerfully that Laura had the impulse to look around for her. But of course *madame* was nonspecific; her mother had been just one among many, and now Laura was one herself. The clerk finished clicking computer keys and said with infinite apology, "I am so sorry, madame. We have no other rooms available."

"In the whole hotel?"

"Yes," said the clerk, smiling as though he were not delivering bad news.

Laura had been looking forward to some

privacy, to regroup, to decide what to do, perhaps to telephone Edward. Would she have to sleep in the same *bed* with Philip?

"Well, that will have to do," said Laura, with a gaiety she did not feel, her mother's voice in her head singing *In for a penny, in for a pound.* "We can share the room. Is that all right with you?" she asked Philip, who nodded.

A bellman appeared, pushing a brass luggage carrier; he plucked the two bags from the carpet, nestled them onto the velvet planchet as lovingly as though they were Vuitton, and led the way to the lift.

When the bellman switched the overhead light on in their room, Laura saw with relief: two beds. She had no baht, but the man accepted a ten-dollar bill. He made a wai — this time Laura had the presence of mind to return it — and then was gone, and she and Philip were alone. Philip sat on one of the beds and she sat on the other. Between them, a nightstand with a telephone, and a chrysanthemum floating in a glass bowl. Across the room there was a desk bearing a figured brass bowl of fruit, and on the wall above that the dull black of a flat-screen television.

"It's a nice room," Laura said. Philip nodded. "Well. I'd love to take a bath. Then dinner? Unless you're starving now."

"Not starving," he said.

"Unless you need the bathroom first," she said.

"No, you go ahead," he said.

The ninnying politeness of their exchange echoed in her mind as she went into the bathroom. It was like any five-star hotel bathroom anywhere, slick and white and clean. She tipped a cascade of bath beads under the faucet blast, and while the tub filled with fragrant foam, got out her phone. The notifications she'd flicked away before obligingly rose to the screen in a stacked array, the most recent one showing on the top: Now I'm worried.

She read them in order.

Edward: Wheels up at six thirty. Look out, I am accessorized! Here.

Here.

Helloooo.

Oh no, she realized. She'd missed the partner dinner. She'd been in transit while Edward was sending these jaunty messages.

Do I need to park and come in? There's nothing on the street.

All right, I'm going around to the back.

Are you in there? Calling.

Laura, are you okay?

Did you forget?

Please let me know you're OK.

Now I'm worried.

She texted I'm okay - I'm sorry - Can't talk now - I'll explain soon.

Then she stripped and got into the bath, huddled in steamy clouds of lather while her phone buzzed and buzzed from the pile of clothing beside the tub.

I can't, she thought. *He knows I'm okay. He can wait.* She lay back, lifted a leg from the suds and put it against the wall, looked down the column of her leg to her toes splayed on the tile, and closed her eyes.

She saw her own canvas-shod foot kicking at a slanted oblong of sunlight — the window in an open car door — and the scowling face of Philip, his fluffy hair making a cockscomb against the light behind him. He grabbed her kicking foot and pushed, doubling up that leg and crossly crowding against her, the back of her other leg painfully unsticking from the leather, while he grunted *Don't be a brat.*

She opened her eyes. It had been memory, not dream. She and Philip had been quarreling over the window seat. The scene had floated up in her mind without effort, as though it had been lying undisturbed and whole just below the surface of her consciousness since the day it happened. She'd never specifically recalled that episode before, although she also knew she'd always remembered it. Why had that moment been selected from all the other possible moments, to be harbored in such perfection and completeness? On the other side of that bathroom door, unless she was very much mistaken, was the same little boy from that memory. It seemed preposterous, miraculous.

Her phone buzzed again. She must have fallen asleep; the bath was cooling. She reached over the side of the tub, crushing one breast against the porcelain, and teased the phone from the pocket of her jeans, where they lay abandoned on the tile.

Sullivan, not Edward.

Am I calling the Bangkok police? said the text. The phone buzzed again: Are you really in Bangkok?

Yes Bangkok, she typed. No police.

The phone rang. She turned on the hot water, to refresh the bath and cover the sound of her voice, and answered.

"Don't ask me to explain," she said.

"Okay," said Sullivan.

"I came here to get my brother," she explained anyway. "Or the man who says he's my brother. I haven't seen him since I was seven and he was eight."

"Okay," said Sullivan.

"He was living in some kind of commune. Shaved heads and pajamas and no electricity, and lots of meditating." It sounded more and more like a cult as she heard herself describe it. "Maybe his head isn't shaved, actually," she said. "Maybe he's gone bald. He's fifty-five," she said, and she was laughing and crying a little at the same time. "Fifty-*five.*"

211

"Are you sure it's your brother?"

"Ninety-nine percent," said Laura, and then recalled *the rest of the Prestons.* "Ninety-five."

"Ninety-five is still very good," said Sullivan. "What's he like?"

"Calm. Otherworldly calm. A real Zen motherfucker." The bath was dangerously full; she turned off the faucet and cracked the plug. Water drained with a throaty gurgle. "I've been acting like some kind of batty hostess."

"Where are you?"

"In a hotel. Both of us. That woman just threw him out of the house."

"All right," Sullivan said. He didn't ask who *that woman* was. "Has he — or anyone — asked you for money? Or banking information? Has anyone handled your wallet or credit card?"

"No." Too loud: the syllable echoed. "I haven't asked him *one thing,*" she whispered.

"One step at a time," Sullivan said. "What's your plan?"

"The consulate tomorrow, to get him a passport."

"Is that the best idea? If you're not sure it's him?"

"It's him," she said. She remembered that first sight, her father's ghost standing in the doorway. "I really think so."

"If you believe it's him, well, then, good,"

he said. "Give yourself a night. Give both of you a night. Have some food, have a good sleep. It's sleep time there, right?" Listening, Laura took one of the white robes from the back of the door, plunged the hand with the phone through the sleeve, shrugged the whole robe on, then put the phone back to her ear. "— have a lot of ground to cover," Sullivan was saying. "He knows you want to know. Don't push."

"Thanks," she said.

"Anytime," said Sullivan, adding before the call ended, "Be careful."

She tied the bathrobe belt more tightly, scooped up her clothing from the floor, took a deep breath, and opened the bathroom door.

Philip was sitting on the bed where she'd left him. Just sitting. Not watching TV, not looking out the window. Doing nothing, eyes closed. Was he meditating? She walked quietly through the room, dumped the clothing onto her bag in the corner, and took the room service menu from the desk.

"How was the bath?" he said.

"Good." Looking down at the open menu, she heard herself say, as if someone else were speaking, "Were you living with Claudette's father voluntarily?" Over her racing heart, she added, "I mean. Was he holding you prisoner?"

A moment of silence, of held breath. Staring at the menu, *shredded green papaya and tomato with spicy garlic-lime dressing.*

"No," he said. "He was my —" He considered, choosing the word. "Teacher."

Cult, thought Laura, *cult cult cult, it* was *a cult after all.* Pounding in her ears. "So you could have come home?" Her voice quavering a bit.

"I was home," he said, the correction gentle.

She looked up from the menu, directly at him. She heard Sullivan's admonition, *Don't push,* but the words came out anyway. "You know what I mean," she said. "You could have contacted us. You could have found us. If no one was stopping you."

He looked back at her; she couldn't read his expression. After a long pause, he said, "I didn't feel that I could." And then, with no change in his voice to indicate the shift in topic, he said, "I think I need medication."

"Are you all right?" she asked, alarmed.

"The doctor Claudette called prescribed some pills. I think they're in the blue bag." For some reason, Laura noticed the article — *the* bag, not *my* bag — as she brought it to him with a glass of water. He unzipped the bag, tumbled some pharmacy boxes onto his lap, and scrutinized them before punching first one pill and then another from blister packs and swallowing them down.

"There wasn't a funeral," he said.

How do you know that? she almost asked, but realized in time he must be talking not about himself but about Claudette's father.

"Claudette had his body shipped to Switzerland for burial," said Philip. "He would have wanted to be cremated."

"I'm sorry." With a hint of a question mark — was *he* sorry? Did he feel sympathy for the wishes of his teacher — or cult leader, or kidnapper, whatever the truth was?

"She has her own healing to do," he said.

Laura watched him tuck the boxes back into the bag and zip it up. What must it be like, to be able to fit everything you owned in the world into an overnight duffel? How self-centered she was. She hadn't even considered that Philip must be in mourning too, or at the very least in shock from the abrupt change in his circumstances. Sullivan was right: no more questions for now. She took up the room service menu from where she'd dropped it on her bed and thrust it toward him.

"You choose," she said. And added, as he opened the menu and bent his head over it, *"Mai phet maak."* His face creased with amusement. She'd meant to say *not too spicy,* the way the Prestons had always said it at home, but probably the family patois had the tones all wrong, and they'd all been saying something like "light my cow on fire" to one another through the years.

He chose from the Western side of the menu, hamburgers and french fries. *Extra pickles,* he said into the phone, smiling at her as he did, and she felt a wave of shame for her scrutiny and doubt. She had loved pickles as a child, had always wanted extra. He'd remembered.

They sat on the beds across from each other, the air-conditioning rushing from the wall.

"You told me about everyone else," he said. "Are you married, do you have children?"

"No," she said. "I'm a painter." It sounded comical, as if the one explained the other. "I never considered doing anything else, didn't even choose a sensible minor in college." *College.* The word hung awkwardly in the air. Something the Preston girls had done as a matter of course, something their brother didn't get to do, as far as Laura knew. Had he had any formal schooling since he was eight? He'd said Claudette's father was his teacher. What did that mean? "I didn't graduate." She heard the air of strained apology and forced herself to stop there. "I was thinking we could go to the consulate tomorrow morning and get you a passport. Or — do you even want to go home?"

The word slipped out before she recalled what he'd said already: *I was home.* Perhaps

America was not home to him anymore.

He nodded. "I think it's time," he said.

She awoke in the night, and at first did not know where she was. It was a disorientation deeper than geography. She could be a little girl again, or herself at sixteen or thirty-five, or someone else entirely. *Who is that breathing?* She turned her head as slowly and quietly as possible, and her heart jumped to see a shape of darkness looming against the backdrop of the city lights in the window.

It was Philip, of course, sleeping sitting up in the other bed. He'd piled the pillows behind him to watch the movie they'd chosen, then stayed like that when eventually she'd turned off the light. Three feet away from her, her brother. Or a stranger. All day he had flipped back and forth in her mind, *brother-stranger-brother-stranger.* Despite the pickles, despite the flashes of physical similarity to her father, despite everything.

As she fell off to sleep again, another memory came into her mind: just a sound, the trickling noise of a coin falling into a vending machine. Bits of narrative crowded up to bolster the fragment: it was Philip's coin, he'd found it in a hotel where the Prestons were staying; he had made the selection and let Laura pull the lever; they'd sat in an empty corridor to consume the candy, their backs against opposite walls and legs stretched out toward each other. Even as more details came to her — shushing each other as they crept from the room where their older sister was sleeping, the scratchiness of the carpet under Laura's thighs — she suspected that much of it was a clinging cloud of memory pollution, a mixture of invention and extrapolation, the way a constellation is confabulated from three stars. The only absolutely true parts were the sound of the coin falling and the glow of a shared secret.

I've missed you so much, she thought. Speaking into the universe, not necessarily to the man a few feet away. *My big brother.*

CHAPTER ELEVEN

The consulate was located in the embassy, on the other side of the park. Laura and Philip took a tuk-tuk; as they idled at a stoplight on Ploenchit Road, she had a thought. She leaned forward and shouted to the driver over the noise of the motor, putting her phone over his shoulder to show him the map on the screen. She wasn't sure he'd understood, but a minute later, instead of turning right on Wireless Road, he stayed straight. The Skytrain ran along in midair high above them; below it a scribbly scrim of electrical and telephone wires coursed from pole to pole. They rode past Burger King, past endless hotels, past a McDonald's with a life-size statue outside of Ronald McDonald making a benevolent wai. And then they were turning onto a small lane, slowing and then stopping.

A beige high-rise tower thrust up from the pavement, to one side of it a dark oblong, the entrance to an underground garage. No high wall, no gates. Not a blade of grass anywhere.

The shining brass number 9 was the only clue that it was the same location.

"They tore it down years ago," said Philip.

Of course that simple two-story house at 9 Soi Nine would be gone now, swallowed up into the *Blade Runner* metropolis that central Bangkok had become. It had been irrational to hope for anything else. Still, Laura felt confounded, as though she'd reached down to scratch an ankle and found nothing but empty air. She hadn't realized until this moment how at the back of her mind she'd cherished the belief that there was a clear, physical path back to the last place her family had been whole. As if they could all go back and start over.

"Where are the khlongs?" she asked, trying to keep her voice steady. "Wasn't there one right behind the house?"

"Most were paved over. They're roads now."

The tuk-tuk driver revved his motor. Laura leaned forward and told him the embassy address again. He nodded without annoyance and drove back the way they'd come.

The U.S. Embassy was massive. Nothing like the vague memories Laura had of a humble box of a building in whose garden she'd burned her fingertip on a sparkler one Fourth of July. The new embassy looked like a cross between an airport tower and a gun turret. It rose above the tall trees lining Wireless Road — the most green she'd seen in

Bangkok thus far — as a sheer cliff of white fenestrated with checkbox windows, presenting such a militaristic and aggressive message that Laura had the thought, *No wonder everyone hates us.*

The passport section was across the street, in a far less ostentatious building; Laura's heart sank when she saw the long line of people standing beneath a sign: CONSULAR SECTION AMERICAN CITIZEN SERVICES AND VISA SERVICES. When they got closer, she realized that there were two queues: a long one in front of the visa window, and a much shorter one in front of the U.S. Citizen window. They joined the latter.

When they reached the front of the line, Laura showed her passport and airline itinerary and told a simple version of Philip's story — this was her brother, he'd lost his passport and needed an emergency replacement — no, he'd lost all of his ID, he could provide no ID.

"Photo ID," said the man, and Laura put her hands wide in an Italianate gesture. *Mai mee* jumped into her head, but she squashed it.

"He lost everything," she said. "All gone." The man called another guard over; they conferred in Thai while examining Laura's passport and ID. After some walkie-talkie consultation with someone on the inside of the building, they were given passes to enter.

They went through security, where Laura's cell phone was taken from her; she expected to get it back on the other side of the metal detector, but after a short confused exchange with the personnel she understood that it had been confiscated for the duration of the visit. She and Philip followed the signs down the hall to the passport section and entered a waiting room, where they checked in at a concierge-like stand, giving the same lost-passport story, again flourishing the airline itinerary, and then took seats to wait. A television on the wall played CNN; they watched desultorily for half an hour before their names were called.

"Have you made a police report?" asked the clerk when they took chairs in front of her desk.

Laura didn't know what to say. *Yes, there should be one on file from 1972?* "Not today," she said.

"You need a police report," the clerk said. She asked Philip, her hands poised over the keyboard of her computer, "Was your passport stolen as part of a serious crime?"

"No," said Philip.

"Do you have a photocopy of the lost passport?"

"No."

"Do you have a picture for the new passport?" She intuited the answer from their expressions. "You must have a passport picture. You may acquire one here." She flicked a small map from a stack to her right, spun it around on the desk, and circled the location in pen with a practiced hand. "It is the next building to this one. You will need to fill out this application," she said, sliding a form beneath the map. "Bring the photograph with photo ID and a photocopy of the lost passport." At the end of this speech, her smile took on a fixed quality: she was finished with them for now.

"We don't have any of those things," said Laura. She leaned forward, lowered her voice. "It's a bit complicated."

The clerk listened with knitted brow as Laura spoke; then she called her supervisor over. Laura told the story again, and the clerks conferred in Thai, shooting glances toward Laura and Philip. Then the supervisor walked away.

"What did they say?" Laura whispered to Philip.

"They think you don't look crazy," he replied. "But the jury's out on me."

There was a metallic click from the wall to their left. A door had opened and the supervisor stood there.

"Please come," she said. They followed her through the door and down a short corridor to another door, which she opened to a room that contained five chairs, a desk, a photograph of the U.S. president, an American flag. "Please wait here," she said with a smile.

They sat for five minutes, fifteen, an hour. No one passed the glass panel beside the door. Laura felt the lack of her phone acutely. The small room, the locks, the photograph on the wall made her increasingly nervous. *We're Americans,* she reminded herself. *We're actually in America right now.* Finally, the door opened and a tall man came in. He had wavy blond hair silvering at the temples and an agreeable face. He introduced himself as the vice consul.

A diplomat to his core, he listened with exquisite attention and no evidence of skepticism as Laura told the story for the third time. She noticed that a small group of clerical staff was gathered outside the door, a half dozen Thai men and women who watched intently as Laura opened the clear plastic bag she was carrying and slid the contents of Genevieve's manila envelope out onto the desk.

The vice consul went through it all: Philip's childhood passport and birth records, the police report, the clippings. One was a front-page headline, AMERICAN BOY MISSING, the other a column from an interior page. While the consul held up the photographs to study them, the heads outside the door jerked back and forth, looking from the downy-headed boy to the bald middle-aged man. When the vice consul had finished examining the documents, he looked up. If he was moved by what he had read, he did not show it. He didn't ask any of the obvious questions of Philip — what happened to you, where have you been all of this time — but focused on the matter at hand.

"The problem as I see it," he said, "is to link this boy" — he held up the child Philip's navy passport — "to this man." He indicated Philip, who was seated and silent, his eyes closed. *Meditating now, really?* thought Laura.

"Yes, that's it exactly," said Laura, her voice bright. She dug a discreet elbow into Philip's side: *Wake up.* This was hardly the time or place for eccentric behavior.

"Time was, we could have accepted your word," said the vice consul. "But things have — tightened up."

"Could we do DNA testing?" said Laura. How stupid she'd been, thinking this would be a simple errand.

"We don't do that here," he said. He looked thoughtful. "But there is a service —" he broke off, asked one of the clerks in the doorway a question in Thai, listened while she answered. "You're in luck," he said, turning back to Laura and Philip with a smile. "There's a company offering something that will suit this situation perfectly. Sibling DNA testing. It's mainly used for immigration." He spoke again to the crowd of clerks, who dispersed. "They're going to hunt up the information for you."

"Thank you," said Laura. The feeble phrase didn't accurately reflect the intensity of the relief spreading through her.

"We've just recently begun to accept the results of sibling testing," said the vice consul, conversationally. "Siblings are harder to match than child and parent, of course." Laura nodded, although her knowledge of genetics dated to one high-school biology class, a foggy smear of pea plants and Chi-square tables. "This particular test is accurate only for siblings of opposite sexes, so — more luck." He seemed sincerely glad. "With a definitive match and your affidavit, plus these," he said, tapping the pile of documents, "we should be able to issue an emergency passport."

"How long will the test take to come back?" said Laura.

"About a week," said the vice consul, and misinterpreted her expression. "I know — it's amazing what modern technology can do."

Outside the embassy, Laura and Philip looked at each other: *What do we do now?*

"A week in Bangkok," said Laura. "It's not the worst problem in the world." She wasn't looking forward to explaining it to Edward or Bea, though. She looked at her phone: two p.m. meant three a.m. back home; so a few hours more of reprieve.

They changed money and ate; they visited a department store to buy Philip some things, then walked back across a smooth concrete plaza, passing tourists taking selfies with the B A N G K O K letters and walking with phones at chest level, filming.

"I don't remember it being like this," Laura said.

"It wasn't like this," said Philip.

"Is there anything else you need?" said Laura. They'd bought some pants and shirts, a pair of sandals, a few toiletries. It wasn't much. It wasn't enough. She felt an impulse to shower him with luxuries, to buy him something that would not fit into that little blue bag Claudette had packed.

She was surprised by Philip's response to the simple question. His face animated, as though a licking fire had caught behind it. "I'd like to ride the Skytrain," he said. They both looked up at the elevated rail.

"To visit anyplace in particular?" asked Laura. He shook his head. "Skytrain it is," she said.

The fare card system was no more complicated than the Metro. The Skytrain stations and cars were beautifully clean, ungraffitied, gloriously air-conditioned. Philip and Laura rode the line from one end to the other, Philip's face avid at the window.

"Look, a Ferris wheel," Laura said. "We would have loved that when we were kids. We had nothing like that. What was that place we used to go, with the trained elephants?" He shook his head, staring out at the city. "You remember," she said. "Lots of snakes in cages. Did Mum take us there? It seems like a place she would have expressly avoided."

"I don't know," he said. "I don't remember."

"Of course you do," she insisted. "You *loved* that place. The elephants stacking logs with their trunks. What was it called?"

"I don't remember," he said again, and there was a deadened quality to his voice, like a hand put over the mouth of a ringing bell. She was astonished into silence.

They watched out the window together without speaking, while the awkwardness ebbed. When they reached the end of the line, the logistics of figuring out the return dissipated the last of it, and back at the hotel they rode the elevator up to the room in a wearied, companionable silence. Philip went to take a shower, and Laura reluctantly got out her phone. Time to face the music.

"I don't even know what to say to you," said Edward. "I'm furious. I'm so relieved you're safe. Do you know how worried I've been?"

"I'm sorry I forgot about the partner dinner," she said. "That was terrible of me."

228

"Not a word," he said. "Not one word in two days."

"I'm sorry," she said again.

"I almost called the FBI."

"I get that you were upset," she said, "but let's take a step back. I took a trip without telling you. It's not a reason to panic."

"*That's* how you see it?"

"That's the situation. Objectively."

A frustrated exhalation. "It's like trying to describe a color to someone who was born blind," he said. "Do you want me to come there?"

"No need," she said.

"I didn't say need," he said. A pause. "When are you coming home?"

"We have to wait for the DNA results so Philip can get his passport. Maybe a week." The rush option she'd chosen had promised a turnaround of five to seven business days.

"He hasn't asked you for money or had access to your banking information or passport?" Then, "Why are you laughing?"

"It's almost word for word what Sullivan said." As soon as the words were out, she wished she could bite them back.

"You talked to Sullivan."

"I texted him," said Laura. Technically true: she had texted him before he'd called and they'd spoken. "Just to let someone know where I was."

"You texted *him*," he said.

229

"Please don't make that into a thing."

"Laura, I am very glad you are all right, but I can't talk to you anymore right now." He sounded far away. "Stay safe. If you need me, call me."

"Edw —" But the phone was dead.

Philip came out of the bathroom, a cloud of steam wisping out behind him. He was wearing the pajamas they'd bought that day, dark blue with small polka dots.

"Are you all right?" he said.

"Ugh," said Laura. "My boyfriend is super pissed. And now I have to call Bea."

"Does she know you're here?" She shook her head. He smiled. "Fun." He sat on his bed, used the towel hung around his neck to pat the moisture from his face and head. Sitting had pulled the pajama cuffs up his legs, and she could see for the first time the source of his limp: a knobbed deformity of his left ankle. When had he been injured there? She forced herself to look away from it as she dialed the phone, hoping he hadn't noticed her staring.

Bea picked up on the first ring.

"I'm in Bangkok," said Laura.

"Of course you are."

"Bea, it's him. It's Philip."

"Has he *proved* that? Has he said something only Philip would know?"

"We sent DNA."

"You could have had that done without going there," said Bea. Laura said nothing; it was true. "Did he give you any resistance about it?"

"No." Philip had dutifully spat into the plastic vial from the test box. "We should have the results in a week."

"I do not have time right now to come there."

"I didn't ask you to," said Laura. Although she realized that she had hoped, until that moment, that Beatrice would come. "Do you want to talk to him?"

"No," said Bea.

Laura looked over at Philip: Could he hear Bea's side of the conversation? She got up from the bed, walked into the humid bathroom.

"He looks just like Daddy," said Laura.

"You tend to see what you want to see." Sounds flared in the background of the call. "One minute," said Bea, apparently to the person seeking her attention, then her voice became clearer again, directed into the phone. "I'm really not happy that you've done this, but it's done now. Just please be careful. Remember that con artists can be ruthless. And very clever. Don't give him anything. Don't tell him anything. And make sure he understands that the family trust is under *my* control."

"She's a tough customer," said Philip, when Laura came out of the bathroom.

"She's not convinced it's actually you." She sat on the bed, then lay back and spoke to the ceiling. "To be fair, there were a lot of false leads down the years. But yeah, Queen Bea still reigns." She turned on her side to face him across the gap between the beds. "Remember the awful games she used to invent?"

He laughed. "And somehow it was never her turn."

If Bea could see this, Laura thought, *she wouldn't ask for more proof.*

"Philip," she said. Her voice almost a whisper. "Tell me what happened."

A wince flitted across his features, the smile dissolving, his face shuttering. The change was unbearable.

"It's all right," she said. Soft, as though comforting a child. *"Mai pen rai."*

Bea would want to hear it for herself anyway. Why drag him through it twice? *I'll bring him home to Bea,* Laura thought. *She'll interrogate him without mercy. He can tell both of us together.*

She lifted her phone to wake it again, touched its surface to bring up a browser window. "Listen," she said. "We have a week here. No point in moping around. Let's be tourists."

They cobbled together a list from the combined resources of the internet and the hotel concierge. A longtail boat down the river in a languid haze of mosquitoes, a slow hike up to the top of Golden Mount, half a dozen temple visits, the butterfly garden, a morning riding the Skytrain again, both lines end to end. Philip was roaring with eagerness, wanting to do it all, as if he actually were a tourist. Although Laura noticed scattered flecks of familiarity — the monkey warrior outside Wat Phra Kaew, the golden spires of the Grand Palace, the Victory Monument in the center of a traffic island, the smell of Yaowarat Road in Chinatown — she didn't call Philip's attention to them. She avoided the word *remember.* It was easy to do: on the whole, the city didn't feel nostalgic. Particularly downtown, which reminded her of other large, modern cities. The solid crowds at the temples like the packed pedestrian traffic on Dublin's Grafton Street, the sidewalks like the East Village when she'd lived there, the walkways hemmed in on both sides by displays of purses and watches and sunglasses and scarves. And food vendors, who were everywhere. Laura had never eaten street food in any city, but Philip was intrepid. After the first street meal, she waited for the onslaught of dysentery. Nothing happened, and after that they got most of their meals from carts, pronouncing each dish the best so far.

With a blend of calculation and spontaneity, they decided each evening upon one main activity for the next day and concocted the remainder on the fly. Laura had never felt so free of striving or worry. Each day was bracketed by Philip's morning and evening meditation; during those times Laura napped or listened to a podcast or audiobook. The third evening, when Philip sat down on his bed and closed his eyes, she clicked the sound off, took her earbuds out of her ears, and asked, "Will you teach me?"

"I'm not sure I'm qualified to teach," Philip said. "But I'll tell you how I learned." The question leapt into Laura's mind, *Who taught you?* but she didn't speak it. "First, sit up." She did. "Get comfortable. Keep your spine straight." Those two directives were incompatible, she thought. "You want to empty your mind. Then draw a line from the top of your head down the middle of your body." His voice was steady, the words unfaltering as though, despite his demurral, he had taught this before. "Then hold that line in your mind and draw a second line, this one around your waist, just above your navel." He paused with a look of mild inquiry, and she nodded to indicate *Got it.* "When you've got both lines, hold them there and focus on the place where they cross."

"I can't empty my mind," she confessed, opening her eyes after what felt like an hour but was probably two minutes. So many things were jostling around in there: not just conscious thoughts but also sensory awareness, the sound of the air-conditioning, the texture of the bedspread beneath her, a belch welling up. "Not even a little bit."

"It takes practice," he said.

"Mum has memory problems," said Laura, surprising herself: she hadn't planned to say it. "She can seem normal, but she often doesn't know where she is, or who anybody is."

He nodded. Impassive. Had his experience, whatever it had been, drummed sadness out of him? Or did he simply feel unconnected to the mother he hadn't seen for so long?

"Bea's in charge of all the Preston money," she said. Thinking, *There, Bea, I told him.*

He nodded again and closed his eyes, and after a few seconds, Laura did too. She concentrated on pushing each thought and sensation away as it entered, then awoke in the pitch-dark room with the coverlet pulled up over her.

Friday morning, they caught a minibus to a floating market two hours outside the city. After a couple of hours of wandering, they sat on a set of stone steps on the riverbank, watching their lunch being prepared by a woman on a boat tied up below.

"In America, everyone thinks Bangkok is

all about drugs and sex," said Laura, accepting the bowl that was handed up to her. It contained a thin omelet, which she broke open with her spoon; noodles spilled out and a fragrant steam rose up. "It's really about food."

"The food is very good," agreed Philip.

"Do you want to go to a muay Thai boxing match tonight?" Laura asked, thumbing through screens on her phone with her free hand.

"No," said Philip, one short syllable. It was so uncharacteristic of his previous *yes, yes, yes* to everything she'd suggested all week that Laura looked up at him, surprised. He was eating, eyes on his bowl.

"Okay," she said. She looked down again at the list on her phone. "We haven't gone on the Ferris wheel yet."

Before he could respond, her phone dinged in her hand and a notification box slid down from the top of the screen. The DNA results were back.

At the consulate, an electric typewriter was rolled into the room — Laura hadn't seen a typewriter since college — and one of the clerks seated herself and inserted a thick triplicate form. She typed as the vice consul dictated a short paragraph that attested to Philip's identity, *based on attached materials.* At the bottom of each page the typist pressed and held the underline key, making long empty lines for signatures. The papers were collated, and each set was stamped with a seal; the vice consul signed under that. A five-minute signature round followed, the papers passing from Philip to Laura to one of the clerks, signing as a witness.

When the process was done, the completed passport application laid on the desk with the affidavit and the DNA results paper-clipped to it, the vice consul looked up. His face became solemn. He stepped across the tile floor and put his hand out.

"Welcome home, Philip Preston," he said. They shook hands.

Laura sent texts to Bea, to Edward, to Sullivan. She copy-pasted the same message, We're coming home, then shut off her phone before they could reply.

"Remember how I used to sleep on the tray tables?" Laura said as she and Philip buckled in on the first flight. She distinctly recalled having lain across two or three of them to nap in-flight, with a pillow and a blanket. She must have been very small. "Where were we going?"

"Australia, I think," he said. Philip's voice was light, but she'd noticed his minuscule flinch at the word *remember*. "Mum took us there the first year to escape the peak of the hot season. We saw a kangaroo on your birthday." He coughed, wheezily.

"I have literally no memory of that," said Laura. He coughed again, and she said, "Did you take your medications this morning?"

He nodded. "I think I'm just tired. It's been an eventful week."

She dug into the bag at her feet for an inhaler, the same kind she'd used since elementary school for her own mild asthma. She so rarely had an attack these days that she'd forgotten to pack her own; she'd picked one up *just in case* at the pharmacy near the hotel. No prescriptions needed in Bangkok, just a pointer finger and cash. "Try this," she said, giving it to him.

He took two puffs, nodded thanks.

It seemed to help: no more coughing. Laura felt reassured, watching him joke with the flight attendant in Thai. Of course he was tired; he was probably also anxious about the return home. No need to be an alarmist.

During the second flight, as the two of them dozed in adjacent seats, Laura awoke to an odd, repeating noise. Not loud enough to rise above the engine sound, it was more of a vibration, at regular intervals. After a few confused seconds, she realized its source was Philip. Each of his sleeping exhalations was terminating in a short grunt, something between a throat-clearing and a cough. She watched him for a little while. His face was peaceful, his breaths deep and regular; the only odd thing was the growl-grunt. He didn't look feverish. She touched his arm: not hot. Whatever it was, it didn't seem serious. She let herself fall back into a fretful sleep.

When the captain's voice came overhead, *Flight crew prepare for descent,* Laura's internal hallelujah was mitigated by alarm when she attempted to rouse Philip. He'd gotten worse while they'd slept. His skin was damp. He opened glassy eyes briefly when she shook his shoulder, closed them again. "Wake up," she said. He nodded and raised his eyebrows high as if to drag his eyes open, failing at that.

During the plane's descent, Laura thought fast. They wouldn't legally be *in* the U.S. until they had been officially checked through Customs. If Philip was obviously ill, would he be allowed to enter? As U.S. citizens, they couldn't be refused entry to their own country — or could they? The climate of welcome had shifted in recent years; long-naturalized Americans were being threatened with deportation. The old rules didn't apply.

While everyone else erupted from their seats into the aisles, Laura hailed a passing flight attendant and requested a wheelchair for *my brother's ankle.* She pointed to the deformity. They stayed in their seats until the plane was empty, and then Laura put both carry-on bags over one shoulder and hauled Philip up out of his seat. Talking to him all the while as though he were simply leaning on her, she manhandled his thin frame up the aisle and deposited him into the waiting wheelchair. "Thanks," she called merrily to the flight attendants as she wheeled him up the short jet bridge to the mobile lounge. She stared out the window as the giant vehicle moved slowly across the tarmac toward the International Arrivals Building, all the while expecting a hand on her shoulder, some voice of authority: *He doesn't look right.* But there was no hand, no voice, and when the mobile lounge stopped, Laura pretended nonchalance as she unlocked the wheelchair and steered it up the gangway to the terminal, not first or last of the crowd but in the middle of the pack, the carry-on bags jumping in double-thumps against her back with every step.

She'd never been so glad for the multilay-ered invisibility cloak she wore, of whiteness, femaleness, middle age. Immigration was a cursory passport check, and they rolled through Customs with no one looking twice at them, down the escalator and out of the building, into the American breeze.

When they got to the front of the taxi line, Laura braked the wheelchair and pulled Philip up, pivoted him into the taxi's back seat, got in on the other side. She turned on her phone and it burst into life in her hands, vibrating as notification after notification floated up onto the screen. She flicked them all away, opened Maps to look for the nearest hospital.

"He doesn't look good," the taxi driver said in a syncopated West African bass. Laura looked up. The man, hand on the gearshift, was eyeing Philip in the rearview mirror.

Laura scooted up the seat to speak through the gap in the Plexiglas. "He can't drink like he used to," she invented. Under the driver's gaze, she affected a languid annoyance. "There was a going-away party last night, and then today we were in the airplane, and he drank only two of those little bottles of water. . . ." She looked at Philip with feigned exasperation. "I think he might still be drunk."

"He needs intravenous fluids," the driver pronounced. He named the nearest hospital. "Okay?"

Laura nodded. She found the hospital on Maps and typed in a text to Bea, adding a dropped pin.

En route to hospital. Philip sick.

The driver shifted out of park but kept his foot on the brake as he asked, "Where did you fly from?"

"Paris." Another lie, to cap the others. No contagious tropical nasties in France. The driver nodded and lifted his foot from the

241

brake. As they merged into traffic, Laura settled back into her seat, pressed Send on the text to Bea.

At the exit for the hospital she said, "I'm not sure how I'll get him into the ER without the wheelchair."

"No problem," said the driver. He swung the taxi past all the AMBULANCES ONLY signs, right up to the glass double doors marked EMERGENCY. He stopped; his eyes met Laura's in the rearview mirror.

"Pay me now, please," he said.

Laura slid her card through the reader and put in her PIN. She tipped twenty dollars; the driver dipped his chin in acknowledgment before pressing the heel of his hand against the horn. Five seconds, ten, of blaring continuous noise before the glass doors parted and personnel surged out. They surrounded the taxi, yanked open all of the doors.

"Where is he shot?" a silver-haired woman in blue scrubs bawled into Laura's face as she scrambled out of the back seat. "How many times?"

"He's not," said Laura, confused.

Young men in burgundy scrubs push-pulled Philip out of the car and dropped him into a wheelchair. They rolled it away at a run as the taxi drove off, leaving the two bags on the ground.

"Come on." The woman in the blue scrubs stood outside the doors, scooping the air in a huge, impatient arm wave.

Laura took up the bags and hurried after, through the doors and down the hallway in the wake of the disappearing wheelchair, the woman firing questions and Laura answering mostly *I don't know.* Any allergies to medication? *I don't know.* Any fever? *I don't know.* Does he take any medicines? *Some pills — I don't know what they are.* From the doorway of the hospital room she watched them heave Philip onto a stretcher and swarm around him. A doctor stalked past Laura into the room, whipping his stethoscope from around his neck, rapping out orders. He asked Laura the same questions the nurse had already asked and some others, with growing incredulity at each successive *I don't know.*

"Well, what *do* you know?" he asked, finally.

"We just got off a plane from Bangkok," said Laura. "Well, from Tokyo, but we started in Bangkok. He's been living there." The doctor waited. "He had some difficulty breathing on the plane. I gave him an inhaler." She produced it from her pocket, and the doctor took it from her, turned it to read the label. "It seemed to help at first."

By that time, Philip was surrounded by machines, an IV going into one arm, wires trailing off his chest, a mist-filled mask over his face. His eyes were still closed.

"Does he have asthma?" asked the doctor. "Let me guess — you don't know."

"He's been taking some pills," Laura said. "I have them here." She crouched to unzip the blue bag, took out the boxes and passed them up to the doctor.

"Okay," he said, a fissure of warmth creeping into his voice: *I can work with this.* "These are for high blood pressure and congestive heart failure. Did you ever hear a doctor say he had those things?"

"I didn't talk to his doctor," said Laura.

"So you came from Bangkok with him, but you know nothing about him." His eyes were narrowed; he was working to make the connection — Bangkok, international city of sin, was this something kinky?

"I'm his sister," she said, feeling like she was lying. "But we haven't seen each other since we were children."

He stared at her briefly, too buffeted by whatever had happened to him already, in his life or just in this day, to summon curiosity or surprise. "You can wait in the waiting room," he said, and went back to Philip.

Bea's eyes were very close, intense like blue fire. Her husband, Clement, loomed behind her with his customary abstracted, genial expression.

"What happened?" Bea demanded.

"He got sick on the second plane," said Laura, pushing herself up from the slump she'd slid down into while asleep. She rubbed her eyes carefully; they felt as though they had grains of sand in them.

The waiting room was half-filled, clusters of people on the joined plastic seats sleeping, or talking in low voices, or staring at their phones. A baby cried against its mother's shoulder; she patted its back as she watched the television playing soundlessly under the ceiling.

"What have the doctors said?" said Clement, moving forward, setting a small cooler down on the empty seat beside Laura and opening the lid, taking out a wax-paper-wrapped square. "Sandwich?"

"Nothing yet," said Laura. She accepted the sandwich, untucked the pleat of waxed paper. A delicious aroma breathed up; she was abruptly ravenous. "My God," she said, with her mouth full. Thick bread, balsamic dressing, brawny tomato, feathery mozzarella, peppery arugula. "This is gorgeous."

"It's just a sandwich," Bea said, but there was a thread of satisfaction in the words.

"I told you the mozzarella came out well," said Clement, and to Laura, "She thought it might be rubbery."

"Mm-hm," said Laura, totally occupied with the eating.

"We took a cheesemaking course last summer," said Clement, producing a glass bottle of lemonade from the cooler and holding it out.

Of course you did, Laura didn't say, taking the cold bottle and twisting the cap; it came free with a breathy pop and she took a long tart-sweet swallow.

She felt a cheerful giddiness, the child's joy of passing a burden to grown-ups. It was done, she'd done it. It had been such a long, bizarre journey. From the Oz moment when the gate in the wall of that drab alley had opened onto the serene green compound, through the week of carefree tourism ending with the vice consul shaking Philip's hand, and the rest: the anxious second flight and the Lucy Ricardo–ridiculous performance that had followed, the wheelchair and the stream of lies, the taxi driver's suspicion, his *Pay me now, please.* Laura took another bite of the sandwich and felt tears prick her closed eyes. *Blessed are the cheesemakers.* Wonderful Bea. Thank goodness for Bea. Her older sister was here. Everything was going to be okay.

"So what did he tell you?" said Bea. "What did he say happened to him?"

"I don't know," said Laura. More *I don't knows* to add to the mountain. "He was living in that house, Claudette's father's house, since 1980."

"What about before that?" Laura shook her head. "You didn't ask him *anything?*" Beatrice was incredulous.

"I did ask," said Laura. "But — you don't

246

know how it was, Bea. You weren't there."
Bea looked unmoved. Laura felt defensive. "I
figured you'd want to interrogate him, once
the DNA matched."

"The DNA *matched*?" said Bea. Her face
alive with astonishment.

"Well, yeah," said Laura. She realized she
hadn't put that information into her preflight
text. "That's how we got him the passport."

At that moment, the doctors appeared. Two
of them, a man and a woman. They announced *Preston* and then crossed the blue
industrial carpet to introduce themselves as
Philip's admitting doctors. They stood like
imperturbable white-coated statues and
catalogued rapid-fire what was wrong with
Philip, their eyes raking the sisters' faces for
signs of comprehension.

He had malaria — *but not the worst kind,*
the female doctor put in — and at least one
kind of intestinal worm, and a moderate
degree of chronic heart failure, and pneumonia. His liver was okay, they said, as if going
down a checklist of organs, and his kidneys
were struggling but not too bad. The real
problem was the heart; it wasn't squeezing
strongly enough. They invited the sisters into
a back hallway, showed them an X-ray on a
monitor screen.

"That's his heart," said the male doctor,
pointing to a slump of white. He moved his
finger to a lacy hovering fog above it and said,

"This shouldn't be there." He dabbed two other places and said, "Neither should that."

"We can give him medicines to help his heart squeeze," said the female doctor. "But those can take time to work. With the fluid backing up into his lungs and the pneumonia on top of that, he's not getting enough oxygen."

"Right now he needs a ventilator," the other doctor cut in. "Has your brother ever expressed strong wishes against being put on life support?"

They both stopped talking. In the abrupt silence after so much information, Laura and Beatrice looked at each other — as if they knew this man *your brother* at all, or any of his wishes — and shook their heads no.

At that, the two doctors whisked away down the corridor and a young woman in burgundy scrubs led Bea and Laura back to the waiting room.

"Did you see him?" asked Clem.

"No," said Bea. "They're putting him on life support." Something washed across her face and she sat down suddenly, in the chair beside her husband. "The DNA matched," she said, her voice hollow and wondering. "It's really Philip." Clem put his arm around her. "He's come back," said Bea. She was staring at nothing, brow wrinkled as though she was working out a puzzle. "And he's dying."

CHAPTER TWELVE

1972

Mondays at 9 Soi Nine were mainly recuperative. Their mother spent the whole morning out — at the salon first, then lunch — while the house underwent an intense cleaning, Choy and Noi going back and forth to the laundry behind the building and Daeng calling commands in a loud voice she didn't use when the parents were there. The children were expected to amuse themselves outside until early afternoon, when the driver would take the girls to ballet.

They played Red Light, Green Light and Mother May I, both exceptionally dull with only three. When they dragged into the kitchen complaining of the heat, of boredom, of hunger, Daeng gave them each a glass of orange squash and told them *Get out, I busy.* They wandered out again holding the sweating drinks and settled onto the swings in the garden. Noi, who sometimes played with them, whisked by in her long black skirt, shaking her head *sorry sorry* when Philip called to her. A minute later, they could hear energetic scolding from Daeng. Who was always scolding the Number Three, but today she sounded more vociferous than usual.

"It must have been a great big tray she dropped," commented Philip.

The children had been dismissed by then, but had heard it all from the top of the stairs. First the crash, then a silence that quickly filled with polite sounds of distress, Robert asking *Are you all right?* and Genevieve: *That's enough, Sarah, leave it.* The carpet had had to be taken away for cleaning.

From the swing, Laura could see Somchit in the driveway, squatting in the hump of shade beside the car. She felt a sediment of guilt for having spied on him from the window the night of the party. She hadn't told anyone about that yet. As she watched now, Daeng came out onto the front step and began speaking to him in a quarreling voice; he crab-walked around the car to the sunny side and squatted there instead, slitting his eyes closed against the sun.

"We could play freeze tag," said Philip.

"It's stupid with just us," said Bea. "Maybe if Jane and Alex come over."

"You always want Alex to come over," said Laura. She sang, "Alex and Bea, sitting in a tree," and Philip joined in, *"K-I-S-S-I-N-G."*

"Shut up," said Bea, her face bright red. She jumped off the swing and put her empty glass down onto the grass. "Let's swim."

"It's Laura's turn," said Philip. He turned to her. "What do you want to do?"

A brief, giddying power. Laura could choose hopscotch, which they never played because Philip hated it. Or army men in the grass, which is what Philip probably would like, but Bea would refuse to participate. Laura could choose swings, but they were sitting on the swings now, so that wouldn't be like taking a turn.

Bea was looking at her, eyebrows raised, expectant.

"Swimming," said Laura. Bea smiled.

They all ran toward the house for their suits; at the side terrace, Laura slowed. She let the other two go ahead of her and went around to the front step, where Daeng still stood, scowling.

"What's he done?" Laura asked, expecting to be told *mai pen rai.*

"Somchit like women," said Daeng. "My daughter very unhappy." She spat another furious volley of syllables toward the car and the man hiding behind it, then turned and went into the house.

In the quiet, Somchit peeked over the car's white bonnet; seeing that Daeng was gone, he smiled at Laura. She smiled back shyly.

Philip, wearing his bathing trunks, raced out of the side of the house toward the pool. "Last one in is a rotten egg," he shouted.

"No fair," cried Laura. "I'm not even changed yet."

Inside the house, Noi was aware of Somchit outside in the driveway, his presence like a burning point of energy focused on her. From his second day of work, he'd been bringing her presents. First a box of candy, sugar-dusty fruit pastilles with soft jelly centers, left on the front step for her to find when she went out at dawn on Thursday to sweep. He'd watched her pick it up, open the lid, look nervously back at the house; when she'd put it into the pocket of her skirt, he'd smiled. In the afternoon of that day he'd stood in the driveway blowing onto a pinwheel made of thin colored foil looped onto notched wooden blades. When she approached, he held it out to her, his fingertips just touching hers as she took it. The next day, Friday, he'd stood at the bottom of the front step, hand behind his back; she'd gone close, then closer, then put her own hand out and he'd produced a sweet iced coffee from the vendor just outside the gate, in a small plastic bag with a rubber band twisted tight around the straw. He'd settled it into her palm like a cool egg. On Friday afternoon, he'd brought her a dress. She, who had never worn anything but a *pha tung* or the Number Three uniform of white blouse and black skirt, beheld the sheath of colored silk with something like amazement.

"Let me take you to a movie," Somchit whispered as she reached for it.

A movie. She immediately thought of her sister. *Enough about cleaning,* Sao's spirit had told Noi just the night before. *Do you ever do anything fun?* Noi turned her head to look into the house — Daeng was deep within, occupied with last-minute party preparations — and then turned back to Somchit, and nodded quickly. Somchit relinquished his hold on the dress; it fell like an empty woman into her arms.

She ran with it to the Quarters, examined it there. Bright red, Sunday color, a shiny-soft material. It would need a little alteration to fit her properly; she could do that on Saturday night. She ran back to the house, got there before Daeng noticed her absence.

Late that evening, when the party was done and the guests gone and the house tidied and closed up, Noi lay on her sleeping mat exhausted, wondering if Madame would make her pay for the carpet cleaning, and how much it would cost. She heard a whistle from outside, peeked out her window to see Somchit standing in the garden below. He beckoned, put a finger to his lips.

Did he mean to take her to the movie *now*? In a Sunday-color dress? It was wearable, although she hadn't yet taken in the waistline — and red wasn't Friday-*un*lucky . . . but she was so tired . . . but a movie! Finally, she slipped the dress over her head. Buttoning the last button, she looked outside, saw that he was gone. She'd taken too long; he had tired of waiting. She was surprised by how disappointed she felt.

When she went out to sweep the front step on Saturday morning, there was nothing waiting for her. Somchit stood smoking on the far side of the car in the driveway. It was the same on Sunday, and again this morning. She'd taken her time pushing the broom over each step, sneaking her eyes at him, but he never even turned his head.

"Look what I can do," said Philip as Laura stepped down into the pool. She stood on the second step, a line of cool water bulging at her thighs, and watched as he clasped his hands together and squeezed. A jet of water shot upward.

"I can do that too," said Bea from the deep end. "I *taught* you."

"No you didn't," he said. "Alex did."

"Let's not show Laura," said Bea.

Laura pretended not to hear them, going another step, watching the butterflies on her swimsuit go darker as the water touched them.

"I'll teach you, Lolo, and then we can have water fights," said Philip.

"Thank you," Laura breathed. Under his direction, she held her hands half-submerged and let him shape her fingers around each other. *Now go,* he said, demonstrating with his own hands, and she pumped her palms together. A small pulse spurted up.

"You're getting it," said Philip. "Maybe more like —" He frowned down at her hands, adjusted her finger placement.

She had an impulse then, to confide in him about seeing the new driver in the garden the night of the party; perhaps it was something Philip could explain. But telling even one person might be a mistake. Some secrets were better when shared; others were weakened. She wasn't sure yet which kind of secret this was.

CHAPTER THIRTEEN

It was the same hotel where the Prestons had stayed upon their arrival in the country, the one at Rajaprasong intersection with the rock-face swimming pool and the three-headed elephant on every towel and sheet and cocktail stirrer. Going into the lobby, Genevieve felt exposed, as though she might be recognized. But of course the hotel staff wouldn't remember her: it had been years ago, and she had been just one wife among so many, stopping with her husband and children at one of the best hotels in Bangkok.

She walked past the desk unchallenged, to the elevator bank; once inside the ascending box she was seized by misgiving. So far her transgression was merely theoretical. When would it become actual? At the moment that the clothes came off, or at some time before? When she had had the driver drop her at the club, telling him to return at four, and then stood outside pretending to fuss with her gloves until he'd gone? When she'd walked back down to the street and caught a tuk-tuk and given the address of this hotel? Or was it when she'd brazenly crossed the lobby with the brisk, assured gait of a guest? Each of those acts had committed her, and none of them had been the first. The first was at her own party, in her own house, with her husband just across the room, when she had looked into Maxwell Dawson's eyes and replied to his invitation in a low, complicit voice.

Of course, she hadn't yet passed the point of no return; she could stop right now. She could simply stay in the elevator when the doors opened, ride it down again and leave the hotel, take a tuk-tuk back to the club and meet the driver at four after a Monday afternoon spent like any other in the last four years, gossiping with the ladies, reminiscing about home. But when the elevator doors opened on the fifth floor, even while imagining her hand reaching out to press the Lobby button, she was walking forward into the corridor. And then she was standing outside the door of 510. She castigated herself for her waffling: Hadn't she decided all of this already? In all of the minutes between Friday night and now, hadn't she gone back and forth a thousand times? She had come, she was here. That must mean she'd decided. She knocked, two quick raps.

When he opened the door and saw her, he

raised his eyebrows, and Genevieve had a moment of chilling panic. Perhaps it had been a joke. Perhaps he hadn't actually expected her to come. But the faint surprise on his face did not birth actual puzzlement; he smiled and stepped aside. As she passed through the doorway he put his hand to the small of her back, not touching her there, but bringing his palm within an inch of the fabric, the heat from his skin driving her on.

It was one of the suites, the main room furnished with soft furniture arranged around a low table, a small desk against one wall and a bar in the corner, a balcony overlooking the pool. Two doors on the far wall, both ajar: one to the bathroom, the other — her mind went blank.

He went over to the bar counter and put his hand onto the familiar green bottle with the red stamp.

"If gin isn't your fancy, I can call down for something else," he said.

"It's fine," she said, her first words in the room, her voice sounding clogged and unnatural. She cleared her throat.

He made the drinks with quick, sure movements. Four cubes of ice rattled into each squat glass, three fingers of gin. He rolled a lime briefly under his palm before slicing into it, crushed a wedge over the mouth of each glass. The citrus tang reached Genevieve where she stood watching. She turned to put her purse onto the desk, heard from behind her the sigh of the tonic bottle as the cap came off, and then the glug of pouring.

"Here you are," he said, and she turned. Their fingers touched as she took the drink. "Cheers," he said, lifting his glass.

She looked into her glass at the tiny bubbles collecting on the ruined piece of lime and streaming upward in hectic lines. Gin and tonic. Genevieve had met wives who'd drunk it in Africa, in India, in Ceylon, in all the places lumped together as *overseas* where they'd found themselves, following their husbands. Whiskey was ubiquitous, of course, in all of its forms, rye and bourbon and scotch, but gin was the expatriate staple. She put the glass to her lips and tipped it up, let the clean juniper taste roll across her tongue. Gin and tonic. When she got home, she would never have another one.

"I'm glad you came," he said. He took a packet of Pall Malls and a hotel matchbook from the end table, shook out two cigarettes. He handed one to her and lit it, brought the match back to his own. The flame throbbed down and up with his inhalations. He blew out the match and laid it, ribboning out a bitter whiff of sulfur, into the glass ashtray with the three-headed elephant cut into the bottom. Putting his glass to his mouth, he took a long drink, scrutinizing her.

"What did Robert do to deserve you?" he

259

said. "You are flawless."

Her bare shoulders felt suddenly obscene, rising in gooseflesh in the river of cool air flowing out of the air conditioner. She cast about in her mind for a gracious way to respond, and then she realized: She had already broken many rules by coming here. No need to respect the others.

"I'm not here to talk about my husband," she said.

He smiled. "Why are you here, then?" he said.

The rain began to pelt the windows, *spat spat.* In Washington, the summer rain beat down like a cleansing curtain, pulling a delicious smell of dirt into the air. The spring before they had left, she remembered, Philip had had a little boat that he'd played with during a rainstorm, dropping it into one of the rushing street gutters and then running alongside. Robert had run with him, to pluck it out before it could swirl down into the sewer through the slot at the end of the street. Over and over they did that, while she watched from the screened side porch. Her two men laughing hugely, the rain falling into their mouths.

"You have the most poignant look on your face," Dawson said. His voice was gentle.

"I hate the rain," she said. She sat in one of the chairs, took a swallow of her drink. "Let's talk about you," she said. Rudely changing the subject. She felt ugly, exhilarated. "Is this your first visit to Bangkok?"

He laughed. "No," he said. "But it's shaping up to be the best."

He crushed out his cigarette, then drained his glass and put it down on the bar.

"Finish up," he said, as though she were a child. "And then we'll go." At her surprised look, he said, "You did promise to take me shopping." He added, "Or did you have something else in mind?"

An odd mix of relief and dejection. She'd sidestepped the yawning pit of adultery; she'd bungled the seduction. She jolted the last of the liquid down her throat, set the glass on the table, and extinguished her own cigarette.

"Shopping it is," she said. She stood up, smoothed her skirt.

"You must show me your secret places," he said as they got into the elevator. His expression innocent of double entendre when she shot a glance at him. "Perhaps the shop where you got those little pots." He pressed the elevator button, stood a decent distance from her in the small enclosure. "There's nothing like being taken around by a native."

"I'm hardly a native," she said.

"Close enough," he said as the elevator doors closed.

"You have that mislabeled," Genevieve told the shop owner, pointing to the cream-colored card taped to the shelf beside a bowl. "This is Ch'ing Pai, not Ting." The man stared at her. "Not Ting," she said again. He retrieved a large book from a shelf behind him, opened it flat on the counter, turned some pages, and squinted down, reading. Then he came around the counter and peeled the card from the wood.

"Sharp eyes, your wife," he told Dawson, turning the card over to its clean reverse, dipping his pen.

"Don't I know it," said Dawson easily. He wandered to another display. "Uh-oh," he said. "This one's broken." He held up a pitcher, turned it to show Genevieve a seam of gold curving around its side.

The shopkeeper, carefully printing onto the card, looked up at Genevieve; they both smiled.

"It's Kintsukuroi," said Genevieve. "A Japanese mending technique."

"I would think a mend would do a better job of hiding the damage," said Dawson.

"The whole idea is *not* to hide it," she said. She went over, inspected the pitcher in his hands. "This is very valuable."

"Not really," he said, looking skeptical.

"Art is not just what it looks like," she said. "It's also what it means."

"This one seems to mean that its owner was too cheap to buy a new pitcher."

She didn't laugh along with him.

"This wasn't reconstruction," she said. "It was creation." She put a finger beside one of the wide seams. "This is urushi. The sap of a specific tree." She took the pitcher from him. "After the repair, it had to dry for weeks at just the right temperature and humidity, in a box built specially for the purpose. Open enough to allow air circulation — but not too open, or the sap would become brittle. If the piece survived without even one fragment shifting out of place, the joins would be painted with lacquer and dusted with gold powder, then given a final coat of clear lacquer to make them shine." She turned the pitcher between her hands; the fracture lines glinted in the dim shop light. "Kintsukuroi doesn't attempt to re-create the original. It acknowledges that the original is no more." Her voice sounded almost mournful. "It celebrates impermanence, and the imperfection wrought by change."

She looked up, saw that Dawson was staring not at the pitcher but at her.

"And of course, every piece is unique," she said, brisk. She placed the pitcher onto the shelf.

"That only Japanese," said the shopkeeper, who had come up behind them. "In Thailand, broken we throw away. Make more." He showed Genevieve the card he'd written out; she read it and nodded approval. Dawson let Genevieve guide him down the aisles of the shop, away from a collection of animal figures, away from an ancient-appearing vase (*cheap reproduction,* she murmured), into a purchase of a Burmese gold-leafed plaster statuette of a monk.

"Not the broken pitcher?" Dawson said as the shopkeeper began swaddling the monk in tissue paper.

"You don't deserve the broken pitcher," she said.

"I think I do," he said. He told the shopkeeper, "I'll take both."

"I should get some fruit," she said when they were outside the shop.

"I thought your servants did that," said Dawson.

"They do," she said. "But I'll need packages." She realized, when the words were out, that they betrayed her scheming beforehand, how she'd planned to acquire props as proof of her innocent afternoon. He didn't remark on it, though, following her into the channel of pavement made narrow by vendors squatting with their baskets of goods.

"Where did you learn so much about Oriental art?" he asked as Genevieve selected a hairy cluster of rambutan.

"I studied it in college," said Genevieve. That wasn't quite accurate: she'd begun to study it in college. Most of what she'd learned had been from reading on her own, after having left college to get married. She pointed to a pyramid of pineapples, held up three fingers to the vendor.

"Did you want to be a curator?" Dawson said.

She blinked. Had she? Had she had any concrete plans for herself at any point in her life, before leaving school to marry Robert? That time seemed so distant, sepia-toned, blurred by a wavy glass of years. She thought of Frances Sawchuck, a high-school classmate — striving, serious, bespectacled Frances. *She* was the kind of woman who worked, who would make a cold, solitary path through the world. At fourteen, Genevieve had known she was not like Frances.

"It's starting to rain," said Dawson, accepting the bags from the vendor.

"If you let the rain stop you here, you'll never go anywhere at all," Genevieve said, putting her change into her purse and snapping it closed. "The club does a lovely shrimp cocktail."

"I don't want to go to the club," said Dawson. He spoke deliberately. "Do you?"

She felt a frisson. Thus far, he hadn't touched her, and apart from letting the antiques dealer assume that they were married, there had been no suggestion of impropriety on his part.

"What do you want?" he said.

He was not standing very close, but she was

very aware of his chest under his shirt; she remembered how his biceps had flexed and unflexed as he tossed the little rooster pot. Her pulse beat in her throat. She understood that the line was behind them now, perhaps had always been.

In room 510, without words they began to undress. He removed his shirt, revealing a powerful torso; she unhooked the eye at her collar and turned her back to him so he could tug the zipper down, the split widening until her dress dropped around her feet. She reached behind herself, unclasped her brassiere, let it fall. Hesitated, then pushed down her underpants, and stepped out of them. She kept her hands at her sides when she turned. The thought came, unbidden: now Robert was not the only man to have seen her naked.

They were almost the same height. She smelled the tobacco on his breath, the echo of gin. He slipped one palm down to the small of her back and pulled her toward him, took his time about kissing her, as though that was all that he'd planned, the single kiss. *Stop it,* she told herself, for she was comparing it to Robert's kisses, those perfunctory preludes to sex or firm dry-lipped goodbyes. Surely there was something not quite — nice — about this kind of kissing, so open-mouthed. That thought chased briefly through her head and was gone.

Now both of his palms were underneath her bottom, and he was lifting her, and they were going backward. She felt a cool surface under her as he released her weight, and opened her eyes enough to see that she was being settled down onto the desk. She closed her eyes again and steeled herself for the next part. She jumped at the touch of his hand, then couldn't make sense of the next sensation, and her eyes flew open. What was he doing? She put her hands on his head, pushed it back and away.

"Let me," he said, his breath warm against her. She let him, but she remained jackknifed, cold, uncertain. Finally she relented, *In for a penny, in for a pound,* and lay back. Closed her eyes again and resolved to think about other things, to separate herself from what was happening: his fingers, his mouth, the soft tickling on her inner thighs from the curls on his head. If she retained no clear memory of the act, the experience would pass over her like water, would not write itself upon her in any detectable way. She thought about the shopping, wilting in paper bags on the floor. She'd bought a lot of pineapple; she'd have Harriet make a fruit salad. She thought about socks: the children needed new ones, she had better order them soon, packages sometimes took months coming from the States. *Isn't this how most women survive?* she asked herself, shakily ironic. *Making lists in their heads while their husbands go about it?*

But this wasn't her husband. He was a veritable stranger, older than Robert, shorter, hairier, thicker around the middle. Far less tentative. Robert had never done what this man was doing right now. What she was allowing to be done. The heady new smells of this man were weaving into one another like the pattern on a fabric, enveloping her: the musk of tobacco, a different musk from under his arms, an unfamiliar hair tonic, a scented soap. Robert always smelled of Truefitt & Hill No. 10 Finest Shaving Cream, shipped from England at great cost.

She squeezed her eyes more tightly closed as a rush of sensations passed through her.

"That's right," Max said, and she realized that she had made a sound, a small moan. It echoed in her head and she stiffened self-consciously, but only for a moment before surrendering again.

Some time later he moved away and she heard the ring of a buckle, his belt falling to the floor, and then the warmth of him returned, his chest hair against her skin. She clung to him as he carried her, laid her down onto a soft yielding surface. He was kissing her again, but now the languor was gone from it; he clutched her upper arms with steel hands and breathed against her throat. And then finally the entrance, violent but not painful, and a still, ecstatic interval before he began to move. She was moving too, an involuntary, automatic series of flexes, her neck arching under his mouth, pressed against the vibrations of the noises she couldn't help making.

For some uncharted time everything hung like that, and there was nothing, absolutely nothing in her mind, while behind her eyes was a shower of flower petals, hurtling toward her like colored snow.

Slowly she became aware again of the world: the separate panting of their breathing, the low noise of a radio on the bedside table, the tug of his hand on her scalp, where his fingers were still looped into her hair. The length of him was on top of her, a dead weight growing heavier until apparently he realized it, and shifted so that they were lying side by side. His chest was damp, the hair plastered dark against the muscle, and there was a small pool of sweat in her navel.

He stretched his arm over her, reaching to the night table for the cigarette packet. She put up her hand with two fingers extended and he settled a lit cigarette between them, then lit another for himself and propped himself on one elbow, smoking, smiling.

"That went well," he said.

"I don't know why I did this," she said. She felt an immense sadness, as if she were at the bottom of an avalanche of despair, watching the great shelf of it moving to bury her.

"Yes, you do," he said. He pressed his lips against her shoulder, his disheveled hair tickling her jaw, and then he pulled his head back, put his cigarette to his mouth. "Or, you know why you did it once." The lines fanned out from the corners of his eyes as the smoke drifted up from his smile. "You may not know yet why you'll go on doing it."

She sat up, fumbled for the counterpane rucked at their feet, found its stiff embroidered hem and dragged it up to her chest. He put his hand on the naked flat of her lower back, his thumb tracing a circle.

"I can have Robert sent upcountry this weekend," he said, the name in his mouth like a slap.

She pulled away from his hand, got out of the bed with the counterpane wound around her, dragging it like a train as she gathered her clothing from the floor. She dressed in the bathroom, balancing her burning cigarette on the edge of the sink, stopping twice to drag deeply on it before dropping it into the toilet. The mirror revealed the wreck of her hairstyle; she combed it with her fingers, catching them on hairsprayed tangles, and ran a wet washcloth under her eyes to gather up the speckled bleed of mascara. How stupid she had been, theorizing coolly beforehand about adultery, deciding that it lay in the consent and not in the act. She had been

270

wrong. It had been nothing beforehand, nothing. It was real now. The soreness between her legs, the oozing onto the cotton panel of her underpants, the places on her body that still felt his fingers. Unwanted flashes in her memory of his head burrowing, burrowing while she made little helpless cries. It was not theoretical at all.

When she emerged from the bathroom, he was standing in the bedroom doorway holding a fresh drink, wearing boxer undershorts and a thin white cotton robe with the three-headed elephant logo of the hotel over the breast.

She turned her back to him, lifted her hair above the gapped back of her dress. He put down his drink and tugged up the zip. He fitted the hook into the eye at the top and his hand paused there, covering the tender neck bones. She stepped away from his hand, her neck going cold with a sensation like pain, toward her shoes, which were lying on their sides on the floor.

"I'll get you a taxi." He went toward the desk — *the desk;* thinking of what had happened there, her breath caught — where there was a telephone.

"No need," she said, her back still to him. "I told my driver I'd meet him in front of the club at four o'clock." Her voice sounded unfamiliar in her head. She put a palm against the window as she eased a shoe over

271

her heel with the other hand, looking down through the glass at the street below, the people and traffic like hectic toys.

"Come back tomorrow," he said.

"I have plans," she said, although she had meant to say something different.

"The next day, then. Any day. In the hot hours. I'll be here."

She took up her handbag, went to the door.

"Jenny," he said in a soft voice. She turned. The gap in his robe showed a narrow strip of chest, wild white and brown hair curling through. "You're forgetting something."

Almost against her will, she stepped toward him. They stood about a foot apart, looking into each other's eyes. The room smelled of sex and tobacco smoke. Still holding her gaze, he extended his arm.

She looked down, saw that his wrist was feathered around with green spears, the crown of a pineapple poking out from the wrinkled mouth of one of the paper bags in his hand.

"Your alibi," he said, with the barest hint of a smile.

CHAPTER FOURTEEN

Robert locked his office door and flipped the light switch on the wall in the corridor. It was a clue to the origins of this building, but one he had yet to decipher, how the ceiling light in each room was controlled from a switch-plate in the hallway outside. He hesitated a moment, patting his pockets: Had he forgotten anything?

It was pointless, and he knew it. No matter how thoroughly he checked now, it would not prevent the need to check again when he was halfway down the stairs. It was one of his lifelong nervous habits. In college those habits had regularly subtracted half an hour of his nightly quotient of sleep, forcing him to turn the bedside lamp on shortly after switching it off to ensure — again — that the alarm clock was set. A few minutes later, he'd have to turn the light back on to check that the alarm had been set to the correct time. Light off. Pause. Light on again: Had he pushed the little pin in the back in inadvertently, shutting the alarm *off,* during the last maneuver? After he'd married, he'd been able to relinquish the bedtime checking ritual, having put his trust in Genevieve to manage the alarms and locks and other minutiae of home. One of the great advantages of married life.

But away from the house the old behaviors dogged him, and it was a rare evening that he didn't have to go back at least once after leaving his office, to check whatever it was that needed checking. Sometimes only once but more usually twice and occasionally three times, before the compulsion retracted its claws and released him, and he would be able to get into the car and drive away.

Today he got only fifteen feet down the hall before turning back. And then the second time to the stairwell, and the third time halfway down the first flight of stairs. The fourth time he made it to the parking space where the white Mercedes awaited him. He had the keys out and in his hand, but the anxiety scrabbled inside him like a trapped animal and he turned away from the car, went back across the garage, and pushed through the door again into the stairwell.

The door fell closed behind him, cutting off the rushing sounds of traffic from the street, and he climbed the stairs with a feeling of dull resignation. He couldn't even remember what he was checking this time.

Not the lights, which he recalled turning off, and which he had already gone back twice to check. Ah, the window. The third time he'd gone back was to ensure that it was closed. Now he was going back to make certain that he'd locked it.

The building was quiet. It was nearly seven. Everyone else had gone home to their dinners; they weren't boomeranging back over and over, to check on things that didn't need to be checked. He knew the things didn't need to be checked; and yet, he also didn't know, and he had to check them. He opened the door onto the second floor. The corridor was dark.

Not completely dark: there was a slim bar of light beneath one of the doors down the hall, a large dim rectangle hovering above it. He was sure that when he'd left just a few minutes before, all of the offices had been dark — yes, he remembered having had some trouble with his footing, feeling around for the stairwell door, pushing it open, the stairwell light spilling onto his feet. Whose office had become occupied since he'd left? He thought at first it was Bardin's, but as he got closer, he realized that the light was coming from his own office. He stood outside the door. No movement apparent through the thick pebbled glass, but from within, he heard a very quiet noise, like someone surreptitiously sliding a drawer closed.

The briefcase in Robert's hand was solid, with sharp corners. He could burst into the room, serve the intruder a wicked backhand with the case — and then what? How was Robert to subdue the intruder after the initial assault? No smack from this fine-grained leather valise — no matter how powerful the swing, no matter how sharp the corners or well-aimed the blow — was certain to render a man unconscious. What if the man was armed? The safest plan was to retreat and look for a public phone. Robert could say *khmoy* to the operator — everyone knew that word, there were plenty of burglars in Bangkok — and give the address. That would surely get the message across. And if the man got away in the meantime, well, then he got away.

While Robert was considering the options and coming to this decision, almost of its own accord his hand floated up and found the light switch on the wall on the near side of the doorway. His fingers grasped the protruding plastic nub and pulled it down.

The room went instantly dark; the small surreptitious noises from within stopped.

The small flare of pleasure that Robert felt when the light extinguished, eliminating the uncomfortable asymmetry in the corridor, evaporated almost as it was born. What now? Robert had a fleeting advantage over the intruder — he knew the topography of his own office better, and so might circumnavigate obstacles more easily in the dark — but that advantage wouldn't count for long. His burglar (Robert had begun to think of him in the possessive) was probably standing with his back to the window, eyes open wide. The longer Robert waited, the better the other man would be able to see. Robert had to act now.

He put his left hand out, grabbed the knob, and turned it. It went an entire revolution: the door was unlocked. He jumped in front of the door, pushing it wide with his left shoulder, flicking the light switch back up with a swipe of his right hand as he did so. He didn't recall later, but he might even have yelled "Aha!"

Bardin stood blinking in the light.

"Good Christ," he said. "Give a man a fright."

"What are you doing here?" Robert almost yelled, his heart hammering in his chest. "You're not supposed to be in here."

"Perhaps you should sit down," said Bardin, his brow corrugated with concern. He motioned toward the chair in front of the desk — *My* desk, thought Robert. "You look quite faint."

"Why are you in my office?" Robert said again. Bardin was so calm, his air of ease so pure, that Robert double-checked that it *was* his own office. Yes, there was the potted plant, and there the photograph of Genevieve on the desk.

"I misplaced something," said Bardin. "I thought you might have it."

"Why — would I — have it?" Robert spoke between deep slow breaths, trying to bring his pulse rate down. "If you wanted something, you could have asked me. I was here all day."

"I thought it might have got mixed into some of the papers that were sent your way." This was news. Bardin saw materials before they came to Robert? "I was hoping to undo the damage, no one the wiser." Bardin pulled the desk chair out, sat. "And no one would have *been* the wiser if I had exerted just a shade more self-control." He shook his head, rueful. "My mother always warned me about the consequences of impatience."

"What are you talking about?" Robert sat in the chair across from the desk.

"I know you always come back once," said Bardin. "You often come back twice. I thought I was being exceptionally cautious, waiting you out for the third time. But tonight — four times! A personal record." He pinned Robert with a frank gaze. "You seem to have extra trouble leaving the office tonight. Problems at home?"

"Stop it," said Robert. His legs were still trembling from the adrenaline burst, but his heart was finally slowing down.

"Can you just forget I was here?" Bardin said. He reached up to slide the file cabinet drawer closed, held up his empty hands. "I've done no damage. I'm not carrying anything away."

"You can't be serious," said Robert.

"It's not as if anything very important would be in this office." Bardin must have realized how it sounded, for he added, "Not with these worthless locks." He continued smoothly, "Even so, you deserve an explanation, and I shall give you one. But not here," he said. "Ears in the walls." Robert had never considered the possibility. "Let's go for a drink."

Robert looked at his watch.

"Are you allowed?" said Bardin, seeing the gesture.

"Don't be an ass," said Robert, picking up the phone receiver and dialing, pushing the wheel round and listening to the clicks. Three rings, and then the fourth ring cut off abruptly, but there was no greeting. "It's Mr. Preston, Daeng, don't hang up," he said into the emptiness. "Is Madame there?" Of course she was there, he thought after he'd said it. Where else would she be?

More emptiness, then "I get," and the clatter of the phone being put down on the hall table.

Under Bardin's amused eye, he waited. By the time Genevieve finally spoke "Hello?"

into the phone, he felt snappish.

"I'll be late coming home tonight," he said. "A bit of a snag at the office."

Was there disappointment or curiosity in the short silence? "All right," she said. "I'll telephone the Whitmans and beg off."

"Damn it, I forgot about them."

"It's all right if we miss," she said. "It's only cocktails."

"I won't be too late," he said.

"All right," she said.

"I'll see you later then," he said, but she'd already put the telephone down.

Bardin was leaning against the wall watching, hands in his trouser pockets.

"Haven't you lied to her before?" he asked with something like sympathy. Then he shoved himself away from the wall with a short bark of laughter. "Of course you have. Let's go."

As they were leaving, Robert looked back into his office. From the doorway, everything looked in order. The file cabinet lock twinkled innocently as though it had never allowed itself to be picked. He pulled the door shut and locked up again, switched off the light.

They walked in silence together down the stairwell, Robert fighting the usual impulses tugging him back into the building. *I locked the door,* he told himself, *I shut the window.*

"Was that the reason for that stupid story before?" said Robert when they reached the street. He remembered that feeling he'd had, that Bardin was peeking at the papers on his desk. "You were spinning that tale to distract me?"

"Knew you'd figure it out," said Bardin.

Robert presumed they'd go to the small bar on the corner, and when they came to its entrance he slowed, but Bardin kept walking.

"Not there," said Bardin over his shoulder.

Robert quickened his gait to catch up and they walked together, too far apart for companions, too close for strangers, down the long dark street and around the corner. Robert felt like an idiot, carrying his briefcase. He should have left it in the office, or put it into the car.

They turned another corner and were confronted by a carnival of neon, signs blinking asynchronously on all sides, people spilling from doorways onto sidewalks, from sidewalks into the street. The crowds were mostly men, and judging from their haircuts, mostly soldiers. Thai girls stood in doorways calling to them sweetly, *Hello hello.* This was the red-light district, which Robert had heard about but had never visited. He suspected that many of his colleagues had come here, but they hadn't told him about it. Other men didn't tend to confide their salacious exploits to Robert. Not that he wanted them to.

Bardin threaded through the crowd; following, Robert nearly bumped into a girl who stepped in front of him. "Pardon me," he said automatically.

"Hello, big honey," she said, smiling, looking up into his face. "Come have drink with me?"

"No, thank you." Scanning the street: Where was Bardin?

"Nice place very nice," insisted the girl, reaching for his arm.

There! Half a block ahead, the cowlicked head was unmistakable among the surrounding crew cuts. It plunged through a doorway under the looping neon script *Baby Lotus.* Robert shook the girl off and followed.

Inside was a damp fug of smoke, a surging tide of bodies, a throb of rock and roll music. A glowing jukebox squatted in a corner and a skimpily clad girl stood in front of it, plucking coins from the open palm of the man beside her. Couples were dancing. A line of tall stools along one side of the bar counter held girls laughing and chatting together, fixing their lipstick, all the while keeping an eye on the door. Like a cabstand, thought Robert. They looked just like cabbies, waiting for a fare.

A woman stood in front of him, wearing a top that tied around her neck and a brief pair of shorts. There was a white flower in her hair.

"I'm Tami," she said. "What you drinking?"

"No thank you," he said, scanning the crowd behind her. Was Bardin somewhere else now, laughing at having given Robert the slip?

"Whiskey soda?" Tami said, as though she hadn't heard him. "Green Spot?"

"No thank you," he said again.

"Bar special," she said. "Good very good drink."

"Will you leave me alone?" Robert said.

He didn't expect her tears, although perhaps he should have done; certainly a girl like her had learnt long ago how to cultivate a useful semblance of grief.

"I'm sorry," he said. "It's just that — I'm looking for someone."

"Girl?" she said, her tears drying at their source.

"No," he said.

Her expression didn't change as she said, "Boy?"

Robert pushed away from her, holding the briefcase in front of him and using it as a kind of prow to part the crowd, making his way to the bar. He snaked his arm between the mass of bodies and placed his hand on the sticky wooden counter.

"What you like," said the bartender, who was uncapping two bottles of Coke at once by shoving them down against a flange of metal that protruded from the edge of the counter. He poured the soda into four glasses, added a measure of clear liquid from an unlabeled bottle to each, and slid the glasses away down the bar.

"I'm looking for my friend," said Robert, speaking loudly over the clamor as a crowd of young women pressed up around him, calling to the bartender in Thai. "He just came in here."

The bartender was rapidly uncapping beers, gathering bottlenecks between the fingers of one hand. He held the hand up and collected money thrust at him over the bar as one by one the bottles were plucked from his grasp. He did this twice more and then turned to a cash register behind him and pressed some keys; the drawer shot open.

"My friend has red hair," said Robert to the man's back.

The man paid no attention, separating the bills by denomination and smoothing the stacks before laying them into the drawer. When he was done, he slammed the drawer shut and turned around.

"What you drinking?" he said.

"I don't want a drink," said Robert. "My friend. Tall. Red hair. Did you see which way he went?"

"Scotch whiskey, Coke, rum, gin. Green Spot."

"I don't want a drink," repeated Robert.

"You buy drink," said the bartender, making the words slow. "Find your friend."

Robert understood: he was expected to pay for the information.

"Whiskey, then," he said. The bartender reached beneath the counter and brought up an unlabeled bottle, glugged a measure of tea-colored liquid into a glass clouded with fingerprints.

"Fifty baht," said the bartender, putting the drink down in front of Robert. His accent made it *fip-ty.* "Special price for find your red hair friend."

Fifty baht was ridiculous, more than two dollars. Robert pried the notes from his wallet and the bartender pushed the glass across the bar toward him, jerking his head to Robert's right as he did so. Robert looked over in that direction but saw no sign of Bardin.

"Special room," said the bartender, and immediately returned to uncapping beers.

Robert looked again, craning his neck to look around a raucous knot of humanity that was gathering in front of him. He could just make out the edges of a closed door in what had appeared at first glance to be unbroken wall. *Special room.* Clutching his drink in one hand and the idiotic briefcase in the other, he headed toward it, trying to divert around the cluster of people, but it surged outward and ingested him and he found himself in a clearing, where a girl was standing on a table.

She was totally naked except for a headband with a tall upright pink feather in it; the smooth V between her legs was almost at his eye level. Her body was like a child's, hairless and neat. Robert had seen girlie magazines, but not many, and he'd seen only one nude woman in the flesh. Genevieve would look like an alabaster Amazon beside this girl. He shuddered at the thought of Genevieve in this room.

The crowd closed in front of him again, and the feather sank out of sight. The girl must have lowered herself to sit on the table; what she was doing there Robert could not see. Men were going up to the table for a moment, doing something there, then moving back. Robert was transfixed: What were they doing to the girl? How could this be legal? A space cleared again in front of him and Robert shouldered into it, whiskey slopping from his glass onto his sleeve.

The woman with the pink feather was getting to her feet again on the tabletop; two grinning men stood on either side, gripping the table to hold it steady. *Jump,* called a man. With her knees tight together, the girl hopped in her high heels. The crowd booed and called, *Higher.* She jumped again, another feeble effort. A man came forward from the crowd and thrust his hand between her knees, levering them apart. A few coins clattered onto the table. *Jump,* the crowd called in a rhythm. *Jump. Jump. Jump.* With each jump, more coins fell. The men laughed like crazy.

"She gets to keep whatever doesn't drop out," said a voice close to Robert's ear. He turned: Bardin. "But of course she keeps all of it. No one wants those coins back." Bardin laughed at Robert's expression. "How is it you've never been to Patpong? Genevieve has you on a short leash, my friend."

"Where the hell did you go?" Robert asked. His hand clenched on the glass he was still holding; he wanted to punch the name of his wife from the smiling mouth. "This place is disgusting."

"This place is safe," said Bardin. He circled a finger, indicating the chaos, the noise. "We can talk here. Come on."

He led Robert around the fringe of the dance floor to a collection of empty tables. As they sat down at one of them, a girl appeared.

"Bring us two closed beers," Bardin said, holding up a bill. She took it and went away. He indicated Robert's whiskey glass. "Don't drink that bile."

"I didn't come here for a drink," said Robert. He put the glass down on the table, pushed it away from himself. After a moment's deliberation — lap or empty chair or sticky table or sticky floor — he put the briefcase across his thighs. "What were you doing in my office?"

"I think the Harch took something off my desk by mistake." Robert had seen the messy piles on Bardin's desk; it would be no wonder if things got misplaced there. "Ah, *khob khun khrap.*" The girl was back with two bottles of beer. Bardin uncapped them with a gadget from his pocket and placed one in front of Robert, vapor misting from its mouth. "Cheers," Bardin said.

"You buy my bar?" the girl asked Robert.

"He already paid," Robert told the girl, nodding at Bardin, who choked with laughter, midswallow.

"She wants you to buy her company for the evening," he explained. "It's a good deal at seven dollars." He rummaged in his pocket, brought out a handful of coins. "Go play the jukebox, darling," he said, holding them out to the girl.

"Why burgle my office?" said Robert when she was gone. "Why not just ask me about — whatever it is?"

"It's complicated."

"Obviously," said Robert.

Bardin dropped the flippancy. He leaned forward, his mouth a grim line. "It was a personal item," he said. "A photograph."

"Oh," said Robert, understanding what happened to photographs that came to him in the envelopes Miss Harch brought. "But even if I did use it, that wouldn't matter. No one would see it." *No one* meant no one but the enemy.

"You're right, of course," said Bardin. But he didn't sound reassured.

A girl with her hair in two high ponytails

was wandering through the place, a small bunch of balloons drifting jerkily above her. Now and then she stopped at a table, detached one balloon from the others and wound its string around a GI wrist, tied a bow. When she approached their table, Bardin waved her away. She pout-smiled and moved on.

"Tell me if you recognize this," said Bardin. Robert looked back and saw that Bardin had his hand out, a photo cupped inside it. He recognized it immediately: the striped shirt, the blurred boyish face. Nguyen Tran.

Bardin's face was intent, questioning: *Yes or no?*

Robert recalled the man's statement earlier that evening: *It's not as if anything very important would be in this office.* He'd meant it as it had first sounded. Nothing to do with the terrible locks on the office doors; he had meant that *Robert's* office specifically would not contain anything important.

Staring into Bardin's anxious eyes, Robert felt his head move as if someone were moving it for him, dragging around on its axis, to signify no. He watched relief spread across the other man's face.

"Master?" said a high voice, very close. Both men looked up.

It was the coin dance girl, the pink feather still bobbing on her head. She was wearing a

289

brief orange dress now, with a plunging neck-
line.

Robert looked back at Bardin. His hand
was empty now, the photograph back in his
pocket.

"*Sawadee-kha,* Master," the girl said to
Robert, with a wai so deep that her thumbs
touched her hairline. *Master.* The word called
up the house where his wife and children
were waiting, only a couple of miles away.

"Preston, you have untold depths," murmured Bardin into his beer.

A loud *bang* from across the room, followed
by whoops and hollers of laughter. Robert
could see a soldier holding up a hand, as if
he were in class asking to be called on; from
between his fingers dangled a string, at its
end the tatters of a balloon.

The pink-feather girl put a hand flat on her
chest. "Root," she said.

"Erm," said Robert. Root? It was impossible to look at her without remembering her
nakedness, the coins falling as she jumped.

"Root," she repeated, nodding harder, the
feather ducking and waving. "Nine Soi Nine."

And then it came to him.

"Ruth?" he said. Her lips burst into a smile
and she nodded even more ferociously, the
feather whipping about.

Ruth. Genevieve had christened one of their
early Number Threes with that name. Robert
studied the girl's face without a particle of

recognition.

"Ruth," he said. "Well. How are you?"

"I am fine," Ruth said. "How is Madame?" She told Bardin, "Madame very beautifun," with that Thai vocal quirk of turning a word's terminal *L* into an *N*.

"She certainly is," said Bardin. His anxiety had vanished after Robert's lie; he appeared to be enjoying this enormously.

Robert had a mental flash of Ruth, decently skirted and bloused, reaching to unpin clothing from a line. She'd bathed his children, made his bed, and laid out his pajamas. She'd probably scrubbed his underwear. Was she a prostitute now? Was this what happened to the girls who were dismissed from the Preston household?

"Incoming!" someone yelled. An injured howl followed, and a chorus of boos.

"This one's aim is not spectacular," said Bardin, around the beer bottle at his lips.

It was abruptly intolerable, all of it: the music, the naked girls, the staccato fanfare of bursting balloons, the raucous whoops of laughter, Ruth's friendly face, the redhead's smirk.

"I have to leave," said Robert. "It was very nice to see you again, Ruth." Nodding at her deep wai.

As Robert shouldered through the crowd, he saw the ponytailed balloon woman, now clad only in her bikini top, lying back on her elbows on the bar with legs apart and pelvis tilted upward. As he watched, she flexed her thighs and something, incredibly, shot out of her and across the room. There was a *bang,* and a round of cheering. He fled.

He trudged back down the street alone, his suit jacket folded over his arm, his shirt adhering to his back, carrying his briefcase in a damp grip, winding his way around the groups of people. Vendors dotted the pavement, cooking over charcoal grills.

That headshake to Bardin, that lie told without words, had been an impulse prompted less by caution than by vengeance. For the insult, the *nothing important.* Also for the general air of mockery, and for taking him to Patpong. Bardin had known that Robert would be uncomfortable there. He'd perceived what Robert had striven for years to hide: how often he felt an onlooker in the company of other men, outside their easy bawdiness and filthy banter. Robert's otherness had made school, that welter of vicious adolescent boys, a misery before athletics had rescued him, and it bred in his adulthood a certain isolation — men didn't invite him along when they went to seedy places, or tell him about their adventures there.

Robert had seen the same otherness in Philip, and had silently worried about it. When the boy developed an interest in judo, it had seemed to be a gift. Genevieve had been dead set against it. *Violence is not the answer,* she'd said. *Sometimes it is,* Robert had said. He had ended that discussion with a fiat: *Find him a judo class.* Imperious, peremptory. His son would not suffer as Robert had. Philip would have the soft corners knocked off while being taught how to fight back, would gain self-confidence so that even if he stayed small he could move powerfully in the world of men. If Genevieve had been surprised by Robert's vehemence, she had not said so. She'd found Philip a judo class.

Robert hadn't eaten since lunch. He stopped at one of the smoking sidewalk grills.

"Is that chicken?" Robert asked, pointing to a cluster of skewers at the side of the grill. *"Gai?"*

"Gai, gai," nodded the vendor, taking a skewer threaded with chunks of pale meat and thrusting it into the flame. "You want spicy?" he asked, lifting a liquid-filled jar with two nail holes in the lid. Robert nodded, and they both watched the meat sizzle for half a minute in the dancing fire one side, then the other, before the vendor withdrew it and spun the wooden stick expertly between his fingers, shaking liquid from the jar over the meat. He held the skewer out to Robert and put his hand up, two fingers. Two baht.

Robert paid and devoured it on the spot, standing with his jacket over his shoulder and his briefcase between his feet, pulling the meat pieces from the stick with his fingers, stuffing them into his mouth. They were searingly hot. The spice of the sauce deadened his lips and mouth and throat. It was delicious. He pointed again, paid for another, gobbled that down. When he was finished, his eyes watering, he saw the vendor looking at him expectantly.

"What?" said Robert. Unconsciously mimicking the speech pattern of the bar girls, "I already pay, four baht, very good."

The vendor reached to the side of the grill and took up a coffee can, wordlessly tilted it toward Robert. Inside, a crowd of wooden skewers, little flecks of meat and fat still clinging to them. Obviously the vendor reused them, washing them clean between patrons — or probably not even doing that. Robert dropped his two skewers into the can, feeling a wave of nausea. Hadn't they all been warned countless times against eating from street vendors' carts? Had it even been chicken meat? How many mouths had that wooden stick been in tonight? He thought of Ruth, the pink feather, the coins dropping.

It'd serve him right if he got sick from this.

Genevieve greeted him at the door and kissed him on the cheek as if nothing were out of the ordinary.

"Sorry I'm so late," he said.

"I sent the servants to bed." Her voice was free of reproof, but Robert could sense the specter of some emotion there, as though strong feelings had been indulged and then erased. "Harriet left a plate for you in the kitchen."

"I had a little something to eat," he confessed. He regretted it now, his lips still slightly numb and a smoldering under his ribs. He put his briefcase in its usual spot beside the hat rack.

Genevieve wasn't looking at him, running a fingertip along the surface of the entryway table, inspecting it before reaching into the vase of flowers on its top, frowning when her fingers came out dry. Was she considering the fate of another servant, was Choy or Noi at risk of being expelled from the household for faulty dusting or inadequate vase filling?

"Do you remember Ruth?" he asked.

"Ruth," she repeated, her gaze drifting up from her fingerpads.

"That maid we had when we first got here. The Number Three."

Her brow cleared. "Oh, yes. Ruth. Intolerably lazy." Robert thought of the half-hearted hops of the coin dance. "I would have sacked her the very first week if she hadn't been that Number One's cousin."

"She was the Number One's cousin?" he asked.

"Darling, they were all that Number One's

cousins, the first ones."

"I wonder what happens to them after they stop working for us."

"I have no idea," she said. "Perhaps they go on to another household. Although that would be unlikely without a reference."

"You don't write them references when they leave us?"

"Of course not," she said, still with that slightly abstracted air. "A false reference isn't in anyone's best interests. Not even theirs: if they're not suited to domestic service, they should find a new line of work." The jolt of dislike took him by surprise. She gave him a puzzled look. "Whatever made you think of Ruth?"

"I saw someone who looked like her to-night."

"What a funny man you are," said Genevieve. "She was only here a couple of months. I'm not sure that I would recognize her now."

He noticed that her hair was loose, not styled and sprayed into magazine perfection as it usually was on Monday. She must have washed it at home.

"You should always wear your hair like this," he said.

He stepped toward her, lifting a hand to touch it, and she went very still, as if she were willing herself not to step back. Surprised, he stood still too: His wife flinching away from him? They stood frozen like that for a second or two before a mask seemed to draw down over her features, and she wrinkled her nose.

"You'd better give me that suit jacket," she said. "It absolutely reeks."

That explained the flinch. Of course, she was repelled by the smell of him, the spilled whiskey, the cigarette and marijuana smoke. As he slipped the jacket off, he cast about in his mind for a plausible explanation — he would not have acquired those smells at the office — but she didn't demand one.

"It'll need to be sent out," she said without pique or curiosity, accepting the jacket from him and carrying it away through the house.

Chapter Fifteen

She hadn't known she was waiting for it, but when the whistle came again, Noi was ready. She dropped the dress over her head and buttoned it as she crept down the steps from the Quarters. Somchit wasn't there; she ran through the garden and opened the gate. There he was. She stepped through with her eyes down, ashamed and thrilled to feel her knees in the open air. He said *That dress is perfect,* his voice proud, its perfection more a reflection on him for choosing it than on her for wearing it well. He patted the flat panel of metal behind his bicycle seat and she climbed on, shyly allowed him to take her arms and put them around his waist. She tightened her grip as they swooped away from the curb, the wind rushing up her narrow skirt. Her heart raced but she wasn't frightened; she wanted to memorize every detail, so she could repeat it all to Sao. How the reflected taillights of cars made long red columns on the wet pavement; how Noi

298

found she could affect the bicycle's balance by shifting her weight to one side or the other. How Somchit swore when she did that but he was laughing, and skilled enough that they didn't fall.

They didn't go to the cinema. The films had all started already, he said, she had taken too long coming down to his whistle. She had taken only two minutes, but she didn't protest. Instead they went to a tiny restaurant, had a meal of glass noodles in a lemongrass broth, her eyes wide to be eating something from a stranger's kitchen. Afterward, they walked close together along the khlong, wheeling the bike. Somchit asked about her family, and she told him about her parents and sisters and her brothers, the river chuckling past the house on stilts. He told her that he was the eldest of five, that he liked the city and didn't ever want to go home. He bought a Coca-Cola and tipped the thick glass bottle to his lips and then to hers, alternating sweet swallows. *I'm sorry you miss your family,* he said, *but it is lucky for me that you came to Krung Thep.*

The bicycle tick-tick-ticked as they walked through the sleeping garden of 9 Soi Nine. She didn't want the evening to end. She floated up the steps to the Quarters, turned at the top to look down at him and wave goodnight. To her astonishment he wasn't at the foot of the stairs — he was right behind her. She made a sound of surprise and he put his hand over her mouth softly, *shhh.* He leaned against her and she let him push her down the external walkway and into her room, where he slipped the hand away from her face and replaced it with his mouth.

She had expected more violence, remembering the animals in the countryside. She kept her hands on his biceps until it was over, thinking: *This is more important than it seems.* She didn't cry. After he dressed again and left, Noi lay on the mat alone as the moon slowly moved out of her window. Once, she thought she heard the clink of amulets behind her, and her heart leapt; but she must have been dreaming, because her sister didn't speak or touch her, and Noi didn't hear the sound again that night.

CHAPTER SIXTEEN

At thirty-three, the bulk of what Genevieve guessed to be true about sex was greater than what she actually knew. She had expected her husband to teach her, but Robert had come to the marriage bed almost as naive as she, and there had never been anything in their demure congress of the wildness she had experienced in room 510, the memories of which now chased her even in her sleep. Two mornings in a row, she awoke into the open air of a shuddering orgasm, Robert slumbering unaware beside her.

It seemed that the encounter had awakened a stranger within her; perhaps that creature she had heard about only in whispers, the nymphomaniac, who craved sex and rotted her body with it. Genevieve willed herself to forget room 510, to dedicate herself to the minutiae of the present and let the past seal itself up behind her. She experienced the weekend parties at a remove, as though from the other side of a thick glass, but woke into

Monday feeling more herself. She marshaled the children through breakfast and went to the salon. Like any Monday.

"Have you heard?" said Irene, her voice juicy with rumor. They were side by side, their bare feet in bowls of scented water. "Maxwell Dawson left his wife. They might be getting a *divorce.*" The last word mouthed without sound as the pedicurist lifted one of Irene's feet from the water and enfolded it in a towel.

After the deafening initial shock — had room 510 been responsible somehow? — Genevieve heard the rest of what Irene was saying, that the separation had taken place months ago, before Dawson had come overseas. In the tide of relief that she wasn't responsible, there was a tinge of disappointment for which Genevieve chided herself: of course their afternoon together hadn't meant anything to Maxwell. She wouldn't want it to.

"Thank God they have no children," said Irene, studying three bottles of nail polish in her hands. She sparkled wickedly at Genevieve, brandishing one. "What do you think? I'm feeling racy." Genevieve nodded, and Irene leaned forward to tap the pedicurist on the shoulder with the bottle, saying in that loud pidgin she sometimes adopted with the Thai *I change my mind* and *I think this color instead.*

That afternoon and the next, Genevieve doubled down, exhorting the servants to greater meticulousness, puzzling the children by accompanying them to their lessons. She stood at the side of the ballet class to watch the row of little bodies at the barre, twinned in the mirror: first position, second position, plié. She stood outside the riding ring as the children went past, posting up and down. Beatrice, posture perfect, paid no attention to her, while Laura kept twisting around to look and nearly fell off. Philip, surprisingly, had a natural seat. How had Genevieve not known that? When Wednesday came, Genevieve announced her intention to attend the judo lesson also, but Philip objected.

"None of the parents go," he said. Frowning, anxious. "And there's nowhere in the shade for you to stand."

"Don't you want me to see how good you're getting?" she asked. He shook his head.

She didn't argue. It felt inevitable. Her resistance had been pointless and temporary, a frail promontory of sand beset by a restless surf, all week the fingers of the tide clawing long crumbling ruts into it. She realized that her capitulation had already been written into her daily choices — she'd forsaken elaborate hairstyling, had been applying only the barest makeup. No longer a stiff-sprayed untouchable doll. She'd known all along that she would go back.

She had the driver drop her at the club, dawdled a few minutes outside the entrance, then walked down again to the street and caught a tuk-tuk. As she settled onto the vinyl cushion, she felt no doubt, no worry about consequences, only a sparkling mindless anticipation. The door of room 510 opened and Maxwell stood there, face brightening at the sight of her; he swung the door wider and stepped aside to let her in.

CHAPTER SEVENTEEN

Now he saw them everywhere: in the streets, in the shops. Not much older than his daughters, in short dresses and garish makeup, leering at men, offering themselves. Had they always been there? Obviously they had. Robert had not been looking.

Bardin didn't appear at work all the rest of the week, leaving Robert in a pother of indecision. Should he tell the Boss about finding Bardin in his office? Robert went through his files and his desk drawers thoroughly: nothing seemed to be missing. Telling the Boss might also entail confessing Robert's lie, that impulsive headshake *No* that had seemed to reassure Bardin so much. It was a lie without consequences: information passed to the Viet Cong wouldn't imperil a boy in Thailand. For that reason, Robert thought the whole story about the photograph might be a fabrication. What had Bardin *really* been doing in Robert's office? Each evening, when everyone else had gone home and it was too late to act, Robert felt fresh outrage about the incident and was sure that he would tell everything to the Boss at the next possible opportunity, but by morning that resolve had evaporated. This went on all week.

He fretted through the weekend, Friday's party at home and Saturday's party out and brief Saturday-night sex with his wife that was complicated by unwanted visuals. Thank God Genevieve couldn't see inside his head.

In the middle of the afternoon on Monday, Robert stood up abruptly and snapped his briefcase shut, carried it down to his car, and stowed it in the boot. He locked the car and left it, walked down the street with a brisk, purposeful gait.

Patpong was muted in daylight, the neon turned off, the streets less crowded. In the Lotus, only a few couples were on the dance floor. Even the cab girls at the counter seemed subdued, talking quietly among themselves.

"Hello, *daa-ling,*" said one of them, as Robert approached the bar. "You buy my bar?"

Although her smile was wide, the invitation sounded half-hearted. He had the impression she'd been enjoying chatting with her friends.

"I'm looking for someone," Robert told her. "A tall Englishman. Mr. Bardin." What in the world was the man's first name? They'd done the boarding-school thing and used last names only. "Red hair."

"*Sie som,*" said the girl. She touched the hair beside her ear. *Orange.*

"Yes," said Robert.

"I maybe know him," she said. "You want dance?"

"Not right now, thank you," said Robert. "The red-haired man. Has he been here to-day?"

She screwed up her face as if considering, while her eyes slid to a spot behind Robert. He knew what was there: the door in the wall.

"Is he in that room? The special room?" said Robert.

She slipped down from her seat and leaned close against him, looking up with a smile. Her bangs fell into her eyelashes and she blinked them free. "Dance with me," she said.

She was terribly young. She might not be out of her teens. There seemed an inexhaustible supply of these sylphs, glossy-haired and miniature, their bodies created with a miracle of economy, not an extra bit of flesh. *We're monsters beside them,* Robert thought, *all freckled and lumpy and hairy.*

"My — *sie som* — friend," said Robert, taking a step back, making a space between their bodies. "Is he in the special room now?"

She looked across the bar at the door in the wall, then back at Robert, and her face changed a little bit. "Two hundred baht," she said.

Did she mean to go into the room, or just for the information? He looked at the anonymous door. Who knew what lay behind it? Apparently, something that cost ten dollars.

"I don't want to go in there," said Robert. "I just want to know if he's there now."

"Master!" cried a voice behind him.

Ruth was fully dressed today by Lotus standards, in a spangly dress with a V-neck that dipped nearly to her navel. She said something in quick Thai and the girl to whom Robert had been talking turned away without apparent chagrin and went in the direction of the entrance, where a group of men had just come in.

"Hallo, Ruth, how are you?" Robert asked. "Or — what is your real name?"

"Root okay," she said. "You want drink? Beer whiskey Green Spot Coke Fanta."

"Beer," he said. She smiled, waiting, and he understood that he should pay her. He gave her the money and she carried it the few feet to the bartender, who produced two bottles, one beer, one orange Fanta with a striped paper straw in its mouth. She brought them back, gave Robert the beer and took a long pull from the straw in the other bottle.

"Fan-ta," she said in a deep voice after swallowing, then giggled. He recognized the advertising tagline from the television, some-

308

thing his own children imitated at home. He felt a deep pang at the thought of his children.

"I'm looking for my friend," he said. "The man I was here with the other night?" He lifted a hand to his head, rolled a pinch of his own hair between index finger and thumb. "*Sie som.* Have you seen him today? Is he in that room?" he asked.

She looked over in the direction he indicated and shook her head.

"No one in there now. I don't think so," she said. Her eyes slid away as she said it. Was she lying? She looked back at him. "You buy my bar?"

How quickly the giggly-sweet veneer scratched off, revealing the grasping beneath. But it was only fair to pay her for her time — and talking to her would keep other girls from bothering him. He looked at his watch. Four o'clock. He didn't need to be home for two hours. Robert pulled a bill from his wallet.

"Only seven," she said, looking at it.

"Um, keep the rest," he said.

"Okay thank you," she said, folding the bill into a packet and magicking it away into her dress. She took his hand, led him to a table. When they got there, he dropped her hand under the pretext of pulling out a chair for her. She smiled and perched on it, but when he took the chair opposite, she moved over to sit beside him. She drank a little more Fanta, gave a delicate orange-scented belch, then covered her mouth and broke into giggles.

"Do you like working here? Is it hard work?" he asked. He thought of the coin dance. "I mean —" What did he mean?

"Dance, talk, okay, easy," she said, her voice matter-of-fact. "Clean floor sometime hard."

"You have to clean the floors?"

"Sometime." She mimicked gagging and put her tongue out, then grimaced, and he realized she was saying that sometimes people threw up on the floor. "Not nice." *Not naiii.* A tiny frown crimped her features, then dissolved into her default smile.

"I suppose not," he said. He didn't know how to ask the questions crowding into his mind, some of them stupid, all of them intrusive: Did she have to sleep with the customers? Was she sorry to have left her job with the Prestons? Across the bar, the door to the special room remained closed. "Do you have family here?" he asked.

"Many family," she said.

"Do they live here in Bangkok?"

She shook her head, pursed her lips again to suck at the straw of her soft drink, and looked up at him through her lashes. Like the other girl had done. Did they realize the seductive effect of that look, had someone taught that to them?

The music subsided from a whining nasal solo to a number that sounded like children shouting. The dance floor livened up accordingly, became a mild mayhem of people jumping around. The dancing Robert had grown up with was partnered and orderly. Society itself then had been partnered and orderly. This chaotic dancing had come to the States before they'd left; he'd thought it a fad, something ephemeral, like the Teddy Boy craze when he was young. It didn't seem to be passing, though, and neither did the societal havoc that accompanied it: glimpses of America from newspapers and television news clips showed a citizenry of scruffy vagrants, long tangled hair on the men as well as the women, giant puffs of hair on the black people, who now seemed to be everywhere.

"Children how big?" Ruth said, putting a flattened hand table height, as if measuring Laura or Philip.

"Bigger," he said, putting his own hand out, showing Bea's height. "Beatrice is twelve now. *Sip-song.*" As he said it he could hear Laura's voice, counting while she skipped rope.

"Sip-song," Ruth repeated with wide disbelieving eyes, looking at Robert's hand as if she could see the girl standing under it.

He took out his wallet, flipped it open. "These are from last year." Ruth leaned close against him to look. The children didn't look like themselves in the school photos, uniformed and neatly combed and brushed. "Philip's lost another tooth since then."

Ruth slipped her finger under the page,

flipped it over to show Genevieve's picture. She smiled, as though this were not the face of the woman who'd fired and forgotten her. "Beautifun," she said. Her smile dimmed. *Mai mee khwam-suk.*

"Excuse me?" Robert said.

"Not happy," said Ruth. "She not like Thailand." With deep sympathy, as if speaking of a terrible illness. "Madame want to go home."

"I want to take her home," he said forcefully. Something he had never acknowledged to Genevieve. And then he said something he had never admitted to anyone. "But I can't."

Robert had never meant to strand the family in Bangkok, and he'd certainly never intended to become a spy. Family expectation decreed that he'd go into law. His father had indulged him when he chose to attend university in the colonies, and as an undergraduate at Harvard he'd dabbled, taking anthropology classes, chemistry, engineering, knowing they didn't matter: the endpoint would be the same.

"You don't have to be a lawyer," Genevieve had said one night at dinner.

She'd taken the bus from Wellesley, as she had done almost every Friday night since they'd met at a party more than a year before, for an early dinner at a restaurant and then a walk, sometimes a movie before he'd see her

312

onto the return bus, back in the dorm by curfew. Wherever they went together, passing men appraised her and nodded their approval to Robert.

"What might you like to do instead?" she said. "Quick, without thinking."

"I'd like to build things," he said, surprising them both.

He realized it was true, though; he'd enjoyed his engineering classes, and building was practical, satisfying work, delightfully lacking in nuance. A structure would fall or stand, a wall hold or crumble, each circumstance predictable, governed by physical laws.

Genevieve was silent after the confession, and he imagined what she was thinking. *A builder.* How grubby it sounded. A step away from manual labor. This would likely mean the end of the Friday-night bus from Wellesley. He felt sadness, mixed with a bit of relief: finally the other shoe had dropped.

When she put her hand on his, he realized that he had been sliding his cutlery forward and then back, adjusting by millimeters the dinner fork, the spoon, the dessert fork across the top, laboring to achieve a precisely symmetrical frame of his plate. A wave of cold shame passed over him: *she had seen.* He lifted his eyes to hers, was surprised to see the affection there.

"I think the world may need builders more than it needs lawyers," she said. And smiling:

"The world certainly does not need a lawyer who wishes he were a builder." He felt an enormous burst of love. She added in meek afterthought, dropping her eyes, "You must do what you like with your life, of course."

His pulse quickened; he chased her withdrawing hand with his own, trapping it. "I was hoping," he said, "that it would be our life."

A long beat.

"Well," she said, one warm acquiescent syllable, the full blue of her gaze rising again to envelop him. "I always hoped to settle near my family in Washington."

That gentle push spun them together on the axis they now shared. Genevieve's father knew someone at an architectural firm in Washington's Dupont Circle; Robert accepted a position there as a draftsman *with a good chance for advancement.* In a whirl after graduation, Robert married, bought his first array of non-hand-me-down ties, his first house, his first new car. Following those chockablock accretions were the more sentimental arrivals of three children, the middle one a boy, which assuaged most of his parents' objections to all the rest.

Genevieve chose the house, a 1920s Tudor that stood on a small dead-end street surrounded by slightly newer upstarts. It seemed dropped into the landscape from some grander place and then forgotten, the landscaping overgrown and the double lot wild from neglect.

When the unobtrusive man came to him, Robert was approaching his ninth wedding anniversary. The neckties in his closet had all been chosen by his wife, the garden around the Tudor had been brought to heel, and his third child was sleeping through the night.

He was playing absently with a Slinky, which was to be a present for his elder daughter. At the sight of the man in the doorway, Robert dropped the toy into his desk drawer and shut it quickly.

The man didn't acknowledge having seen the Slinky as he approached Robert's desk, and launched a bewildering chain of questions: Was Robert happy here? Did he find the work challenging? What kinds of projects did he enjoy most?

"You're asking me to come work for you," Robert interrupted as understanding dawned.

"That's right," said the man.

"Well," said Robert, "they keep me pretty busy here." His glance fell onto the closed drawer and his face went hot as he remembered the Slinky.

The man nodded at the drawing on Robert's desk. "What's that, a bridge?" he asked.

"Yes," said Robert.

"You can build much more important bridges than that," the man said. Something in the man's voice or eyes, some hint of mockery, pricked Robert.

"I like these bridges," said Robert, not mentioning the sorry truth that this bridge in all likelihood would never come off the paper; he was a very junior member of the firm.

"It is critical that everyone give their special talents in this time," the man said.

He didn't need to explain what he meant by *this time:* It was 1968. America was at war, abroad and at home. Riots had shut down the city just a few weeks before, the arson and looting and gunfire like something from a third-world country. The fires downtown had been so extensive that the Prestons had been able to see the smoke from their house.

"I don't have any special talents," said Robert.

"Oh, but you do," said the man. He leaned forward over the desk and dropped his voice.

Robert listened to the man's speech with an odd sense of nostalgia. Something about its rhythm was striking. The ellipses, the escalating content, the emphatic punch word . . . He recognized that the man was using a method of persuasive technique as observed by Robert himself as an undergraduate, nearly a decade before.

"You've read my senior thesis," Robert interrupted.

"I have."

Robert knew that a copy of "The Elements of Persuasion," the linguistic study of argument that had won him honors and capped a small flourish onto an otherwise unremarkable academic career, had been bound and added to the stacks in the great campus library along with all the other theses. He had never imagined that anyone might go in search of it, might find and open it with a crack of age-stiffened crimson leather. He wasn't even sure where his own copy was; perhaps in one of the boxes in a basement storage room of the Tudor, nestled among the softening sheaves of paper, the handwritten notes and forgotten syllabi and other detritus of a liberal arts education.

"Is this about Columbia?" Robert asked. Perhaps they wanted him to help with negotiations in the student protest that was currently making headlines.

"Bigger than that," said the man, and Robert understood.

"I don't want to go to war," said Robert.

"You're already at war," the man said. "Every American is."

"My father is English," said Robert. "I spent my youth in England." Not meaning it wholly as it sounded, as a sniffy disclaimer of responsibility for the current antics of the colonies, but yes, partly exactly that.

"But *you* are American," said the man, his voice sharp. "Courtesy of your American mother."

"I have wonky knees."

317

"We don't need your knees," said the man. "We have plenty of *knees.*" He looked furious. Robert had seen the television images, everyone had: the parachutists jumping from airplanes, brown mushrooms scattered against the sky. "We should already have won this war."

"Are we losing?" Robert spoke with incredulity. America didn't *lose* wars. No matter what dismal statistics appeared in the news, victory was inevitable. Everyone knew that.

"It's not a fair fight," said the man, sounding defensive. "They don't even wear uniforms most of the time. They hide from us like rats. They've built whole cities underground, grandmothers digging with teaspoons." His jaw was grim. "Ordinary warfare won't win against them." His unblinking eyes on Robert. "We need a different kind of weapon. We need you."

"I know very little about guns," said Robert.

The man's expression changed fractionally, as if he were adjusting his original estimate of Robert's intelligence. "I'm not talking about guns." He hesitated, then said, "You must not share anything of what you are about to see and hear."

Robert nodded, and the man took something from his inside jacket pocket, held it hidden in his palm. Robert had the wild thought *Grenade*? He had no time to do anything but clench his teeth and squint a wince before the *click.* But no explosion came: Instead the room filled with an unearthly noise. Hooting and wailing, creaking and moaning. Robert's heart paused, then gave one giant beat, and he felt the hairs on the back of his neck rise.

Another *click* and the noise stopped; the man returned the unseen device to his pocket.

"What the hell was that?" said Robert.

"A psychological weapon," the man said, with not a little relish at Robert's expression. A *psychological weapon:* the phrase made no sense.

"I mean the thing in your hand," said Robert. It had to be a recording device of some kind, but any tape recorder he'd ever seen was far too large to be hidden in a person's hand. Reel-to-reel tapes were the size of a briefcase; even the recently introduced compact cassette tape player was far too large to fit into a pocket.

"Never mind that," said the man, irritated. "The sound you just heard is the weapon."

"I don't understand," said Robert.

"There's a Vietnamese superstition that if a person dies and is not buried near his home, his soul will suffer and wander forever. We took Vietnamese funeral music and added voices to it, the spirits of wandering souls, urging soldiers to go home and save themselves from the same terrible fate." Robert

319

hadn't heard any words, just unintelligible moans. "First we pop off a tiara grenade — a canister of phosphorescent marker gas — and then deploy the recording. It's an *incredible* effect."

"Does it work?" said Robert.

The man looked aggrieved. "It enrages them," he admitted. "It makes them shoot the hell out of everything."

Of course they would shoot, thought Robert. Even if they believed in the spirits, they weren't stupid enough to shoot at the spirits themselves. They'd shoot at the enemy who had brought them. *I could do so much better than that,* he thought, surprising himself.

"We've tried guns and bombs," said the man. "We've tried fear. We've dropped enough chemicals to make the whole country bald. I think we need a new tactic. I think we need to try to *persuade* them." A pause. "And you're uniquely suited."

Robert understood that all he had to do was say no. He had no reason to change anything about his life; he was on a good path, a gradual climb to a comfortable career plateau, fifteen or twenty years of that before retirement. He opened his lips to say no and put an end to this strange conversation.

And then he realized with a stab of alarm that if he said no, that might well *be* the end of it. In another few years, this crisis would be over. No one would be interested in his *unique suitability* or his potential then. He would no longer *have* potential then; he would have become the thing he was doing, and the nondescript path he had chosen on a blind impulse, into which he had settled as a consequence of inertia, would be the only path he ever saw.

"I wouldn't have to kill anybody," Robert said, the question mark faint at the end of the statement. A triumphant light appeared in the other man's eyes.

"There is always killing in a war," the man said. With a short mirthless laugh, he added, "But no. You wouldn't have to do it." He added casually, "You would have to move to Asia, but that's no hardship: year-round summer, all the pineapple you can eat. Paradise."

"I have children," said Robert. "Three small children."

"They'll be quite safe," said the man. "You'll be living in a different country entirely, far away from any actual fighting. Safer than here." With a glance at the window, where the horizon still smoked. "We can brief you on enemy culture, and you'll find the weak points and devise ways to penetrate them. Depending on how well you do, things should wrap up in a year."

"What would I tell my wife?"

"You could tell her the truth," said the man. "Or," he amended quickly, seeing Robert's expression, "you might tell her that your company's taken on a humanitarian project, building a dam in the north of Thailand. We can arrange it to look that way."

With surprisingly little difficulty the family relocated across the world to a rental home near the center of Bangkok, with a swimming pool and a large garden all surrounded by a high wall. As the unobtrusive man had promised, Robert did not have to do any actual killing; he toiled instead in a penumbra outside the conflict, unstained by the frankness of blood. The work wasn't as glamorous as he been led to expect by the unobtrusive man's flattering speech. Robert was a small cog in a machine, one he never saw the whole of: he made minor innovations on established projects or smartened up already-written text. But the other promises held: there was plenty of pineapple to eat in the perpetual summer, and his children did seem safe.

Genevieve didn't question the cover story, that the engineering firm had lent Robert to the government project for a year; she pronounced it a good barter, a year abroad for a career advance, and she threw herself into the planning. She thought of details he would never have considered, down to the five light sweaters she packed into her suitcase, three of them sized for the children's estimated growth by year's end. *To wear on the airplane home,* she'd said. *Who knows if you can even buy a sweater over there.*

When a year had passed, the Boss said they were making headway. In the second year, the Boss said *The goal is in sight.* That was the year the draft came at home, the call-up order determined by birthdate, 366 slips of paper plucked one by one out of a jar. Both Robert and Philip were ineligible, of course, but Robert couldn't help but note the numbers assigned to each of their birthdays — what their draft numbers would have been: Philip's was 26, Robert's 280. If he'd been eighteen years old, Philip would have gone in the first wave.

At the three-year mark, the Boss had spoken of *finishing what we started,* and been uncharacteristically frank: Robert could quit if he liked, but he'd be given no covering letter of reference if he did. Such an unexplained hiatus without references would be career poison, the Boss didn't need to say, and Robert understood that he'd been backed into a corner. By pride more than money, more than either of those by his love for his wife. There was no way to tell Genevieve the truth now without revealing the broad sweep of his dishonesty — in four years, that first lie had fathered a million others — and he couldn't bear to think how things between them might change if she found out. He did not fear her anger as much as her contempt. *A junior*

G-man, she might exclaim, and then he would see it too, how ridiculous it all was.

He told Ruth a halting, extremely abridged version of the story. It wasn't clear how much she understood, but she listened intently. When he was done, she said something in Thai, the last vowel sound crooning to its end, and put a hand on Robert's chest, making him jump. What would he do if she tried to kiss him?

"Buddha people have many life," she said, in English.

Was that supposed to be comforting? Was Ruth acknowledging that he'd made a cock-up of this life but he needn't worry, he'd have a fresh start after death, another chance to get things right? Maybe that philosophy explained why the Thai were always laughing and never seemed to take anything too seriously.

Her eyes moved from his to something behind him, and her smile broadened. She took her hand away from his chest — he felt a mild sorrow at the tiny loss of its removal — and waved it enthusiastically. He turned to look: Was Bardin coming out of the special room? It would be just Robert's luck to be spotted sitting cozily with a prostitute.

It wasn't Bardin, or anyone he knew; Ruth had been waving at a girl, another tiny doll with long shiny hair, wearing white boots and a skirt so brief that her matching underpants showed. She waved back at Ruth and led the man she had come in with onto the dance floor.

"Prem have good boyfriend," Ruth said, watching the couple. "They go Hong Kong already."

"How nice," he said. Uneasy: Was Ruth angling for him to be "good boyfriend" too? He didn't know how to make it clear to her that he was to be no kind of boyfriend at all. He had not touched her and he didn't intend to do so. Perhaps letting her touch him had muddied the waters. But how did one reject a woman's hand? It would have been rude to push it away.

He felt no desire for her, only a kind of camaraderie, the warmth one might feel for a peripheral character from a shared, beleaguered past, a classmate who'd suffered under the same cruel head boy. He also felt gratitude: the act of confessing, although it hadn't brought absolution, had lightened his load. To sit with Ruth a while longer, and buy more drinks, would be a way to return the kindness. She might not get another customer today. She was not as pretty as some others here, not so young. There were just so many to compete with, all beautiful, all willing. And all just seven dollars.

CHAPTER EIGHTEEN

Each morning now, Noi slipped the buttons of the white blouse through their buttonholes and zippered the skirt without thinking, before hurrying through the garden at dawn. No more lingering on the paving stones and hoping for a whiff of khlong to be carried over the walls, and Sao's amulets never made their delicate rattle behind her anymore in the dark. News from home told her that Sao had married Tee and had a baby, a little boy called Moo. From his play name, Noi guessed he was fat as a piglet, and she wondered what his ears looked like, although it didn't really matter. Whatever his fortune was, pebble or weed or water buffalo, in one way at least his luck was assured: he would spend this life as a boy.

Noi knew that what she and Somchit did together brought babies, and she wanted a baby to come. She ate pomelos and eggs, round hopeful things that might woo a child into her womb, and visited the shrine to the spirit who lived in the trees near Khlong Saen Saep, bringing as offerings a circlet of jasmine and a long smooth stone she'd found in an oil-paisleyed puddle in the street. She dreamed of her own baby lying naked, waving its little fists and laughing; it had Somchit's beautiful eyes and her own small mouth. She knew she should want a boy, but when she saw the bunched cleft between the fat kicking thighs, she was delighted. *Come soon,* she told her daughter. *Come to me soon.*

Somehow, Noi's virgin sensibilities had remained intact: a crude comment would make her blush like fire, and she could not have described aloud what she and Somchit did together in the dark of her room in the Quarters, in the cool of the garden at night, once even, ineffably daring, on the warm red leather of the Mercedes. Still, she felt a thousand miles away from the child she had been. She felt her world changing, expanding, filling with sensation; she understood more of the beat that drove everything. At night, she undid her long braid and let the hair fall, thick and shiny, tickling her shoulder blades; she admired herself when she bathed, running the washcloth over her stomach and legs. She dreamed of the countryside where she was born, the swollen, always-moving river, the rice plants poking up from the flooded lowlands in brilliant green lines. She awoke with a longing to see her sisters.

■ ■ ■ ■

Somchit had greater ambitions than driving for the Prestons, although he assured Noi often that it was a very good, high-class job, and he loved the car. Affection came into his voice when he talked about it. *It's not good, all the stop-and-go, stop-and-go in the city,* he told Noi. *A fine engine requires speed.* Sometimes when his eyes jerked back and forth behind their lids in sleep, Noi guessed that in his dreams he was driving. As fast as he wanted, no traffic ahead of him, no one in the back seat telling him where to go.

He had plans, he said, but he didn't offer specifics; when Noi pressed him, all he would say was *I'm waiting for my luck.* She conjured up details in her own imagination. Perhaps a little grocery store. A stall in the market to begin, then in time a real shop with a counter and an electric fan on the ceiling. She could see herself shaking out paper bags with a snap and making change after a purchase, counting up the coins and dropping them into the customer's palm.

She would prefer a dressmaking shop to a grocery. There was plenty of custom. Farang women bought clothes in Europe and had them copied in Bangkok; their husbands ordered handmade shirts by the dozen. Noi was good at sewing. In her room in the

Quarters, she had studied discarded Preston garments carefully, taken them apart and put them back together again and again until she knew their secrets: how to set a dart, how to bury a zipper invisibly into a side seam. A tailoring shop would be perfect for her and Somchit. And the baby, who could sleep while Noi sewed, kicking its legs and cooing in a basket in the corner. When business grew, they could hire on another girl to help; perhaps her cousin across the city, or Choy, the Preston Number Two, who had poor vision and troublesome joints and needed an easy job without much standing. Choy could cut cloth, sweep the floor, mind the baby.

Noi had a lot of time to think about these things while Somchit talked. He barely spoke all day; he believed it was better if farang didn't know how well he understood English. Each night when he came to her, the words rushed out of him as if they were under pressure. About the car; about how stupid the farang were, how careless; about how spoiled the children were, how whiny. She paid little attention, mostly waiting for the fountain of speech to turn into compliments, as it reliably had in the beginning. But now when he stopped complaining about work and talked about her instead, it was usually to chide her lack of ambition.

"You could make much more money than you are making," he said.

"Shhh," she said. "Daeng will hear you." The Number One's room in the Quarters was two rooms away, on the other side of Choy's.

He put his lips next to her ear. "Two or three times more money," he said.

"I don't want to work in a different house." She didn't contradict the ridiculous claim, *two or three times more.* The Prestons paid well. Nine Soi Nine was a good job: a lot of rules, but Noi was accustomed to them now, and the parties were relatively modest, confined to weekends and usually over by midnight. Nothing like the near-nightly bacchanals that went on in the house where her cousin was currently employed.

"Stupid girl." His kiss took the sting out of it. "I'm not talking about another Number Three job."

From this she understood that he meant a Number Two position, and despite herself, she was intrigued. As Number Two she would be shielded from the most unpleasant and dirtiest tasks. Perhaps the Number One at the new job would be nicer than Daeng, who of late seemed to invent arduous chores for Noi — this week, she'd had to empty all the khlong jars that stood at the back of the foyer holding emergency water for use during cutoffs. Her hands still stank from scraping out the slime that had accumulated at their bottoms.

"I'm too young," she said. Most Number Twos were at least twenty-five. She drew his arm over her and turned on her side, hoping he would do the same. She loved that part best, when they nestled together. He didn't turn; he stayed on his back.

"Madame goes to the Erawan almost every day," he said. "I leave her at the club, but then I see her come out again and get into a tuk-tuk."

"Mmm," said Noi, not listening. She was waiting for his words to run down and the rest to begin: the kissing, and the closeness. "Why would she go there?" She turned back toward him, nuzzled the soft place behind his ear that reliably made him passionate.

"Why do you think?" he said.

She lapped her tongue around his earlobe; there was no more talking for a while after that.

"Come with me tomorrow night," he said before he left. "I'll introduce you to the man with the job."

A man? Usually the lady of the house did the hiring. Perhaps it was a bachelor — that *would* be much easier than looking after a family with children.

"Maybe," she said.

From the window she watched him push his bicycle through the garden, his hair glossed with moonlight; she felt her heart go with him out of the gates. Her future was entwined with the luck and love of this handsome man. She hoped his luck would have a dress shop in it.

That night she dreamed that the baby she'd prayed for entered her womb, small as a millet seed, and settled in to grow.

CHAPTER NINETEEN

"What do you tell people?" Genevieve said into the hum of the air conditioner. "About where you are."

She was sitting naked in one of room 510's chairs, which she'd pulled up in front of the laboring window unit. She lifted her heavy hair from the back of her neck and held it bunched against her nape with one hand.

"I don't tell them anything," Max said. He was lying on his side on the bed, his head propped on one fist. "They don't ask." He patted the mattress to invite her back to it, and when she didn't move he reached for the packet of Pall Malls on the night table. "They probably think I'm with a Thai girl," he mumbled around the cigarette as he scratched a match into flame. "Most of the men here have girls."

"None of the men I know." She imagined Giles Benderby with a Thai mistress, his naked pale belly slopping over his pants as he pulled his belt from its loops. The girl would have to be on top, a mosquito riding a hippo, otherwise he'd crush her. Genevieve shook her head as if to toss the thought out of it: her mind went such disgusting places when she was in this room.

"Do you always know where Robert is?" said Max.

"Yes," she said.

He patted the bed again.

She rose, walked over to the bed, and sat down on it, swung her legs up and leaned back against the pillows.

"I like your knees," he said, putting his mouth to her kneecap.

"Robert doesn't keep secrets from me," she said. "He's not like that." *He's not like me.*

"Everyone has secrets," he murmured into her thigh.

"Not him," she said. "He's perfectly dependable. I can practically set my watch by him."

"Good old Robert," Max said, lifting his head away from her, rolling back onto his side and putting the cigarette to his lips. "Punctual as a train."

"Don't make fun of him," she said. "He's a wonderful father." She didn't know of any other husbands who took such an interest in the doings of their offspring. It had sometimes struck her as distasteful, effeminate almost, how Robert tracked the mundane details of the children's lives, inquiring about Bea's sniffles, Laura's insect bite, Philip's mystery rash.

"If he's such a paragon," said Max, his eyes on his own hand where it played with the curly hair over her pubic mound, "what are you doing here?"

"I really don't know," she said, drawing the sheet up over herself, knocking his hand away. He put his head down and breathed on her through the linen, then pulled himself up and kissed her neck.

"What do you wish for?" he murmured. "If you could have the world as you want it. If you could change anything. What would you do?"

"I'd go home," she said immediately.

He pulled back; his eyes searched her face.

"Back to Washington," he said, his voice flat. "Back to your life there." She nodded yes. He leaned back on an elbow, brought the cigarette to his mouth. "What is it that you miss so much?" he said. "Tell me."

After a pause, during which her thoughts went around like a carousel, every horse beloved, she said, "My house." Adding the disclaimer, "It's not modern or fancy; it's old and it has its problems. But I chose it. And every stick of furniture in it. All antiques, all priceless."

"How did Robert enjoy paying for all of that?" Maxwell said as he reached to stub his cigarette out into the ashtray.

"He didn't pay for it," she said. "It's mine. Family heirlooms. My mother used some pieces when I was very young, but everything went into storage when they began traveling." Words wouldn't quite suffice to explain how it had felt to rescue those abandoned, beautiful objects, those artifacts of her childhood, from the dark, climate-controlled vault where they'd been waiting. "They kept the Washington house mostly empty."

"Your *parents* traveled," he said. "You didn't go with them?"

"I boarded at my school. I saw them on holidays. I'm not complaining," she said. "It was a very nice childhood."

He lit another cigarette, the light jumping in the hollows of his face and the flesh under his chin folding on itself in an unattractive way. She might not even recognize a photograph of him as he looked at that moment.

"And when you grew up, you did as your parents did," he said. "Put the furniture into storage and took flight."

Was he mocking her? "Not by choice," she said. "I long every day for the life I left."

He cocked his head, still that unattractive stranger. "You believe that life is waiting for you still? Everything just the same?"

"Not exactly the same," she said. "Who knows what's happened to the garden by now. I'll have to start it all over again."

"I don't mean your house," he said. "I

mean your country." He turned his head, breathed a cloud of smoke away. "It's not the same place you left four years ago."

"Nonsense," she said tightly. "The fundamentals never change. Something dire is always happening, some group is always protesting. It's all just headlines."

"It's more than headlines," he said.

He reached for the ashtray on the bedside table, placed it on his stomach.

"Albert Einstein had a famous thought experiment," he said. "About identical twins." As he spoke, he was rolling the tip of his burning cigarette against the thick glass rim of the ashtray, making it into a point. "One of them leaves Earth and travels on a rocket ship at the speed of light for a year, then turns around and spends another year coming back. When he steps out of the ship, he's two years older than when he left, but in that same time his twin has aged a decade."

"What are you talking about?" said Genevieve, flooded with impatience, her fists balled in the sheeted valley of her lap. "My family is not on a rocket ship. We're not traveling at the speed of light. We're buried at the end of the world, for the best years of our lives. For what? For what?" She gulped a furious sob. "A project that doesn't seem to matter to anyone enough to complete it." She did not care how rude this was, or that she was speaking to her husband's superior.

"You misunderstand me," he said. He took a last pull on the cigarette, then crushed it into the ashtray. His voice held a grave pity. "You're not the twin in the rocket ship. You're the one who was left behind."

"Please," she said. She felt the world outside bulging the walls of their idyll inward, and closed her eyes. "Please don't ruin this."

The clatter of the ashtray back onto the bedside table, a shushing of sheets, and then his arms were around her and he was whispering *Jenny,* and all was forgotten for a while.

Sometimes it seemed to Genevieve that she was living in two separate geographies, as if the afternoons in room 510 were a chain of islands off the mainland of her regular life. She didn't feel divided; oddly, it was quite the opposite — she felt whole. If in room 510 she had discovered something unexpected within herself, a kind of whirling, consuming physicality, well, that was all it was. It wasn't love, and honor, and the bonds of marriage, and raising three children. Room 510 was simply a tonic, a welcome wildfire that burned messy underbrush away. It anesthetized her longing for home into a distant throb; she felt less trapped and frantic. She was more patient with the children, with the servants, with her husband. When the electricity cut off, she shrugged *mai pen rai* and they made do with candles. It was clear to Genevieve that the hot hours in room 510 were good for everyone.

CHAPTER TWENTY

Make the sheets tighter, Daeng barked at Noi
and Choy, ripping the covers away from
Beatrice's freshly made bed. *Do it over.* Just a
few days before, Noi would have scrambled
to obey, fearful of Daeng's displeasure. But
now, thinking of the new Number Two job
and the millet seed, Noi calmly gathered the
linens from the floor under Daeng's glower-
ing eye and she and Choy remade the bed
together, lifting the sheet high between them,
letting it billow and settle before pulling it
tight and smoothing it flat, folding the top
over the way Madame liked. Daeng made a
tch sound with her tongue against her teeth
and stalked from the room; they heard her
feet slapping down the stairs.

"Make it tighter," mimicked Noi, smiling at
Choy, who did not smile back.

"Disrespectful," Choy said as they each
took up a pillowslip and a pillow.

"She is so harsh lately," Noi said, finding
the inside corner of the pillowslip with her

fingers and snuggling a pillow ear into it. But she felt chastened; rudeness to an elder was indefensible. "She was nicer to me for a while. I don't know what changed."

"Somchit is married to Daeng's daughter," Choy said.

She placed her pillow at the head of Beatrice's bed, gathered up the pale stack of folded sheets, and went out the door, leaving Noi in the middle of the room holding a half-sheathed pillow in her arms.

Married. How could Somchit already be married? How had Noi not known? She had never asked; she had never even considered it. How could they have the grocery store or the dress shop with the baby kicking its legs in the basket in the corner? No wonder Daeng was angry. She was boxed in: she couldn't report the dalliance to get the Number Three fired without having the driver, her own daughter's husband, fired also. It was clear why Daeng had been working Noi so hard again: she was provoking her to fail and supply a separate excuse for her dismissal.

Noi finished forcing the pillow into its case, placed it at the head of Laura's bed, and then joined Choy in the parents' bedroom at the end of the hall. They went silently about the work there, making the bed, wiping the windowsills, cleaning the floor. While Choy swept a line of dust into a pan, Noi polished

Madame's mirror, keeping her eyes on her work, avoiding her own reflection.

That night, when Somchit whistled and Noi went down, she found him already straddling his bicycle; when she came through the gate he made a wordless head-jerk toward the space behind him: *Get on.* She ignored that, stood a few feet away.

"You're married." Her voice did not come out purely angry as she had intended; a tremor of sadness warbled through it.

His face tightened with annoyance. He got off the bicycle and leaned it against the wall. When he turned around again, his expression was calm.

"My wife knows about us," he said. "She approves."

"I don't believe that," said Noi.

"It's a customary arrangement," said Somchit. He took a step toward her, his voice coaxing. "One wife for babies, another for fun. It's the way modern people live." Another step; he put out his hand.

Babies? "Her mother doesn't approve." Noi leaned back from his outstretched hand, put her arms across her chest with her fingers tucked into her armpits.

"Daeng is a peasant," he said, dropping his hand, the softness fled from his face and voice.

"I am a peasant," said Noi. He knew that.

342

He had made an endearment of it: *my country rabbit.* The memory of that made the tears start.

"You are not a peasant," he said, sweet again. "You are my beautiful lotus blossom." He stepped closer. "I married too young. Our parents wanted it." Another step. "She is ugly. I don't love her."

He must have seen something in Noi's face that would permit it, for he closed the last bit of distance between them and took her in his arms.

"You are the wife of my heart," he said.

She didn't embrace him back but she also didn't resist. She was like a rabbit frozen in the grass. His arms went tight around her; she stood feeling his heart beating against hers and imagining the third, secret heartbeat below. She could have stayed like that forever, but after only a minute he pushed her away gently, with hands on her shoulders.

"Why aren't you wearing the red dress?" he demanded.

It was disorienting how quickly he could go from affectionate to businesslike. Noi looked down at her uniform, confused: Why would she wear that dress to interview for a Number Two position?

"Let's go," Somchit said. "He's waiting." He pulled his bicycle away from the wall, got on, and waited for her to get on behind him.

She didn't want to go to a job interview

now. But she might not have another chance — as Somchit had made clear, the man was doing Noi a favor by scheduling the interview so late in the evening, after her workday ended. *Three times the pay.* Noi felt the millet seed stir in her womb. Three times the pay would buy the basket, and the corner, and the shop. It would pay the taxes for her parents, pay for Sao to visit Bangkok.

She climbed onto the back of the bicycle, pulling her skirt forward and tucking it under her legs so it wouldn't catch in the chain. Somchit pedaled fast, weaving around cars and turning recklessly across traffic, and in a quarter of an hour they were on a long dark street, the branches of flowering trees reaching above them from either side, making a fragrant tunnel with a far light at its end. That light turned out to be a noisy, busy neighborhood, blinking tubes of light everywhere and sidewalks crowded with farang. Somchit stopped and waited for her to get off the bike.

"What are we doing here?" Noi asked.

The front door of the nearest building swung open, music blaring out behind a man and girl, muting again as the door fell closed and they stood entwined, kissing on the sidewalk. Noi averted her eyes.

"This is where he works," said Somchit.

Maybe Somchit didn't want her to see how big the man's house was, how much work would be required to keep it clean. She got down from the bicycle and spanked road-dust from her skirt, telling herself that she would not agree to the job until she saw the house itself.

Somchit hurried her through a crowded, sticky-floored room filled with beery smoke and loud Western music, at its center a group of girls in bikinis dancing. Noi wasn't sure she wanted to work for someone who worked in this kind of place. Who knew what his home would be like? *Still,* that voice inside her said, *three times the pay.* She watched as a flashlight beam cut through the crowd and lit on a small square of paper pinned to a bikini bottom, with *14* written on it. The beam moved up to the face of the girl wearing the number; squinting in the strong light, the girl began making her way toward its source.

Somchit pulled Noi out of the room before she could see what prize the girl had won, down a corridor to a closed door. Before knocking, he put both of his hands on Noi's shoulders and looked into her eyes.

"Smile. Be friendly," he said. "Make a good impression."

She stretched her lips into a smile that must have satisfied him, for he knocked at the door. A voice shouted for them to enter.

"Here she is," Somchit said, pushing Noi in and stepping in behind her, closing the door. He made a wai to a man who sat in a chair behind a cluttered desk.

The man didn't wai back. He was Thai, perhaps forty, wearing a purple patterned shirt, the collar open in a wide V, its points splayed nearly to his armpits. He was smoking; the air of the room was hazy.

"Fresh from the rice paddies?" he said, looking at Noi but talking to Somchit.

"No, I told you," said Somchit. "She works for farang." He put a hand against Noi's cheek. "See how fair. She hasn't been in the fields for a long time."

"Turn around," the man told Noi, who did so, puzzled. He grunted. "How old?"

Somchit looked at Noi.

"Fifteen," she said, and then remembered she had to give a good impression. She smiled hard. "But very strong." She was beginning to suspect she was being hired to clean this building — clearly no one else was doing it. This room was filthy, every surface cluttered with stacks of paper and filled ashtrays and half-empty glasses and soft drink bottles. The ashtray on the desk was a stupa of cigarette butts; a few had rolled off the mound onto some papers underneath and lay like bent elbows in a gray nimbus of ash.

"Very strong," echoed the man, with a wheezy gust of laughter. He tapped his cigarette onto the heaped ashtray. "Any babies?"

"No babies, no scars," said Somchit.

"I do have a scar," said Noi, showing her forearm, the shiny place where she had been burned by a stove. The man sat forward to look, then sat back again.

"Okay, let's go," he said in English, waving the hand that was holding his cigarette. When she stared uncomprehendingly, he said in coarse Thai, "Take your clothes off."

She couldn't believe her ears. She looked at Somchit, certain that he would share her outrage. He himself had never seen Noi completely naked. And now this man — this stranger — was expecting her to undress? She had heard of employers trying to take advantage of servants, but usually it happened after they had started working in the house, not before.

Noi backed away from the desk. Somchit, standing behind her, put his hands on her upper arms and held her in place.

"Go ahead," he said into her ear. "He won't touch you."

She shook her head and closed her eyes, tears slipping down her cheeks.

"She's shy," Somchit told the man. "Innocent."

"Innocent." The man sucked on his cigarette and narrowed his eyes, looking at Somchit. "I bet not completely." Noi bowed her head, tears dropping onto the dirty floor. "Okay. But she had better not be shy by Friday at eight o'clock."

"She won't be," said Somchit. He opened the door and Noi went through it gratefully. He didn't follow. "Wait here."

She stood in the hallway just outside the closed door, facing it so she wouldn't have to look toward the big room. The music made her feet vibrate; the strong smells were nauseating.

When Somchit came out a few minutes later, he looked jubilant.

"What did I say," he told her. "Twice as much as you make now."

"You said *three* times," said Noi, following him with relief through the big room, keeping her eyes down. "I won't work for that man," she said as they went out the front door. "I would never clean this disgusting place."

"Silly girl," said Somchit, hugging her with one arm, inadvertently trapping her braid and jerking her head back. "You won't have to clean anything." He let her go, taking the bicycle from where it leaned against the wall. "I'll buy you an outfit for Friday. You can pay me back." He straddled the bicycle, still talking, motioning to her to get on. "Maybe pink," he said. She usually loved it when he was this way, enthusiastic and happy. "Pink would make you look like a little girl. Some men like that."

All of a sudden she understood. And felt like an idiot for not understanding sooner.

Somchit had never been talking about a Number Two position. He wanted her to be one of those bikini girls.

"I'm not doing that," she said. "Are you crazy?"

"Are *you* crazy?" he said. "This is easy work! You can be a Number Two in five years, when you're old and ugly. Plenty of time for cleaning toilets then."

She felt the tears rising again. She had been so stupid. She began walking; he followed her on the bike, walking it along with his legs on either side.

"It's just dancing," he said. "Talking to the men, getting them to buy drinks."

She shook her head. She knew it was not just dancing and talking. Her cousin had told her about the unfortunate girls who came to Krung Thep on the promise of domestic work but ended up in bars like these.

"Popular girls make a lot of money," said Somchit. "You would be the most popular, Number One."

"I would rather be Number Three in a house than Number One in a bar," retorted Noi.

"This is the best opportunity for you," said Somchit, still walking the bike in that awkward waddle. He kept beside her for a block or two, kept up the wheedling patter, but when she didn't stop or reply or even turn to look at him, he finally yelled, "Stupid peasant," and cycled away.

She had to walk all the way back to Soi Nine in her thin shoes; she was footsore and miserable by the time she reached the gate, lifted the hasp, and slipped inside. She undressed quickly and lay down on her mat. Only a few hours to sleep before the workday began.

Chapter Twenty-One

The girls didn't bother Robert by this point. They didn't try to sell him drinks or nag him to dance or harass him to buy their bar. When he came in, they'd wave at him from their cabstand seats, tittering behind their hands, and call *Root*. Within a few minutes Ruth would appear from somewhere, saying *Hello, Master,* smiling enormously as if it were a spectacular reunion and she hadn't seen him just a day or two before.

He liked to go at lunchtime, when the bar was relatively empty. Nothing improper took place. He taught the girls to play gin rummy; sometimes five or six would try to play at a time, which made for giggling chaos. He was also teaching Ruth to foxtrot, and in turn she was teaching him to *rockanro dance.* They'd alternate choosing songs on the jukebox. Her choices were ridiculous: the Monkey, the Pony, the Funky Chicken. He felt an idiot as he made wings of his arms and flapped them about, but somehow it was all right to laugh and be laughed at here, no sting in the light rippling laughter of these women. When his turn came to choose, he punched up one of the three Frank Sinatra numbers in the jukebox and they danced slow-slow quick-quick, stepping and turning, Ruth keeping her head down to watch her feet, with an adorable frown of concentration. *Those fingers in my hair.* She was much shorter than Genevieve.

He hadn't seen Bardin since the night he'd caught him rummaging through his office; perhaps he was *in the field* again. Robert had decided not to report the incident to the Boss. It had been poor judgment on Bardin's part but not blatantly criminal, and if the materials Robert had created for the photograph were to be implemented, that would have already happened. What was done was done.

When the Sinatra song finished and another fast number began, Robert went to sit at a table and Ruth brought him another beer.

"I think my mother die soon," she said, sipping her Fanta.

"My God," he said. "I'm very sorry."

"I want visit but," she said, "too much money."

He reached for his wallet, opened it. Only two hundred baht and twenty U.S. dollars left inside. He pulled out the baht. "You go see your mother," he said. "Get her a good doctor."

"Thank you, Master." She took the money from his hand. "I buy many flower."

"Not flowers," he said severely. "Doctor. Medicine." She nodded.

He felt protective toward her, as if she were one of his daughters. It wouldn't be so terrible if his girls were more like her, sweet and kind and always laughing, although he'd fight until his last breath to keep them from living her life, so dependent on a thin river of generosity from men. They'd have their own money, he vowed then and there, watching Ruth tuck the bills away. From now on, the family would live only on his salary; he'd put the family trust that was currently earmarked for his heir, Philip, into all of the children's names, divide it equally between the three of them. His girls would never have to depend on a man.

CHAPTER TWENTY-TWO

In midmorning, Noi stood on the side terrace beating dust from one of the front hall rugs, keeping an eye out for Somchit. Just the night before he had called her a stupid peasant, had left her standing on the street, yet while she was sweeping the front step at dawn he'd whistled to her from the driveway and squeezed his face up into a wink, as if none of it had happened. She'd gone inside and stayed away from the front of the house since then, to avoid him.

She saw something moving in the garden, low to the ground, just at the edge of her vision, and leaned far over to look. Was it Somchit, weaseling his way along the wall toward her with a present in his hand, hoping to win her back?

No, it was Philip. He was in the space behind the swing set where the dirt was bare and grassless; he was on his knees leaning forward and back, over and over, in a floor-scrubbing movement. She left the rug hanging over the side rail, went down the terrace steps. She saw what he was pushing back and forth along the ground: his judo robe.

"What wrong," she said, kneeling beside him, putting her hands onto his. "What wrong?"

"I hate this, I hate it," said Philip. He sounded frenzied, near tears. "It's too white, it's too — clean."

"Not clean now," said Noi, smiling, looking at the garment bunched under their hands.

"I've asked Choy over and over but she doesn't understand." There was a despairing gravel in his voice. "Every week it looks brand-new."

"The other boys not so clean," said Noi, understanding.

Philip nodded.

"Okay," said Noi, getting to her feet, taking Philip's hands and making him stand too. She jumped on the robe, stamped on it, ground it under her heels. She stepped back, beckoned to him to do the same. They took turns for a while; then Noi gathered the defeated robe from the earth.

"I wash," she said, holding it in a bundle against her hip. "I do, okay, not so clean."

"And not so hard?" asked Philip, hope cracking through the words. "It cuts me under here." He lifted a pale arm and pulled up his shirt, to show her the red chafing just below his armpit. "Softer," he said. "Please."

355

"Soft," promised Noi. She looked into his pleading face. "Soft." She put a hand out and scrabbled her fingers over his lower ribs, tickling him in the vulnerable place he was exposing.

"Stop," he cried, clamping his arm to his side and twisting away from her, laughing.

Later, when the policeman asked questions about Philip — was he unhappy, would he have run away? — the parents were united in their vehement negative. Philip had such an even disposition, they said, he never threw temper tantrums, not like the girls. *He's always been our sunny child,* Madame's voice trembling as she said it, and Master put his arm around her.

Noi didn't speak then — no one expected her to, no one thought to ask her anything — and she sometimes wondered afterward if she should have. She'd seen the look on the boy's face that morning, the desperation. She'd also seen his laughter while she tickled him; it had made her realize how long it had been since she'd seen it. Philip used to laugh all the time. He had been happy by nature, as Madame had told the policeman. That was true, but it had not been the whole truth about him.

■ ■ ■ ■

PART 3

■ ■ ■ ■

Chapter Twenty-Three

2019

After he'd been put on the ventilator, the sisters were allowed in. Bea went forward to the stretcher while the nurse waylaid Laura near the door with updates: he'd be going upstairs to intensive care soon, he'd be sedated all night, they should probably go home and get some sleep and come back tomorrow.

"Why did this happen?" Laura asked.

"The low oxygen pressure in the airplane, maybe?" The nurse sounded like she was guessing. "A long flight could have stressed his heart, tipped him over into failure."

Bea didn't look up when Laura joined her at the bedside. She was staring at Philip. His face looked swollen, and was distorted by the tube taped into his mouth; Laura couldn't see the dimple under his eye. Was it even the same man? She had an urge to twitch away the sheet and check for the deformed ankle.

Bea's phone buzzed and she looked at it, then put it away.

"Clem's getting the car," she said. Meaning: *Let's go.* "You can stay with us tonight, no point battling traffic."

As they walked toward Clem's hybrid crossover, crouched at the curb in front of the hospital like a gigantic shiny beetle, Laura's phone vibrated in her pocket. She pulled it out: a text from Sullivan.

How's our zen MF? How are you?

"Is that Edward?" asked Bea, opening the car door, getting in. "What does he think of all this?"

Edward. The name tolled in Laura's chest. They hadn't spoken since that conversation in Bangkok.

She walked over to the car but didn't get in. Bea's window slid down.

"What now?" said Bea. "Don't make a scene."

"There's nobody even here," said Laura, spreading her arms. But she dropped her voice. "I'm sorry," she said. "I shouldn't have gone there by myself." Her head felt hollow. "Big surprise: I've fucked everything up."

Without waiting for a response, she turned and walked away.

"Are you okay?" said Sullivan. "Where are you?"

"NoVA," said Laura. She had walked for a while on the side of the street that faced traffic, so that Clem and Bea couldn't easily follow in their car. They hadn't followed. Now

360

she was sitting on a bus stop bench, talking on the phone.

"Do you want me to come get you?" Into the brief hesitation before the offer she read an entire scenario: Kelsey, the young gallery receptionist, naked between million-thread-count sheets, pouting *Come back to bed.*

"I'll get a car," Laura said. She pulled the phone away from her face to look at the time: nine thirty p.m. So not Kelsey abed, tousled and sleepy, but elegantly dressed Kelsey in a hip restaurant, mouthing *Who is it* across the table. She put the phone back to her ear. "Where are you?"

"At the gallery, doing paperwork. My fancy life. How's your brother?"

"Sick." She rubbed her eyes with thumb and index finger. "They told us fifty different reasons he might not make it."

"I'm sorry," he said. "There's nothing to do tonight, though, right? You need to get some sleep."

"I'm going home." She took the phone down again and navigated to the ride-sharing app, tapped in the request, put the phone back to her ear. "Mohan is six minutes away."

"Okay," he said. "I've got a six-minute story for you. Titled, 'The Man Who Made Art with Bodily Fluids Not His Own and Got Himself and His Gallery Sued.' "

Laura sat on the bus stop bench with the phone to her ear, listening, shivering in her

T-shirt and thinking longingly of the cardigan in her bag, the one Clem had put into the crossover and taken home with Beatrice. Sullivan's anecdote lasted longer than six minutes; it wasn't done when the car came. She got into the car still listening and fell asleep with his voice in her ear. Sometime later she awoke outside her own house, hand lying on her lap still clutching her phone, her cheek smashed against the window glass.

"Sorry," she told the driver, sitting upright, ripping a tissue from the box in the console and wiping the faceprint, turning it into a giant cloudy smear. "Ugh, that's worse."

"Lotion tissues," said the driver brightly. "No worries. I'll hit it with Windex."

Her phone screen blinked on as she went up her front steps, the display showing the call still active, the elapsed time counting up. She raised the phone to her face. "Sullivan?" she said.

"Are you home now?" he said.

"Yes," she said.

"Signing off," he said.

The banging on the door wove itself into her dream: it was a drum, it was a dozen drums, it was snakes dancing a conga line around a circle of drums.

"Go away," she moaned into the bedclothes, burying her head.

Her phone buzzed on the bed surface

beside her ear and she swiped her hand around the sheet to find it, peeked with one eye at the blinding brightness of the screen. Then sat straight up in bed and answered the call.

"It's two a.m.," she said. "Is that you at my door?"

"Yes," came the response. "Let me in?"

She went down the stairs at a run.

Her nephew Dean stood on the front step, looking bedraggled. It was raining in earnest now and he was drenched, drops fattening on the tips of his hair and falling onto his shoulders.

"For God's sake," she said. "Get in here." She closed the door behind him. "Kitchen," she said, and he followed her pointing finger. "Stay," she said.

She got towels and Adam's old terry-cloth robe; while Laura stood with robe held open, Dean stripped to his shorts and put the robe on, then bowed his dripping head and let her scrub it with a towel. She put his clothing into the dryer, laid a fresh towel on the seat of one on the bar stools before letting him sit, used another towel to wipe up the water from the hardwood.

"This place is nice," he said, looking around. "It's so — empty."

"I don't like clutter," she said, dumping the wet towel into the sink. "Dean. What are you doing here? Does your mom know you're here?" His face told her the answer. She retrieved her phone, and under his baleful eye told Bea's voicemail, "I have Dean here, he's fine and safe, I'll get him back to you in the morning."

"I can't believe you," Dean said, his voice thick with disappointment, as she clicked the phone off and put it down.

"Dean," said Laura. "I had to call her. Our brother *disappeared*." She watched the accusation fade from his expression: he hadn't thought of that. "What are you doing here?"

"I was just in the neighborhood," he said, trying for silly. When she didn't smile, "I was with someone."

"On a date?" she said, surprise scaling her voice up unintentionally.

"Sort of," he said.

Laura felt a sudden sympathy for Bea. How frightening it must be for a parent, when the child whose whole baby skin you knew, whose every moment you supervised for years, develops his own separate, secret life.

"I'm making tea," she said. She ran cold water into the electric kettle, switched it on, got two mugs down from the cupboard. "So — a date," she said. Was that why he was here, had it gone badly, had he been dumped? "How did it go?"

"Good." Uninflected, unrevealing. Still annoyed that she'd phoned his mother.

She found a package of cookies in the

pantry, expensive English biscuits a friend had given her, put some onto a plate and set that before Dean. He looked at them, then up at her, then took one, as if conceding a détente.

"We've been seeing each other for a while," he said around a mouthful of cookie. "He's older. Don't tell my parents."

He. Older.

"How much older?" said Laura, carefully, a cape of fear-prickles moving over her shoulders. She didn't look at him as she dropped tea bags into the mugs.

"Eighteen."

Eighteen, only two years between them. Laura had forgotten how once upon a time, *older* might mean such a sliver of difference. A rushing noise rose from the kettle as the boil gathered, the first reluctant bubbles welling up. It was hard to know what to say next, to prevent the clamshell that was wavering open in the warm current of their conversation from snapping closed again.

"Your mom loves you, you know," she said. "You can tell her anything."

"Probably," said Dean. "But." He wrinkled his face up. "Did you tell your mother everything when you were my age?"

"Fair enough," said Laura, thinking *Who knows — I might have, if she'd been there to listen.* The kettle was boiling now, the bubbles jostling furiously against the glass. "Are you

— out?" she asked, lifting the kettle and pouring into the mugs, amber swirling from the tea bags. "I mean, do your friends at school know you're gay?"

"I'm not gay," Dean said, curling his hands around the mug she put in front of him. Laura looked her confusion: *But you just said you're involved with a man.* "I am who I am. I don't want to label it." He took another cookie.

"Okay," said Laura. Baffled. There had been no spectrum to sexuality when she was young: boys were boys, and paired with girls. Nothing else was even imaginable. She and her generation had crossed the chasm of sexual awakening as if blindfolded on a wavering rope bridge, starting out clueless as dolls and reaching the other side either harrowed or unscathed, depending on sheer luck. Still, the crossing then might have been easier than it would be today, carrying the burden of so much information and nuance. Her gay and trans friends would probably chastise her for that thought, remind her that *without nuance, we don't have a bridge at all.*

"Glad the date went well," she said. "And why are you here?"

"It was his idea," Dean said. He studied the surface of his tea, where a broken moon trembled, a reflection of the overhead light. "I told him about Philip, about you going to get him." He raised his eyes to hers. Laura bit back her objection — *You talked about our family with a stranger?* — and nodded. "I want to see Philip," he said. "You need an adult to visit the ICU, and Mom said no."

"So your boyfriend suggested you come here and wheedle me into taking you."

Dean nodded. "He said you sounded cool."

"Uh-huh." Not taken in by the flattery. "How did you meet him, anyway?"

"Loop." He slid a hand into his pocket and pulled out his phone. "Want to see his profile?"

What is Loop? she didn't ask, as he turned the screen to show her a colorful collection of photos and an emoji-sprinkled bio, the font so small it was almost unreadable. *That's one way to filter out older users,* she thought. Dean turned the phone back toward himself.

"Isn't he cute?" he said with fuzzy fondness.

It was wonderful, and painful, to think of him striking out into that vast gulf of unknowing, the giant world ready to break his heart over and over. She felt happy for him, and frightened, in equal parts.

"He's not my boyfriend," said Dean, more soberly. The unspoken, hopeful *yet* shivered in the air at the end of his sentence. "I'm not even sure how much he likes me." He clicked the phone off and put it down, picked up his mug and took a sip.

367

"Are you having sex?" asked Laura. Dean smiled into his tea and said nothing. "Are you being safe?"

"Yes, Grandma," said Dean.

"Good Lord, my grandmother would have died before she'd ask me anything like that," she said. He said nothing, the clamshell now firmly shut.

Her phone skittered across the counter: Sullivan, all-caps.

GO TO SLEEP.

"That's a booty call," said Dean with a grin.

"Hardly," she said as she typed in I *WAS* ASLEEP THANK YOU. She pressed Send. "What do you know about booty calls?"

"I'm not a *child*," he said. "We've been able to get around parental controls since we were ten." Unconsciously speaking in the first person plural. What must that be like, going through life as an automatic *we*? "Mom's basically a cavewoman technologically, and Dad — he trusts us." He had the grace to look guilty, saying that. With an interested glance at her phone, "So, do you and Edward have an open relationship?"

"Oh my God," said Laura. "That was my gallery owner."

"That's not an answer."

"Not that you're entitled to one," she said, "but no. Edward and I do not have an open relationship. And I'm older than Sullivan."

"So?" Dean said. "It's a patriarchal construct that the man has to be older than the woman, derived from ancient gender roles that defined *man* as provider and *woman* as bearer of children. Insanely irrelevant in 2019." He smiled at her expression. "Aunt Laura, everyone understands that now." *Everyone.* Youth, society's prow, cutting a path into the future. "Why didn't Edward go with you to Thailand?"

"I didn't tell him I was going."

"What?" He looked incredulous.

She laughed: apparently even a teenager understood basic relationship etiquette better than she did.

"Why not?" he said, starting to laugh too, his whole face transformed by it, the resemblance to his mother slipping to reveal a resemblance to his father.

"He didn't want me to go," she said. "And I didn't want to argue about it."

"I would have gone with you," he said.

"I know," she said. And she did know: she had this young ally, like a knight, ready to do battle on her behalf. How does anyone deserve that, she wondered. "Listen, I have to crash," she said. "My body says it's three thousand o'clock. We can talk more in the morning."

In the doorway of the guest room he lingered, fingering the molding around the door.

"Why do you and Mom always seem like you're in a fight?" he said.

"Sibling stuff," said Laura. "It goes way back." Why a heart-to-heart now, when she felt like a dead person walking?

"Dustin and I fight sometimes," he said. "But it's just, like, a blowup. Then we're okay."

"You and Dustin naturally get each other," said Laura.

"We're not *exactly* the same," he said, and there was an undercurrent there that she read as twin frustration, at so often having been treated as interchangeable, one of a pair of clones. His voice strangled and emphatic, he added, "Please take me to the hospital with you in the morning. *Please.* I want to meet my uncle. Even if he doesn't wake up. Even if he dies."

"Okay," she said.

His hug surprised her.

"I think you did the right thing going to get him," he said. Earnest, impassioned. Perhaps thinking of his own brother, what he would do if Dustin were lost and then found. "I think you're a hero."

Well, that made exactly one person in the whole world, thought Laura, hugging him back. Still, it was amazingly comforting to hear.

The next morning, Philip was still sedated and immobile, bags of nameless liquid ticking into him and the ventilator puffing breaths down the tube that went into his mouth. The ICU nurse updated Laura and Dean on his status, alternating good news and bad news as she did — *oxygen's good, kidneys are still struggling a little bit, fever is down, white count's still high, his anemia is stable* — the pattern of it hypnotic.

"When will he wake up?" asked Laura. The nurse nodded, as though she'd expected that question.

"We have to keep him sedated until the tube is ready to come out," she said. "And that can't happen until the lungs are doing better." *The lungs,* as though they, like *the tube,* were independent entities from the man.

"Can I talk to him?" asked Dean.

"Yes, we encourage that," said the nurse, smiling. She went to the head of the bed, beckoned to Dean. "You can stand here. It's okay to touch his hand if you want. Just be careful of the IVs." She moved away to the other side of the room, began clicking an entry into a computer there.

Bea was suddenly beside Laura in the doorway. She had both Laura's bag and Philip's blue duffel over her shoulder, and she slid them down her arm and held them out; Laura put the straps over her own shoulder.

"Thank you for leaving the voicemail," Bea said in a low voice. Laura nodded. Bea looked at Dean, who was bent over at the bedside, his back to them. "What's he doing?"

"Talking to Philip."

"Is he awake?"

"No."

They watched together for a minute. They couldn't hear Dean's words; his voice was a quiet rumble beneath the rushing and beeping sounds of the machines around the bed. "Our lawyers are requesting another DNA test," said Beatrice.

"What?"

"They require it before they'll accept his identity."

"The U.S. government accepted the DNA test I got," said Laura. "The result was unequivocal."

"The sibling test isn't standard," said Bea. "It won't hurt to get another."

"That's ridiculous," said Laura.

"They're just being prudent," said Bea. "They need to be absolutely certain before they legally declare him Philip Banford Preston. Entitled to a third of the trust."

"Money?" said Laura. "Really?"

"The only people who say it like that have never wanted for it," said Bea. "I'm in charge of it for a reason."

"Oh my God," said Laura. "That again."

The nurse came over. "Maybe talk outside?" she said, with an edge to her voice. She slid the glass door open, stood there waiting; like bad dogs, Bea and Laura went through. The door slid closed again.

"Mum will know if he's Philip," said Laura in a low voice suited to the surroundings, the hush of critical illness, all the glass-doored rooms and muted beeping.

"Mum doesn't know who I am half the time," retorted Bea. "We can't tell her about this. What if he dies? What if we tell her and she does understand, and then he dies here?"

"What if we *don't* tell her and he dies? How could we let that happen?" A thought struck Laura. "Do the lawyers really want another test, or is that something *you* want?" Before Bea could respond, "Why am I even asking? Of course my DNA test isn't good enough. Only your DNA test will do."

"Oh, for God's sake," said Bea.

The glass door slid open again.

"Waiting room," said the nurse firmly through the gap.

They'd been in the waiting room for ten unspeaking minutes, side by side in a row of chairs in the corner under the hanging television monitor, when the door opened. The scattered conversations around the room ceased and heads turned toward the doorway. Dean came through, followed by a man in a white coat. All eyes followed the doctor as he walked across the room, silent questions pulsing from every side: *Whose doctor are you, who is getting an update, is it bad news or good?*

"Are you the Preston family?" the doctor asked, stopping in front of Bea and Laura. They nodded. "I'm Dr. Gomez. May we speak in private?" He told Dean, "I'll bring them back in a few minutes."

Philip is going to die, thought Laura, her head light, as they followed the doctor through the door and down the hall. She thought of the mild man riding beside her on the Skytrain, his face alive; his smile as he said *extra pickles* into the phone; how he'd taken the inhaler from her on the plane without demur. He'd trusted her. Had her impulsiveness killed him?

FAMILY ROOM, said the sign beside the door near the elevator bank. It was a small space, furnished with hospital-issue furniture: a settee and some chairs upholstered in apricot vinyl, an end table holding a bulbous lamp and a box of tissues. Bea and Laura filed in and sat. The doctor closed the door and sat in one of the chairs facing them. For the first time, Laura read the name tag swinging free from his collar: CLINICAL PSYCHOLOGY.

"You're a *psychologist*?" said Bea. She must have noticed the ID just then too.

"For God's sake," said Laura. Dr. Gomez looked confused. "We thought you were a real doctor."

"She means a medical doctor," said Bea.

"About to give us bad news."

"I'm sorry," said Dr. Gomez. He didn't seem bothered by the *real doctor*. "Didn't the team tell you I'd be coming?"

"No," said Beatrice. "They didn't. We haven't even met *the team*."

"I was consulted because they noticed some tension between you two." He looked from Laura to Bea, then took an index card from his pocket and looked at it. "From what I understand, it is an unusual situation."

"I'll say," said Laura. Without warning, it all struck her as hilarious. Dr. Gomez's long, concerned face, this room, the awful chairs and terrible lamp. The Kleenex box discreetly placed with its flame of tissue at the ready. *What did that index card say?* She snorted with laughter. "I'll say it's unusual."

Bea looked startled, then furious. "Stop it," she told Laura, who was bent forward, overcome. "She's jet-lagged," she told the doctor.

"I am," said Laura, squeaking it out. "I'm sorry."

"We have no need for a psychologist," Bea told Dr. Gomez. She hissed at Laura, "Pull yourself together."

Laura sat upright, cleared her throat, composed her face. As Dr. Gomez put the index card away, another wave of hilarity crashed down; Laura squeezed her eyes shut and shook with suppressed laughter.

"From what I understand," Dr. Gomez said

to Bea, "you haven't seen your brother since you were young."

"He was abducted in Thailand in 1972," said Bea. "Not a trace of him since, not a word."

"Miraculous," said Dr. Gomez. "Missing since 1972." A pause for quick calculation. "He was nine years old then?"

"Eight and a half," said Bea. "It *would* be miraculous," she said. "If it's him."

"It's him," said Laura. The giggles were stopping, finally. She took a tissue from the box and wiped her streaming eyes. She blew her nose, told Dr. Gomez, "I got a DNA test."

"A *sibling* DNA test," said Bea. "Those are not perfect."

"Nothing is perfect," said Laura. "Especially something *you* had nothing to do with."

They glared at each other.

"Forty-seven years," said Dr. Gomez in a quiet voice. Both sisters looked at him, wary. "Has he told you where he's been all this time?"

"She didn't ask him," said Bea. "She didn't ask him *anything.*"

"I feel bad enough about that," said Laura.

"But apparently he wasn't locked up," continued Bea, ignoring her. "He could have just walked out. Gone to the police. Used a telephone. Used the internet. *Something. Sometime* in the last forty-seven years."

"I don't understand that part either,"

admitted Laura.

Dr. Gomez nodded for a few seconds after they'd stopped talking, as if he were listening to extra information in the after-echoes of their speech.

"This event injured your family — it likely shattered your childhood," he said. Laura nodded; Bea did not. "You do have a right to want to understand it. But Philip — *if* this is Philip" — looking at Bea — "also has a right to his own story; how much to tell, and when. As for why he didn't contact you before now, I can't know that, of course. But if I imagine being eight years old and taken away from everything I knew —" He paused, as if to let Bea and Laura imagine along with him. "In that terrible situation, I would need to trust the adults caring for me. Even if the adults didn't do it very well. Even if they sometimes hurt me." Laura felt a queasy pain at the pit of her stomach. "The person who was feeding and sheltering me might even become a person I loved."

"He called the man he was living with his teacher," recalled Laura. Bea looked at her sharply: Laura hadn't mentioned that before.

Dr. Gomez nodded. "Children adapt to the most extreme situations in order to survive."

"He hasn't been a child for a long time," said Laura.

"We're all still children," said the psychologist. "That never stops."

"There's no point in discussing any of this," said Bea. "Until we have *definite* DNA confirmation of his identity."

"Another DNA test probably won't be possible until he's awake and can give consent," said Dr. Gomez. "You should check that with your lawyers."

"I have," Bea said. "I also called Uncle Todd," she told Laura. "He's out of the office, but he'll get back to me."

"Out of the office, at his age?" murmured Laura. They both knew what *out of the office* meant. Of course Bea had called Uncle Todd; it was her reflex, when anything of importance happened in the family. It was annoying. Uncle Todd couldn't replace Daddy. Laura felt a sudden terrible yearning for their father, and its aching corollary: how happy he would have been to see Philip again.

"Since you can't agree," the psychologist said, "and you can't do anything right now to settle the question, I suggest a truce. A time during which each of you can focus on preparing yourself for whatever the future holds: the verdict of a new DNA test as well as the medical outcome for this patient." Avoiding the name, keeping things neutral. "I'm happy to meet with you again, separately or together." He looked from one stony face to the other. "Or not. And when he's awake, I will work with him, if he wants me to. Whoever he is."

378

■ ■ ■ ■

They collected Dean from the waiting room and rode down in the elevator as a silent threesome; on the sidewalk they parted, Dean giving Laura an *I'm doomed* grimace, drawing a finger across his neck, before turning to follow his mom. Laura wondered what punishment Bea would mete out, hoped she'd cut him some slack.

As she walked to the Metro, Laura took out her phone and called Edward. Two rings before voicemail clicked in — so his phone was on, but he had declined her call. He had declined her call: that knowledge pounded through her, erased the script of what she had been planning to say.

"It's me," she said after the voicemail beep. "But you know that." She watched a father stop at the subway entrance and lift his small daughter to his hip to carry her down the steps. The girl's hand curled around her father's ear as if it were a handhold. "I guess you're not ready to talk yet, huh." It wasn't like the old days, when you could ramble on into an answering machine until the person got annoyed enough to pick up. Voicemail was a windsock, a blind pouch. "Um, okay," Laura said, watching the heads of the father and daughter bob out of view. "I guess I'll wait for your call."

She clicked the phone off. She felt a giant emptiness, as though she stood on a wind-scoured plain, totally alone. It was devastating, but also warmly familiar: she'd been here before.

CHAPTER TWENTY-FOUR

No change, said the ICU doctor the next day. *Not better — but not worse.* She gave Laura a pinched smile. *So that's something.*

During the journey to the hospital that morning, Laura had girded herself for confrontation. But Bea had not been in the lobby, or the elevator, or the ICU waiting room where Laura sat most of the day with a book open on her lap but not actually reading it, looking up every few minutes at the door. Once an hour she rose to spend the permitted fifteen minutes standing at Philip's bedside, placing her hands on the rails between the drooping vines of tubing and watching him in his chemical sleep.

When visiting hours ended, she left the hospital and walked to the Metro, rode it two stops past her own. She shopped at the gourmet grocery for things to tempt Genevieve, who was always having to be coaxed into eating, and called a ride-share car to carry her and the bags down Albemarle

Street, into the warren of placid green lawns where she'd grown up.

When she entered the kitchen of the Tudor, Noi was sitting at the table with one of her daughters.

"I brought plenty of food if you're hungry," said Laura, setting the bags on the counter.

"We eat already," said Noi, as the daughter — Vanessa, that was her name — said, "No, thank you." She was a serious woman; Laura remembered her as a serious toddler. She was a doctor now, in Boston.

They watched Laura unload the bags, get cutlery and clean napkins from the drawers, go to the cupboard for plates. As she unlidded the tub of pasta salad, Noi got up from the table, came over.

"Philip," said Noi. *Pillip.* The two syllables in her accent came out of the past like a punch. "You think it's really him?"

Laura nodded.

"Did he tell you what happened to him?" said Vanessa, from behind them.

Laura shook her head, then cleared her throat. "Not yet." She unwrapped one of the butcher-paper-wrapped sandwiches, took a knife from the block.

"Is he requiring any intravenous medicines like dopamine, dobutamine, norepinephrine?" A doctor Laura had dated before Edward had done this too — offered medical-information processing as an expression of

382

caring. *I changed your diapers once, kid,* Laura didn't say.

"He's on a lot of IVs," Laura said. "I don't know what they are."

"You stop fighting with your sister," Noi said.

She had seemed so tall when Laura was a girl. Now she was tiny; Laura could see a scattering of white strands along the part in her hair.

"*She's* fighting with *me,*" said Laura. She set the blade of the knife across the sandwich and pressed it down, then turned the plate and did it again, cutting the halves into quarters.

Noi looked skeptical. "You always fighting with everybody," she said.

Laura felt the heavy silent phone in her pocket: still no message from Edward. The thought of him was like pressure on a bruise.

"It would seem so," Laura said. For the first time in her life she heard her mother in her own voice.

Genevieve raised her eyebrows at the pasta salad but managed two sandwich quarters, enough to make Laura feel a pang of victory. The visit was quiet, their conversation genial and vague. Afterward, she stood on the sidewalk outside the Tudor with her fingertip hovering over the Call Car button on her phone screen. It was early evening, but the light was still strong. Spring was in full glory up and down the street, dogwoods sheeted with pinched white blossoms, front gardens brimming phlox like lavender ponds. She used to know every inch of this street and every street around it, every shrub and sidewalk crack. When they had returned to America the lack of walls had been astounding to Laura, and she had taken full advantage, roaming barefoot through neighboring backyard grass sugared with dew and venturing down the alley behind the house to the busy road at its foot, dashing across to find the surprise of a creek clattering cold and clear. Walking a landscape was so different from riding through it. She hadn't really looked at the old neighborhood for years.

On an impulse she closed the app and pocketed her phone, set off walking. The same route she and Bea had taken every school morning, fifteen minutes to the city bus stop where they'd wait for the first bus that would take them to the transfer point for the second, the one that would stop across the street from the school and flap open its doors so they could exit in a hot grind of exhaust.

Here was the house where the scary dog had barked and barked as they passed, leaping against the diamond-wire barrier. No dog now, and the fence was split-rail, merely decorative. Across from it, the house with the tire swing, the tire gone but the tree still there, extending its empty branch. In the next block a flowered hedge had hummed with bumblebees in two seasons and required a wide berth, first Bea and then Laura stepping into the gutter to pass. No hedge now, and no remnant of it; that house sat revealed on its emerald lawn.

How miserable a walk this had been in the cold, in the rain, struggling to keep up with Bea's long strides. It had seemed such irony to Laura, to work so hard every morning to get to such a hateful place. At least, Laura had hated it. Bea intercalated herself without apparent effort into the popular mainstream of the Upper School while Laura gutterballed her way through the Lower, keeping her head down, weird but not the weirdest, smart but not the smartest. Remodeling her accent and vocabulary, making herself say *Really* when she meant *I agree,* squealing *Gross* about anything she didn't like. She learned to call Mum *Mom* when a friend came for a sleepover, sometimes making two complaining syllables of it: *Mah-ahm.*

Not that she saw very much of Genevieve, who was always packing or unpacking, calling to Noi or the au pair to get or leave things, riding away in a taxicab and returning after a month or more in another one, an exhausted, stringier version of herself. Their dad traveled too but not as much, and never for as long. He didn't talk about where he went; Laura didn't ask. By some process of osmosis, she understood that while some of the girls at school had famous fathers — in the White House or cabinet or on the Hill — some other fathers were the opposite of famous. Their daughters were scattered throughout the student body like a broken string of beads. A null quality made them recognizable to one another and they resisted aggregation, keeping the string broken, the beads safely dispersed.

The only good thing about the American school as far as Laura was concerned was the Art Room, which took up the whole top floor of the Lower School building. Skylights cut into the ceiling poured sunshine onto the bounty below: easels, pottery wheels, bolts of drawing paper, cups of charcoal and colored pencils, cubbies filled with cloudy bottles of tempera. Students were free to use it all when a class wasn't in session, as long as they cleaned up after themselves. Laura spent every minute there that she could.

She brought a painting home when she was eleven. As she passed the sitting room, her mother looked up from her Smith Corona. Feeling caught by the beam of her gaze, Laura went into the room and unrolled the stiff curl of painted paper with a depersonalized sense of playacting. Wasn't this what television children did, they showed their mothers their artwork, for praise and proud display on the refrigerator? The only thing ever magneted to the Harvest Gold surface of the Preston refrigerator was Genevieve's itinerary.

Genevieve stood up from the desk and took the picture from Laura, carried it into the light from the wall of windows.

"You have talent," she said, after two or three long minutes. "Is this something you want to do?" Laura only stared, made speechless by the compliment. Her mother rolled the picture up again, gave it back. "The life of an artist is difficult," she said. "Be sure you want it very badly before you go down that path."

"Do you really think it's good?" Laura asked, greedy for praise. She had thought so herself, but she'd been too shy to show it to anyone, even the teacher.

Genevieve, back at her desk, bent a disappointed look upon her. "Don't make anyone tell you anything twice," she said. She adjusted the half-glasses on her nose, looked through them at the document she'd been typing. "Luckily you won't have to worry about money." She lifted the metal bar that held the paper in place, scrolled the page up a couple of inches. "You won't have to get married."

This was a revelation: People *had* to get married?

"Are you sorry you married Daddy?" Laura asked, her heart racing at her own audacity.

"That's not the point," said her mother. She scrolled the page down again, dropped the metal bar back into place. "There weren't other choices then. Everyone got married and had children."

Laura heard only what her mother didn't say. Her mother didn't say *Of course not.*

"Are you sorry you had us?" Laura said.

"No," said her mother, after an unpardonable latency. "But one does give up a lot when one has children." She pressed the backspace key and began typing again.

Recalling that event more than forty years later, Laura wondered at her own passivity. She hadn't said — or even thought — *I'm eleven, I made a picture, not a life decision.* She hadn't pushed beyond those two timid questions. She had carried away a confused skein of impressions — that children were obstructive and only grudgingly chosen, that marriage was a trap. She'd also borne away a jewel — the notion that she had talent. Enough to catch her mother's attention, to raise her eyebrows and interrupt her work.

The untidy forsythia that had once made the halfway mark in the walk was gone, but Laura recognized the Dutch colonial on the opposite corner, its winding front walk and its window boxes bursting with pansies, and felt an unpleasant chime of memory. The clapboard was a different color now, but nonetheless she recognized it as one of the Drills houses. On the next block, another one, stone flowerpots flanking its door.

Bea had invented the Drills game one morning on the walk to school when Laura was about ten. She chose houses along the route, one or two per block, and told Laura *If I say Drill, you run as fast as you can to one of those houses and bang on the door.* The game added an extra element of anxiety to the morning walk. Bea might say the word at any time — in the middle of a conversation, twice during the same morning, not at all for days. Hearing it, Laura would take off, heart slamming in her chest, beelining to the nearest Drills house, sometimes getting halfway up the front path before Beatrice would call her back. Once Beatrice didn't call in time, or Laura didn't hear her calling, and the door opened to a concerned elderly woman who looked down at the girl crying with embarrassment and fear on the doorstep.

"My sister is playing a prank," Bea had told the lady, marching up the walk and taking Laura's hand as if she were a very little girl, leading her away. "We're very sorry." Laura had been so mad at Bea for that, she'd walked three feet behind her all the rest of the way.

Of course, Laura could have refused to go along with it. But she always played Bea's games, no matter how awful they were, even while steeped in shame for her own cravenness. So eagerly had she thirsted for even this kind of miserable attention from her sister. But considering it now, Laura realized there had been more to it: Bea had always invented games, and Laura had always played them. It was something that hadn't changed about their lives, while every other thing had. The Drills game went on until Beatrice got her driver's license and was able to drive them both to school. When Bea went off to college, Laura made the morning walk alone. She put away the memory of the Drills. Bea might even have forgotten them entirely; they had been just one game among many devised to bully her little sister, such a long time ago.

At the bus stop, someone had planted a stand of lily-of-the-valley. It was the flower Bea had chosen for her wedding; the chapel had smelled beautiful from the frilled, fragrant bells. Laura at nineteen had been sneeringly dismissive of the event, the expense and planning, the big white dress. She'd stood at the altar in her bridesmaid dress and dyed-to-match heels, clutching her tasteful bouquet, just barely stopping herself from rolling her eyes when the bridal fanfare sounded. But watching her sister walk graceful and tall and alone down the aisle, a wave of admiration passed over Laura: how confident Bea was, how dignified. Bea caught Laura's eye and twinkled a smile at her; Laura grinned back. A rare moment of solidarity, in which Laura knew that she and her sister were inescapably bonded, like a twin-trunked tree diverging widely from a wounded base, united forever by what was missing: their father. And by the other, earlier loss, the one that went unacknowledged. They never spoke of Philip. It was almost as though it were an ordinary thing, to have had a brother once and lost him, like a favorite toy you carried every day and couldn't imagine being without, and then one day noticed you carried no more. With no memory of the last time you'd seen it, not knowing where, or exactly when, you'd put it down.

The city bus lumbered into view, wheezed to a stop. Laura boarded, stuffed two dollar bills into the glass box at the front, and took a seat. Watched through the scratched windowpanes as the old neighborhood fell behind her.

Edward didn't return her call. He came to her house instead, rang the bell.

"I've been back for a week," she said, standing in the front doorway.

"I was in Philadelphia," he said. She saw that his suit was rumpled, his face fatigued. "Wall-to-wall meetings."

"You sent my calls to voicemail."

"I thought we needed to talk in person. And I needed to cool off."

"I thought we were broken up," she said.

"Laura," he said. His voice soft: *How could you think that?* "I was angry. Not fifteen."

They stood staring at each other, a foot of space between them.

"Someone caring about what happens to you is not the same as someone trying to control you," said Edward.

"I know," she said.

"Do you?"

"I'm working on it," she said. She remembered the texts she'd ignored — happy and then confused and then worried. "I'm sorry I missed the partner dinner," she said.

"I really wanted you there."

"I know," she said.

"The things I want matter too."

"I know," she said. Her voice cracked. He put his arms wide, and she stepped into them.

"How are you?" he said into her hair.

"I don't know," she said. She was, she realized, just so relieved to see him.

"It really is your brother?" She nodded against his shoulder. "Incredible." He pulled back to look into her face. "I officially apologize for not believing you." His expression was penitent. "I have hated being away from you."

"Me too."

"Shall we put all of this down to extraordinary circumstances?"

She nodded, stepped back to let him into

392

the foyer, closed the door behind him. They went into the living room and sat together on the sofa.

"Tell me," he said.

"Philip's still in intensive care," she said. "He has fluid in his lungs. They think it was the plane ride that tipped him over." The nurse's phrasing, as though Philip were a vase or a Weeble. She bit her lip. "I should have taken him to a doctor in Bangkok."

"You couldn't have known," said Edward. "Laura. You couldn't."

"I was an idiot." It was like a dam bursting, the things that she'd been thinking without putting them into words, no one to tell. "I was living out some kind of fantasy, having a holiday with my brother. Doing all the things we might have done —" She realized she was crying, and scrubbed a hand across her face. "You should have seen him riding the Sky-train."

"What did he tell you about his disappearance?" said Edward, giving her a packet of tissues from his breast pocket.

"Nothing." She blotted her eyes. "My fault again. I should have pushed him to talk. I should have. Even though it felt really wrong when I tried." She remembered Bea in the ER waiting room, her puzzled, helpless face. "I failed my sister," she said. "I failed my mother."

"Have you told your mother anything?"

"No," she said. "I'm done making bad unilateral decisions. Bea and I need to discuss how to handle telling Mum." She blew her nose. "If Bea ever talks to me again."

"You haven't been painting, have you," he said.

"No," she said. "How can you tell?"

"You always seem — weighed down — when you're not working," he said. She'd been feeling the opposite: empty, dry as dust, floating over the landscape of her life. "It'll come back," he said. He put out his hand and she took it. His clean, sure hand. "Remember the good part: You rescued your brother. You recognized him and you went."

"But that was wrong too," she said. "I mean, the way I did it. I could have arranged for DNA testing first; then Bea and I could have gone together. Bea would have thought to take him to a doctor. She would definitely have asked him more questions than I did."

"You didn't want to wait," he said. "You were eager to bring him home."

"True. But that's not all of it." She confessed, "I didn't want anyone to go with me. I wanted to go alone. I was being the hero." She took a deep breath, released it in a shuddering sigh. "And now."

"And now," Edward said, taking her hand, "we wait."

CHAPTER TWENTY-FIVE

Two more weeks passed, in which there was no good news about *the lungs* in the daily litany of updates delivered sometimes by a doctor, sometimes a nurse. Laura and Edward fell into a new pattern, spending about one night in three together, not all of them at Edward's. Laura cleared a space for him in the closet, a drawer in the bureau. She went to the hospital every day and visited Genevieve three times a week, always half hoping and half fearing running into Beatrice, but it didn't happen. The ICU nurses didn't mention whether Bea had been there, but the evidence of her was in the Tudor when Laura visited: food in storage containers in the refrigerator, more squares filled in on the dry-erase calendar on the kitchen wall. When the month changed, a multicolored star appeared around the third Saturday, accompanied by Bea's neat capitals: GENEVIEVE'S BIRTHDAY.

Are you painting? texted Sullivan.

I'm thinking, Laura texted back.

Thinking about painting?

She sent a straight-line-mouth emoji in reply.

She didn't tell him that she *was* painting. Only not in the studio. She had begun repainting the interior walls of her house, telling herself it was something she'd meant to do anyway. Room by room, she clustered the furniture into the middle of the floor and outlined the walls with the square brush, then filled in with the roller, two coats. She didn't miss the subtext: this was paint she could control, that didn't defy her. The smell hanging in the air of her house — although it was a low-VOC, water-soluble weak kin to oil paints — was comforting. Stripping away the long blue tails of tape when the paint was dry, admiring the neat lines, she felt a mild echo of accomplishment.

She was prying the lid off a quart of bruise-colored paint in her second-floor guest room one evening, the furniture huddled in the middle of the floor under a drop cloth and every ding and crater in the walls spackled and sanded to velvet, when she felt a stirring at the back of her mind, like a tickling. She wasn't sure at first, but then it happened again. She jammed the lid back in place and climbed the stairs into the studio, pressed the control panel on the wall to flood the workspace with light. Thinking, *Thank God.*

She took one of the ready canvases and propped it up, cleaned the dust from the thick pane of glass she used for mixing colors. From the drawer of crumpled metal tubes she conjured a palette, stood for a little while looking at the blank canvas surface. Then she took up a brush and dipped it into the bright butter of paint, and with a pell-mell feeling of releasing hounds from their traces, let her mind connect to her hands.

And then it was a chase, a long blur of hours punctuated at intervals with pacing or lying on the floor, sometimes swallowing from a bottle in the refrigerator, the long cold slash down her throat tasting like paint. From time to time, she went outside onto the terrace, hunched at the rail like a gargoyle in a warm spitting gust of morning, again in the broad light of midday, later in a steady curtain of afternoon rain, the roofs of the neighborhood slanting wet and gray all around.

It was early evening when she put down her brush. She stood before the filled canvas for five minutes, paced for five minutes, then back to the canvas. Finally, she took up the wide plastic blade that she'd bought at a kitchen store and stepped up to the painting, set the tool at the upper right edge. She pulled it across, the paint rising in rumpling ribbons over the blade, over her hands. She made a second pass just below the first, and then a third, like cleaning a window.

Quick steps behind her; before she could react, hands came over her shoulder. They grasped the blade, wrested it away. She staggered back, heart in her throat, wheeled around to see Sullivan.

"What the fuck," she spat. Breath heaving.

"Gotcha," he said. He raised the blade high above his head, out of her reach. There was paint on his cuff, she saw with satisfaction. "I want to *see* one of these paintings before you destroy it."

"There's nothing to see," she said.

"Art is not private," he said. "Let me look."

She moved aside; as he leaned close to the half-scraped canvas, she stood looking away, hands gummed with paint, heart still going fast from the shock of his arrival.

"I *knew* you were still in there," he said, finally, turning away from the painting.

She realized she had been holding her breath only when she let it out.

"Here," he said, offering her the blade. "Do what you need to do." She didn't take it; he set it down onto the paint-smeared glass pane. "But ask yourself *why* you need to do it."

"If I knew why," she said. She finished the sentence with a shrug.

"I have a theory," he said. He went to the sink, pressed down on the pump-bottle of vegetable oil there, rubbed his palms together to dissolve the paint. "You're not enough of an asshole." He pumped soap onto his hands, lathered. "You let yourself be distracted by personal stuff. Your mother's illness, now your long-lost brother." He stepped on the foot controls and put his hands under the water to rinse. "But in a hundred years, will any of it matter?"

"In a hundred years," she repeated, incredulous. "*You're* an asshole."

"Never said I wasn't," he said. "It doesn't mean I'm wrong. Real artists put the work first." He took a towel from beside the sink, turned to face her, wiping his hands. "I only want what's best for you. And the art. Which is also you." He put the towel down. "Be an asshole," he said. "Let other people take care of the trivial shit."

That night as she tried to fall asleep, she mulled over what Sullivan had said. Was that it, then, was that the answer? Had giving attention to personal issues compromised her work? The timing was right: her block had begun shortly after her mother's diagnosis. Also, there was a certain economy to it — empty her mind of everything else, and inspiration would flood in to fill the empty space. Human connections were messy. She'd been a loner back in high school, after all, hadn't minded it much; maybe that was her true nature.

She'd arrived in New York for college thinking what most freshmen probably feel: *My life starts now.* The city was huge, filthy, fabulous; by comparison, Washington seemed a prissy hamlet. Laura made friends, had fun, did well in her classes; her work got attention and praise. It was everything she'd wanted, until junior year, when she took an advanced studio course led by Professor Davis. *Everyone cries in her class,* Laura's roommate, Allison, said. *Ev-er-y-one.* Laura had seen Professor Davis from a distance, short and wide, her gray-streaked black hair in a Buster Brown cut with a blocky fringe. Laura didn't see anything scary about her.

The world is not gentle, Professor Davis said in the first session, looking around at all of them with small bright eyes. *Better get used to it now.* Laura sat smug, unworried. She was one of the class stars, on track for the senior prize; Professor Davis wouldn't be making her cry. The crit began, students going one by one to put work up on the easel at the front of the class and stand beside it, stolid or blubbering, as the professor made her comments. When Laura's turn came, Professor Davis stepped close to the canvas, studied it for a quiet minute. Then she turned to the rest of the class. *Here we have, ladies and gentlemen,* she said, *a fine example of the School of Mediocre.*

Although it became clear as the weeks went

on that any effort to appease Professor Davis only exacerbated her scorn, Laura couldn't stop herself, like a moth fluttering again and again toward a flame. She worked as hard as she ever had but Professor Davis was unimpressed. One week, as Laura lifted her painting onto the easel at the front of the room, the professor actually groaned.

"Fuck you," said Laura.

The class went silent. The professor stared hard at Laura. Then she smiled, dark dirty pearls of smoker's teeth.

"That's right," she said. "Fuck me. What does my opinion matter?" She spread her arms wide and waited as if expecting Laura to reply, but then answered herself, thundering, "It doesn't!" She dropped her arms. "*Yours* does. So why are you trying to please me?" She stepped closer to Laura. "I can see that you have talent. But week after week, you give me —" She waved at the canvas. "You know that this is no good. *You* know."

Laura stood frozen, the words going straight into her soul.

Professor Davis walked a few steps away, toward the windows. "They won't let me have the freshmen," she said, as if talking to herself. "They say I'm *too mean*. But then this is what happens. Those nice professors — everyone loves them, nobody cries in *their* classes —" She turned back to Laura. "Whenever you tried to push yourself, they corrected

401

you. Am I right? They told you no no no." With sorrow: "They made you insipid." With disgust: "And you let them."

"What should I do?" Laura heard herself say.

"Don't ask me," shouted the professor, enraged again. "Stop listening to other people. Stop looking at other people looking at your work. Stop accepting praise. Stop telling yourself it's good enough. *You* look at your work. *You* decide." She flung her hand back at the canvas. "And get *this* out of my sight."

For the rest of that day and the next, it was as though Laura had been deafened by a bomb blast; she could barely hear anything through the ringing in her ears. On Sunday morning, when the rates were low, she called her boyfriend, Adam, who'd graduated and moved to Washington to attend law school the year before.

"I think I'm going to quit school," she said.

"You can do it," he said, sounding sleepy. "If I can make it through torts —"

"It's not because it's hard," said Laura. "It's because it's bullshit. I've been making bullshit."

"Okay," said Adam, after a slight pause. "But how will dropping out help with that?"

"I need to get away from here," she said. She couldn't explain the urgency she felt — the professor had rung a bell inside Laura that had not stopped chiming since: it was too long already that she'd been wasting precious time.

"So, what then?" said Adam again, sounding a little more awake. "Are you going to look for an apartment?" Always the first concern of a New Yorker: real estate.

"I was thinking of coming to Washington," Laura said.

A long pause.

They'd been drifting apart despite the ease of the no-reservations-needed, twenty-nine-dollar Eastern Shuttle. Lately, Laura had begun to suspect that their relationship was fueled by negatives, inertia and fear of AIDS, more than by true love.

"Leaving New York?" he said. "Isn't that basically giving up your career?"

"People make art everywhere," said Laura. "DC is home. And it's away from all of this." She made a gesture that he couldn't see, that took in the dorm, the school, the whole island of Manhattan.

"It seems a drastic response to one nasty professor."

"It's not because of her," said Laura, and then reconsidered. "Well, it is, actually."

"Just as long as you aren't doing it for me." Hard, cautious.

"I'm not doing it for you," said Laura.

A beat of silence, then "Okay," he said. His voice warmed. "It *would* be nice to see you all the time." Suddenly expansive, as though her assurance had uncorked a river of affection, he went on, "You could live here. Maybe it would help me eat better. I'm a terrible cook." As if Laura weren't a terrible cook herself.

Laura quit college and moved back to Washington. She didn't move in with Adam, who didn't repeat his invitation; she hadn't taken it as sincere the first time. She went instead to the Tudor, which was standing empty, and set up a studio in the walk-out basement. She cleaned the cobwebby mullioned windows of the big playroom where she'd had middle-school slumber parties, set her easel in the light, and stopped answering the phone to Beatrice's angry diatribes.

The next few months were like a slow rehabilitation for Laura, unhobbling her instincts, learning to ignore the criticisms that wailed from her memory: she didn't need to use *so much* paint; and those colors! They were too violent, too blatant; they robbed her work of finesse. Over time, she saw that by *finesse* the professors had meant caution, they meant femininity, they meant she ought to dab and dottle, make something pastel and pretty. She caught herself again and again, following a path that had been carved by her desire to please. She gritted her teeth and painted on. When darkness fell, she turned on the clamp lights.

The work enveloped her completely, an amniotic sac. It did not feel like loneliness. She saw Adam most weekends but not all, and occasionally met a friend for lunch or dinner, the rest of the time eating from tins or making sandwiches. It was a golden, selfish time: no one to report to, few bills to pay, no real responsibilities apart from finding her way through the paint.

When Genevieve returned to the Tudor, she seemed only mildly surprised to find Laura there. She listened without alarm to Laura's explanation, descended into the basement to inspect the studio, commented merely *You need better light — and much better ventilation if you insist on oils* before heading upstairs to unpack.

So maybe Sullivan *was* right, thought Laura, sleepless, thirty-three years later. She'd gone wrong when she'd tried to please others, when she thought too much about what they might want. Only selfishness and isolation had allowed her to break through. But selfishness had probably also been the thing that ended her marriage, that had taken her alone to Bangkok, been the final straw in her always-contentious relationship with her sister. She didn't know how other artists managed their personal lives. As her career had climbed, she'd connected with some, had done some invigorating collaborations, but that wasn't exactly friendship.

She had kept in sporadic touch with her college roommate Allison, who'd been a brilliant sculptor but whose career had bumped along in obscurity. *I have kids,* Allison had said the last time she and Laura had talked. *The days just — go.* That whole conversation had been skew, two monologues without any shared points. Allison hadn't seemed envious of Laura, or regretful. She'd seemed happy. Still, Laura had judged her, thinking after they'd hung up *Such a waste.*

Sullivan was wrong, Laura realized, turning over in her bed, punching her pillow into shape. She was already an asshole. No epiphany there.

The next day, three weeks after being admitted to the hospital, Philip woke up.

CHAPTER TWENTY-SIX
1972

It had been incredibly stupid, Genevieve realized later, to take him to the wat. The place was always thronged, but only with Thai and tourists; she didn't think she'd see anyone she knew. The truth was that Genevieve hadn't been thinking at all. She'd been operating in a bubble of delusion, feeling invincible. Being out with Maxwell in public was exciting, the tension like a twanging cord between them.

"Pay attention," she scolded, moving away as Max stepped up close behind her. "Be respectful. This is the most important Buddha in Thailand."

"What, this fellow?" he said, squinting up at the statue poised at the top of its pedestal, its jeweled headpiece as tall as itself. "There's a dozen bigger Buddhas within a mile."

"This *fellow,* as you call him," said Genevieve, "is so important that only royalty may touch him. The king himself performs the costume change each season."

"Is he actually made of emerald?"

"Maybe jade," she said. "Or green jasper. No one will risk damaging him by testing." She put her head back, to look up at the little figure. He was wearing his summer decoration, her personal favorite, with the gold flame shapes at the shoulders and knees. "According to legend, he's the first known image of Buddha." They had stopped too long; a crowd was massing politely behind them. They moved away while she told Max the story: how the statue had been made by a saint with help from the god Vishnu himself, been fought over by various kingdoms for hundreds of years, and then disappeared until the fifteenth century, when a lightning strike on a Chiang Rai temple severed a lump of stucco from the roof. The crude statue that fell to the ground was taken inside and kept with other minor works until some months later, when the plaster nose began to crumble away and the glowing green peeked through. "They say he's performed miracles."

"Speaking of which," Max said. They were in a quiet corner; she turned toward him. "Abracadabra."

He produced a silk pouch from an internal pocket. She took it, loosened the drawstring, drew out a tiny gold Buddha on a delicate chain.

"It's beautiful," she said. The Buddha's scalp was studded with little bumps and his eyes were closed, his lips turned upward at the corners. One hand was on his knee and the other was raised, palm out: the pose of the Protection Buddha.

Max took it from her. "Let me put it on." The chain made a featherweight against her skin. He put his nose to her neck. "You smell nice."

"This is a holy place." But she smiled as she protested, angling her head away. Between the lashes of her slitted eyes she saw a familiar face across the room and froze. She brought her head to upright and took a giant step forward, away from Maxwell.

"What?" he said.

"The Ladies," she said. She thought fast. "We'll have to say hello."

They went over to the group of four women, three of whom greeted her with unalloyed welcome. But as Irene turned to her, Genevieve's heart sank; both the artificial slowness of the turn and the exaggerated surprise on Irene's face made it clear that she had seen Maxwell Dawson nuzzling Genevieve from across the room.

"I'm giving Mr. Dawson the penny tour of Bangkok," said Genevieve, her voice tinny and false in her own ears. "Mr. Dawson, you remember Mrs. Duncan, Mrs. Pettis, Mrs. Martelli, Mrs. Green."

"So nice to see you all again," said Max.

"We're here doing homework," said Clara Pettis.

"You're taking a class?" said Genevieve, panic chased out of her mind by surprise. "Through the university?"

"Irene is our teacher," said Renee Martelli. "Every Monday we have a slideshow and lecture, then Wednesday mornings we go on a field trip."

Genevieve turned to Irene. "Really," she said.

"An introduction to Oriental art," said Irene. She added, her eyes level on Genevieve's, "I would have asked for your help, but you've been so busy this summer."

Genevieve saw then what should have been obvious: Irene had felt abandoned. It had been a lonely time, solo in the salon chair for a solid month, after so many cozy Mondays and Wednesdays and Fridays. Genevieve hadn't even made decent excuses — *busy with the children* the first few times, and then nothing at all.

"Have you already been through, or did you just get here?" asked Julia Green. "We're going on to Wat Pho."

"As a matter of fact, so are we," said Genevieve, cutting off whatever Maxwell had been about to say. "We'll join, if that's all right."

She ignored the baleful look on his face as she fell in with the other women, strolling through the Chapel Royal and past the guardian monsters at the gate.

Max caught her elbow as they rounded the feet of the giant reclining Buddha at Wat Pho.

"This is interminable," he said.

Genevieve said nothing, letting the Ladies move ahead. She gestured toward the incised designs on the soles of the statue's feet, as if pointing out an interesting feature. "Irene knows," she said when the Ladies were out of earshot. "She saw."

"Will that be a problem?" he said.

"Of course it's a problem," she said through a clenched-teeth smile. The panic felt like a cold liquid washing around inside her. Irene wouldn't tell Robert directly, of course, but she might tell her own husband. Would he then tell Robert? Genevieve had no idea how gossip spread among men. She darted a glance ahead; the group of Ladies had reached the doorway, stood waiting for them there. "Come on." She walked briskly to catch up.

"I'm all in," said Clara when Genevieve and Max reached them. "We're going back to the club."

"I'll ride along with you, if that's all right," said Genevieve.

"Five is too many for one tuk-tuk," said Irene. She looked at Max. "We've barged into your tour for long enough. You two should

411

carry on with your day."

The Ladies disappeared in a cloud of parting noises.

"Finally," said Max.

Genevieve pushed his hand away from her arm. "What is wrong with you?" she said. "I told you, Irene knows. This could ruin my whole life."

"Change," he said. "Not necessarily ruin."

"What?"

"This doesn't need to end," he said. At first the words made no sense; it was as if he weren't speaking English. "We could see each other every day — and night," he said, while she stared at him. "We'll travel. Go anywhere you want." It was at once thrilling and horrifying, the thought of herself floating around the world like a loose balloon. "You could even have a job if you like." He touched the Buddha nestled between her collarbones. "The man who sold this to me said it meant 'overcoming fear.' "

"I have children," she said.

"They're not babies," he said. Dismissive, casual.

She remembered cooing over infant Beatrice, marveling at the miracle-tiny feet, pressing lips against one warm pink sole. *They're not babies.* It was sickeningly true. They would not be babies again. How long had it been since she'd touched any of her children in that motherly, affectionate way?

412

Her interaction with them had become a litany of *don't*s, always chiding and correcting. She had a sudden quick pain under her ribs at the image that rose in her mind then, of Robert coming through the front door, that way he always did, with that light step, already half smiling, pleased to be home and to see her, to be mauled by the children's welcome while Genevieve said *Stop it now, stop jumping on him like animals.*

"Enough," she said, although Max had stopped speaking. She put her hand out to hail a tuk-tuk, and when he tried to step in after her she said "No," in a voice as cold as she could make it.

She got caught in a snarl of traffic, a vendor cart overturned ahead of them, a river of steaming coffee running along the side of the street, a lot of shouting. She fretted in the idling tuk-tuk: What if Irene had gone home, had already told her husband? When they finally reached the club, Genevieve walked through its doors with a sense of nostalgia. She'd spent so many afternoons here; after having their hair and nails done, she and Irene would lunch in the air-conditioned rooms decorated with hunting prints and oil portraits. Had the last time really been only a month ago?

Irene was in one of the parlors with the other ladies; they were playing bridge.

"One no trump," said Clara.

"*That's* why I have no face cards," said Renee. "Two hearts."

"Pass," said Irene, before looking up and seeing Genevieve. At first her expression held only untainted pleasure and Genevieve had a brief hope: perhaps Irene had seen nothing after all. But then Irene's smile scattered a little, reassembled itself.

"Long time no see," said Renee, looking up also.

"Hello again," said Genevieve, setting down her handbag and seating herself on an adjacent banquette, taking off her hat. "I have a few minutes before my driver comes."

"Pass," said Julia.

"Three hearts," said Clara.

"That's impossible," declared Renee. "You can't go from one no trump to three hearts."

"I'm sorry," said Clara. "I'm not sure I understand this part."

"This is the hardest part," said Irene in a soothing voice. "Don't worry, Clara, we'll let you do it over. You probably want to go either two no trump, or pass."

"Two no trump," said Clara, after a few seconds of studying her cards.

"And I pass," said Julia.

"Pass," said Irene.

"Pass," said Renee.

"That makes me the dummy," said Irene, laying out her cards: not nearly enough face cards to support the contract. They all watched Clara play and lose the first trick.

"Let's take a walk," Genevieve suggested to Irene. "I need an iced tea."

"They'll bring it," said Clara, not looking up as she spoke, plucking at the cards in her hand, frowning at the ones on the table.

"Let's go to the outside bar," said Irene, getting up.

The heat bellied through the door as they opened it, like a rude guest not stepping aside to let them out. They walked slowly toward the outside bar at the other end of the swimming pool. There were a few shrieking children in the water, some adults on the chaises under umbrellas.

"At least now I know why," Irene said. She was looking straight ahead. Tears trembled in her voice. Not angry, then; hurt. Bewildered by Genevieve's sudden absence. "I thought I had done something wrong."

"I'm so sorry, Irene," said Genevieve. Irene sniffed and nodded.

They ordered iced teas at the outside bar, then didn't turn back the way they'd come but kept walking, carrying the glasses with them, toward the deserted tennis courts, no one out playing in the strong sun.

"Are you in love with him?" Irene asked.

"I don't know," said Genevieve, and realized immediately that she ought to have said yes. Being in love might mean absolution to a romantic like Irene, who devoured cheap novels and cried in movies. "Maybe."

"I just don't understand," Irene said. "Robert's so good-looking." She lowered her voice. "Are you still — do you still — with Robert?"

Genevieve recoiled slightly at the question. "It's been thirteen years," she said. "It's not always — you know."

"I don't think," said Irene with a puzzled face, "that it was *ever* — you know — with Don."

The two women stopped walking, looked at each other, and simultaneously burst into laughter.

Well, how about that, thought Genevieve as Irene, overcome, put a hand out to Genevieve's forearm to steady herself. *I might have told her everything all along.* This woman to whom she had condescended as a follower might have been a real friend, a confidante. Genevieve had had bosom friends, in high school and during her two years at college; in due course they had fallen away. She hadn't thought to mourn them, believing that the sacrifice of friends to the altar of marriage and family was part of growing up.

"It's wonderful," she confessed now. "It's just wonderful — and terrible, too."

"I think I would just feel terrible," said Irene. "I think I couldn't relax enough to enjoy the wonderful part."

"You'd be surprised," said Genevieve.

They began walking again.

"I kissed Giles Benderby once," Irene said. "At a party. Well, he kissed me. But I didn't stop him."

"Heavens," said Genevieve, truly astonished.

"So I do understand how things can get carried away. But it meant nothing. I'm not in love with Giles Benderby."

"Of course not," said Genevieve.

The main building came into view again at the end of the long looping path.

"Are you going to *leave* Robert?" asked Irene. "What about the children?"

Straight to the soft place. Perhaps this was the reason one shouldn't have real friends as an adult; they understood things.

"They're not babies," said Genevieve. It bubbled to her lips involuntarily. Why had she said *that*? She could have said any other true thing — that she knew she needed to put an end to it, that she wanted to repair her marriage. Instead she'd repeated Maxwell's callous comment to her, in a close facsimile of his flippant tone. "I didn't mean that," she said. It was true, she hadn't meant it, but it was too late; she could see that Irene was scandalized. Betraying the husband was one thing; betraying one's children was unforgivable.

"I didn't mean that," said Genevieve again.

"Why would you say it, then?" said Irene. The moments of spontaneity between the two of them, of honesty and closeness, might never have been. "I just don't understand you." She began walking quickly; Genevieve hurried to keep up. "And you don't have to worry," said Irene, still in that cool voice. "I won't say anything to anybody." Her expression making it clear that distaste would make a cautery to this particular bit of gossip: that disappointment, not loyalty, would seal her lips.

Clara had thoroughly disgraced herself by the time they returned to the table: nearly all of the cards were massed in a facedown pile beside Renee's elbow. The women were chatting. Seeing Genevieve and Irene approaching, Julia scraped the cards toward herself, began a shuffle.

"Would you like to play?" Clara asked Genevieve, pushing back her chair and beginning to rise. "You can take my place; I'm hopeless."

"No, Clara," said Irene, seating herself and putting her hand out to Clara, who lowered herself back into her chair as Julia began to deal. "You need all the practice you can get. You have only a few more days to sort out bidding." She lifted her eyes to Genevieve's. "We're having a tournament on Saturday. Come if you're interested; maybe there'll be a group who needs a fourth." She picked up her hand, fanned out her cards, began rearranging them.

Genevieve lingered a few minutes, sipping her iced tea and watching the bidding, seeing how the other women deferred to Irene, how they courted her opinion, and how Irene accepted their homage, like royalty. No doubt she had organized the bridge tournament, as she had the class in Oriental art. After so long in the wings of the stage, Irene was now standing at its spotlit heart.

Genevieve set her empty glass onto the table and made her farewells. The message had been transmitted and received: Irene would keep her promise and not say a word to the others, but whatever path Genevieve chose from here, whatever happened with Maxwell Dawson, the rift was complete. There would be no more tandem salon appointments, no more cozy manicures. No room for Genevieve in the salon chair beside Irene, nor in any of the chairs at the bridge or luncheon tables from now on, not with any of the Ladies, old or new.

CHAPTER TWENTY-SEVEN

Noi was alone in the house when the telephone in the front hall rang. Master was at work; Madame had gone out after breakfast and shortly after that Daeng had left too, supposedly to the market, but more likely to the temple. She couldn't actually pray for something bad to happen to Noi, but she could make merit to increase her own karma, which might affect the balance of things. Choy was in the Quarters, taking a surreptitious nap. The children were in the swimming pool. They weren't allowed to answer the phone. Neither was Noi. Nonetheless, she walked toward the heavy black instrument as it made its shrill loud call, again and again, like a fretful baby. *Something to tell Sao,* Noi said to herself. *If she ever visits me again.* Better than the other things she did not want to say, about Somchit and how foolish she had been. She put her hand out, crept her fingers around the receiver, lifted it up.

It was heavier than she'd expected. She held

it to the side of her face the way she had seen Daeng do, and said nothing.

"Hello?" A fierce voice came into her ear. She almost dropped the receiver. "Hello?" It was a man, a farang. "For God's sake. Hello. Say something."

"Hello," she whispered.

"Hello, I'm calling for Mrs. Preston. Put her on, please."

"Madame not home," said Noi. "You call back." She'd heard Daeng say that too. Usually Daeng put the receiver down immediately after saying it.

"Damn," said the voice. "Will you please tell her that I called?" Noi nodded, not thinking that the phone couldn't see that. "Are you still there?"

"Yes," said Noi.

"Tell her that I called. Mr. Dawson. Tell her," commanded the voice. "Say it back to me. Mr. Dawson."

Noi couldn't believe it. Had she heard wrong? Was he joking?

"Say it back to me," said the voice.

"Mister *dort sun,*" whispered Noi. Mr. Short Penis. The man didn't laugh.

"Tell her I telephoned. Tell her —" Hesitation. "Tell her to call me. Or come here. She knows where." Noi nodded again but did not speak. "Do you understand?"

"Yes," said Noi.

She waited, but the voice didn't speak

again. She heard a click, and then a hum rolled out from the earpiece. Eventually it became a siren, bouncing rudely in the air. She put the receiver back into place.

She didn't know what she had been so frightened of; the telephone was easy.

CHAPTER TWENTY-EIGHT

Laura, last one into the water, was It for the game Philip chose. Surfacing with eyes closed, she called "Marco" and from the blend of noises tried to pick out the important ones: the curt splash of Beatrice or Jane diving under the water, or the flutter-splash of Philip kicking across the pool. A giant splash: Who was that? "Marco," she called again. The hoarse, bellowed "POLO" told her that Jane's older brother, Alex, had arrived and cannon-balled into the middle of the game.

"No fair," said Laura, the wake from his entry slapping her lips. Keeping her eyes closed, although the rules were already being broken.

"Keep your hair on," said Alex, making Philip and Beatrice laugh.

Laura found herself tracking four bigger children by sound. *Marco,* she said, and *Polopolopolo,* the whispers came back to her, tangling themselves with the bees, with traffic honks from the street, a radio playing Thai music somewhere. She'd lunge with hand outstretched — and touch nothing. It was a long, lonely turn, the others laughing as they evaded her. She could hear wet footslaps around the pool, but no one called fish out of water. They were cheating, she thought angrily, but she kept her eyes closed, determined not to be a baby about it. Finally, through sheer luck, she tagged the edge of a heel kicking past her, and opened her eyes, triumphant: Jane. Now it was Jane's turn to be sightless and seeking in the water.

"Marco," said Jane, standing very still in the water, eyes closed.

"POLO," shouted Alex. He let Jane get very close to him before he dove away and swam to Philip, whispered something into the younger boy's ear. Philip looked at Jane where she was turning slowly around and around in the shallow end with her eyes closed, and the two boys began laughing together. Jane went under the surface and began tunneling in their direction. If they noticed, they didn't seem to care; they didn't move to evade her, and when Jane surged up from the water and slapped Alex's shoulder, *Got you!,* he just laughed harder.

"See?" said Alex. Philip nodded, his mouth open as he laughed. Laura didn't like how Philip was when he and Alex were together. He could be harsher, cruel, something of a stranger.

"See what?" asked Jane.

The game seemed to be over. Bea and Laura swam over from opposite corners of the pool and the three girls stood puzzled in the shallow end, looking at the two laughing boys.

"Jane's got boobies," crowed Alex. "Want to see?" He lunged over to his sister and tugged at her swimsuit straps.

"Get off, pig," cried Jane, pushing at his hands and kicking back away from him.

Laura hadn't noticed before, but now she could see the soft little points on Jane's chest, under the fabric of the bathing suit. Had they been there the week before? Jane's face was growing red as she struggled with her brother; Laura put her own hands over her suit straps in sympathy.

"Make them stop," Laura cried to her sister, but Bea had retreated to the deep end of the pool and was treading water there. Laura didn't like Bea either when Alex was around; she got shy and giggly. Normal Bea would have waded in and sorted them all out in a moment. Laura swam toward the boys. "Stop it," she shouted at Philip.

"You'll have them too," said Philip, with a kind of hysterical glee. He used both hands to press Laura's head under the surface. Her gulp of surprise took in water as she went down. Philip held her there, her panicked eyes open in the green froth-streamed underwater world while she tried to twist away, pinching desperately at his arms and legs, her fingers slipping on the muscle.

Finally, when her lungs felt as though they were bursting, the pressure came off Laura's head and she came up choking and sobbing and gasping. Jane and Alex were still grappling, Jane holding both of her swimsuit straps with one hand at the root of her neck and using the other hand like a blade to drive water into her brother's face. Bea was still frozen at the other end of the pool.

"Bea!" screamed Laura, still coughing. "Bea! Make them stop!"

"What is going on here?" said Genevieve, appearing at the side of the pool, carrying her gloves in one hand and her handbag over the same wrist. At the sound of her voice, the knot of children burst apart. "I could hear you all the way from the street. What on earth were you fighting about?"

"Nothing," all of the children said in ragged unison.

"We'll be quieter," added Beatrice.

"I'm going home," said Jane, getting out of the water. She slapped her feet angrily on the wood all the way around, and down the steps that led to the little side gate between the neighboring gardens. They all watched her go.

"What did you do to Jane?" asked Genevieve.

"Nothing, Mrs. Preston," said Alex as the gate banged behind his sister. "She's just like that."

"Mum, come swimming with us," said Philip.

A weak ploy, thought Laura. Intended to distract, destined to fail. Genevieve didn't swim. She had a bathing suit, but not a swimming kind; hers had a little skirt and a cluster of daisies appliquéd to one shoulder. She'd worn it at Pattaya last year, where she'd mostly stayed under an umbrella on the sand, and gone only knee-deep into the sea. She had never put even one toe into the heavily chlorinated blue water in the swimming pool at 9 Soi Nine.

"Play Marco Polo with us," Philip coaxed. "I'll teach you. It's easy."

It was hard to tell what their mother was thinking as she stood there looking down at them all. The sunglasses hid so much of her face.

"Thank you for the invitation," she said, finally. "But I must decline. Philip, you have judo in an hour. Don't forget to get the water bottles from Harriet."

"I won't," said Philip. His voice was dull; he was no longer smiling.

"No more rough playing," said their mother. "Or you'll all be out of the pool until tomorrow."

When she was gone, Laura pulled herself

427

out of the water with a suctioning heave and slapped her feet hard on the wood like Jane had, until she reached the steps down to the garden. She ran across the grass and up into the house, past her mother, who was taking her hat off in the foyer, up the long stairway to her bedroom, where she closed the door behind her. The air-conditioning wasn't on, since it was the daytime; the room was dense with humidity. She peeled off her suit and wriggled clammily into a pair of shorts and a shirt.

"Lolo," said Philip from outside the door.

"Go away," she said.

He pushed the door open, stood in the doorway.

"I'm sorry," he said softly. She shook her head, buckling her legs to sit on the bed behind her, clutching her balled-up dripping suit and looking down so he wouldn't see the tears trembling on her eyelashes. He took a step toward her. "I'm very sorry."

The kindness in his voice broke the sorrow open in her then, and to her horror she was sobbing like an infant, gasping and shuddering and bubbling snot from her nose.

"Why did you?" she said. She could still feel his hand on her head, the betrayal and terror and surprise.

"I don't know," he said. He sat on the bed and she drew her legs away from him and clutched her knees to make herself small, so that no part of her would touch him. "I have to go to judo soon." She could hear tears husking his voice.

She kept her head bent to her knees, her shirt growing wet from the bathing suit against her chest, and she wouldn't look at him. She cried into her wet ball of bathing suit, and he didn't try to come closer or hug her. He stayed where he was and let her cry, bearing the punishment, accepting the loss he had caused her, accepting it as his loss too.

CHAPTER TWENTY-NINE

Genevieve had felt a moment of dislocation, looking down at the children as they bobbed in the water, slick-headed like a group of seals. She had that impression again, of a shutter blink and a jump forward in time. They'd been pale and small and obedient; now they were brown-skinned and loud and wild. And they had secrets. *Come swimming,* Philip had said; there had been something hidden in it, something the children were not telling. How had they grown old enough to have secrets from her? And then Laura running into the house, and Philip chasing after. Clearly, there was something going on.

Those neighbor children were a bad influence. They'd been at the Preston house almost every day this summer, inviting themselves to swim. Genevieve had met the mother once or twice over the garden gate; she seemed a careless type with her frizzy hatless head and perpetually sunburned nose. Genevieve couldn't forbid the children playing together — that would be immensely awkward — so she'd redoubled the discipline among her own children to counteract the poor example. *When we get home,* she thought, *they'll go into a good strict school, first thing.*

"Annie," Genevieve called, and when Sarah appeared instead, Genevieve pointed. "Do you mind wiping?" Wet marks from the children's feet, across the floor and up the stairs.

"Mr. Dawson," Sarah said, pointing to the telephone. The girl looked embarrassed for some reason, saying the name.

Genevieve stood still. "You answered the phone?"

Sarah stammered the message *He say call him.* "Thank you, Sarah," Genevieve said.

She climbed the stairs, head ringing. How foolish she'd been to think of Irene as the only danger. Maxwell Dawson could reach into her life and destroy it if he chose. She had put that power into his hands. She reached the second floor and looked into Philip's room; it was empty. She heard murmuring from the girls' room next door, and she found Philip and Laura there. Some childish spat between them, Laura crying and Philip looking remorseful. "What's happening, Laura, are you hurt?" The girl, face against her knees, turned her head from side to side.

Genevieve had a feeling she should do more, should say more, but there were too many things jostling for her attention at the moment. Whatever this was could wait.

"Get dressed for judo, Philip," she said. "We'll have to leave now; I need the driver to drop me somewhere on the way."

Noi listened with exquisite anticipation to each sound of departure. First the slam of the car door after Madame and Philip got in, then the growl of the engine moving up the driveway, finally the clang of Kai shutting the gates.

When they were gone, she went out to the outdoor laundry area. The house next door was playing loud radio music, and she hummed along as she unclipped dry clothing from the line. She folded everything carefully before laying it into the basket. She took the whites from the washer, pushed them through the wringer, then hung them up on the line. Rain would come later, it was inevitable, but now the sun was strong and hot and with any luck everything would be dry before then.

"How dare you telephone my house," Genevieve said.

"How dare you try to end this," Max said. "How dare you pretend this means nothing."

They stood apart from each other in room 510.

"I never said that," she said.

His face softened a little. "Tell me you don't long for this room," he said. "That you don't live in these hours. And the rest of the time is just . . . waiting."

It was so close to how she'd been feeling for the past month that she found herself nodding.

"I want to be the one to take you to parties," he said. "I want to quarrel and make up. I want to be the only one who shares your bed." His breath was coming short. "That's what I want. What do you want?"

No one had ever asked her such a thing; she'd never asked herself.

"I am offering you a life," he said. "Your whole life."

She wept then, great tearing angry sobs. She cried the way she had never cried in front of Robert, or in front of anyone, or perhaps ever at all, making ugly noises.

"What can I do?" he asked, his arms around her now. "What can I do?"

Send us home, she wanted to say, but she realized that she didn't even want that now. She didn't want to live in room 510, but she also didn't want to live in a world without it. She could not leave her children; she could not take them from their father. It was an impasse, a smooth unclimbable wall with

433

misery on both sides.

"Jenny," he said into her hair. "It's all right, it'll be all right."

Another name she hadn't chosen for herself. She was Mum to her children, and Madame to the servants; in this room she was Jenny. Selfish, careless Jenny. She felt like Laura, weeping for the broken toy that she'd been explicitly warned to treat gently. *You knew better.* Genevieve had known better, and yet she'd gone ahead, a stupid Pandora lifting the lid on the box of evils, and now everything was ruined and wrong.

"It will only be difficult for a short time." His lips at her ear. "We'll get through it together."

After she finally stopped crying, she felt a profound emptiness, a sterile soundless peace like the surface of the moon.

"My brave little Green Buddha," said Max.

"Emerald Buddha," she murmured automatically.

"My precious Emerald Buddha," he said. His fingers worked the buttons of her dress front, his warm hand slid inside. "You've waited so long, for me to break you free from your hard, drab life."

My life wasn't always hard and drab, she thought but didn't say, lifting her face to his as the fabric dropped away from her shoulder. *And you didn't break me free. I fell.*

■ ■ ■ ■

As Noi walked back to the house with the filled basket of clean folded laundry, Somchit was suddenly there. Behind him, the Mercedes in the driveway. She had failed to hear him return, the radio music to blame, her own happy singing along.

He laid his hand on her arm and she jerked away, nearly dropping the basket, walking faster. Just a few more feet and she'd be at the terrace; he wouldn't follow her inside.

"Why won't you be friendly?" he said.

He moved in front of her, blocking her path to the house, feinting and dodging as she tried to get by. He laughed, as though they were playing a game.

"Just one kiss," he said. She could smell the alcohol on his breath.

How had she ever found beauty in the midnight black of his irises? Had she really once traced her fingertip along the rim of his ear reverently over and over for minutes, loving its curve? She couldn't imagine it now. His face was too round, his legs too short. His eyes were beady and his ears were just ears, not beautiful in any way, and she had no desire to touch them.

"Come for a drive," he said, stepping near, closing a hand over her wrist. "We can have a picnic."

She pulled away, threw the basket at him, turned and ran. Away from the house, away from the moist creased palm and stubby fingers, toward the Quarters, up the ladder-steps and into her room. She closed the door and sat with her back against it, pressed her feet hard against the floorboards, felt his heavy steps shaking the structure.

"Noi-Noi-Noi," he said. Leaning his weight against the door. "Let me in."

"Go away," she said, pushing back with all her might.

He put his head through the window.

"Lotus petal," he wheedled. "Why won't you be nice?"

"I won't tell your wife that you've given me a baby," she hissed, grateful that the window was too small to permit him to climb through. "That's how nice I'll be."

Instantly she regretted having said it.

His head disappeared from the window and he thudded his whole body weight against the door. She pressed her hands and feet and bottom against the floor as hard as she could, but each blow scooted her forward and widened the gap between door and frame. Somchit's hand slipped through; then his elbow was curling around the door and his fingers clutching at her while she leaned as far away as she could. Now his head and whole arm up to the shoulder were through. He would soon be in the room.

Suddenly he disappeared, Noi's head bouncing back against the wood as the door shut behind her with a bang.

"Worthless dog." Daeng's voice. "Get out of here." Then she hissed, "Have you been drinking?"

"Not much," he said.

"You have to collect Madame soon," said Daeng. She sounded alarmed. "She must not smell the alcohol. Go ask Choy to cut some *phak chi* from my kitchen pots for you to chew. Go."

Vibrations of his feet stamping down the stairs. Noi waited a minute, then got to her feet and opened the door. Daeng was standing on the landing outside, looking across the garden in the direction Somchit had gone.

"Did he seem very drunk to you?" she said.

"I'm — not sure," said Noi. She had no idea how to assess drunkenness.

"Tch." Daeng made an impatient noise with her tongue. "Maybe it would be better to find someone else to drive." As she said that, they both heard the Mercedes starting up, the squeak of the gate being pulled open. "Where is he going?" said Daeng. She shook her head. "My unlucky daughter." She turned back to Noi and her features sharpened. She looked Noi up and down and said bluntly, "When did you last bleed?"

Noi put her face into her hands.

"Stupid girl."

"I don't know what to do," said Noi.

"Go home," said Daeng. "Have the life you would have had if you never came here."

"I can't," said Noi, weeping into her hands. She knew that her family would welcome the child; there would be no shame to a baby, however it arrived — especially if it was a boy. But her family needed her wages. If Noi went home, she would be bringing two more mouths to join her parents and little sister and brothers, her grandparents and aunts and uncles, while also ensuring the loss of the house where they lived and the land that fed them all. How could a millet seed have the power to put so many lives in jeopardy?

"I didn't know Somchit was married," Noi choked out. "I'm so sorry."

Daeng said nothing for a minute. Then she spoke in a low voice. "I was young once. I know what it is, believing whatever is promised to you." She reached out, took Noi's chin between her fingers, shook it. "Stop crying. Look at me." Noi took her hands down from her face. "There is another way," said Daeng. Her eyes were bright black stones. "I have medicine you can take. Do you understand?" Still jerking with sobs, Noi nodded. "It would not be killing," said Daeng. Of course not: no good Buddhist would advocate that. "It would make your womb unfriendly, that's all." Daeng released Noi's chin. With a glance downward at Noi's belly, she said, "You don't have much time. You decide soon. Now, go rewash the laundry you dropped in the mud."

Afterward, they lay on their backs, looking up at the ceiling. Genevieve turned her head to look at him, his brown eyes very close, a fine network of lines branching from their corners. Was this the face she would wake to for the rest of her life? Other women had done it, divorced. They disappeared from social circles, weren't spoken of above a whisper. Could she be one of those, an object of pity banished to a universe untraveled by anyone she knew? Max had a small bump on the bridge of his nose. She put a finger out and pushed there, finding the bone, then took her finger away and watched as the pale mark left behind filled itself again with pink.

He kissed her lightly, then turned on his side and pulled her against him, her back along his front, and draped an arm over her. Their bodies fit together perfectly.

"Max," she said, her voice an octave lower than usual from the crying. "Is there really a dam?"

He didn't answer right away. "What makes you ask that?"

"Let me put it this way: Should I believe in the dam?"

Another little pause.

"Yes," he said, his breath lifting the hair by her ear. She closed her eyes; she could feel the heat of him through the sheet, all the way down her back. "Yes, I think it best that you do."

Chapter Thirty

His shoulder tingled with that maddening feeling of needing to be evened. It was beginning to pulse, in a ragged shape where his usual sparring opponent had rudely bumped against him while they were getting into position for the stretches. Philip had staggered backward but not fallen, had coughed up an automatic *Pardon me.* Ever since, that shoulder had been feeling heavy and wrong. Philip reached up to his left shoulder to press it; out of the corner of his eye he saw the boy watching him with a smile. He must think Philip was rubbing the sore place. But it wasn't sore; it was *urgent,* which was far worse.

He tried to put it out of his mind during the stretches. He counted the seconds — *one one thousand, two one thousand* — as he pressed his forehead to his knee. The counting didn't help. He hadn't really expected that it would. Counting rarely helped with the need to even things out. By the time the slow-motion exercises ended and it was time for the short break before sparring, the urgency had expanded to fill Philip's mind. It was all he could think about: things needed to be evened out.

He didn't mean to do it — what insanity, to provoke his nemesis intentionally — but the thing got itself done. As the boy crossed in front of Philip, Philip bumped him hard, his non-tingly shoulder meeting the shoulder of the other boy with a jolt that sent them both reeling. Philip barely had time to savor the relief that rolled through him before the boy hurled himself at him.

Philip went down on his back in the dirt, the boy straddling his torso while he punched Philip's face and chest. There was a warm taste of snot and blood and a choke of dust, and then the boy leaned forward and took Philip's head in both of his hands, gripping and twisting the ears painfully as he lifted Philip's skull and banged it back against the ground.

Philip found his arms free, loose beside his body, and he thought something like, *I suppose these could be useful.* He thrust them up against the boy's inner forearms, pressed them outward, hard. The boy's hands came away from Philip's head, and he fell forward just as Philip doubled his knees to catch him, then gave a mighty push. The boy flew backward.

Now Philip was on top of the boy, punching him hard on his bony chest, kneeling on the boy's upper arms with all his Nitnoy weight, the bone on each side rolling under his kneecaps. Philip took the boy's head between his hands and lifted it, then banged it back into the dirt. *Turnabout is fair play,* as his father would say.

It seemed to go on forever, the roaring in Philip's ears, the blood drooling from his lip onto the boy's neck and face, before someone had hold of Philip's collar and was lifting him, the cotton coat rising up under his chin and choking him a little. He was dropped onto his bottom a short distance away from where the other boy lay on his back coughing.

It was the judo master who had pulled him off. He motioned to Philip to stand, lifted Philip's head with one hand beneath his chin, looked at the skin of his neck. Examined his ears, pulling them forward and peering at them as if to be sure they were still properly attached. Then he put his hand in the middle of Philip's upper back and pushed him toward the side of the yard with a gruff command, chopping a hand at the other boy, who got to his feet. The two of them trudged over together toward the tree where Philip's cloth bag with the water bottles lay. The two boys squatted as far as possible from each other, within the blot of shade.

Philip opened the bag and took out one of

443

the bottles, while the other boy gingerly pressed each nostril in turn and blew bloody mucus onto the dirt. Philip drank a mouthful, then shut his eyes tight, tipped back his head, and poured some water over his face. He saw the boy watching. Their eyes met and the boy lifted a hand; Philip flinched but the boy only brought the hand in front of his own mouth and held it there, fingers curled toward his lips, as though he were going to bite into an invisible apple. He smiled broadly, and Philip understood: he was saying that Philip looked funny with his swollen lip. Philip put down the water bottle and lifted his own hands to his head and made spiky fingers, to show the other boy what he looked like with his muddy-bloody hair standing up. The boy laughed. "Buhn," he said, pointing to himself. "Philip," said Philip. He pulled the other bottle out of the bag and held it out.

They watched the sparring together, squatting beside each other in the Thai way, drinking the water. Philip hurt all over but he felt a rising elation. He had defended himself. He had beaten the other boy. He realized another thing also: This was the end of judo — or Thai boxing, or whatever these lessons had actually been. Once his mother got a look at him, he would never have to come back.

He hoped that it would be his father who came today to collect him. It had been an honorable fight; his father would understand. He might even be proud. And surely the universe would see fit to reward Philip with ice cream today.

When the lesson ended, Buhn stood up, capped the empty bottle carefully and handed it back to Philip, then made a wai, which Philip returned. As the boys dispersed, Buhn called something to Philip in Thai. No chorus of laughter or *Nitnoy* followed from the others, so the words must have been at least neutral. Maybe *See you next week.* Maybe *Good fight.* Or *Good luck when your mother sees you.* In boy-speak any of that would be intimate as a kiss. Philip realized that he hadn't heard *Nitnoy* all day.

It began to rain as Philip stood alone at the edge of the street, holding the cloth bag with the empty bottles, waiting for the Mercedes. All of the other boys had left; the master had gone into the building at the back of the lot and shut the door. Philip amused himself by walking along the edge of the road, a few feet this way, a few feet that, one foot in front of the other as though on a tightrope. The rain collected on his neck and ran down inside his collar. *If I count to twenty and look up, the car will be here,* he told himself. *If I count to forty.*

The rain stopped, leaving the late-afternoon sun low in the sky. Philip sat right down on the dirt at the edge of the road. His upper lip was so swollen that if he looked straight down, he could see the blurry edge of it. He touched it gently: it felt huge, alien. He wanted very much to see it in a mirror, but that would have to wait for home. His body had consolidated into a symphony of pain, his lip a dull, throbbing bass line, the scratches on his neck a shrill pizzicato. Despite that, he felt good. The soreness encompassed his whole body evenly, no one place more painful than any other.

They had never been so late coming to get him before. He looked up the empty block, toward the big busy street from which the Mercedes always came. Perhaps it was caught in a traffic jam on that street. Perhaps it was sitting just out of view, its side light blinking and blinking, unable to make the turn through the solid unyielding lanes of cars. He decided he'd walk to the corner, just to see.

■ ■ ■ ■ ■

PART 4

■ ■ ■ ■ ■

CHAPTER THIRTY-ONE

2019

Beatrice's text came when Laura was making the midmorning pilgrimage to the hospital, carrying her coffee past the corner kiosk near the zoo. A new flyer had been stapled willy-nilly across all of the others, bearing a vivid color-printed image of a stuffed pink pig, with the caption LOST: MY THREE-YEAR-OLD'S BEST FRIEND — REWARD $50. The alert rang from Laura's pocket, and she dug her phone out.

He's awake. The doctors are taking his breathing tube out now.

Laura ran the rest of the way to the Metro, down the steps and onto a train, her mind percolating with questions. When had he gotten better? She'd been at the hospital every day except for yesterday, which she'd spent in the studio making the painting that remained half-scraped. But she'd kept her phone with her the whole time. Why had no one called her?

When she arrived at the ICU breathless, the nurse buzzed her in with a smile. Bea was in the hallway outside Philip's room talk-ing to the doctors, both the older, rarely glimpsed one and the younger, haggard one. The doctors smiled at Laura and recapped, without impatience. *He's got a good strong cough — his heart's improved on the medica-tions — looks like he might do okay.* The curtain was pulled across inside the glass doors of Philip's room; in gaps between the panels of cloth, Laura could see the motion of nurses whisking past.

The doctors' air of celebration revealed the concern they'd downplayed before, made clear how very ill Philip had been. Their codicil *Do you have any questions?* was for once not perfunctory; they seemed to want to prolong the happy moment. When they'd finally run out of things to say, they pressed the button on the wall to open the double doors of the ICU and shooed Bea and Laura out toward the waiting room with the promise that they could come back in to see him together *when the nurses are done with him.*

In the corridor, Bea turned to Laura, who steeled herself.

But Bea was laughing. "You were right, Lolo," she said. "It is Philip."

Laura felt her own mouth gaping, a slack jaw of surprise. "Why did they call you, and not me?" she asked, a beat behind, still work-ing out the questions she'd had on the way.

"I was already here," said Bea. "I've been

here every morning. I leave before you get here. Didn't you hear me? You were right. Look."

Bea put out her hand, opened it to show a plastic toy nestled there: a prancing red horse tossing its head, one hoof raised.

"I had no idea you kept one of those," said Laura, taking the figure, turning it between her fingertips. For a mass-produced object, the horse was beautiful work, the bell-shaped hooves, the separate curling locks of mane and tail.

"I kept them all," said Bea.

Laura hadn't even known she'd held this memory, but it sprang perfect into her mind: pulling a cellophane strip around the sides of a small box to unroof it, plunging forefinger and thumb into the opaque white sugar beads within, rooting around to find the treasure. Usually a monkey or lion; very rarely a horse. The Preston children had been obsessed for a season, ears cocked for that specific vendor's bicycle bell outside the garden wall, spending whole allowances. Laura's two horses had been her most precious possessions until Bea said they were stupid and that she'd thrown her own collection away.

"You told us you threw yours away," said Laura.

"I lied," Bea said without a trace of shame. "I said that so I could take yours."

"You were such a shit," said Laura, shaking

451

her head.

"They let me in to see him for a minute right after they took the tube out." Bea was beaming, taking no offense. "I showed it to him and he recognized it immediately, just like you did. He laughed and said, 'I should have known.'"

"You just happened to be carrying this?" Laura asked Bea. "You came this morning, and found he was awake, and you just happened to have this with you?"

"I've *been* carrying it," said Bea, taking the little horse back from Laura and tucking it into her purse. She didn't specify whether she meant she always had, like a talisman, or had been doing so only recently, in case Philip woke up. "I'm very sorry," she said, looking Laura in the eyes, her voice soft and sincere. "You recognized him, and I didn't. I should have listened to you."

"Well, it was kind of crazy," said Laura, dazed. Not only by the apology: it was nice to see Bea happy. Like the doctors' worry revealed only in retrospect, it was suddenly clear how anxious Bea had been, and for how long.

"We'll have to figure out how to tell Mum," Bea said. This task, which Laura had expected to be a bone of contention between them, now appeared to be simply a bullet point on a joyful agenda.

■ ■ ■ ■

Within the week, Philip was moved from intensive care to a regular floor, where the nurses took his meditation hours very seriously; twice a day, they put a sign on his door and kept everyone out. The twins came to visit, Dean and Dustin shaking his hand solemnly, *Hello, Uncle Philip,* as their mother blinked back tears.

"I met you when you were asleep," said Dean shyly.

When a social worker made noises about eventual discharge to a rehabilitation hospital where Philip could regain his strength, Bea squashed that idea: home meant the Tudor. She began mobilizing forces to get a bedroom prepared, and arranging in-home therapies: physical, occupational, respiratory.

Dr. Gomez stopped the sisters in the corridor one day, warned them *He's not ready to talk,* but it was an unnecessary caution. Bea had pivoted completely on that subject; she seemed to have lost the need to know what had happened to Philip on the day he went missing, or all the years he was gone. She instead threw herself into the task of telling Philip what had happened to *them* during that time, bringing photo albums to the hospital and marching him through the pages.

"That's Great-Aunt Patricia," said Beatrice,

pointing to a woman with heavy eyebrows. "Do you remember her? She used to pinch us if we did something wrong."

"I remember the pinching," said Philip.

"These are Mum's parents," said Bea, turning a page. "They had that big house in Chevy Chase. We saw them for holidays before." *Before* meant before Bangkok, the time they'd lived in the Tudor as small children, Bea for eight years and Philip for four and a half, Laura for barely three. "And these are Dad's parents. They lived in England. They didn't visit very often."

Page after page, photo after photo, Washington and then Bangkok. Christmas in the long living room of the Tudor becoming Christmas in the party room, baby Laura mouthing a candy cane on Robert's lap becoming five-year-old Laura opening a package while Philip and Bea watched. In the backgrounds of both, the fuzzy lights of a decorated tree.

"I used to think you'd be an engineer or architect," Bea told Philip, pointing to a snapshot of him building with Tinkertoys. "When the boys were small I thought about how much you would have loved Lego."

"Don't do that," he said, the first sharp words they'd heard from him. "Don't talk about me like I died."

"But I thought you were dead," said Bea, surprised into frankness. "We all did."

A fragile silence jittered between them all.

"I'm sorry about that," said Philip.

Another beat of silence, and then Bea turned another page in the album. A monochrome photo of Genevieve and Robert at a Bangkok party, her perfect bouffant, his crew cut, cigarettes and cocktails in their hands. They were smooth-faced, beautiful, young. On the facing page were color snaps of Laura and Bea in their new uniforms for the school in America.

Here was another before and after, with nothing to mark the transition. No gap in the photographs, no blank pages. The images simply changed from black and white to color, Robert and Genevieve stopped appearing together, and Philip no longer appeared at all.

The doctor was beaming when she signed off on Philip's discharge.

"You'll live another thirty years," she said, then added in an earnest rush, "If you take your meds and wear your seat belt and don't smoke."

Philip said nothing during the drive from Northern Virginia into the District. Not a sound as the car navigated the sweep along the parkway with the monuments in the distance, postcard landscapes that predictably elicited cries from tourists. No reaction as they got closer to home, turning off Beach Drive and driving up Brandywine, emerging among the plush lawns and spreading trees.

Noi stood in the entrance of the house like a tiny Cerberus, watching them come up the long slate front path. When they reached her, Philip made a wai, spoke to her in soft Thai. She blinked tears, her mouth working as she returned the wai.

"Madame napping," she said as they went inside.

Philip stood still in the middle of the foyer and looked up. Laura watched him. Was there a spark in his memory, of this house he'd last seen when he was four? Superficial things had changed since then, but the bones — the wood, the slate, the wall of mullioned windows in the sitting room straight ahead — would be the same. He climbed to the center landing, looked to the dining room on the right, the living room on the left, then stepped forward into the sitting room that jutted out from the back of the house, twenty feet above the sloped backyard.

"Who cleans those windows?" he asked.

"Intrepid people with enormous ladders," said Bea. "This house is ridiculous."

"But it's beautiful," said Laura.

Yes, they all agreed. It was beautiful.

They went slowly through the rest of the main floor, Philip occasionally pausing in front of something and his sisters providing commentary, *There used to be wallpaper here,* and *We took out that wall when the kitchen was redone.*

Philip stopped in front of the elevator at the back of the kitchen.

"We put that in four years ago," said Bea. When Genevieve was diagnosed, although she had no mobility issues at the time, Bea had arranged for the old back staircase to be hollowed out for a small lift, saying *I'm thinking ahead.*

Clem and the boys arrived in a hubbub of unloading: flowers, stacks of food containers, a large chest cooler. Edward's silver sedan pulled up and he got out, wrestled a case of wine from its trunk into the house. Bea called orders from the kitchen; minions Laura and Clem and Edward ferried silverware and glasses and napkins out to the screened porch, where Philip was already seated at the long table, while the boys filled the cooler with ice and buried cans of soda and bottles of beer.

"Oh my God, can you do this please?" Beatrice said to Clem, laughing, gesturing to the large watermelon into which she'd sunk a knife. "It's like the sword in the stone." She sounded purely happy. Had Laura ever heard her laugh like that?

On the screened porch, everyone was chatting as they went about the final tasks, Clem and Bea placing serving bowls on the sideboard, the twins filling the water glasses. Laura and Edward were switching on the electric candles down the middle of the long table when the chitchat noise died away and Laura turned to see Genevieve standing in the doorway from the living room. She was holding Noi's arm, and her eyes were on Philip.

"It's Philip, Mum," said Bea. Gentle, as if every word were a sharp object being placed into their mother's hand.

"Of course it is," said Genevieve, without a flicker of amazement.

Noi helped her navigate the step down onto the porch, and Genevieve walked the rest of the way alone, seated herself in the chair beside Philip. "Did anyone get you a drink?" she asked him in a brisk hostess voice. The sisters looked at each other and shrugged: who knew what she understood.

Before the meal everyone raised their glasses to Philip; then Dustin made a charming toast to "our grandmother and matriarch," dipping his head to Genevieve. *Hear, hear,* everyone said; Laura watched Genevieve sipping with the others. She would never have made the faux pas of drinking to herself — she had not realized that she was the grandmother mentioned in the toast. Bea's eyes caught Laura's: she had noticed too.

"You're trending, Uncle Philip," announced

Dean, looking down at his phone. "They're using the hashtags #returnedfromthedead, and #miracle, and #nevergiveuphope. Barf."

"Hashtag no phones at the table," said Bea. She took Dean's phone, looked at the screen, tsked and clicked it off. "Where are they getting their information? I presume none of *us* talked to a reporter." She looked around the group; everyone shook their heads no.

"I'm sorry," said Philip. "Hashtag?"

"You're like a time traveler," said Dustin, slipping his napkin from its ring.

"*Please* let me be the one to explain the internet to him," Dean said to no one in particular.

As the long table naturally broke into groups of conversation, Laura watched her mother talking to Philip. She seemed relaxed with him, familiar — was it simply the unguarded friendliness of Genevieve 2.0, or did it signify recognition on some level? Or did she think he was Robert? At the other end of the table, Beatrice laughed at a story Dean was telling. Noi, who'd sat for a brief time at the table but had soon found a reason to get up, was standing beside her seat, talking with Clem. Dustin was deep in a discussion with Edward. It could be any homecoming, any happy reunion with a soft spotlight on the returned one.

"Edward," called Bea down the table. "Would you mind choosing another bottle of wine from that lovely selection you brought? Laura, could you help him?"

"Subtle," said Laura, rolling her eyes, but she got up and they went together to the pantry, stood in front of the wine rack. "She wants us to make up," she said.

"We have," he said. "Haven't we?" He selected two bottles, stood studying them. "California or Spain?"

"We have," she said. She felt a surge of huge affection, watching him frown down at the labels. "I've been really stupid," she said. He looked up. "You're a brick." It was something Robert had used to say, a high compliment for strong character and loyalty.

"Thank you?" Edward said.

"After all, we are both going to die," she said. He raised his eyebrows and she added, "Someday." Then her mind went blank; the thoughts that had seemed so eloquent in her head the moment before had curled in on themselves, away from her tongue. "You don't disappear for me," she said.

"How drunk are you?" he asked, smiling, setting the bottles down and putting his arms around her.

"I couldn't drive home," she admitted. "But in another way, I feel extremely clear." She leaned against him, spoke muzzily into his chest. "What I'm *trying* to say is, okay. Let's jump off the curb. Let's get married." She added quickly, leaning back, "But no fuss."

"No-fuss curb jumping toward certain death," he said, kissing her. "Sounds excellent."

Laura and Edward didn't announce anything — *no fuss,* she repeated to him — but when they returned with the wine, Bea gave them a little smile. The rest of the meal was a gauzy blur. In a rush of sentiment, Laura found herself telling the story of Philip's birth to the table, Genevieve listening with an expression of delighted interest, as if she'd never heard it before. At the *just like a little Dutchman* part, Philip rounded his eyes and batted his eyelashes, and everyone laughed.

"That must have been scary," Dean said to Genevieve.

"Oh, yes," she said. "*You* remember," she told Philip, and everyone laughed again. Again, the sisters' eyes met.

It was full dark when the event began to wind down, the boys in the living room on their phones, Edward on a call in the dining room, Clem and Laura clearing the table while in the kitchen Bea battled with Noi over the washing-up. *Laura, get the napkins, we need to put them in to soak* said Bea, and Laura went out onto the porch, which was empty now except for her mother and Philip. They had their backs to her and were carrying on a murmured conversation, the candle

461

flickering on the table in front of them. As Laura came up behind them, Genevieve put a hand on Philip's forearm and leaned toward him. Laura stood still, the words she'd been about to say dying on her lips.

"The girls must never know," Genevieve said.

At that moment, Bea came through the French doors.

"Laura, did the night nurse call you?" she said. She seemed agitated, all the soft ease of the day gone. "I totally lost track of time. She should have been here half an hour ago." She bent toward Genevieve. "Mum," she said, "it's time for bed." She drew back Genevieve's chair, helped her up. Looked at Laura pointedly. "Philip, do you need help getting up?"

"Bea," said Laura, the words covered by the scraping noise of Philip's chair as he pushed it back. She put out an arm to him, helped him get to his feet. "Bea, I have to talk to you."

"Whatever it is, it can wait," said Bea, one arm under her mother's, going with her into the house. Laura and Philip followed; when they were all in the living room, Bea said, "I can stay, but Clem is flying out in the morning." The airport was a quick drive from Bea and Clem's house, an impossible journey from the Tudor through DC morning traffic. "And I'm sure Noi wants to get back to her own family."

"I'll stay too," said Laura. "Edward can go home. We'll make it an all-Preston night. You and I can sort out the nurse situation together tomorrow."

Bea's face softened, surprised.

"Okay," she said.

"I can use the stairs," said Philip, realizing that they were making their way toward the elevator in the kitchen.

"Not on your first day," said Bea in a voice like a general's. "Mum and I will wait here while you and Laura go up."

"I'd love a hot toddy," said Genevieve as the elevator doors closed.

"Do you think it's solely birth order that made Beatrice so bossy?" Philip asked Laura as they were creaking upward. "I mean, what if you or I had been born first?"

"Bea would never have allowed that," said Laura, and they shared a smile.

Philip's room had been in use as a guest room until recently. Bea had had it whipped into shape, new clothes put into the closet and fresh navy paint on the walls. An adjustable bed stood beside a nightstand, upon which sat the black box of the CPAP unit, a gooseneck lamp, and a small brass bell.

"If I ring this, does a butler come?" said Philip when he was settled in bed. He touched the bell. "Or maybe a genie?"

"If you ring that tonight, I'll come," said

Laura. "I'll be just down the hall." In her old bedroom; but had it actually been his once upon a time, she wondered, had her crib been in this room next to the master? She couldn't recall anything from her years in this house before they left it for Bangkok. "Bea's probably working on an intercom system."

His smile was weary. It had been a long first day home. She had intended to ask him about his conversation with Genevieve on the porch, but decided: not now. She wished him goodnight, left his bedroom door ajar.

At the end of the upstairs landing, Bea and Genevieve were just getting out of the elevator; Noi was coming up the front stairs.

"Laura and I are staying," Bea told Noi. "The night nurse hasn't come."

"I fire them all," said Noi.

"When did you do that?" said Bea, as Laura said "Why?"

"Too noisy," said Noi, flapping a hand. "Watching TV, talk-talk-talk on the phone. Madame not sleeping."

"Who's been with Mum at night?" asked Bea.

"Mai pen rai," said Noi. She ducked under Bea's arm and replaced Bea's body with her own, put an arm around Genevieve's waist. The two of them went down the hall, Laura and Bea staring after.

"Nighty-night," called Genevieve as they turned into the master bedroom.

"Noi has been sitting at Mum's bedside all night?" said Laura. "And then she's up all day? When does she sleep?"

"I vote for one crisis at a time," said Bea. "We can deal with it tomorrow."

Sometime after dropping off to sleep, Laura woke again in her old bedroom tucked into the corner of the second floor. Through the partly open door came the rushing noise of Philip's CPAP machine. She realized that down the hall were her brother and mother and on the other side of the bathroom, her sister. She felt something like vertigo, as if history had rolled them all back into the past. All except her father. With the miracle of Philip's return, and the rest of them restored to the house, it seemed deeply unfair that Robert was not there too.

She slipped out of bed, and went down the front stairs.

Bea was in the sitting room, in one of the chairs that looked out the windows, drinking brandy from a balloon glass.

"There's more of this," she said, lifting the glass; Laura shook her head.

"My mouth feels like sand," Laura said. She got a glass of water from the kitchen and brought it back, took the other chair. They sat for a minute in the darkness.

"Mum seemed totally okay with Philip," Laura said.

"I think she might believe that he's Dad," said Bea.

"I overheard her telling him something when she didn't know I was there," said Laura. She described what she had heard. "What do you think she meant by that? *The girls must never know.*"

Bea shrugged. "Parent secrets. The Easter Bunny, Santa Claus."

"She wouldn't have said *never* about the Easter Bunny or Santa Claus."

"You sure you heard correctly? You had a good amount of wine tonight, if I recall." Laura didn't grace that with a reply. "What did Philip say in response?"

"He didn't say anything," said Laura.

"Very Preston," said Bea. She sipped some brandy. "We're less a 'read between the lines' family and more a 'hallucinate something onto this blank sheet of paper' family."

The wall of windows was black, moonless.

"You know, I never really understood about Philip," said Laura. "No one actually sat down and explained it to me. He was just gone. And then we came home."

"We had to come home sometime," said Bea.

"What a horrible decision for Mum and Daddy to have to make." Curiously, "What would you have done?"

"I wouldn't have lost him in the first place," said Bea.

466

"That's not fair," said Laura. "It just happened."

"It happened to *them* because they weren't paying attention," said Bea. "Because they entrusted their children to the servants."

"What did the servants have to do with it?" said Laura.

Bea gave her an odd look. "We all knew it was the driver."

"What?" said Laura. A flash in her memory, of guilt and stealth. She felt some truth looming just outside of her consciousness, a berg floating in dark water.

"The creepy one. Somchit," said Bea.

"Everyone knew that?" said Laura. "Mum and Daddy knew that?"

"Especially Mum and Daddy," said Bea.

"Why didn't I know that?" said Laura.

Bea shrugged. "No one could prove it." She leveled a look at Laura. "Is it really better than simply not knowing?"

"Yes," said Laura.

Bea lifted her glass and spoke before the sip, her voice echoey. "I always wondered why Mum and Dad didn't divorce, after."

"Why would they? They never argued," said Laura.

"They didn't have to," said Bea. "They were hardly ever in the same place. Did you ever see them kiss?"

"On the cheek," said Laura, but she couldn't call to mind any specific memory of it. "Not much PDA in that generation, though."

"It was the 1970s," said Bea, wry. "Plenty of their contemporaries were wife-swapping and dropping LSD." She shook her head. "Mum and Dad made a deliberate choice to stay in their 1950s bubble. And they tried to keep us in that bubble with them. Remember the saddle shoes?"

Those first years in America, after the return. Bea and Laura had never discussed them.

"I remember the Drills," said Laura. "That was an awful game."

"We were always alone," said Bea, shaking her head. "We went everywhere alone. Two little girls, like the Lyon sisters."

Just the name put a chill through Laura. The Lyon sisters, ten and twelve, who had stepped into oblivion in 1975 while walking together to the mall near their Maryland home. The mystery had been recently solved, the perpetrator identified after more than forty years, but for Washingtonians of that era the horror was indelible, like an enormous fire that chars an entire geological stratum. No degree of later recovery, lush forests blooming on the same spot, could eradicate the bitter ash.

"You'd think Mum and Dad would have been super paranoid even before the Lyon sisters," said Laura. "But we were free to wander."

"They lived in a different world," said Bea. "Remember having to curtsy when we were introduced to a grownup?"

"Oh, God, yes," said Laura. "Remember the white gloves?"

"Those didn't last long."

For the first time, she and Bea poured their separate glittering hoards of remembrance out between them, letting the precious bits mix up together, not getting defensive when a memory didn't match exactly. Why had they kept them separate for so long? What did it matter if Bea's recollection was slightly different from Laura's? But it had mattered so much, for so long.

Remember the green station wagon?

Remember Dad's parents visiting?

The station wagon had those wood side panels, or it didn't, but they both remembered how wonderful it was on long drives, how you could lie in the very back and watch the trees go by. The Preston grandparents, they agreed, were awful.

"There was a reason for that," said Bea. "They were extremely annoyed that we went away with two girls and a boy and came back with two girls and no boy."

"Which of us do you think they would have traded for Philip?" mused Laura.

"Definitely you." Deadpan. "They probably expected Mum and Dad to try for a replacement boy. They could have, you know. Mum was only thirty-three when we came back."

That seemed impossible, but Laura did the math: it was correct.

"It does explain some of their choices," said Laura. "Like deciding to make a road trip through the snow belt in December when Mum was eight months pregnant. She was only twenty-five then. At that age I wasn't even responsible for a houseplant."

Bea sipped from her glass. Charitably not saying, *You're not responsible for a houseplant even now,* thought Laura. But when Bea spoke, it was clear that wasn't what she had been thinking at all.

"Did you happen to notice that I am not mentioned in that story?" Bea said.

"You were in the back of the car sleeping."

"That's right. But I disappear, didn't you notice? I'm not there when they get to the hospital."

It was true, Laura realized. Bea had not been mentioned in the story after the blizzard began.

"They forgot me," said Bea. "They got out of the car at the hospital and left me there."

"No," said Laura.

"I remember it vividly. I woke up alone, in the freezing darkness. The car's front doors were open, the snow was blowing in. I couldn't open the back doors because the snow was too high. I was afraid to climb over the gear shift."

"What did you do?" said Laura.

"I just waited," said Bea, "and I cried." Her voice sounded sad. "Eventually a man came and got me. A stranger. He turned off the engine and took out the keys, and then he lifted me out. He called me Peanut. *Poor little Peanut.*" She looked thoughtful. "I suppose I was lucky the doors were open — otherwise the exhaust from the blocked tailpipe would have done me in." She tipped up the glass, drank the last of the brandy.

"They were remarkably focused people," said Laura, after a moment's silence.

"There's no excuse," said Bea. "You don't have children. You don't know."

The memories of their parents were like that, sometimes filled with fury, sometimes love, sometimes sorrow. Unforgivable things mixing with dumbfounding things and tender things, the same event in equal parts hilarious and enraging. There was no one way to think of their childhoods.

Laura watched the shapes of the trees through the windows, dark moving against dark. She had known that she missed her brother; she'd been told so all her life — *you two were so close* — but she'd had no idea how much she'd missed her sister, who'd been with her all this time.

"Edward asked me to marry him," said

471

Laura. "I said yes."

Bea looked genuinely pleased. "That's wonderful. Isn't it?"

"I don't know," said Laura. "It's just — it feels like giving in. Or giving up. Something."

"Oh, come on," said Bea. "Join us ordinary mortals in our ordinary lives. Have some ordinary happiness."

They sat for a while longer, two sisters up far past their bedtime, the old house creaking and sighing around them, always in the process of settling, never completely at rest.

CHAPTER THIRTY-TWO
1972

It was the children's bedtime, and still the parents weren't home. Both cars were gone, the driveway empty. Philip wasn't home either, so the parents must have taken him somewhere. They'd never done that before; the girls were jealous. They were fed dinner and Noi supervised their toothbrushing and saw them into bed, turned out their bedroom light.

When Noi went down the stairs, Daeng was standing at the bottom.

"I don't think they went to a party," Daeng said. "They always come here first." It was true: they always came back to the house before a party, to bathe and change their clothes. "When Master will be late he telephones."

"Master did telephone," said Noi in a small voice. "He said he was working late, that he would miss dinner."

"You answered the phone?" demanded Daeng.

It had been almost easy the second time,

just a few hours after the first, putting the handset to her face and speaking into the pierced plastic circle of the mouthpiece, her voice traveling into the master's ear. Noi had still been sniffling after the encounter with Somchit, gathering up the dropped laundry from the ground, when she heard the ring from inside the house. Daeng was outside the gate, looking down Soi Nine after the disappearing Mercedes, as if Somchit would turn around and come back for the *phak chi* to cleanse the alcohol from his breath.

"It rang and rang," said Noi.

"You should have come to get me," said Daeng crossly. "All right, so Master is late at work. But what has happened to Madame and the boy? Did Madame telephone too?" Noi shook her head, eyes down. "I will wait for them," said Daeng. "You go to bed." She went into the kitchen; a minute later Noi heard the metered drum of chopping.

In the Quarters, Noi fretted. Why did she do such foolish things? Big mistakes like Somchit, little mistakes like answering the phone. As she drifted into sleep, two memories slid into her mind and collided, and Noi came awake again. She knew where Madame might be. She got up and dressed, took the small bag of her savings from its hiding place, and crept quietly out of the Quarters.

The hotel doorman looked her over with

disdain as she passed by him into a flower-thronged foyer and then an elegant lobby with a grand staircase curving away out of sight. Ahead of her was a tall counter and behind it, a man in a blue suit who watched Noi steadily as she approached.

"Sawadee-kha," she said when she reached the counter, making a deep wai. "I am looking for —" Her voice failed her. How could she say that name to this man? She whispered, "Mr. Short Penis."

The man behind the counter looked disgusted.

"Get out of here," he said.

"It's a farang name," she said desperately. "I don't think it means the same for them." She invented, "His son has been in an accident. He needs to come right away." The man looked uncertain. "Please look through your book, to see if there's a name that sounds like — that."

"I don't have time for this," he said, not even looking down at the large book open before him.

There was a familiar undercurrent to the words. That tone of indignation from a vendor in the market meant *Guess my price.* Could it mean the same here? Noi turned away from him, dug under her blouse for her money pouch, worked the drawstring open. She fingered the coins. The brash noise they made sliding against one another was too

475

vulgar for this elegant place. It would need to be one of the bills, soundless and discreet. She pulled out a ten-baht note, and turned around with it in her hand. "Will this help?" she said, holding it out to the man, trembling a little. The bill's shadow fluttered on the surface of the counter.

The man's face focused; he moved just his eyes, looking right and left; he reached and the money disappeared from her fingers. Then he turned some leaves back in the big book in front of him.

"Nothing," he said, after having run his index finger down four pages.

Perhaps she had been wrong. Maybe she had misremembered the name of the hotel Somchit had told her about, the one where Madame spent her afternoons. She almost turned away, but then she remembered the quiet, frightened faces of the Preston girls, getting into their beds without complaint.

"Look again," she ordered in a gruff imperative, an imitation of Daeng.

He raised an eyebrow but looked again, making a big show of turning each page.

"There is a Mr. *Dawson* in 510," he said, finally.

"Yes, yes," she said. "How do I get there?"

"I can't permit you to go up to the room." Real indignation this time.

"You can send someone up with a message," she said, using the bossy voice again.

"That's a lot of trouble," he said.

She reached into her pouch, not bothering to turn around this time. The slim soft packet she pulled out was warm from lying close to her skin. She held it for a moment. It was not enough for the land tax; it was just enough to buy her passage home. But even if it had been enough for both, all of it was tainted by the bad path she had taken, her bad choices.

The clerk accepted the money with a slight sneer, as though the bribe was so paltry that it dirtied his fingers. She thought for a moment he might send her away anyway; what recourse would she have? There was nothing left in her pouch but coins. But the man lifted the receiver of the black telephone beside him and pushed the dial around. They waited nearly a minute on opposite sides of the counter, both of them listening to the double-burr sound of the rings.

CHAPTER THIRTY-THREE

"I don't know any Noi," said Max, impatient, into the phone.

The loud ringing had awakened them both. *My God,* thought Genevieve, *what time is it*? The room was dark. She got out of bed and went over to the window, saw the lighted strings of traffic below. They must have slept for hours.

"I don't know any Sarah either," Max said.

Sarah? She froze. It couldn't be, it couldn't be.

"Tell her I'm coming down," she said, scrambling into her clothing.

"What are you doing?" he said, putting his hand over the telephone receiver.

"It's my Number Three," she said frantically, pulling her dress over her head, buttoning it wrong, rebuttoning.

"Tell her to wait," Max said into the phone, and hung up. "What is your Number Three doing here?"

"I don't know," said Genevieve. "I have to

go." She pushed her feet into her shoes while still buttoning her dress front, scooped up her hairband from the desk and put it into the purse, went toward the door with the purse under her arm, combing her hair back from her face with her fingers.

"Do you want me to come?" he asked.

"God, no," she said. "God."

"I hope everything's all right," said Max as the door was closing behind her.

The utter humiliation of coming out of the elevator bank and seeing Sarah there, waiting.

"What is it?" Genevieve asked. "Is it Mr. Preston?" During the slow descent of the lift, she'd had time to generate numerous dreadful scenarios, Robert killed in a traffic accident or felled by a coronary.

"Philip, Madame," said Sarah.

Philip had been in an accident? It was Wednesday. Robert had been supposed to get him today from judo.

"What happened to Philip?" Had they both been in a car accident while she lay for hours sleeping next to her lover? She wanted to vomit. How in the world had Sarah known where she was?

Sarah was shaking her head. She kept saying *Philip,* not *Master.* How had Philip alone been in an accident? Maybe they had both been in the accident and Philip alone was

479

injured. He was so small; she saw the hurtling heedless bus as it crushed the passenger side of Robert's Mercedes, Philip's face right before the impact, his mouth an O through the glass.

"Where is he?" Genevieve asked, hurrying toward the hotel exit. If he was at a Thai hospital, he'd need to be transferred to Fifth Field. The embassy could help — if she could raise anybody on the telephone at this hour. Maybe Robert had already called them. Where *was* Robert? On the apron of concrete outside the hotel, she stood confused: Where was the car?

Sarah was following behind, talking in a mix of Thai and English, urgent, incomprehensible. Genevieve turned and grabbed the girl's hands, clutching them and pulling the girl's arms up, as though they were reins that could halt her speech. Sarah stopped talking.

"Is Philip in the hospital?" Genevieve asked slowly, each word separate.

"No, Madame." Sarah shook her head. "Philip not come home."

This made no sense at all. Genevieve let go of Sarah's hands and backed away a few steps, as if distance would help to bring the situation into focus.

"Mr. Preston was supposed to collect Philip from judo," she said. Wasn't that right, hadn't they arranged that? Her day's plan had been derailed after encountering the Ladies at Wat

480

Phra Kaew. "Where's Mr. Preston?" Sarah shook her head. "Both of them didn't come home?" She looked around. "Where's our car?"

"Come," said Sarah, beckoning to her to follow, in that Thai way of holding a hand by one hip and patting the air. Genevieve just stood there, so Sarah took her by the hand and led her to a waiting tuk-tuk. She spoke in Thai to the driver first, then gently pushed Genevieve in and climbed in after.

"Where are we going?" Genevieve sat forward on the vinyl seat. The oblong of rearview mirror showed the driver's curious eyes on her.

"Home, Madame," said Sarah. "We go home." Her voice soothing, like a mother talking to a frightened child. She said something else, which Genevieve didn't understand. "Master *mai ru,* Madame."

"No," said Genevieve. But she couldn't think of where they should go, to find her husband and son.

She'd never taken a tuk-tuk at night; without window glass between her and the dark streets, the city seemed frighteningly close. They idled at a stoplight, the open sides of the vehicle not ten feet from the people on the wet sidewalks.

"Master *mai ru,*" said Sarah again.

Genevieve still had no idea what that meant. But they were already pulling into the gate at 9 Soi Nine. Genevieve would have to find out whatever Robert was, or would be, later.

CHAPTER THIRTY-FOUR

When he finally understood the situation, Robert was still holding his briefcase, standing in the entry to the party room, whose door was wide open despite the air-conditioning. All the ground-floor lights had been on when he'd pulled into the driveway, and two police vehicles had stood one behind the other in his usual spot; he'd had to park in the place usually occupied by Genevieve's car.

"Our driver took him to his judo lesson at two," Genevieve told the policeman. She looked terrible, her hair disarrayed and dots and flakes of mascara on her cheeks.

Robert asked, "Was I supposed to collect him today?"

Genevieve didn't look at him. She gave the address of the judo lesson, and the policeman's eyebrows rose. He spoke in Thai and two of the uniformed men left.

"They will go there now to look," he told the Prestons.

"We should go too," said Genevieve, rising. "He'll be scared."

"Not a good place at night, Madame," said the policeman, frowning.

"All the more reason," said Genevieve, going past him through the door and getting into the Mercedes. She still hadn't looked directly at Robert.

Until he saw the empty street beside the judo lot, Robert didn't realize how clearly he'd been visualizing Philip there. How much he'd expected to see him sitting on the grass or on the packed dirt, his back against one of the trees and legs tucked up, stolidly watching the street, or face pressed against his knees, sobbing. Waiting and whole and safe. But there was no one out in the street at all, just a yellow soi dog snuffling in the gutter who lifted a wary head as the car went by.

The police had arrived already. Their headlamps were lighting up the judo yard and the small house at the back of the property, where the policemen stood talking to the judo master. He was shaking his head *no — no* in response to whatever they were asking, cutting the air with one flattened hand. Robert felt the car jolt, looked to the passenger seat and saw it was empty, then saw Genevieve running across the dirt toward the little house. He got out of the car and followed her.

"Where is he?" she was shouting at the judo

484

instructor, who looked up at her, blinking in the glare of the headlamps. "Where is he?"

"Not here," he said in English. The flat of his hand, slicing again. "Not here."

The policemen translated. Philip had been there that day; during the lesson, he had fought with another boy. The judo instructor made a punch with one fist into his other hand, then put fingertips to his eye, his lips. The fighting stopped and the judo lesson finished, everything the same. Everything the same as always. The instructor didn't see Philip leave. When he last saw him, Philip was waiting by the side of the road for the white car. The judo master didn't see the white car come. When the judo master went inside the house, the boy was waiting by the road; when the judo master came out again later, the boy was gone.

The policemen looked through the small house, pulled open every box and cabinet, any place a small boy could be hiding, and places smaller than that. They walked the judo yard with their flashlights, foot by foot. A burst of Thai from the perimeter and the head policeman went over, toward a cluster of flashlight beams trained on a spot under a tree. The judo instructor was brought over to look; he stood remonstrating, making motions to his nose and outward, like taking a mask off over and over.

The policeman came over to where the

parents stood.

"There is blood under the tree," he explained. The Americans stood expressionless. He gestured at the judo instructor. "He claims it is from the nose of the boy your son punched."

"Philip wouldn't punch anyone," said Genevieve.

Through his agony of fear, Robert felt a lancination of pride: *Good for him.*

The judo instructor was wrestled roughly, objecting loudly, into the back of the police car.

"You're taking him away?" Genevieve exclaimed as the car pulled out of the yard. Panicked, as if the man, the last known to see Philip, were a bloodhound they needed to keep here, as if he could be put on the scent to track their son to wherever he'd gone.

"We'll find out what he knows," said the policeman, without a smile.

The remaining policemen banged on the shutters of the houses on the street one after another, rousing occupants who listened to the questions, squinted at the farang couple standing together and apart, then one after another shook their heads.

"No one remembers seeing him," said the head policeman, coming back to the Prestons.

"He's a resourceful boy," said Robert. "When no one came for him, he might have walked to find a telephone."

They walked slowly the way they'd come, the way Philip might have walked. As they approached the large street, Genevieve gave a cry and her pace hastened. She ran right through a crush of smashed fruit to the edge of the curb, and would have stepped off into traffic but Robert reached her first, held her back. The policeman followed her pointing finger, putting his hand up to stop the cars, a chorus of honking rippling around him as he retrieved something from the roadway and brought it back.

Seeing it, Genevieve started to cry.

"What is it?" said Robert. Dirty patterned cloth; he couldn't make out the shape. Was it a shirt? But Philip would have been wearing his white judo outfit with no shirt underneath.

"It's the bag he carried the water bottles in," said Genevieve.

The policeman peeled the damp fabric apart. They could all hear the tinkle of broken glass.

They drove to the hospitals, Fifth Field and the Australian Nursing Home and then the Thai ones. None of them had treated an American boy from an accident that day. Genevieve pushed past the nurses as though she didn't believe them, stalked through all of the treatment rooms and out again to the front where the cars were parked.

"Where else?" she asked. "Where else?"

"Genevieve," said Robert. "Where's *your* car?"

Genevieve looked blank.

"Your car. It wasn't at home," said Robert.

"Sam had it," said Genevieve. "He drove Philip to judo at two."

Robert turned to the police. "Our other car is missing," he said. "Our driver Somchit had it this afternoon. It's just like this one, and the license plate number is almost the same — a three at the end instead of a two."

The policeman wrote down the car make and model, the license plate number, Somchit's name and description.

"Maybe he did collect Philip," said Robert.

"But he didn't take him home." Genevieve looked alert, like a dog listening to a far-off noise. "Where would he take him? Where would they go?"

"We will keep looking," the policeman told Robert. "You go home." He repeated himself gently to Genevieve. "You go home, Madame. You can do nothing more tonight."

Something in Genevieve went slack then, like a puppet string had been cut. She slumped where she stood and Robert put his arm around her, folded her gently onto the front seat of his car, scooping a trapped frill of skirt inside before shutting the door. They drove home in silence. Robert shut off the engine and got out, went around to open the

488

passenger door.

Genevieve didn't move; she was looking down, her hair loose around her face, putting it into shadow. He squatted before her, put his hands on her hands where they were knitted together in her lap.

"What do we do now?" she said, a reed of sorrow in her voice.

"I don't know," he said. He stood, and after a moment she swiveled slowly, like a very old person, to put her legs out of the car. She gave him her hand to help her out, but dropped it again as they walked toward the house. At the bottom of the front steps she turned back toward him. She looked at once much younger and much older than herself, like an exhausted teenager.

"Where were you?" she said.

"At a bar," he said.

She nodded and turned back. He watched as she climbed the steps away from him. The door opened, a bright slice of interior widening to admit her, then sealed up again.

CHAPTER THIRTY-FIVE

It was very busy during the first few days, lots of grownups in the house, people from the parties whom the children had never seen in ordinary dress, men standing with a hand in a pocket jingling change, wives with their hair under scarves. Once or twice the ambassador himself. They congregated in the party room as if it were a joyless version of one of the weekend parties, no music or fancy food and voices hushed. Mum sat inert on one of the sofas while the women bossed the servants to produce drinks and sandwiches, bending sad gazes on Laura and Bea as they passed them.

Philip wasn't home and their mother's Mercedes was missing from the driveway. There was no sign of Somchit. No one explained. It was obvious to Bea that Somchit must have crashed the car, which explained two of the three absences, but how that related to Philip wasn't clear.

Bea cornered Noi alone to ask, "Where is

490

Philip?" She stood straight to receive the answer, as if to proclaim that she was adult enough to hear it: he'd been injured, he was sick, he'd been horribly naughty and sent to live with grandparents.

"They looking," said Noi.

On the second day a policeman was escorted into the party room by Choy, his appearance banishing the low chatter; he strode down the long room toward Mum and Dad on the sofa, made a wai. The other grownups withdrew to the other end of the room, to stare over the rims of their drinks and pretend not to listen.

"We have verified the story of the fight," the policeman said. His ears stood straight out from his head, like the Pinocchio illustration in Bea's old storybook. "The other boys agree that Philip stayed afterward, to the end of the lesson. At four-thirty, he was waiting by the road. At six, he was no longer there." *What fight?* thought Bea. "We have not been able to find your car."

"It can't be that hard to find a Mercedes in Bangkok," said Dad.

"Your driver may have left the city," said the policeman. "He was not at his home, and his family and friends do not know where he is."

"They could be hiding him," Mum said. She stood, shakily. "His family and friends. Did you actually interrogate them?" Her voice was loud, aggressive. "I don't care how un-Thai it is. Have you been forceful enough to get the truth?"

"We have not been excessively polite," said the policeman. Calm, although Mum had basically been shouting at him. "We are looking for him. We are continuing to seek witnesses." He made a deep wai before leaving.

Her mother's rudeness to the policeman; that was a first. It was followed by a ream of other firsts, spilling off one after another like pages from a stack. One of the ladies going over as the policeman left, crying *Oh, my dear,* arms open for an embrace, and Mum pushing her away, actually shoving her so that the woman staggered, then walking right out of the room. In the amazed silence, Dad followed her. Both of the parents went upstairs and stayed there while the abandoned guests drank and smoked and finished the sandwiches and eventually drifted out without proper goodbyes from anyone.

Dad came down eventually, but Mum didn't. She didn't come down to dinner, nor to breakfast the next morning, and when two ladies visited that afternoon, Mum didn't come downstairs to greet them. *She'll see* me, said Mrs. Duncan in a confident voice, and Daeng shook her head, standing on the bottom step. The two women lingered there for a few baffled minutes, then finally left and didn't return.

The calendar was blown apart. Without the clockwork of the parties and the lessons, time blurred, grew indistinct; the days ground forward indistinguishable from one another. Dad didn't go to work. He brooded in the party room all day, smoking and pacing, alone. The parents' bedroom door stayed closed, with Mum behind it. The whole house seemed quenched, Daeng and Noi and Choy going through the daily chores in silence, Noi taking trays up to Mum and bringing them back down with the food barely touched. At meals, the girls ate alone at the table, the orange place mat at Philip's place terribly empty.

It rained a lot, but even between rainstorms they didn't go outside to play. Laura didn't skip rope; neither of the girls swam. They stayed in their bedroom together, went down to meals together, never far apart, as though a new gravitational force had sprung up between them. Jane came over once, neighbor Jane who still had a brother — that thought provoked a thorny blankness in Bea's mind — and who hissed in a fascinated, eager whisper *Do you think he's dead?* and tried to make Laura leave the room *so grownups can talk.* After that visit Jane was not invited back.

Bea was beginning to be impatient: Why hadn't they just found Philip and brought him home? Where was he hiding, and why? He would be in a lot of trouble when they finally found him. Somewhere inside herself there was a hard, dull kernel of understanding — that he was not hiding or being naughty — but she pushed it down in her consciousness. She wasn't sure what Laura comprehended. Laura asked no questions and seemed tranquil, even pleased by her older sister's new willingness to tolerate her company. She had always been the baby of the family, difficult matters ever out of her purview. Bea had no words to explain what was happening; she was glad Laura didn't ask.

Bea kept herself busy by reading. She did it methodically and without enjoyment, working her way through all of the books on all of the bookshelves in the house, even the grown-up ones, no one to stop or redirect her. If she didn't understand something, she dutifully passed her eyes over the words and turned the pages just as if she did, every page until the last one. She took comfort in the way the pages followed each other, the earnestness of the printed words, as if they were the most important thing in the world. As if there were an orderly, ordinary world outside of this one, where everything was in chaos.

During the daytime, the house wasn't frightening to Bea, surrounded as it was by bright sunshine, warm rain, or both, and filled with the servants busy at their tasks and the benign companionship of her little sister and the books. But at night, with darkness at the windows and the servants in the Quarters, the parents in their bedroom all the way down the hall, Bea lay awake, rigid with terror and planning, straining to hear through the hum of air-conditioning. The girls' bedroom door always stayed closed to keep in the cool, but it didn't have a lock and she watched the handle, expecting at any moment to see it turning.

She built spindly Tinkertoy creations, tall enough to make a clatter if they fell over onto the wooden floor. After her sister was asleep Bea stood two on the windowsills, leaned two more against the inside of the unlocked door. In the morning she arose before Laura, to remove them. Seeing the wooden sentries in the early light, Bea always felt foolish; but each night it was impossible to sleep until they were all balanced in their places.

On the fifth day without Philip, Bea was positioning one of the statues on the windowsill when she saw something in the garden below. There was no moon, so it was not a thing exactly but an absence of thing, a shape of darkness, larger than a person or an animal. Its smooth motion was familiar somehow, and after a few seconds she recognized it: the Mercedes, with headlamps off, was gliding slowly across the grass.

A wide panel of light fell onto the garden

— the ground-floor wall below had been flung open. As if in reply, the car's headlights went on. Through the glass of the closed bedroom window, Bea could hear shouting; then Dad was there running along beside the car. It kept rolling, pushing tunnels of light along the grass while Dad pulled at the driver's door handle and banged a hand against the window. Just at the edge of the swimming pool the car stopped. The driver's door opened, and Dad lunged at the figure who got out. A new tall shadow fell across the grass then, its base at the house and its head nearly reaching the conflict: Mum was on the terrace. The shadow began jerking and shortening, Mum running to join the men. From the dark garden beyond the car, faces appeared: the servants, almost unrecognizable to Beatrice in their sleeping garb. Mum opened the back door of the car, crawled halfway in.

There was a loud *crack,* and the car lurched and settled a little lower on one side, then more cracking and the car lurched again, the luminous channels from the headlamps angling downward into the water. Bea realized what was happening: the tiles around the pool, under the car's front tires, were bursting from the weight. Dad released his hold on the figure, who by now was recognizable to Bea as Somchit, and pulled Mum out of the car, both of them falling back onto the grass. Somchit threw himself at the Mercedes, grasping the upright of metal behind the open driver's door and planting his feet. He was dragged along briefly before he stumbled and fell onto his knees. With a long shuddering slide, its undercarriage scraping the pool edge, the Mercedes slipped into the water.

It floated for a few moments before rolling to the left, geysering water upward from the open driver's door. Debris on the surface whirled in the vortex, making tattered bobbing shadows on the lit blue water as the car rolled lazily back onto its belly and, headlamps still on, sank to the bottom of the pool.

The police came and took Somchit away; the servants filtered back to the Quarters, leaving the silhouette of the parents standing together. Finally they came toward the house, up the steps to the terrace beneath Bea's window, and disappeared inside; shortly after that the wide light was extinguished as the house wall was drawn closed. The swimming pool glowed in the dark garden for several more minutes before the car's headlamps went off. Bea watched for a while longer after that, a rectangle-inside-a-rectangle in her vision fading with each blink. Across the room, Laura had never stirred.

CHAPTER THIRTY-SIX

Noi couldn't forget the sight of Somchit in handcuffs, pleading and crying. She would never have believed he would harm a child. But Philip was missing, and Somchit had been drunk and angry when he'd driven off that day. What had he done?

Daeng went to the police station the next morning, stayed away all day. Choy reported later to Noi that Daeng had waited hours there with her daughter, but hadn't been allowed to see Somchit. The next day she did the same, and again 9 Soi Nine was left in the care of Noi and Choy. They did the cleaning, then Choy prepared lunch and Noi served the girls at the table and the master in the party room before carrying a tray up to Madame.

On the third day, Noi noticed that the larder seemed to be emptying itself. At first she thought she was imagining it, but the next morning she looked again, saw bare patches where drums of cooking oil had stood. That afternoon she saw some young men behind the house carrying a large bag of rice between them through the laundry area to the back gate, where Daeng was waiting; she closed the gate after them.

"The farang won't stay long enough to eat all that rice," said Daeng when she noticed Noi. "They won't find the boy. And then they'll go."

"Where did Somchit take him?" asked Noi.

"He swears he had nothing to do with it," said Daeng. "He says he went for a drive."

"He was gone for days," said Noi.

"He says he was afraid to come back," said Daeng. She looked at Noi, and a frown crept over her face. "All of this is *your* fault," she said. "He's besotted with you. It was your responsibility to resist him. Men are weak. Women have to be strong."

"I didn't make him drink and steal the car," said Noi. "I didn't make him hurt Philip."

"He didn't do anything to Philip," said Daeng, impatient. "Somchit is a coward and a liar, but he wouldn't hurt the boy. He's not capable of that."

Wasn't he, though, thought Noi. Not that he would have done so intentionally, but she could easily imagine Somchit having an accident while Philip was in the car, and simply driving away from the consequences. But what had he done with Philip? She had a brief image of his small face, eyes closed, sinking under brown river water, and she put a protective hand over her own belly.

Daeng saw the gesture.

"Have you decided about the medicine?" she said. Noi shook her head. "You need to do it soon. For your own good. When the farang leave, you won't get another job — not with a baby coming." She seemed struck by an idea. "You can make up for your mistakes," she said. "You can come with me tomorrow, and tell the police that Somchit was here with you that afternoon."

"But he wasn't," said Noi.

"Yes, he was," said Daeng. "He was here at three o'clock, fighting with you." She made it sound like a lovers' quarrel, that terrifying experience when Somchit was forcing his way into Noi's room. "Whatever happened to Philip happened between four-thirty and six, all the way across town. If you say Somchit was here at five o'clock instead of three . . ." She saw that Noi understood. "Tell the police exactly what really happened, but add just two hours to the time. It's not such a big lie. You can say you were ashamed to tell anyone before now. They'll believe you." She smiled, but it wasn't friendly. "And then I'll give you the medicine. And I'll teach you to read and write English. Someday you can be Number One like me. Better than babies."

Noi sat at prayer that night with a blank

mind, uncertain what to pray for. Philip's safe return, of course, but what after that? She felt unable to entreat the millet seed, who might be the size of a longan now, to stay or go. So many decisions to make. Should she tell the two-hour lie? Or tell Madame or Master about the theft? Their house was being robbed blind, all the valuables being removed. Only the bedrooms on the second floor and the party room where Master sat smoking alone day after day were untouched. He didn't seem to notice the disappearance of all the little statues, the urns, the gold-leafed panels and pressed-silver boxes. The Preston girls asked no questions, staying most of the day in their room. The household that had been like a solid locomotive felt now like a rickety cart, oxen bolting without a driver.

I want things to go back to the way they were, she whispered. How far did she want to go back, though — before Somchit, yes, but before Krung Thep also, before the fortune-telling? Everything that had happened since was bad, a tangled mess of bad. *Seven times bad, seven times good.* Her grandmother had often repeated that proverb, which counseled optimism and *jai yen,* encouraging a long view of any situation, reminding that good always came along with the bad. This situation seemed no exception: Noi could come out of it reading and writing English. Daeng wasn't exaggerating about the value of such skills: they could vault Noi to a Number One position. But first would have to come the medicine, and the two-hour lie. Maybe sometimes bad things had to happen, to make way for the good.

Noi took the breakfast tray up to Madame the next morning, pushing the door open into the cool, shuttered room. After setting the tray on the chest at the foot of the bed, she didn't withdraw as she usually did. Instead, she went to kneel beside the bed on the side where Madame lay. Madame turned over toward her.

"Are the girls all right?" she said. Her voice thin as gossamer.

"Yes, Madame," said Noi.

"Then whatever it is, Noi, you decide," said Madame. She turned away, put her face into the pillow so that the next words were muffled. "Please. You decide."

Noi sat back on her heels, then rose and left the room.

She went to Daeng, said, "If I am to lie, I need one promise: the farang must not find out."

"That's not a problem," said Daeng. "I'll tell the police you're afraid for your job. They'll believe that." She smiled. "Good girl. You'll see. This is the smart thing to do."

CHAPTER THIRTY-SEVEN

Bea was taking down a book from the book-shelf on the landing outside the girls' bedroom when she heard the bell from below. She peeked down the stairs and saw Daeng leading the Pinocchio policeman toward the party room, opening the door and ushering him in. Then Daeng ascended the staircase, went into the parents' bedroom at the other end of the hall from where Bea stood. A few minutes later Daeng came out of the room with someone who had to be Mum, but who was almost unrecognizable. The woman who had told Bea *Never greet the world looking less than your best* was dim-faced without makeup, her hair in a braid, her eyes cupped with darkness. The two of them went down the stairs and into the party room; Daeng came out again and pulled the door almost closed but not quite, holding the doorknob and listening at the crack.

Nothing audible at first, and then Mum, loud. "You can't do that!"

503

"I am very sorry," said the policeman. "It is a strong alibi." His voice devolved into an unintelligible murmur.

"They're *lying.*" Mum's voice arched up and cracked. "Whoever it is is lying to you."

More murmurs; footsteps. Daeng pulled the party-room door shut and moved around the corner just before it opened again and the policeman emerged, with Beatrice's parents behind him.

"I want him kept in custody," said Mum, summoning a frail imperiousness.

"I am very sorry," said the policeman again.

He made a somber wai, left the parents standing together in the foyer.

Mum turned to Dad. "You just stood there. Being *polite.*" Her eyes dry and bright. She put her hands onto his forearms, looked up into his face. "I can't fix this," she said. "*You* have to." Her voice was harsh. "You have to do something. You need to be a man." She was breathing hard between the words. "For once. This is the time." Dad didn't move, his eyes locked on hers. She repeated, still in that ugly voice, "This is the time."

She drew away from him and went back up the stairs and into the parents' bedroom, closed the door.

Dad stood for a minute, then went back into the party room. Beatrice heard the click of the big brass lighter, smelled cigarette smoke. It was quiet for a few minutes. She

504

reached for the book again, then started at a shattering crash from below. Another followed, and then a series of them, and then her dad strode out of the room and out the front door. From the driveway, the sound of his car starting up.

Bea crept down the stairs, went to the open party room door, and peeked in. There was a field of rubble in the near corner of the room, sharp shards and ceramic dust. From one of the larger pieces, still spinning slowly with the violence of its destruction, she recognized the pots her mother had loved. What had been precious, or merely priceless, was now worthless, beyond repair.

The doorbell went again later that afternoon. The girls were in their bedroom, Bea reading and Laura drawing at her desk. The bell rang a second time; Bea looked up. No footsteps from below. She laid a bobby pin in the book to keep her place and got down from the bed, went out to the landing. The house was deadly quiet. When the bell sounded a third time, she went down the stairs. She had never answered the door, but she'd never been told not to. She pulled the heavy door open by its central knob.

"Beatrice," said the man on the front doorstep. "How are you?"

"Very well, thanks, and you?" It was a reflex, something that popped out of all of the Preston children when the proper trigger was given, just like *Thank you for coming* provoked *Thank you for having me.*

It was irritating that he would think she'd remember him, out of all of the adults she'd met in this house. It was obvious who *she* was, the only twelve-year-old at 9 Soi Nine. But then again, he was right, she did remember him; he was one of the men Daddy worked with, who sometimes came to the parties. He was *charming like a cobra,* her mother had said of him once, and *butter wouldn't melt.*

"Where are your parents?" he said.

"Mum can't be disturbed," she said. Another stock response, used when Genevieve was having her bath.

"And your dad?"

Bea shrugged.

He looked up at the sky. "It looks like it might not rain again for a little," he said. "Let's go outside to the pool, shall we, and put our toes in the water."

At poolside, they sat on the edge, a foot or so between them. Beatrice pulled her flip-flops off and set them beside her, and the man unlaced his shoes and set them side by side, pushed the rolls of his black socks into their oval mouths.

"There's a car in your pool," remarked the man.

"Our driver drove it in there last week."

506

She lifted one foot in and out of the water, watching the drips falling from her toes. Water was clear when it dripped and blue when it all collected together, as if it could disguise its nature when isolated, but en masse some hidden essence was revealed.

"Are you and your sister all right?" asked the man. "Being fed properly, and all that?" Beatrice nodded. "Your mum and dad are very distracted right now."

"They're busy," she said, leaving off the end two words *finding Philip,* because that's what she very much wanted to believe. No matter what she'd overheard. If Beatrice let them focus on that, if she read all of the books in the house from start to finish and kept Laura quiet and occupied and didn't ask any questions, they would find Philip and all would be well.

"Do you need anything?" asked the man.

This was more puzzling. Of course she wanted things — but was that the same as needing them? This man didn't have the power to give Bea what she really wanted: Philip to come home, Mum to get out of bed, Dad to joke around the way he used to, pretending to take their allowance coins out of their ears.

She tucked her hands under her thighs and held her legs out straight, letting the water drip from her heels while she considered his question. There were water-walkers skating

507

across the pool, and dragonflies hovering and darting. Two or three pieces of green swirled in the eddy Beatrice had created by lifting her feet; along the water's edge where it lapped against the side of the pool a long clinging crust of white petals rose and fell. A little breeze kicked up, and more petals drifted from the trees to scatter themselves on the water.

"I want to help," she said, finally.

"You're very like your parents," he said. She nodded: everyone always told her how much she resembled her mother. "You have your dad's good heart." That surprised her; she looked at him directly for the first time. "You're old enough to understand this," he said, and she wanted to stop up her ears, but instead held her breath to hear the rest. "It's not going to go back the way it was," he said. She let her breath out. "No matter what happens. It's going to be different now."

"He's not coming back, is he?" she said in a small voice.

"We can hope," he said.

He looked away to give Beatrice dignity while she cried.

"You'll be all right," he said. He put his arm around her. It wasn't awkward, the way that it might be to have a grownup she hardly knew hug her. He smelled a little bit like her dad. He gave her a handkerchief to blow her nose, and took it back afterward with no hint of disgust at its burden of tears and snot. "Tuck this away," he said, giving her a small ivory-colored card. She stared at the thick pasteboard. It had nothing on it but a telephone number and a mailing address. "If you get into difficulty, you can send a letter to that address, or call that number and ask for Uncle Todd, and I will get the message. I will help in any way I can. And I will always tell you the truth when you ask."

She looked up at him, and realized what seemed wrong, what was missing. "Will you have a drink?" she said. Flooded with shame because she'd forgotten. In a clogged voice, she said, "The cook is out but I can make orange squash. And there's bottles of things in the party room." Too late, she remembered the mess of broken pottery, still lying there on the floor.

"Another time, perhaps," he said. "You go look after your sister. I believe she's alone in the house."

After Mr. Todd left, Bea went in search of the gardener, found him out back sitting and chatting to Choy.

"We need to arrange for someone to remove the car from the swimming pool," she said. "Can you do that, please, Kai?" He looked at her steadily for a few moments, then nodded. "After that, the swimming pool will need to be drained and cleaned." As Kai put down the Coca-Cola he'd been drinking and got to his feet, she turned to Choy. "Will you please come with me to the house?"

She showed the Number Two the destruction in the party room; Choy went to get a broom. After the first sweeping, Bea passed a light hand over the tile and felt a grinding tumble under her palm. "A wet cloth will get up the sharp bits," she said, and stood watching to be sure that it was done correctly, so the floor would be safe for Laura's small bare feet.

She went upstairs again, past her mother's closed door and into the girls' bedroom, where Laura was playing on the floor. Bea got onto her own bed, opened the book she'd left there, slipped Uncle Todd's card into the back of it, and lay down on her side to read. She'd turned only a few pages before looking up in annoyance to say, "Be quiet, you two."

But it wasn't *two,* it was only Laura, sitting on the round rug with a toy in each hand. She was making the toys talk to each other in small voices, the bristly stuffed fish whispering to the monkey, the monkey squeaking back. Was she playing both parts of a game meant for two? Laura and Philip had often played together. They were so much closer in age to each other than to Bea that it had almost been like having twin younger siblings. She watched for a few moments longer. Laura's chin was curved and soft like a baby's; her hands were so small.

"Let's play paper dolls," Bea suggested, closing the book.

"Really?" Laura got up immediately, abandoning the fish and the monkey. She ran to get the pad of paper while Bea drew two chairs up to her desk and set out the colored pencils.

They spent the rest of the afternoon side by side, drawing and coloring outfits, carefully cutting them out. Folding the tabs over the paper ladies' shoulders, they gave them stories: *She's going to the museum; She's going to the zoo; Time for tennis!* The events themselves were perfunctory, uninteresting: the preparation was all. Laura was completely absorbed, and Bea felt just the tiniest bit better, seeing her smile.

CHAPTER THIRTY-EIGHT

Anger kept Genevieve awake after the policeman left; she went back to bed but couldn't reenter the void she'd inhabited for a week. She wept bitterly, expecting Robert to appear, to sit by the bed and try to comfort her. She'd said terrible things to him; she would need to apologize. But he didn't come and she lay alone through the afternoon and evening in a dull envelope of grief. The door opening, the smells of food from a dinner tray, the door opening again later, then closing; she didn't move. The windows filled with darkness. She must finally have slumbered, because she was startled awake by the sudden stumbling shape of a man in the room. Truefitt & Hill No. 10 Finest, and a scent beneath it, one that activated some animal alarm in Genevieve and made her sit bolt upright: blood.

Robert fell onto his knees beside the bed, put his hands on the mattress, and dropped his head onto them. There was the source of the bleeding: his tattered, swollen hands. More like paws than the elegant hands she knew so well.

"What happened?" she said, resting her own smooth hand over the back of his neck. "What did you do?" He told her the whole long story in a hoarse whisper; she leaned close to hear. Halfway through she started to cry. He crawled up onto the bed and they wept together.

When she woke, the sun was up. Her head felt clear, the grief in her chest focused and sharp. She put her lips against the vertex of Robert's skull; he stirred. They kissed. At the end of the kiss, she drew back. "The girls must never know," she said.

He nodded.

"There's something else," he said. "I should have told you a long time ago."

"I understand," she said.

"There's more I need to tell you."

"I understand, Robert," she said, and the smooth pebble of his name in her mouth seemed to surprise them both. "There's nothing more I need to know."

He fell back to sleep but she did not. She touched her lips very gently to the broken skin over his knuckles, then slid out from under the weight of his arm and made her light-headed way to the bathroom. She opened the bottle of boiled water meant for toothbrushing and rinsed her thick-tongued mouth, then drank the rest greedily. She was repelled by her own smell rising from her crotch and armpits, by the lank greasiness of her hair. She showered, then applied careful makeup.

The girls appeared on the landing as she descended the staircase, tying a scarf over her still-damp hair.

"Are you going out, Mummy?" asked Laura.

"Just for a little while," said Genevieve. They looked big-eyed, younger than when she had last seen them. She bent and opened her arms. Laura thundered down the steps into her embrace; Bea followed more slowly. Then they were both hugging her, hard. "My goodness," Genevieve said.

"Where are you going?" said Laura.

"She's going to the salon," said Bea, scornful. "She has her scarf on."

"I'll be back soon," said Genevieve, avoiding the lie. There had been lies enough; she was choking with them. She kissed each girl. "Don't worry. I'll be back very soon."

"You're looking very thin," Max said. He was just out of the shower, still in his robe, his face ruddy and his hair curling wet over his forehead. "Let me order up a meal."

She shook her head, sat on the bed but

didn't take off her headscarf or gloves: a signal.

"The Thai police will never find him," she said. "They let the driver go yesterday. Some false alibi; I don't know why they are pretending to believe it." She kept her eyes on his. "Can you help?"

There was a long moment, something passing between them.

"We've done what we can," he said, finally. "We've had men in every back lane of this sewer of a city." His eyes soft, sorry. "We think he might have been taken out of the country."

"But why?" Puzzled. "We've had no ransom demand. Why would they keep him?"

He didn't respond, and something in her brain went white and empty.

"No," she said. "No."

He sat on the bed beside her. As he put his arms around her, she felt the gold Buddha that she wore under her clothes roll against her collarbone. The amulet of protection. Why hadn't she given one to Philip? To all of the children. To protect them against the evils of the world, not least her own poor mothering. She'd thought she'd countered every threat she could think of, down to the two oily drops pipetted daily into each small ear canal to ward off the organisms that swam invisibly with the children in the backyard pool. Yet she herself had been the danger.

Even though she loved them. Particularly Philip, who aroused a fierce protectiveness in her that the girls never had, not even Bea, who was her firstborn and who looked just like her. Philip was her son, who had come to her too early, too small, who needed extra care. Beatrice had been bottle fed with formula as was customary then, science deemed superior to nature, but Genevieve had opened her blouse for Philip, scandalizing the maternity nurses. He had lain in the curve of her arm and suckled eagerly, as if he understood how much he needed the sustenance that came from her body. *Thank you,* she'd felt. *Thank you.*

She pulled from Max's embrace, got up from the bed.

This was the last time she would ever see this room, she realized. This had been the place where she had been Jenny, thinking only of herself, pretending that she might choose her life. As if a person could direct a life instead of letting it happen. Stupid Jenny.

Genevieve raised her arms, unclasped the chain around her neck, let it cascade with a chattering rush of links into the hollow of her hand. Held it a moment, regarding the serene Buddha, before opening her fingers and tilting her palm. The necklace fell onto the carpet without a sound.

"Jenny," said Max as she went to the door.

She shook her head but said nothing, turning the knob and stepping through, closing the door of room 510 firmly behind her.

In the lobby, she stopped at the front desk; the concierge smiled and made a polite wai, *Good morning, Madame,* with no light of recognition in his eyes. She remembered the last time she'd been here, and what Noi had said again and again in the tuk-tuk, all the way home: *Master mai ru.*

"What does *mai ru* mean?" she asked the concierge. "If someone tells you that someone else *mai ru?*"

"Not knowing," the man said. "If you have secret — someone never know it."

"Like a promise," she said, remembering Noi's earnest eyes.

"Khrap khrap khrap," he said, nodding. "Yes. Someone keep your secret for you."

CHAPTER THIRTY-NINE

Philip would have loved the vehicle that came to take the car out of the pool, Laura thought. She watched from the bedroom window as it drove through the front gate, a truck with a crane in the back, hook swinging as the truck took a hard left off the driveway and cut a second set of ugly lines across the grass. A group of men jumped out of the truck's bed when it stopped; two of them dove into the pool with the hook while the others stood dry, smoking cigarettes and watching. After what seemed an interminable time, the wet men pulled themselves out and the dry men began cranking the winch mounted on the truck, the handle going around and around, the thin black cable slowly losing slack.

The car broke the surface with its grill and shiny front fender and hung there, the sun dazzling off the Mercedes symbol, the cable taut as the two men strained at the winch. Nothing except the water was moving. Everything stayed like that for what felt like a long time. Then the car seemed to surrender, coming steadily up out of the pool until it hung high from the hook, deadweight and vertical like a fish from a line, great fountains of water coming from the opened windows. All of the men struck up cigarettes as the gushing slowed to dribbles. The car hung there dripping while they smoked.

At some unclear signal the cigarettes were crushed out and one man hopped into the truck cab. The rest arrayed themselves in two rows on the truck bed as the crane swiveled and the car swung over their heads. They reached up, touched fingertips to the tires' black rubber, then their fingers and then their palms, guiding the wet beast in its descent. When the car settled onto the flatbed, the men swarmed around it with straps. Laura had a pang of sympathy for the car then, as though it were a captured animal. All of the men braced themselves against the sides of the truck and the vehicle jerked into motion. More deep ruts across the green sweep of grass, a crushed hibiscus plant, a hard right turn onto the driveway. Then it was out of the front gates and gone.

Laura played the whole episode in her head again and again, so she could describe it perfectly for Philip when he came home. Particularly that time of balance, the blunt emerged snout of the car unmoving, its peace-sign hood ornament sparkling in the sun and the reflection of the sky breaking again and again around it in the water. She memorized it so carefully that she dreamed of it for a long time, but then as the years went on she slowly forgot it all.

Their father drove them now wherever they needed to go, only two of them in the back seat so there was no need to argue: they each got a window. There were no more lessons and no more weekend parties, neither at home nor out. Their mother read them a bedtime story each night. At meals, the empty orange place mat stayed for weeks on the table with that chair pushed in, and when one day the girls came down for breakfast and Daeng had set the table with the red and green and blue and yellow place mats only, neither of the girls said anything.

CHAPTER FORTY

"We've lost the war," said the Boss.

Robert felt a rush of astonishment, although it shouldn't be surprising news. American troops had been withdrawing since August. Nonetheless, defeat seemed tall-tale impossible, the stuff of a fable, mighty steel tanks and beef-fed men vanquished by a diminutive, poorly armed peasantry.

"There will always be another," said the Boss as Robert seated himself in the chair before the desk. Robert looked at him, at his watery gray eyes and long nose. He had worked for this man for four years and did not know what he really thought of the war, of the work they had been doing. The Boss was compartmentalized, as Robert was, completely neutral. They aimed themselves where they were pointed, without ethical compunction, without underlying ethos or dogmatic zeal. It was part of their *unique suitability.*

"Has there been any word?" the Boss asked.

"They've stopped looking," said Robert. That was enough to say. No point in sharing the sickening possibilities suggested by the policeman. *By now, he is most likely out of the country. They often use luggage for transport.* Thankfully Genevieve had not heard any of that. Robert would never have expected that even such a terrible loss would have undone Genevieve as completely as it did. That was exactly how he'd describe it — she'd been *undone* as completely as a knotted rope falling open, the halves slack and separate, retaining the memory of the knot but never able to be twisted together in exactly the same way, with that same fresh perfection, again.

"Terrible," said the Boss. A sigh. He offered Robert a cigarette; he declined. "Did you want something?"

He had, of course. He'd had a purpose when he'd marched down the corridor past Miss Harch to knock on this door.

"I need to confess something," said Robert. The Boss, who was lighting his cigarette, raised his eyebrows. "About Bardin. I found him in my office one night looking through my desk and files, and he told me some rubbish story about a photograph of his being mixed into my materials by mistake. He didn't take anything," he said. "I'm not sure what he was really doing there."

The fan cranked slowly on the ceiling above

their heads.

"When was this?" the Boss asked.

"Three months ago. I should have said something."

The Boss smoked, thinking. "Which photograph?"

"A boy in a striped shirt. I told Bardin I didn't use it, but that wasn't true."

"I remember," said the Boss, nodding. "You made him an informant. That was good work." He tapped his cigarette ash into the brass ashtray with a *ting.* "Why didn't you report this before?"

"It seemed like a personal matter," said Robert. "I was wrong not to tell you."

"All right," said the Boss. "Thank you for telling me now."

Robert nodded, but didn't rise. He flexed his nearly healed knuckles where they lay hidden on his thighs, below the desk surface.

"Is there something else?" asked the Boss.

"After we go home," said Robert. "I'd like to do something more — practical."

The Boss's eyes met Robert's, and for once did not slide away. "Why?"

"I have talents that are being wasted." His heart galloping beneath the boastful words. Under the gray gaze, Robert added, "And if this is going to be my work, then I should actually *do* the work. Not play about."

A long pause.

"I agree," said the Boss.

Robert got up from his chair. He was at the door, hand on the doorknob, when the Boss spoke again.

"All we can do now," the Boss said, "is hope that when we look back, we'll see that all of this will have been worth it."

His voice held honest emotion. Robert knew that if he turned, he might glimpse the man's real face. Or maybe not. Perhaps, by this point in the man's long career, there was nothing to see.

Robert didn't look. He didn't need to see.

"I can tell you right now," he said in a rough voice. "It wasn't."

In his office he packed up his briefcase, putting Genevieve's picture in, leaving the hat rack and the potted plant. He left the building and went straight down the stairs to the car, drove away without looking back. His own life forked ahead of him: one reality in which Philip was found alive, and the other in which he was found dead. He couldn't bear contemplation of the third possibility: that he would never be found at all.

CHAPTER FORTY-ONE

Genevieve stood very still as Robert came up behind her and put his hands on her upper arms.

"It looks like we're going home," he said.

"We can't leave," she said, not turning. "Robert. We can't."

"Sweetheart," he said. "He's not here. If he were still here, they'd have found him."

That was wrong, she thought. He was so small. He could be hidden anywhere.

"We can't stay forever," said Robert. "You know that."

From the floor below, she could hear Noi and Choy working together to clean the dining room, their murmured Thai, the little noises as they lifted each chair and set it down the way she'd taught them, so that the floor didn't get scraped.

She walked out of his arms, toward the window. It was bright midafternoon. At the front of the house, one Mercedes sat dusty in the driveway; in the side garden, Kai clipped a flower border with long-bladed shears. The swimming pool had been emptied and cleaned and refilled after the car was taken out of it, and Bea and Laura were in it, leaping like two ivory dolphins. Little wavering lines of heat danced off the vivid tableau of fuchsia flowers, emerald grass, blue water.

To be seven again, thought Genevieve, watching Laura windmill her arms, sending arcs of water up against the sky. Seven and pure, in that clean baptismal water. To wash it all away, and start again. She wanted to walk into that oblong font, to lie back in it and swallow it and feel it cover every part of her skin. But of course that water would be sullied by her entry. Nothing had the power to absolve her.

Perhaps Master mai ru, she thought, *but I will never allow myself to forget.*

"We'll take Noi with us," she said, not turning. "If she wants to come."

CHAPTER FORTY-TWO

Noi's family was uniformly enthusiastic about the proposition of her move to America. They were saving for Nok's wedding, which had to be grand enough to befit a royal lotus blossom. Choy, however, was skeptical, asking why Noi would travel so far to be a servant when she could be a servant right here. Daeng said nothing then, but that night she came to Noi's room.

"Why haven't you taken the medicine yet?" she demanded. "You can't wait much longer. Especially if you're going to America. Farang don't like babies made without husbands." Without waiting for Noi to reply, she added, "And you shouldn't go to America. You'll be trapped there, a slave."

"Madame said I could go to school," said Noi.

Daeng made a scornful noise. "Even without a baby, there wouldn't be school," she said.

"How is Somchit?" Noi ventured.

"That dog," said Daeng. "He must have another girlfriend already; he went to her after getting out of jail. Hiding from his responsibilities. Don't worry about him. Worry about my daughter, trying to feed her children." She gave a short laugh. "Worry about yourself."

After Daeng left, Noi's mind rattled with all that she'd said. Would going to America be stepping into a trap? That the Prestons wanted to take her reassured Noi that the police hadn't revealed what she'd told them. She'd had to repeat the two-hour lie over and over while they interrupted her and tried to confuse her. *How do you know what time it was?* they'd demanded. *I could hear the radio playing next door,* she'd said. *The five pips went just before Somchit came.* Finally, they'd written it all down on a paper and made her put her name at the bottom. It hadn't helped anything that she'd done it — Somchit had been freed from jail, yes, but according to Daeng, he'd now abandoned his family. It hadn't hurt anything either, though. It had been an unimportant lie after all.

Daeng had said: *Worry about yourself.* But Noi was making choices not only for herself now. Maybe the medicine was the right choice for the longan. Which would be more terrible: to be born only to suffer and starve, or to be given a chance to go back, and be born into a different life?

She thought of the basket, the fat kicking legs.

I can't do this, she thought. She was a weed trying to hold back a boulder of destiny. She sent a silent cry into the universe: *P'Sao, I need you.* She didn't expect an answer. For the first time Noi thought that perhaps she had invented all those visits from her sister; maybe they had been nothing but homesick dreams.

You should go back, she told the baby in her mind, just before falling asleep. *You deserve a better mother than me.*

When the rush of blood came in the middle of the night, Noi knew that the baby had heard her.

Choy pushed open Noi's door in the morning, took in the situation at a glance, went away and came back with a sheaf of broad leaves from the banana tree and a bottle of juice. She made Noi roll onto her side and smoothed a leaf onto the mat beneath her. She put the bottle to Noi's lips, held it there for a long swallow.

"Stay in bed and drink the rest of that," Choy said. "If anyone notices you are missing, I will tell them it is your *pracham duan.*"

Noi's body took two days to expel the longan; she lay sweating on her sleeping mat with her *pha tung* over her and a banana leaf beneath her to collect the blood. She dozed when the turmoil in her belly would let her, and woke sticky every few hours in the small room that increasingly smelled like damp metal. She moved only to drink the juice that Choy brought, or to add a banana leaf when necessary, putting a clean one on top of the bloody one and lying down again. Choy came in the evening with more leaves, took the others away.

On the second night the skies burst open with rainstorms, and the clenches of pain grew longer and longer, the pain-free intervals shorter. Noi felt cold despite the heat, shivering alone on her pallet with the cushion of leaves below her pelvis. Her vision went white and green and she saw things in the corners of the room, scurrying animals that turned into shadows. In the middle of a long cramp that made her want to cry out — surely she would die from this — she felt her sister's hand on her brow. Noi jumped with surprise: no sound of amulets had heralded her arrival.

Nong Noi, said Sao. *This will end soon.*

"It feels like it will never end," said Noi through gritted teeth.

Drink some water, Sao said.

Noi drank from the jar of water beside the mat, then held her breath through another long spell of pain.

Drink more, said Sao, *and then I will sing to you.*

Noi drank again, lay back against her sister's body. She teased shakily, "You don't sing very well."

I sing to Moo all the time, said Sao. *You have to sing to babies, to help them sleep.*

"Oh," said Noi, at the mention of babies. "Oh."

I'll sing a song about rain, said Sao. *It is a very pretty song, with many verses.*

Noi closed her eyes and watched the patterns swirling on her eyelids; Sao smoothed the matted strands of hair that lay over Noi's forehead and ears and began to sing, in a deep timbre that was nothing like the high off-pitch crooning that Noi remembered from their childhood. The low sound filled the room like water, rising to Noi's bare knees, and then to her chin, and then to the sill of the window; it rose almost to the ceiling before it dropped and sank around Noi like a blanket, and she slept.

When Noi awoke, she was alone and the pain was gone. She tied the *pha tung* around her and went through the garden on trembling legs, through the back gate and across the alley to the khlong. She stepped in and squatted, skirt floating up around her waist, scooping water over her thighs and up between them, using her fingernails in places to

531

loosen the crusted, clotted blood. She crouched for a long time in the warm water, letting the current rock her, until the sky overhead began to lighten. A water taxi went past, carrying a row of orange-garbed monks, their shaved heads like peas lined up in a pod. She stood, squeezed the soaked cloth of her skirt, made its hem into two tails and tied them. In the heat of sunrise she waded out of the khlong.

Choy helped her burn the banana leaves in the alley.

"Maybe he'll come back to you later," Choy said as they watched the smoldering pile. "When you are ready."

"It was a girl," said Noi.

The baby had decided for both of them. Noi would go to America. The weed would blow a little farther, that's all, a little farther away from home.

On the day of departure, Daeng gave Noi a small paper bag.

"Lunch," Daeng said in her growling voice. Then, "You're stupid to go." She turned and walked away.

When everyone was asleep on the airplane, Noi opened the bag. She found a small fabric-wrapped square at the bottom, below the packages of food. Inside, an amulet for her neck chain, a Phra Kring Buddha in a silver surround. She shook it beside her ear, listening through the roar of the airplane engines for the noise from inside, the sacred bead repeating the Buddha's name. The amulet would have cost a good deal in the shops, but Noi knew it was one of Daeng's own; she'd seen it in the cluster on the chain around the woman's neck.

There was also a note on a folded paper. It was written in English; Noi studied the light pencil strokes that wobbled like spider legs. She had no idea what the note said; she folded it carefully and put it away, until she could find out.

Chapter Forty-Three

Genevieve left the loose linen dresses and the sandals, the ruined, sweat-stiff gloves. All of the wide-brimmed hats. Over Philip's clothing she hesitated, the soft stacks of shorts and singlets and the green school uniform, the white socks with the colored line of stitching across their toes. He'd worn them all, they'd lain against his skin. She lifted a shirt, pressed it to her face, smelled nothing: it had been laundered into anonymity. She laid it down again, told Choy to dispose of all of it.

She did keep one of the going-home sweaters, the one originally intended for Beatrice to wear on the airplane ride back to America at age nine, after the promised single year in Bangkok. It would just fit Philip now. It was a sensible navy, good for a boy or a girl. Just in case they found him. She would button him into it and say, *You'll need this, it gets cold where we're going, it's not always hot like here.*

PART 5

PART 5

CHAPTER FORTY-FOUR
2019

Laura awoke to a smell of breakfast. She found Bea and Philip in the kitchen, Bea at the stove cooking eggs and sausage, Philip slicing tomatoes at the counter.

"Hello, sleepyhead," said Bea, seeing Laura. She looked chipper and well rested, no sign of effects from the brandy or having been up much of the night. "Take Mum a cup of coffee, will you?"

Laura chatted with Genevieve in the sun-dappled dining room, sipping Bea's excellent coffee and listening to the noises from the kitchen, rattles of cooking and a low murmur of conversation punctuated with occasional laughter. Bea brought the food out on platters and called upstairs to Noi, who came down with her phone at her ear.

"I hire too many stupid people," Noi said after ending the call. She took a plate and sat to eat, joined the loose conversation. It was Monday but no one was hurried; to Laura it all felt low-key festive, like the comfortable interstices of a holiday after the main events were complete, Boxing Day brunch or the morning after a wedding. "Someone needs to see about the tree," said Genevieve at one point, as if she too perceived a holiday vibe.

"I've reached out to Uncle Todd about Mum's birthday," said Bea from down the table. Laura nodded, mouth full, feeling heroic for not rolling her eyes. "And Noi, we have to talk about the night nurses."

"Later," said Noi, taking her vibrating phone from beside her plate and getting up. "What," she said into the phone. "I *told* you." They could hear her uninterrupted speech as she carried the phone through the living room and out onto the side porch.

A few minutes later, a *Hellooo* from the entry hall heralded the arrival of Philip's physical therapist; as the two of them went into the living room, Genevieve's day nurse arrived and took her upstairs for a *washy-uppy,* Bea scowling at the nursery language. Laura and Bea cleared the table and washed the dishes together, then headed upstairs to strip and remake the beds.

In the basement laundry room, Laura dropped the puffy tangle of linens into the hamper, then dug out her phone and texted Edward: How's the day going?

No response: he was probably in a meeting. She had a gritty-eyed, sleep-deprived feeling, but apart from that she felt good, energetic. Maybe she'd go up into the studio today.

When Laura came out of the basement, Bea was coming down the main staircase.

"I was thinking," she said. As she came to stand beside Laura in the center hall, Philip's physical therapist urged from the sunken living room, *Keep your shoulders back.* "Since we're both here without a car. Maybe we could use that app you're always using, to call a ride and go to your house? You could give me a tour." Into the pause after this astonishing statement, the physical therapist's voice floated, *Good work. See you Wednesday.* "We could stop by that shop on Connecticut and pick up some of that jam Mum likes."

"That would be nice," said Laura.

Bea and Laura moved apart as the physical therapist crossed the center hall between them, smiling, then ran down the few steps to the flagstone entry hall and out the front door.

"Apparently I *hunch,*" said Philip, navigating the steps up from the living room to the center hall where his sisters stood. "It weakens my rotator cuff."

"Join the club," said Bea.

"Right," said Laura. "She of the perfect posture."

"I hunch," protested Bea.

"I have a hunch you don't," said Philip. The girls groaned at the pun.

As he reached the top step, the light from the upper-landing windows fell across his face, lighting his scalp like downy blond hair. There were his eyes, the shy crooked smile, that horizontal dimple, like their father's. Like Laura's own. He wavered, and Bea put out her hand to steady him just as Laura did the same. The three Preston children stood balanced together, in the center of their family home. Laura felt a pure tone of happiness in her chest — and then a sudden quiet.

"Where *were* you?" Laura demanded.

"What?" said Philip.

"You could have contacted us. You could have come home long before now." Harsh, angry. "I saw the doors in that house; there were no locks on them. There wasn't even a lock on the gate. Why did you stay away?"

"Laura," said Bea, a sharp syllable. "Stop it."

"*You* stop it," said Laura, dropping Philip's arm, turning on her sister. "Stop treating me like a child."

"Stop behaving like one," said Bea.

It was the first discord between them in weeks, yet it jumped up instantly and enormous, like a spark applied to a chronic invisible hiss of gas, a giant panel of flame appearing out of the air.

"We were having such a good day," Bea said. "Why do you have to ruin it?"

"I'm not the one," said Laura, but she knew she was, she was ruining things. She felt a tsunami of rage building inside her. "We could have all grown up together," she said. "He took that from us."

"He didn't take anything," said Beatrice. "He was the *victim.*"

"I'm not —" began Philip, but Laura rode over his voice.

"Yes, let's all get into our boxes," she told Bea. Hearing her own snotty tone and hating it, unable to stop. "Philip's the victim, I'm the baby. You're the perfect one."

"Are you not happy unless others around you are *un*happy?" said Bea.

"Girls, stop squabbling," called Genevieve from upstairs.

"Sorry," chorused the girls. They glared at each other.

"You think only of yourself," hissed Bea.

"*Someone* has to," said Laura.

Bea's face went very white.

"That's all I have ever done," said Bea. Her words evenly spaced, emphatic. "I have babied you your whole life." She spat out the next sentence: "Where were you when the boys were born?"

"What?"

"I asked you to be there, and you didn't come. I know — you thought I didn't need you." It was exactly what Laura had thought. "I was forty-three years old, Laura. The odds weren't great. I was scared. I wanted my sister."

"You could have told me," said Laura. Bea,

scared? It seemed oxymoronic.

"You shouldn't have had to be told." Bea was furious. "You *are* a child, Laura. I have spent an enormous amount of energy allowing you to be a child. And you — have squandered all of it. You threw away college; you married an idiot, then threw your marriage away. And what do you have now? An empty monstrosity of a house, paintings that no one will buy. A nice man who loves you, but you're doing your damnedest to sabotage that."

"What?" said Laura.

"I shouldn't have said that," said Beatrice. Her face stricken, the anger suddenly gone.

"What did you mean, *paintings that no one will buy*?" said Laura.

"Please," Philip said in his soft, not-quite-American voice. "Please stop fighting."

Laura rounded on him.

"Talk about being babied," she said. "We've all been tiptoeing around you. *Why* haven't you told us anything about what happened? *Why* didn't you come home? Mum spent her life grieving you, looking for you. Daddy *died.*" Their father's death hadn't been caused by Philip, but Laura wasn't making sense now, rage flowing out of her like a malignant honey, indiscriminate, engulfing everything. "You broke our family," she shouted.

Iron fingers were on her arm.

"Quiet," Noi said.

"I'm only telling the truth," said Laura. She stared around at the ring of faces. "Why do we never, ever tell the truth to each other? Why do we keep so many *secrets*?" She tore her arm from Noi's grip. "I'm done," she said. "I fucking quit this family."

She went the back way, through the kitchen and out the side door, down the path that ran through flanking panels of herbs, to the back gate that led to the alley. The way she used to go when she was new here and exploring. Down the alley, a sprint across the parkway whizzing with cars, down the grassy bank to the buried creek. She began walking, balancing on the domed stones with the traffic going by above her, ignoring the phone alerting from her pocket. When the creek swelled into a broad rush, she stepped to the bank and kept going.

When finally she ascended the slope of grass to reach the sidewalk, she was at the back entrance to the zoo. She made her way through the clumps of selfie-taking tourists and emerged through the front gates with feet squelching and wet, walked to the corner and waited at the light beside the kiosk where the notice of the stuffed pink pig still cried LOST.

Only a few more blocks to get home. Or rather, what she called home: an empty house, a quiet studio, a half-scraped canvas. Bea's words came back to her: *Paintings no one will buy.* And *I have babied you your whole life.* Those two sentences collided in her mind; in a flash Laura understood.

She took out her phone and flicked away all of the notifications, opened the ride-sharing app.

Chapter Forty-Five

"I need to talk to him," said Laura, pushing through the front door of the gallery.

A startled Kelsey looked up. "He's not here," she said. And then, "Are you okay?"

Laura looked down at herself: sopping shoes, jeans cuffed with a crust of mud.

"Not really," she said. And then she burst into tears.

Kelsey's face froze for a moment, lips pulled back from her teeth in a mask of fearful repugnance. Then she stood, strode to the front door, and turned the OPEN sign to CLOSED.

"Fuck 'em," she said when Laura tried to protest. "Come on." She bustled Laura through the main gallery room into the back office, gently pushed her onto the Le Corbusier knockoff sofa. "What's happening?"

"I'm a fraud," said Laura. "My work is bullshit."

"Your early work was great," said Kelsey, perching at the other end of the sofa. Clearly unaware of how crushing it sounded — *early work* and *was.*

"I mean the Ghost Pictures."

"Well, *I* don't get them," said Kelsey carefully. "But that's just me. I don't get a lot of the art that we show here."

"Sullivan has been lying to me," said Laura. "No one has been buying those paintings. He's been letting my sister buy them. They've *both* been lying to me."

"Ugh," said Kelsey. She produced a small crackling bag from her pocket, took something from within, tucked it into her mouth. "Want one?" She held out the bag. Laura looked: a single translucent amber gummy bear. She shrugged and took it, put it onto her tongue.

"Why couldn't he just tell me?" said Laura. "I trusted him."

"He must have thought he was helping," said Kelsey.

"He wasn't." Laura's mouth was filled with juicy pear, the gummy bear's flavor seeming to intensify as it melted. "This is delicious," she said.

"Right?" said Kelsey. "And super mild too. Just takes the edge off."

"What?" said Laura. She had just swallowed the last fragment of bear.

"It's an edible," said Kelsey. "Weed." Then carefully, with an air of translating to a foreigner, "Marijuana."

Laura's only experiences with pot had been back when it was still called that, surreptitious joints with high school friends in Georgetown alleys, bitter smoke in burning lungs that brought paranoia more often than pleasure. It was *weed* now, and from what she'd heard a totally different substance, much more sophisticated and potent — also locally legal.

"Sorry sorry sorry," said Kelsey. "I thought you knew. Should you make yourself throw up?" At Laura's look, she said, "I mean, maybe that would work?"

"I don't know if it would work, but I know I'm not doing that. How long does it last?"

"A few hours?"

What the hell. "I guess I'm here for a while." She sighed. "You can go back out front and open the gallery again. I don't want you to get in trouble."

Kelsey shook her head. "Sullivan's in New York, prepping a new show."

A pang. Laura hadn't had work in the New York space since 2015.

"I can't believe he lied to me," she said. The drug hadn't hit her yet. It was like being a teenager again, the endless checking on herself — *Am I high yet? How about now?*

"Did he, though?" said Kelsey. She had pulled a lock of her long hair straight between pincer fingers and was examining the ends.

Laura remembered Sullivan saying *gimmick.*

"I guess he did try to tell me. And I guess I shouldn't have had to be told." It was almost a relief to say it: "I haven't made anything good in years. If anything I made was ever really any good." That was a thought: maybe her artistic block was less of a block than an epiphany. Real artists couldn't afford the indulgence of a block, had no safety net like the Preston trust. Real artists painted through a crisis, painted their way out of corners. Maybe Laura had been deluded, thinking she had talent, following a shred of attention from her mother. Like a puppy crawling toward the smell of milk.

"It was," said Kelsey. She released the hair she'd been examining, swept it back into the rest of her mane. "Your stuff from the two thousands was insane." Almost twenty years ago; it felt like a minute. "Maybe you're just in a slump. You know, like a baseball player with the yips." On the heels of that surprising analogy, "You just need to snap out of it."

"Sullivan said I need to be more of an asshole."

"*Sullivan* can be an asshole sometimes." Kelsey looked an *Oops*. "Um, are you guys — ?"

Laura shook her head. "I actually thought that you two might be."

"Eww. I mean, no offense, but dude is old," said Kelsey.

"He's younger than I am," said Laura.

Kelsey had a faint silver scar under her chin. Wait. Why was Laura looking up at her chin?

"Fuck," said Laura. She realized that she must have slid off the sofa at some point; she was lying on the floor. "You said this was mild."

"It is," said Kelsey, leaning over, her face floating above Laura, flanked by two curtains of hair. "Very mellow."

Crown molding ran all around the office ceiling, of the exact type Edward had been seeking to restore a broken bit in the parlor of his house. *Edward.*

"I'm getting married," Laura told the ceiling.

"Wow," said Kelsey, not so much in congratulations as in wonder. She began to laugh. "That's awesome."

Laura wasn't sure why it was funny, but she was laughing too.

And then she was telling Kelsey about Adam. How at first it had seemed to be that rare thing, a marriage of equals. Neither of them wanted children, and they were each tolerant of the other's long working hours. Marriage didn't change their lives much: Laura still stayed overnight at the Tudor pretty often, still made solo trips to New York to haul slides around to galleries, collecting rejections until one day a young gallery assistant with a freshly inked MFA said *Oh, wow* as he put one slide up against the light.

Her first piece in a group show was singled out by reviews, described by one critic as *muscular* with more than a whiff of insult, of *How dare she.* More group shows followed, in Long Island, then Brooklyn, then Manhattan, hand over hand across a gorge of striving years. Until the watershed: a one-woman show at Sullivan's Upper East Side space. Laura attended the opening alone; Adam had had a last-minute work thing. It was like a dream: flutes of champagne, red Sold dots speckling the walls, collectors buttonholing her to discuss her work — all rather overwhelming after so long painting alone in a basement. After one particularly heady conversation with a critic, Laura had taken refuge in the gallery office and used the phone there to dial Adam on his flip phone, gabbling a giddy flood of detail into the receiver after he said hello. *That's great, babe,* he said when she paused for breath. In the background, a muffled trill of female laughter.

Laura hung up the phone, went robotically through the rest of the evening, stayed at the Tudor for a sleepless night. When she confronted Adam the next day, he said *What did you expect?*

"It wasn't the sex," Laura told Kelsey. "Well, it was and it wasn't." After the 1980s, sex wasn't just intimacy anymore, it was risk. Laura and Adam didn't use condoms — she was on the pill — and she had known without asking that Adam wouldn't have used condoms with those faceless women either. "He took my life in his hands," said Laura.

"In his dick," said Kelsey solemnly.

"In his dick," agreed Laura.

Kelsey was prettier than Laura had remembered, lips plump with youth, eyes clear and bright in their spiky settings of eyelash.

"You're really pretty," said Laura.

"Thanks," said Kelsey lightly.

"My sister has been buying my paintings," Laura said. "Out of pity."

"You told me."

"And Sullivan lied to me."

"I know," said Kelsey, mom-patient.

"He wants me to be more of an asshole," she said. "And Edward wants me to be a wife."

"It's not about the men," said Kelsey. "It's not about what they want."

"Maybe I need to be free," said Laura. "Maybe that's the answer."

"Maybe you should talk to someone, dude," said Kelsey. "I mean, not me. Someone real."

"You're too young to know how it is," Laura said. "We're all bursting with sadness."

"I will not be bursting with sadness when I am old," declared Kelsey.

"Hashtag life goals," said Laura. She closed her eyes. "I quit my family," she murmured.

"Let me know how that works out for you," said Kelsey.

When Laura got home, she climbed the three flights up into the studio and stood in the stagnant, sunbaked air. She'd been so proud of it. She'd been thirty-four when her marriage ended, and she didn't want to paint in a basement anymore. She'd scoured the city listings looking for light and space, and finding nothing suitable, had bitten into the trust against her sister's objections and *added* the light and space she needed to the top of a rundown town house on the crest of a hill. She remembered the day the renovation was finished, how she had sat in the cupola of light inhaling the sawdust-clean smell of new construction, longing to share the moment with someone. One of her art school friends, or her mother, who was across the world, or even Bea, who had been so po-faced about the expenditure. The person she really wanted, she realized, was her father. As a child, she'd sometimes helped him with hobby construction projects, birdhouses and small repairs to the Tudor; she'd loved those hours with him, the grave, preoccupied man she knew replaced by someone warm and humorous, even silly. Stupidly, as though it were a discovery, she realized how final it was, death. She had looked around at the (all hers!) giant box of glass and air, and thought:

I will start again from here.

And she had. She *had* created good work here. It wasn't a whim of childhood. Her mother may have ignited the flame, but hadn't had anything to do with the rest of it, the utter deep wild joy of it. With a sudden flush of conviction, Laura understood that whether or not she had real talent didn't matter: whatever the truth was, if she had it all to do over, she'd still choose the paint.

Her eye fell on the half-scraped canvas still propped on the easel, and she felt brought up short. How could she explain that? Why the joyless, rote Ghost Pictures, why four years of *paintings no one will buy*? Just a slump, as Kelsey had said, something to snap out of? Laura had done some of her best work when she was angry and sad — after leaving New York, and after Adam — but she was no longer young. She was fifty-four and weary. Could she find her way through the paint all over again?

She went out onto the terrace, into the summer evening, and stood at the rail. To the south was a row of narrow town houses that had been rehabbed into condos with wide glass windows; in one of those, Laura could see a young family. It was toddler mealtime, the child bouncing in her seat, waving her spoon, the parents on either side all business: *Eat up.* The child threw her spoon at the window, making a green splat on the glass.

She froze, her face purely astonished. Then her mouth shaped into a joyful caw and she pointed, turning her head to her parents, one and then the other: *Look. Look!* The parents broke into smiles. Happiness ricocheted between the three faces before the mother bent to retrieve the spoon from the floor and the father rose to wipe the window. Laura felt herself smiling too. Then had a scorching thought: In fifteen years those parents might be separated, by death or betrayal or resentment; that child might be suffocating in adolescent sadness. This bright moment, this happy day, would have amounted to nothing.

All we have is now, she thought.

She recalled the damp, rain-puckered poster on the kiosk outside the zoo, the forlorn pink pig who was almost certainly lost forever. Another nidus of sorrow: the lost pig, the child who mourned him. She felt a swell of anger toward the well-meaning parents who had posted the sign. Who had taken the cowardly path, pretending there was a fix to the problem instead of doing the more difficult thing of teaching the child about loss, about its inevitability and how to live past it.

It was abruptly obvious to Laura, what she and everyone usually managed to forget: Life was a sucking cornucopia of loss, everyone teetering on its edge all the time, all the precious things at risk every moment. Childhoods and pink pigs and best friends, lovers and brothers and parents and children, whole lives and histories perpetually rushing into the ravenous funnel of oblivion. It wasn't possible to cherish them enough before they were taken away.

CHAPTER FORTY-SIX

1980

Robert is at work when his life ends.

He has a pencil in his hand; he's tapping it against the desk in couplets, three of them in a row, then space, then repeat. It's a habit that he indulges only when he's in this office, alone. It cropped up last year after he quit smoking, cold-turkeying it without telling anyone, while Genevieve was out of town. Bea was at college and teenage Laura didn't notice; she was always on the phone or in her room listening to music or babysitting or out with friends. Noi probably did notice that the ashtrays stopped needing to be emptied, but she said nothing. With the crutch of tobacco whisked away, Robert had at first leaned on drink; after several fuzzy evenings he eased back on that and entered a short period of volatility, mood swings perceived only by his secretary, before finally reaching an endpoint of brisk clarity — accompanied by the new pencil-tapping habit.

Quitting smoking wrought other changes, imperceptible to him. Without the constant pinching effect of carbon monoxide, his arteries relaxed, providing less resistance to each squeeze of his heart. Without the chemical irritation, the inflamed interior of his blood vessels began to heal, their deposits of yellow cholesterol to disintegrate.

This day, Robert's last, he's stayed late at work. After his secretary left for the day, he'd locked the door behind her and taken a large envelope from beneath the desk blotter, slid out the heavy stack of satellite surveillance photographs and begun to scrutinize them methodically. Top to bottom, left to right. They're a new technology, grayscale and grainy, difficult to read, but by now Robert has accumulated a good bit of practice. On the fifth image he sees it: the boy who could be Philip.

He can't let himself look more closely until he has cleared his desk surface completely, putting everything away into drawers and file cabinets. When that is done, he centers the photograph perfectly on the blotter and begins to examine it all over again, starting in the upper left corner. When he gets to the collection of gray and white shadows near the middle of the picture he is snagged again by the figure's posture, the way the head is held. It could be Robert himself as a teenager. He checks the coordinates printed on the margins of the image, goes to retrieve an atlas from the bookshelf across the room. At that moment, a cholesterol plaque ruptures in the wall of his left main coronary artery.

The exposed interior of the plaque is fluffy, like stuffing burst from a plush animal. The fluff doesn't itself impede blood flow, but it releases a host of attractant humors that call to platelets floating by in the passing blood, and like unreasoning, obedient infantry, the platelets respond. They have one power, to turn sticky, and they do that, clutching together on the soft exposed material of the ruptured plaque, building a precarious bramble of clot. Robert is reaching for the atlas when a pinpoint of clot breaks off and rushes down the open channel, entering the left anterior descending artery and passing into one of the diagonal branches. Down the narrowing diameter it hurtles until it sticks, corking up the flow of blood to the heart muscle beyond. Robert feels a twinge of pain, touches a fist to his chest, and coughs, as though to dislodge something.

That bit of clot dissolves; the pain goes away. Upstream, clot is still growing on the ruptured plaque. For some time, while Robert takes the atlas down and opens it on his desk, there's a balancing act going on, enzymes in his blood working to break down the clot as fast as it accumulates. The artery is nearly the diameter of a pea, the clot fluttering frantically at its margin. While Robert is paging through the atlas, the dissolution begins to outpace the accumulation: the battle is being won.

But then a large portion of clot detaches from its fragile mooring and tumbles down the left main coronary artery, into the mouth of the left anterior descending artery. Robert, bent over at his desk with his finger on the tangled blue and green of a map, feels a suction of air from the room.

He thinks, *Not yet.* He thinks, *I'm only forty-four years old.*

There's still some space around the obstructing clot at first, allowing a small amount of blood flow, but platelets attach themselves and patch up the opening, and then Robert is on the floor. No one hears him fall. No one would hear him if he were to cry out. The office was expressly built to make eavesdropping impossible; there are sound-deadening buffers within the thick walls. *I haven't fixed things yet.* That's his next thought, as he reaches a heavy hand upward, toward the telephone on the desk above him. He hasn't known consciously that he was planning to fix things, but suddenly he does know it. He had meant to find a way to lead Genevieve back — not necessarily to happiness, or to his bed, but to some kind of peace. She'd stop inventing excuses to return to Asia, she'd find a focus at home on which to expend her restless energy. Maybe her two daughters. He's meant to fix them too. He has things he wants to tell them: Bea needs to drop whatever burden she is carrying, or she'll end up too hard to be happy; if Laura doesn't grow up soon, she never will.

With a monumental effort, he grasps the hanging cord of the phone and pulls, and the whole thing falls down with a crash beside him, the receiver jumping away from the base and droning a dial tone into the air. He rests his hand on the quilt of push buttons: Whom to call? His elder daughter is at college. His younger daughter is spending the night with a friend. His wife is out of the country. Again.

He and Genevieve had argued before she left — or what passed for arguing between them at this point. He'd asked her *Should we have a funeral?* and when she'd raised her eyes to his he'd gone on, *Some kind of good-bye? It's been eight years. We have two children who might benefit from closure.*

We have three children, she'd said.

And then he said it, the thing that he'd been afraid to say.

She had to know he'd been thinking it. Robert was an only son, of a sparsely fruited family tree. His sister could not carry the name, nor his daughters. Robert's parents' effusiveness after the arrival of Philip had made clear — by contrast to their restraint after firstborn Beatrice — how much this had

560

mattered to them. In retrospect, it seemed almost destined that the boy would slip away: that wizened pale sultana of a baby had been far too small to bear the weight of a dynasty.

"We could have more children," Robert had said softly.

At forty-two Genevieve is still beautiful, and few would suspect her age, but Robert knows that it's possible his point is moot — there may be no plush womb there anymore to nurture an infant. He has no idea how all that is progressing. He doesn't peek into the bathroom drawer where she keeps her female supplies, doesn't know if the drawer holds pads or tampons or hormone supplements or anything at all.

When he said those words, *more children,* Genevieve's expression changed.

Robert's grandfather had been fond of safari, the walls of his den at home crowded with hairy heads. As a small boy visiting that house, Robert had been unable to turn in any direction without encountering the indictment of their glass-eyed stares. Not that Robert's grandfather had dug out the eyeballs himself, or cut the heads off himself, or carried any of the pelts or heads himself. Those tasks were accomplished by the attendants who stared out from some of the framed black-and-white photos also on the wall, the whites of their eyes making glowing dots against their dark skin. Robert's grandfather spoke of them with affection, pointing them out and using their names — *Maba, he was little but so strong* — but also in a way that made them seem like children or beasts, excluded from having their own motivations, or preferences about what they might rather be doing in place of serving the whims of the *muzungu* hunter.

Looking into Genevieve's eyes that evening after he'd said *more children,* Robert had been reminded of those taxidermied heads. It had been the same gaze: the trophy regarding its collector.

At one point, he had envisioned the two of them as something like the game the girls played in the backyard of the Tudor, punching a ball strung to the top of a metal pole back and forth at each other. Genevieve was the orb, flying around stick-in-the-mud Robert. If he stood immovable, she'd wrap around and around on her string until she was nestled close. He had had that analogy in mind six years ago, when he'd refused to help in any way with her first return to Asia. Instead of discouraging her, the solitary venture had taught her self-sufficiency, and when Robert did accompany her on a later trip he felt like an acolyte moving along in her shadow. She traveled through the slums with flabbergasting ease. *Take your vitamins, Lolly,* she'd call to a giggling Thai girl on the street, and *Okay, Miss Gen,* the girl would call back. They called her Miss Gen, not Madame, another shock. Robert hadn't known about that nickname. He felt reduced by it, appendiceal — *Madame* had incorporated his own existence. *Miss Gen* stood alone.

After saying *more children,* he finally realized that his ball-and-stick analogy was fatally flawed. No matter how deeply he'd planted himself, her orbit had grown only wider, the fettering string stretching to its limit. Just a matter of time until the ball broke free and sailed away.

His compulsions had returned after Genevieve began traveling; they came back stronger than ever, as if he had been holding his breath for years and had to gasp. Not just the checking, but new behaviors, so insidious that at first he did not notice them. Tapping his fingers against his thumb, one-two-three-four and back again, four-three-two-one. Both hands, each finger touching separately, exactly the same. Others noticed, though, and one day he saw a subordinate across the office imitating him, hands held up beside his head like a man adjusting his mustachios, mincingly tap-tap-tapping the fingers while an appreciative audience snickered. From a good distance away, Robert recognized it instantly, felt a hot sweep of embarrassment. His impulse was to swerve into the men's room before he was seen, but instead he continued walking, steadily approaching the group, the laughing faces spotting him over the shoulder of the joker, the laughter dying away.

"Hoskins," said Robert.

The joker froze.

There was a delicate silence. The faces before Robert displayed a range of expressions. Merry or avid or cringing or aghast, each revealed the personality of its owner. All but one. One face was completely without expression, neutral in an unstudied, unmanufactured way. Like a bus passenger, looking at nothing.

"Sir," said the man, turning, ashen-faced.

Robert smiled around the group as if he had seen nothing, made small talk with them while at his side Hoskins festered with uncertainty. Before he went on his way, Robert nodded at the stolid face — its owner was earmarked now, better things in her future, while Hoskins would be given tasks that amplified his faults, not unlike the jiujitsu principle Robert had heard about, an opponent's inertia used against him. Two years after that day, Robert had gained near-total control of his tics and compulsions and could suppress them when necessary, Hoskins's career was puddled around his ankles like fallen knickers, and the bus-rider woman who had been given graduated responsibility had done very well indeed.

There is a sudden mechanical ululation by Robert's ear. Is someone coming to help? A hot tear streams from the corner of one eye.

He sometimes wondered what he and Genevieve might have become without the stain of sorrow seeping across their union, tainting and bonding them, sticking them down in place. The unsullied Robert and Genevieve might have been swept up into the current of the changed American culture, its irreverence and self-gratification. Instead, they'd indulged only in small changes. Robert laid in a new supply of wide ties in adventuresome colors, and let his hair grow out a little bit. Genevieve had her own hair sheared off to a pixie cut that made her eyes look enormous.

The girls, on the other hand, had plunged right in. They backchatted, they agitated to be given things: record albums, pocket money, trendy ugly shoes to wear with their school uniforms. Robert gave in more often than he should have; Genevieve was usually the one to say no. When she was present to say it. Sometimes Robert wanted to blame her absence for the girls' metamorphosis, but he suspected that no disciplinary measures could have held them back. They were young women plunged into a new world, riding the back of a wave of upheaval, the crest of which they'd missed.

Women were different in the new America, braless and shameless and more overtly sexual. Some were forward enough to make overtures to Robert, what he would have called *making a pass at,* what was now called *coming on to.* He'd been too startled at first to find them tempting, their hair worn wild and down, their tight blue jeans defining their buttocks. There was nowhere safe to look: hemlines brushed underpants, breasts with nipples like gumdrops floated under diaphanous blouses. Eventually, rebuffed by his wife, he'd yielded. Sometimes for a night or two, sometimes for several months. He didn't lie to them, but they didn't care that he didn't offer permanence; they didn't want that from him. To his surprise, they merely wanted sex, enjoyed it in a way he didn't know that women could. The most recent, and longest, affair had been with an upbeat freckled blonde named Mary, about whom Robert occasionally had the thought, *If only we'd met before.* But of course that wouldn't have been possible. When he'd married Genevieve, cheerful Mary was in primary school. That sort of mathematics was always ill-advised.

Mary had reassured him when he worried about leaving Laura alone so much, Bea at college and Noi working and Genevieve so often out of the country. "Teenagers do not want parents around," Mary had said. "If you were home, she'd be in her room with the door closed." *But I'd be home,* he thought. *She'd know I was there.* "Your wife is the one who should stay home," said Mary. "A good mother would be with her children." He'd felt cold toward Mary all of that evening.

And Laura wasn't always in her room. Just the other day he'd spotted her in George-town, sitting cross-legged on a low stone wall, in intense conversation with a person he didn't know. He'd had to look closely to be sure it *was* Laura, so unexpected was the sighting. Robert had been stopped in a long rail of traffic waiting for the light on M Street, and he'd looked out his window idly, seen the girl with sand-colored hair wearing the blouse Laura had been given for her last birthday. The girl put her hand to her lips in an unmistakable gesture: she was smoking. She inhaled, didn't cough; this was a habit, not bravado.

Robert rolled down his window to call to her, but then she put her head back and laughed, showing her throat. He'd never seen any Genevieve in Laura, but there it was, unmistakable. Fifteen years old. She'd soon be a woman. Or was she already? Watching her from the car, he'd been gripped by certainty: No, she was not a woman, she was his baby daughter and she should not be with a bearded stranger, inhaling poisonous chemicals into her tender lungs. Again he almost called to her, but again he stopped himself. He didn't want to see what would happen when she saw him. She'd stiffen and scowl and slouch, pull her hair forward over her shoulders as if trying to hide herself with it. It was nice to see her like this, happy and open, even if it *was* like this, with a cigarette and an older man, during hours when she should be at school.

That evening at dinner, he tried to talk to her about it obliquely, saying "You know smoking is very addictive," while she blinked at him wide-eyed, *I know, Daddy.* "It causes cancer and heart disease," he said. "I had a terrible time quitting. You should never start." She'd nodded.

He'd retreated, galled at her ability to lie. On how many other occasions had she lied to him, and about what? He planned to speak to Genevieve, although who knew what she might say: she sometimes shrugged off things now that in the past would have incensed her. She had drifted away from all of them, each time she returned from her travels a little less recognizable as the woman he'd married. She barely wore makeup anymore, and the tailored clothing was gone. She dressed in a way that deemphasized her bosom, the lines of her body merely suggested through the cloth. Her hair was grown out from that pixie into a soft bob. He was more attracted to her than ever.

It feels as though a person is sitting on Robert's chest. His fingers and toes are tingling; he's gulping open-mouthed like a fish. For some reason what enters his mind at this moment is Bardin, the redheaded coworker he hasn't seen since Bangkok, and his story about the woman with the burst aorta. At the time, Robert had dismissed it as meaningless palaver, a tactic to distract Robert so Bardin could peek at the documents on his desk. But since that day the story had cropped up in his mind again and again like a never-solved riddle, along with Bardin's smug *I'm sure you'll figure it out.* People told tales on themselves without meaning to; even their lies carried truth. Robert had finally decided that the story was about futility, and destiny. The woman had carried her own end within her, ticking away like a bomb. All of that good behavior, eating properly and exercising and crossing only on the green, had not mattered; her end was long foretold. That's what Robert would have said to Bardin, if they'd ever met again.

But now, dying on the floor like the woman in the story, Robert sees that that answer is wrong. The woman had had a good life until it ended — she wouldn't have changed a thing. That was the real point of the riddle: It didn't matter how she died. It mattered only how she had lived.

And how had *Robert* lived?

He hadn't remembered to collect Philip that day; he'd left him to the mercy of that driver. But his failure hadn't started there. The thread that ended with the loss of Philip meandered back through events. He had known Philip was unhappy. Robert's own boarding school years had been miserable; perhaps he should have shared that with his son. Instead, he'd told stories of victory, intending Philip to understand that *If I could get through it, you can too.* He'd meant *I believe in you.* What he'd said was *Buck up.* The sacking of the old driver was an act that could be laid at Genevieve's door, but Robert had made the decision before that to let Philip take judo lessons, over Genevieve's objections. *Violence is not the answer,* Genevieve had said, and Robert had responded, *Sometimes it is.* Then the rest unfolding from there.

But the germ of the disaster wasn't any of that. It was Robert sitting at his desk, the Slinky in the drawer, letting himself be seduced by the unobtrusive man. Driven by boredom, selfishness, ego, by the nagging thought *I'm made for more important things,* by his fear that his potential had been spent. The potential that had barely been touched upon, as it turned out. Robert was put into recruitment when they got home, and he'd blossomed. He was able to speak to others' secret hearts, their frightened-rabbit hearts, their miserable ashamed hearts. He ferreted out the nooks inside them where the frail hope of redemption lingered, he convinced them that they were still capable of good. He'd become the unobtrusive man.

And yet, despite all that intuitive power, he had not understood his wife. He'd thought Genevieve hard and selfish, how she wrapped herself up in her grief and held herself apart from him and the girls. But he sees now that she had invited him in. When she had said *Why don't you come with me?* he'd said *One of us has to be sensible* instead of *Why are you going?* When she had told him *I can't be trusted to care for the girls,* he'd replied *That's ridiculous, you're their mother.* Instead of *We can care for them together.* He'd been the one to rebuff her. And she'd made something of her grief, while he buried his.

He remembers her packing to go to Bangkok, chattering to the children about the *adventure,* smiling at Robert as she folded the going-home sweaters. Trusting his word that it would be only a year, twelve months of summer, of paradise and pineapple, and that no harm would come to them.

571

Guilt was a coiling snake with its tail in its mouth, no beginning and no end.

Hands balled up against his chest, clammy with sweat, Robert admits the truth: he hadn't done any of it for his country, not any of it, and not for his family, but solely for himself. His whim had carried them to the place they'd come apart.

With that thought, the pain roars up, the one he has long gauzed over and diminished and turned away from, in order to carry on. At last he allows himself to feel it: the full loss of Philip. All that he's felt and thought before has been but a preamble, a dithering, like a fly buzzing and buzzing before finally settling down to the meat, stepping its feet delicately into the rot and the blood.

Drifting in his body now, no longer feeling pain or suffocation, arms dropped by his sides, Robert's mind clears of thought like a windowpane wiped of fog. What surfaces in the emptiness is not more regret, or sorrow, or self-recrimination. Not worry for his daughters nor anguish for his lost son, nor longing for his wife, who is also lost to him. Instead, what comes into his mind is the little dog he had as a child.

As fully as if it is happening right now, he is experiencing the day his parents surprised him with the animal. While Robert lies on the floor of his office with his heart muscle whitening and stiffening and his pulse slipping from its rhythm, syncopating and then uncoordinating until his ventricle is at a quivering standstill, he is with the dog in the moment they met. Kneeling on the ground with his hands curling into its white soft coat as it leaps its nose up to his lips again and again, its tail slapping its own flanks. Robert can't stop laughing. He tells his mother and father, *Thank you, thank you.* He's there again, nine years old on the best day of his life, as though he never left that day, as though his whole complex, inscrutable life has been just a path looping out from that moment, in order to loop back to it so that it will shimmer once more, all of its beauty and power fresh forever. *Thank you, thank you.*

He dies with a heart full of joy.

CHAPTER FORTY-SEVEN
1972–2019

The farang funeral was solemn and brief, Master in a closed box in the church that was then buried in the ground. Very soon afterward everything went back to normal. Bea returned to college, and Laura to school; Madame left on a plane again. So easily did the master slip from this life. Noi felt sad and shocked at the disgrace of it, but while she prayed for him, she too resumed her life.

When they arrived in America, at first it had seemed that Daeng might be right: there was no mention of school. There was a lot of cleaning. Noi didn't do it alone. A thirtyish woman named Birgita came to live in the other attic bedroom; she was difficult to understand but friendly. She showed Noi how to manage the growling hole in the kitchen sink basin. *Use a wooden spoon,* Birgita said, *never your fingers,* guiding food scraps into the hole. She flicked the switch on the wall to start the growling, water sputtering back up between the toothlike rubber flaps as if some animal were eating, deep inside the house.

It got progressively colder during that first month, a chill unlike anything Noi had known, wetter than air-conditioning and more aggressive, reaching into her bones through coat and scarf and hat and mittens, through the quilts piled on her bed in her room at the top of the Preston house. Her bedroom window revealed a slanted woods of backyard, and she watched the trees go bright colors, then shed their leaves, revealing between their naked branches a rough twinkling of water in the distance. Snow fell in a broken blanket of white over the dead landscape.

Once Christmas was past — a somber holiday by comparison with years before, the tree and presents and holiday visitors not enough to overcome the sad fact of two stockings on the mantel instead of three — Madame sat down with Noi in the kitchen.

"I've found you a school," she said. "It teaches reading and writing English to adults from other countries." Madame was blade thin those days, taut with energy; she'd cut her hair very short. "It teaches other things too, but that's a place to start."

The journey to school, two afternoons a week, was both easy and difficult. The easy part: the walk to the bus stop, a brisk fifteen minutes, Noi's breath fogging in front of her like cigarette smoke, and then the bus ride ten stops to the front of the school building. She memorized the pattern of coins that she needed to drop into the glass receptacle at the front of the bus, the fattest silver coin the least valuable.

The difficult part of going to school was the men. They were everywhere — on the street, at the bus stop, on the bus, in the hallways of the school. Some of them followed Noi and said things to her; she didn't understand all of the words, but the gist was obvious. On the bus they stood very close even when there was plenty of room, and leaned over her when she was sitting. She tried to make herself as small as possible in her seat, turned her face away from their hovering bellies. "Please," she said, when she was standing and they rested their weight against her body from behind. She considered telling Madame that she did not want to go to school anymore; she dreaded every day. Until one morning on a crowded bus, Noi standing and holding the looped metal handhold on the back of a seat for balance (she was too short to reach the overhead straps), when a man leaned against her from behind. She tried to squirm away, but the crowd was solid on both sides. He pressed harder, until she was bowed forward, nearly touching the seated passenger, whose eyes were strenuously averted. Noi's eyes filled with tears.

Please, she whispered, but it came out in Thai.

Suddenly the man's heat was gone, the pressure gone. Noi straightened up and turned, to see him staggering. The standing bodies that would not move for her drew aside and allowed him to fall to his knees, one hand at his crotch and the other flat on the dirty ridged bus floor.

"Far cough," said a cool voice. It came from a blond woman not much taller than Noi, who stood looking down at the man. "Bastard." She stepped deliberately onto the hand on the bus floor and ground her heel. The man moaned.

The bus driver called from the front, "What's going on back there?"

"We have a dirty motherfucker," the blond girl called back.

"Language," said the driver. The bus stopped with a wheeze of brakes, and the back door clacked open. Not at a bus stop, not even at the curb. The man got to his feet and stumbled down the steps, still clutching his groin, hobbling toward the sidewalk.

"Pig," the blond girl called after the disappearing figure. The door flaps slapped closed again and the bus jerked back into motion. The girl gave Noi a brilliant grin; Noi smiled tentatively back. "We use what we have," said the girl. "I have good sharp knees." A few stops later, she rang the bell and was gone.

577

Far cough. Whatever it meant, it worked. Noi never had to use her own sharp knees. She knew that words would not suffice in all situations — not if she was alone or on a dark street, for example — but when she tried these, they were magic. *Far cough* grated in a deep voice out of Noi's chest made the men's eyes widen; they'd withdraw as if she'd spat poison at them. It was a powerful weapon and Noi hoped to see the blond girl again on the bus sometime so she could thank her, but she never did.

"You've done very well," Genevieve said to Noi at the end of two years. "From here, you have some choices. You could work toward a high school equivalency exam, and after that, maybe college." Madame looked tired. The night before, Noi had heard her and the master arguing. Sound came up from the big bedroom into the attic through the vents. *It's just not reasonable* from Master. Then, *Sweetheart,* and a muffled noise. Then *No* in Madame's voice, the syllable like stone.

"You could be anything you like if you work hard enough," said Madame. "Even a dentist or doctor. That would take lots of school." Looking down at the report card. "And you'd have to improve your reading."

Noi didn't want to be a dentist or doctor. Not because of an aversion to hard work or the need to master English. The thought of people's mouths, their hot moist innards, made her recoil. Also, while she enjoyed school, it didn't seem like real work to her. Real work brought in money, it was how you made a life for yourself.

"I know what I want," said Noi. Hesitant, although she felt sure. Madame, who was still talking about being a doctor, fell silent. "I don't want to work for anyone anymore." Noi blushed painfully, for it sounded impolite. "I like to sew. I want to own a shop."

In the ensuing silence, Noi sneaked a glance up at Madame's face. She looked thoughtful, not upset.

"All right," Madame said. "I'll get some fabric for you to make some samples, and we can see where you are."

It had been difficult to say *I want.* Noi had done it though, and she felt the world pivot beneath her. Now things would stop happening *to* her. She would make all of the choices for herself from here.

Madame had already seen an example of Noi's sewing, although she didn't realize it. Noi had designed and sewn the water-bottle bag for Philip, making the two compartments just the right size, layering the fabric to create an extra-thick cushion; Noi had seen how carelessly the Preston children dropped things they were finished with, just opened their hands and let them go. Madame kept that bag, filthy and wrapped in plastic, in her bureau drawer. Noi didn't mention it. She made an array of samples and Madame examined them, exclaiming *Where in the world did you learn to do this,* and that same week a sewing machine was delivered and carried to the basement, into the large playroom the children rarely used.

The playroom was lined with cherrywood shelves of a perfect depth to hold pattern forms; it had closets where Noi could hang projects in progress and finished items. She cleaned the big windows at the end of the room so the light there would be good for fittings. Madame spoke to some friends, and soon Noi had as much work as she wanted. Within a year, she had paid back the money for the sewing machine and the materials, and two years after that, she climbed into a stuffy rental space above a drugstore and pulled down brown paper from the windows to let the light pour in. She had the money for the lease, but Madame had to cosign. *It's because you're young,* Madame said, but Noi knew that was not the only reason.

Noi still went to school two days a week, taking an accounting course. One morning when she was late, running up the steps, a man coming down caught her by the elbow. She wheeled around, too surprised at first to summon the weapon words.

"You dropped this," he said. He proffered a paper, a test that must have fluttered out of the notebook under her arm. "One hundred percent," he said with a low whistle as she took it from him and tucked it away. "You must be very smart."

He was taller than she was but not too tall, and older than she was, maybe twenty-five. She did not say *Far cough* to him. He walked up the steps with her, talking; she learned he was an instructor in one of the classes she did not take. She agreed to have lunch with him after her class. "You correct me," she ordered him during the meal. "When I say something wrong, you correct me." He nodded, his face serious, as though he understood how personal was the request.

More lunches, then some dinners. His name was Tom. He was patient and calm, none of the American hurry-up energy that could sometimes tie Noi's tongue. He made room for the words to come from her; he didn't guess what she was trying to say, or jump in to finish her sentences. He asked Noi to tell him about Thailand. She began to think, again, of a basket in the corner of her shop.

One day she showed him Daeng's note, which she had never been able to make sense of.

"I'm not surprised you had trouble with

this," Tom said. "The spelling is — not good."
He studied it for a moment. "I think it's *try-ing* to say, 'If you can read this I was wrong
and I hope you are happy.'"

Noi laughed. So like Daeng to wish Noi
well only if she didn't need those wishes.

She sent letters home and wired money, and
she heard back sometimes from one of her
brothers or Moo, a polite thank-you with
family news. Noi had not been surprised that
Sao's spirit did not visit her in Washington. It
was such a long way, across so much water.
Still, sometimes when she lay in the little
room with the window raised and the sounds
of the American night breathing through the
screen — rustling in the high branches of the
trees, an occasional animal call *whoo-hoo-hoo-hoo* — she would turn onto her side and
close her eyes, and wait for the sound of
amulets.

Then the master died, and Noi told Tom that
marriage was not possible.

"The family can't expect you to live with
them forever," he said. They were in her shop;
he'd brought her lunch and they were having
what he called a "windowsill picnic," the food
spread between them on the wide wooden
sill that ran under the big windows.

No, they didn't *expect* it, Noi tried to explain.

Her tongue was baffled, her mind filled with jostling thoughts. Madame was always gone now. Birgita had been replaced by a series of worthless au pairs who were always wanting to go sightseeing and to meet American boys. Beatrice was at college many hours away. Noi could not leave Laura alone in the house in all of that stunned, empty silence. *The choices I've made have consequences,* Noi wanted to say. *We're connected by a tough net of karma, it's more complicated than you see.*

"Don't you want your own children?" he said, for the first time interrupting her while she was groping for words.

"I'm doing what I am doing," she said, her voice emphatic, her English rushed and nonsensical. She slapped her hand on the wooden sill, angry.

He left, and didn't come again.

After two months apart she went to wait outside the building where Tom taught a morning class. He came out in a chattering clump of students that filtered away, leaving him standing with one girl, a laughing chubby American with a bushy side ponytail of hair. She held her books in one arm and kept touching him with her free hand: now his forearm, now his shoulder. He was listening to her, smiling, before he spotted Noi walking toward them.

"Far cough," Noi told the fat girl.

"Sorry," called Tom, laughing in surprise, as the girl walked away. "What?" he said to Noi. He couldn't stop laughing.

"I will marry you when Laura is older," said Noi.

"She's fifteen now," said Tom. He knew all about the girls, although he'd never met them. "As old as you were when you came to this country."

That was true, but although Noi was not much older than the Preston daughters, she had always felt the gap keenly. At each stage, they seemed to her much younger than she had been.

"I'll wait," Tom said, putting his arm around her. "But not forever."

He waited until Laura was off to college. Noi was twenty-six then. By that time, her business was solidly established, the lease in her own name. The sign outside said EXPERT CUSTOM TAILORING and inside there was a counter and a telephone. No basket in the corner, though, no fan on the ceiling, no Choy sweeping the floor. It was the American version of her dream — not quite as good as Noi had wanted, but better than she'd hoped.

She became pregnant right away, as if her body had been waiting. When Tom insisted she close the shop, she smiled and kissed him, and did not argue. She went down to the public library and put a notice up in Thai and English: SEAMSTRESS WANTED. At six the next morning she arrived at the store to find three Vietnamese women already waiting outside. She made them sew some samples and chose the best one and trained her, until Noi was so big she couldn't stand for more than half an hour without her ankles swelling unbearably. She hired a second girl then, and spent half a day at home with her feet up before realizing she could lie around at work exactly the same way, so she did that, supervising the two women from a recumbent position, until the minute her pains began.

It was nothing like that terrible night alone in the Quarters; the hospital room was bright and her husband was there. There was that same bigness to it, though, the feeling of being in a place outside of time. She gave birth to a healthy girl and looked hard into her squalling face — was this the baby she'd sent away? She couldn't tell.

When Noi returned to the shop she was pleased to see that not only had the women not stolen from her, but they'd beautifully completed all of the work that had been waiting. They had made her a welcome lunch, a variety of Vietnamese dishes of which she ate a little to be polite, and an American cake from a supermarket box, with grainy frosting and writing on the top, *Happy Baby.*

Noi kept Vanessa with her every minute; in the small brick colonial in Alexandria or kicking her legs in the bouncy seat in the shop, the baby made a tight bubble of home. Noi resolved not to speak Thai to her, so she wouldn't grow up with an accent. Noi had been called all kinds of things in this country — Ching Chong Chinaman and Mama-san and Goddamned Boat Person — and she didn't want any of that for her daughter. She hoped Vanessa would have only the good traits of being American — the big-heartedness and optimism and self-confidence — and none of the bad ones: the laziness, the selfishness, the entitlement. But as Vanessa grew, it was obvious that the balance in her was wrong. She was an argumentative child, an insolent teenager.

"It's normal," said Tom, after another door-slamming tantrum.

"Unacceptable," said Noi.

She increased her strictness, hoping to fatten the Thai flame within the girl. Vanessa, however, seemed impervious to Noi's biggest weapon, maternal disapproval. Instead of shamed acquiescence, Vanessa responded with defiance. In defeat, Noi left her more and more to Tom's management and focused on the two younger girls. With them she had spoken in Thai from the first minute — she had felt lonely with Tom and toddler Vanessa speaking together so quickly that Noi could not always follow. The younger girls spoke perfect American English and also very good Thai, switching easily from one to the other. They looked more like Noi than Vanessa did, although they would never pass as pure Thai at home.

In a vulnerable moment before they were married, Noi had told Tom about the first daughter, the one she had sent back. He had said, "Did you ever have a test?" and she'd looked at him, unsure what he meant. "To confirm the pregnancy," he clarified. She shook her head. "So maybe you were never actually pregnant," he said. She clucked her tongue — she shouldn't have expected a man to understand, how a woman knows when there is life in her, and then when there is no life.

In the winter of 2004, a tsunami killed the twenty-one-year-old grandson of King Bhumibol, and Noi was inconsolable. She wept and wept. For the prince who had been half-American like her children, who had broken the heart of his grandfather the beloved king and his mother the rebel princess; she wept for the sorrow of his grandmother Sirikit and his sisters. She wept more than she ever had for losses in her own family, her sister Pla and her grandparents. Tom was baffled; the two daughters still at home, their own eyes swollen with crying, pleaded with their mother to get up, have a little bit to eat.

Vanessa came home from the faraway college she attended. Noi's eldest girl, her loud, tall, big-nosed American, crawled into bed with Noi and held her, fed her, bathed her. The child who looked so much like her father sang to Noi the only Thai words she knew, the lullabies Noi had sung to the other two when they were babies, and at last, Noi recognized her.

"I'm sorry," she said in Thai. "I'm sorry I sent you away."

Vanessa answered in English, "It's all right, Mom, it's all right."

And finally Noi fell into a dreamless sleep.

When Madame was brought home from the hospital after her diagnosis, Noi paid a visit to the Tudor and was distressed when she comprehended the situation: although Bea and Laura visited often, grocery shopping and fixing meals and ferrying their mother back and forth to medical appointments, neither of them slept in the house, and they didn't manage any of her physical care. For that, they hired nurses. Beatrice went back to her family each evening, and Laura went to the empty house she called home, leaving Madame alone with strangers.

Noi hadn't had the privilege of caring for her own elderly parents. She had seen them twice before they died — she and Tom had taken the children to visit once, and she had gone once by herself after that — and the money she sent every month had made their lives easier, but it wasn't the same as daily care. It was obvious to Noi that Laura, who had no children and no husband, should move into the big house and take care of her mother. Noi hinted at this strongly, but when nothing changed, she moved in herself, taking her old room on the top floor.

Vanessa FaceTimed her disapproval from Boston, where she was now a doctor. "They have all the money in the world, Mom," she said, frowning from the iPad. "They can hire help. She has two daughters of her own."

"That's right," said Noi. She meant, *See what it is to have weak daughters. See how daughters can disappoint you. See how lucky I am.*

"Are they even paying you?" said Vanessa. "Dad. Why are you allowing this?"

"Your mom is loyal," said Tom. "One of the things I love about her."

"Your sister takes good care of your father," said Noi. The middle girl was unmarried and living with them in the colonial, working as a pharmacist.

"Hey," said Tom. "Your father takes good care of himself."

"You're not an old retainer, Mom," said Vanessa. "This is not *Downton Abbey.*"

"You worry about yourself," Noi told Vanessa. "You are getting too old for babies."

Beatrice and Laura also argued with Noi when she arrived with a suitcase. Noi ignored them, taking charge, inspecting the house cleaner's work, supervising the nurses. Eventually, Laura and Bea stopped arguing and arranged to pay her. She managed her shop from her mobile phone. It had been years since she had done the sewing herself. She'd captured the costuming contracts for two area theaters in the nineties, and had hired more seamstresses then; when the real estate market dipped, she'd bought the building and expanded her business to fill all of the space. The store had a manager now, but Noi phoned many times a day and examined the work by FaceTime. She visited the store two or three days a week and spent most of each Sunday at home.

Over time, Noi assembled a corps of reliable day nurses for Madame, but night nurses were less satisfactory. After a week in which she found one asleep for the second time and another inspecting the contents of the drinks cabinet in the butler's pantry, Noi dismissed the lot and kept watch herself, sleeping in snatches. She descended the stairs from the attic for regular checks, or whenever the pressure-detecting mat beside Madame's bed shrieked to announce that she had gotten up.

Once, the sleep mat alarmed and Noi came

down the steep stairs to find Madame already on the landing, standing erect and slim at the leaded windows, amber moonlight falling on her through the diamond panes. She turned, her still-beautiful face tormented. *I've lost something,* she said. Noi took her hand and walked her back up the stairs to the bedroom, got onto the bed with her, made *shhhh* into her ear. What have I done, said Madame. Where is everyone? *I'm here,* said Noi. She said it in English and in Thai and in English again. I don't want to forget, said Madame, and Noi said *I won't let you forget,* and Madame said, I've done something terrible, and Noi breathed *Kha kha kha,* and Madame closed her eyes and Noi's two amulets slid together on her neck chain with a little noise, and she held the abandoned woman as her sister's spirit had held her long ago.

CHAPTER FORTY-EIGHT

∞

Genevieve knows she is losing her mind well before anyone else does. It began with little things, lapses any senior citizen might expect: the house keys in the vegetable crisper, the electric kettle put onto the stove. She told herself it was simple absentmindedness; after all, she hadn't tried to lock the door with an asparagus stalk, she hadn't gone so far as to ignite the flame under the kettle. When her memory began to unravel, she hid that from everyone until it was nearly bare, like an un-picked embroidery, what had been a compli-cated scrollwork dwindled to a scattering of fuzzy knots.

It is not wholly unpleasant to be free of the framework of overbearing facts, *who* and *when* and *where*. Genevieve particularly enjoys how her timeline pleats occasionally, the past touching the present, allowing her to cherish the details of lost ordinary days. Magically, her girls are grown and at the same time also children; she can be talking to adult Bea about her twins' tenth birthday party while also reminding herself to get new ballet tights for eleven-year-old Bea, Laura having cut the feet off with scissors "to see if they'd grow back." Genevieve knows that Beatrice is past fifty and yet there are the tights, pink size small, on Genevieve's shopping list. No one sees that list, not even Genevieve's snappingly efficient assistant, with whom iCloud shares information with a blithe openhandedness. There is still the secrecy of paper in the pocket.

But then she gets lost in Bangkok, a city that she knows as well as the back of her hand. Walking from somewhere to somewhere, within an eyeblink nothing familiar, the buildings glassy and looming just like tall buildings anywhere, the sun reflecting into her eyes. She felt terrified and yet lightened, as though she'd shucked heavy layers of clothing underwater while drowning. Then a man walking beside her spoke, and she realized that he knew her. And that she knew him: her assistant, André. The rest cascaded after: she knew where she was and where they were both headed, and why.

After that meeting, she begged off cocktails, saying she needed to rest — no one questioned that after you turned seventy — and went back to the hotel room, André walking with her. She was clearheaded, the landscape familiar all the way. In the hotel room, she removed her shoes and her earrings and sat on the bed in her clothing, putting both of the pillows behind her to prop herself upright. She didn't want to sleep. She had to plan.

The disorientation had come on without warning, and resolved just as suddenly. It had been, in fact, very much like her old temperamental slide projector that would sometimes stick, the motor whirring and clunking and failing to drop the next slide while a white dirt-speckled square hung on the screen. She'd coddled that machine, learned its every infinitesimal whim. In the end, an unnecessary roster of skills: a slide presentation could now be carried on a chit of plastic-wrapped metal as small as a thumbnail.

Genevieve has so many useless talents. How to tie Windsor knots and half-Windsors, four-in-hands — you never know what your husband will favor, her mother said — and bow ties; the exquisite nuances of etiquette and place settings and proper forms of address. So many, many rules; her young life had been poured into their conduits. Not to mention all of the hours she had spent on her hair. Sleeping on enormous uncomfortable rollers, backcombing and brushing, crafting spiraling pin curls. Whole mornings and afternoons in a salon, each appointment counting double in woman-hours, if one considered the hairdresser's time as well. Cropping her hair short after the return to America had added an almost bewildering amount of time to

Genevieve's day.

She finds that she's closed her eyes after all, sitting up on the hotel bed. She touches her hairstyle, jokes to herself that now perhaps hair can take on a new usefulness: when she feels herself unmooring she can put a hand to her head and by the feel under her fingers — soft or stiff or feathered or shorn, or the current old-lady cotton-candy texture — orient herself.

Not a joke she can share.

She takes the paper from her pocket.

I'm in Bangkok, she adds to the list. *I am going home on Wednesday.* Checks the day on the glowing glass telephone. *That's tomorrow,* and adds the date. For completeness, she writes *Home:* and puts the address of the Tudor. She doesn't think she could possibly forget something so basic, but she keeps surprising herself.

She regrets so deeply now her inactivity in the weeks after Philip vanished. How she'd opted out and elected to sleep. It had been selfish, a way to limit her own suffering; she'd allowed others to do the looking. And after the sleep ended, she hadn't fully returned to herself. She'd remained elsewhere, loose in her body like a ghost. How else could she have left him there? He hadn't discorporated into fog; he was *somewhere.* Yet she went back home without him, docile in a way she

595

had never been, sleepwalking through nearly two years before coming awake abruptly in 1974, while watching the television news. The American president had resigned, something that had been until that very moment inconceivable. Watching Nixon waving goodbye, Genevieve realized suddenly: she could go back.

At the thought, she felt a tug in her chest, as if something were pulling on a thread from her heart to Philip's, wherever he was. She wanted to jump up, go quickly before the thread stretched too far and broke. She turned to Robert. *Let's go back,* she said.

He looked confused at first; then as she talked his face grew sad. *Darling,* he said, *there's nothing we can do there. You know that as well as I do.* He talked for a while and she nodded, not hearing, still feeling the thread pulling, pulling. He went up to bed while she shut up the house, turning the lights off and locking the doors. The next morning she rose, fed everyone breakfast, kissed them off to school and work, and telephoned a travel agent. She had to repeat herself half a dozen times: yes, she was traveling alone; no, her husband wasn't traveling with her.

She tended to a thousand details before she left, battening down the household against her absence. Still, she boarded the airplane feeling like a criminal, the world dropping away below her, the taut thread pulling her to Philip while the threads that stretched from her to the girls paid out, rattling their spools.

Many of the Bangkok policemen remembered the lost American boy from two years before and were sympathetic, but they did not seem to know what to do with Genevieve, why she was there, what she hoped for. After a dazed minute — what *was* she doing there, what *did* she hope for — she collected herself and left. She caught a tuk-tuk to go back to the hotel. As it bumped along through traffic, she felt a jangling collection of regrets: Robert had been right, this trip was wrongheaded, purely magical thinking. She'd return home the next day, do what she could to gather the fragments of her life together.

The tuk-tuk slowed going over the bridge on Sang Hi Road; she sat with the sun beating on the back of her head and looked out at the brown surface of the khlong, dimpling and moving, going away and yet staying in place. Upstream, a woman was bathing a child in the shallows; downstream on the opposite side, a man washed melons. Two or three longtail boats puttered along in the middle of the water. An ordinary day in Bangkok.

Somewhere in this city. Philip was *somewhere*. Wouldn't Genevieve have felt it if the thread between them was broken? Wouldn't she know? She was gripped by the thought:

she could not leave him here again.

Back in the hotel, she began making phone calls. She reached out to the embassy and hired an interpreter, and the next day began going everywhere, talking to everyone. Always the same question — had they ever met or seen this little American boy in the picture, his name is Philip? He would be older now, almost two years older.

The city was very different now that the war was finished. The sprawling red-light district had shrunk significantly; many of the cheap R&R hotels had shuttered. As Genevieve walked through the streets with the interpreter, stopping everyone, asking everyone, she saw a lot of unaccompanied children, too little for school, begging or playing together or just squatting on the sidewalk. Again and again, Genevieve would presume that one or another nearby woman was the mother, but that woman would move on and the child would not follow. They hadn't been there before, these babies all alone — or had they, and Genevieve had tuk-tukked past them fretting about the heat and whether her makeup was running?

"Where are the parents?" Genevieve asked the interpreter, Bun Ma.

Bun Ma grimaced. "Not nice, Madame." The classic Thai response when something was too unpleasant to discuss.

A little girl of about eight pointed at the

photo and nodded; Genevieve's heart leapt.

"She says she knows this boy," said Bun Ma. She spoke some more to the child.

"Where?" said Genevieve, almost breathless. "Where did she see him?"

Bun Ma said, "She wants a pancake and she will tell you. Madame, she is lying."

Genevieve bought the pancake; the girl snatched it and ran. Other children crowded around Genevieve.

"They want pancakes too," said Bun Ma, with an air of reproof: *See what you started.*

But why not? Genevieve was already buying more pancakes, handing them out, the children surging around her, calling out words she didn't understand. She waded through the bold ones at the front of the crowd to the wary ones hanging back on the fringes, made sure they ate too. She gave Bun Ma money and they bought from all the stalls on that block, the children dividing into two flocks to follow.

An old man who had been watching called over something in Thai.

"He's saying feeding one time does nothing, Madame," said Bun Ma, reluctantly translating after multiple *mai pen rai*s had failed to put Genevieve off. "He's saying, they're American, you take them." Eyes down, embarrassed by the man's rudeness.

"What does he mean, they're American?" said Genevieve.

599

"They are *luk khrung,* Madame," said Bun Ma. "Fathers not Thai."

"Are you sure?" said Genevieve. The children looked completely Thai to her.

Bun Ma nodded, and Genevieve understood. Apparently, when the Americans had evacuated from Bangkok like water rushing toward a drain when the plug is pulled, they'd left behind not only gifts like the beautiful Fifth Field Hospital, built at stupendous cost, but also a sediment of children.

The idea was born then, on that street. It was simple, and selfish. Not a grand altruistic plan, but merely a way to justify Genevieve's presence there and allow her to come back. A way to *do something* while keeping the thread taut, following it to her hidden son.

"You can do good *here,*" said Robert, when she returned and explained her idea to him. From this she understood that he wouldn't financially support it. "Your own children need you."

She knew that wasn't true. She knew what kind of mother she was.

"They see more of us than we ever saw of our parents," she said. It was true: she and Robert had both gone to boarding schools.

She raised the money from her own pocket — more accurately, from the pockets of her ancestors. An only child of two only children, Genevieve had been born at the bottom of a funnel of antiquities, a precious legacy rattling down to her from grandparents and great-grandparents and great-greats. She had loved these things, had cared for them like holy objects. Now she saw them only as a fragile and needy clutter of goods through which she'd waded all of her life, and she sold it all off without a pang. The girls came home from school to an emptier and emptier house. They said nothing and asked no questions, but one evening Genevieve came upon Beatrice standing beside the Sheraton desk. It had already been cocooned in packing cloth for transport to auction the next day; the girl rested her hand on it as if comforting an animal going to slaughter.

"Beatrice," said Genevieve, and the girl startled. "Do you like that desk?"

Beatrice nodded, her jaw tight. She would not cry.

"Do you understand why I am selling things?"

Beatrice shook her head.

"You know there are hungry children in the world." Beatrice nodded; she knew about those from the orange UNICEF boxes she and Laura had carried at Halloween. "I am going to use the money that people are paying for these things to help some of those children." She looked at the swaddled desk, at Bea's hand. "This desk needs a lot of care," said Genevieve. "All the little niches need to be kept clean. No spray polishes. A lightly moistened cotton swab and a dry swab immediately after. A dry soft cloth for the rest. *Never* wax. It mustn't be kept too close to a radiator or a fireplace. Climate-controlled storage, if you ever have to store it. Can you do all that?"

Beatrice nodded.

"Why this desk?" asked Genevieve. "You could have asked for any of these things."

When Genevieve revisits this moment during time slips, she wants to whisper to herself, *Why didn't you offer, why did you require her to ask?*

"You used to write letters at it when I was little." Bea's face was flushed.

Long-ago early-morning Saturdays when the nanny was off and Robert was still sleeping, Genevieve would take an hour or two in the quiet to do paperwork: bills or the Arts Council newsletter, thank-you notes, cards for one occasion or another. Beatrice would play quietly with her dollies at her mother's feet. Beatrice was only four when those Saturday mornings came to an end, with the birth of first Philip and then Laura. How much memory did one store before the age of four? But, Genevieve recalled, Philip had had a whole life in eight years; that early time was not negligible.

Beatrice sighed; Genevieve saw that although the girl could not follow the path of her mother's thoughts, she knew their destination. Back to Philip, always back.

"You don't have to do the same things I do," said Genevieve.

"I know," said Beatrice. "Thank you for the desk. I'll take good care of it always."

That money provided the capital for the first fundraiser. As a social event, it was a great success, but at the end of the night, couples swept out of the door without having donated, gushing *It's so good to have you back, Genevieve,* and *You'll need to give me the name of the caterer* as if it had been a party and not a benefit. These same people gave freely to allay every kind of disease, wrote generous checks to support the habitat of a bird not one of them had ever seen. Why would they shun hungry children? Genevieve was puzzled, until one woman remarked as she was leaving, "It's terrible, how they're neglecting their children over there."

Their children. Southeast Asia was a generic beige swirl to most Americans; Genevieve realized that to the fundraiser attendees, the Thai children in her slideshow might as well be Vietnamese. Children of the enemy, in a war freshly ended. Genevieve hadn't mentioned the probable mixed heritage of many of them; even hinting at the sex industry to this audience would ensure that no one attended any of her events again.

At the next fundraiser Genevieve showed the same slideshow, with one additional slide at the end. A photograph of Philip, which she could barely stand to look at, could barely stand to look away from. In the dark room, no sound but her own voice and the whirring projector, she told the story of how one Wednesday afternoon her little boy had gone to a lesson and never come home. How, in his memory, she wanted to feed hungry children and help keep them safe. At the end of that evening, the donations poured in, and when the next event was packed, Genevieve knew that word had spread. They were avid for the spectacle of her pain, and she gave it to them in a quiet clear voice, Philip smiling on the screen behind her. It never became a routine recitation; it felt each time as if she were peeling away her skin to show her beating heart. But those pindrop-quiet minutes also felt necessary. They felt like penance.

Once she thought she saw him. It was just after dawn on an October morning in 1976, and Genevieve and her interpreter were going into the market when she noticed a slender, tanned tall boy with dark blond hair, not thirty feet away from her, staring. He looked like Philip would, if he'd been washed with coffee from head to toe and pulled thin and long like taffy. She stood still, staring back, her breath astonished from her lungs, and then she started toward him. He turned and fled. She ran after, in her slight shoes not designed for more than a stroll, tripping and catching herself, keeping her head up, keeping him in view. He plunged into a narrow street and she followed.

A burst of firecracker sound, then long wails of screaming, a mob of humans crying and shouting and running toward her. Genevieve clung to the side of a building while the crowd surged past. She saw the white iron fence around Thammasat University and realized that she had broken a promise to Robert. He had warned her before she left, speaking from some deep well of secret knowledge, to stay away from that area. Genevieve had chased the boy into Sanam Luang square, right beside the university where students had been protesting for weeks.

Across the square, Thai police crouched outside the white fence, holding long black rods. Guns, she realized. They were taking aim. She felt her arm being pulled and she resisted, watching the police remove a panel of fencing and disappear through the gap.

"Hurry please." Her interpreter's voice in her ear. He pulled Genevieve's arm again, and she allowed herself to run along with him, out of the square and into an alley. Through that alley, stumbling over cooking pots on the pavement and through washing flapping on lines, into another street, where they hailed a tuk-tuk. As they bumped through traffic, the interpreter, a college student, wept.

"They are my friends, Madame," he said.

They stayed in the hotel the rest of that day, the rain thick outside the windows, with the television on, hoping for news, but the screen was a snowy square, no programming on any channel. The radio played only Thai marching songs until the evening, when the music was interrupted for an announcement: a curfew had been imposed, and anyone out between midnight and five a.m. would be shot on sight. After that terse declaration, the military songs resumed.

When she finally got out, Robert met her at Dulles, something he didn't always do.

"I still don't know what happened," said Genevieve, staring out at the colorful autumn landscape flanking the highway.

"The students put on a puppet show," said Robert. The show had a lynching scene, and the rumor had started that one of the hanged puppets resembled the prince. Insulting the royal family was a crime; the perceived slight instigated a strong pushback. Genevieve had seen only the beginning of the police action: after shooting into the courtyard, Robert told her, they had crashed buses through the gates and flushed the students onto a soccer field, where they stripped them of shoes and shirts, watches, eyeglasses, religious jewelry. Some students were herded onto the buses under arrest while others were left to the mercy of a growing mob and executed, shot while lying on their bellies on the grass, or lynched, their hanging bodies beaten and set on fire.

Genevieve felt dazed, listening. She couldn't imagine the sweet-natured Thai beating or lynching anyone.

"Was that on the news here?" she asked.

"No," Robert said shortly.

"They had grenade launchers," she said.

His face darkened at that; he hadn't known she'd been so close to the action.

"I told you to stay away from that area," he said.

"I thought I saw Philip," she said. She put her head against the car window, felt the rumble of the road transmit itself to her skull.

She hadn't meant to say that. Robert had tired of the sightings, the false leads that popped up every now and then, whipsawing them both with hope, every time leading nowhere. She waited for Robert to say something that would widen the chasm between them: *You need to accept that he's gone* or simply *This has to stop.*

"He would be almost thirteen now," Robert said.

She nodded, the window glass rolling under her temple. They said nothing else, all the way home.

■ ■ ■

The Foundation progressed from simple feeding stations to a school with an attached dormitory and a wiry nun, Sister James, who lived in. That first school enrolled just twenty children, most of them orphaned or abandoned, but not all — permission was obtained from any existing family. In time, they added some older children to the little ones; a disastrous move, reported Sister James. Older children were disruptive and greedy; they bullied the younger ones, came for the meals and slept through the lessons, stole whatever they could from the classroom. Many of them were addicts.

"They've been too long on the street," said Sister James. "After a certain point, a person might not be rescuable."

"Surely we are all rescuable," said Genevieve. Shocked: she'd expected more mercy from a nun.

"Idealism has no role here," said Sister James, a Scot who had spent her life in Asia. She might have been forty or seventy, her skin roughened by sun. "We can help the young ones, give them a good start in life. The older ones are sinking the ship." Genevieve gave in. She let Sister James set the age cutoff at twelve years old.

■ ■ ■ ■

After Robert died, Genevieve had the odd thought *Laura's alone now.* Odd but not inexplicable: purely on the basis of resemblance, the family could be sliced down the middle, Genevieve and Bea on one side, Robert and Laura on the other. Without Robert, the family was asymmetrical. Genevieve was dozing on a plane when that thought wandered through. Followed by another: *Too bad we don't still have Philip.* At that, she came fully awake. *Too bad.* As if the central tragedy of her life, that dark omphalos into which everything was always slowly migrating as if drawn by some terrible gravity, were a mild misfortune. Something to tut-tut about, like rain at a garden party. The airplane was flying through a storm; she turned her face to the window, where raindrops wriggled like short translucent worms. She and Robert had not been companions for a long time, but they had been connected in a way that could not happen again. She felt a loneliness to her core.

In the nineties, when the Foundation was considering expansion into Cambodia, Genevieve made an exploratory visit. She spent a morning talking to survivors of the genocide, whose lack of self-pity was humbling, and in the afternoon she visited Angkor Wat. Her guide was disappointed that Genevieve would not be able to return for the sunrise the next day, and took it upon himself to show her a spectacular sunset, urging her past the Apsaras in bas-relief, past the benevolent Buddhas smiling down from the stone of the Bayon, to the foot of a near-vertical stone stairway at whose top, he promised, was the *best sunset place.*

She climbed to the flat stone terrace, stood looking out at the enormous temple complex. According to the guide's crisp history, it had been built originally to the glory of the Hindu god Vishnu, was reconsecrated to Buddhism two hundred years later, and eventually was abandoned to be eaten by the jungle. The ruins were a testament to thousands of lives spent and lost, over centuries come and gone.

What Genevieve was building was so tiny. The Foundation elementary school enrolled four hundred children at that point, with uniforms and dormitories and a battalion of teachers. By many measures a success, but Genevieve had her doubts. The week before, she'd seen Bangkok bar girls protesting government attempts to regulate the sex industry, marching with signs that said BETTER AIDS THAN STARVATION. She had been bemused, wondering what their pimps had offered or threatened to make the girls demonstrate against their own interests, when she recognized one of the marchers. And then another, and another. They were former Foundation girls, each of them fed and housed and educated through their early years. Their rescue had been temporary after all.

She knew that when Foundation children were released at age twelve, some went on to middle schools run by cooperating charities, and some back to their families, but most were returned to the streets. She *knew* that; but the chart illustrating eventual outcomes was one figure on one page in a thick annual report, easily flicked past, and Genevieve had allowed herself to be dazzled by the positives: the improved vaccination numbers, the falling mortality rates. She had believed in Sister James's *good start.*

Genevieve saw now that they had both been naive, thinking they could ignore the sex industry, that dark space that had been dilated in the Bangkok economy in the sixties and seventies from the influx of farang, that did not collapse when the war came to an end. Through the succeeding decades it had expanded into a voracious maw, into which the Foundation delivered the children just as they grew out of simple needs, for food and medicine and the alphabet. A good start was not enough to protect them.

Standing on the terrace of Phnom Bakheng, Genevieve thought of the girls marching for the right to prostitute themselves, to risk AIDS and death. It had seemed wrong-headed, insane. But if one took the sex out of it, weren't the marchers simply saying what they needed? Employment, a means of support. More than charity running across their palms like water. What if the girls had something to sell other than their bodies?

A chorus of *ohhs* broke out from the group of tourists standing on the terrace with her: the sun was beginning to set. Genevieve barely noticed.

It wasn't that older children and adults weren't rescuable, she thought; it was that the Foundation didn't know how to rescue them. It was that *Genevieve* hadn't known how. The Foundation's mission could adjust; it could teach skills. They could take the older ones after all, they could take everyone.

She stood under the bowl of violent orange and pink sky working out the details, the vision of her life's work spreading out before her like bright veins on a leaf, the good futures possible for other people's lost children.

As the colors dimmed to gray and flashlights began flicking to life around her, the guide touched her arm, *Was beautiful, yes?* and she realized that the guides were herding the tourists toward the set of stairs equipped with the farang handrail, to make their way back down to the ground. Genevieve descended apart from them, down the middle of a stairway cut so steeply that each next step was invisible. Stepping again and again into nothing, all the way down.

She saw Maxwell Dawson again at a Foundation event at the turn of the century. He must have been in the crowd when she was onstage narrating her slideshow. She no longer needed to use a picture of Philip, nor any euphemisms. The world was hardier now, ready to understand that sex trafficking made the unappetizing mortar between the tiles of a vigorous tourist trade all over the world. Still, Genevieve's presentation was curated carefully: enough truth to inspire outrage, not so much as to provoke hopelessness.

She recognized Max immediately when he came up to her afterward.

"At this point, you've spent more time in Southeast Asia than I have," he said. He had aged well; his hair had stayed full and his body trim.

"Needs must," she said. She might have expected to feel guilt at seeing him, but instead felt a wave of nostalgia. For herself as she'd been before, for the passion they had shared. "I even speak a little Thai," she said. "Very badly indeed — but I do understand *kha kha kha.*" He smiled: so he remembered that conversation.

"Do tell," he said.

"Hard *kha kha kha*" — a light staccato — "means yes. Soft *kha kha kha*" — a zephyr — "means no."

A pause, both of them smiling. Then his expression became grave. "I was sorry to hear about Robert," he said. She inclined her head to acknowledge the statement. "I'm alone now too."

His eyes held the same adoring spark she remembered; that spark in men's eyes had lighted her path through the world. She had not had much formal education, no marketable skills, but no one wanted those from her anyway. They had wanted her attention. The attention of a beautiful woman, without even a hope of sex, was enough for so many men. Genevieve hadn't seen that light in a man's eye for a while; what men — and women — wanted from her now was absolution, to accept their check and tell them that they had done their part.

"You know, in certain circles, you're thought of as a saint," said Max.

"You know I'm not," she said. Lightly accenting the *you,* letting the word stand for all that had been between them. She dropped her voice and confessed, "I loathe these functions."

It was true; she heartily disliked playing Lady Bountiful, being called good or generous. Her actions weren't pure, didn't originate in goodness. She had brought Noi to

614

America, for example, neither from a burst of generosity nor because she thought of her as family. It had been a barter. Noi kept certain facts sharp and present. Like a hair shirt, over time the torment familiar, a kind of comfort. Genevieve could offer her America, in return for that.

"One would never guess," Maxwell whispered back to her. "You're the model of graciousness."

Had it really been thirty years? His warm brown eyes were exactly the same.

"They never found your boy," he said. He spoke it as a declaration rather than a question, the habit of a man long in authority.

"No," she said.

His face took on a repentant, furtive look; he leaned closer, to say something for her ears alone. But before he could say that next thing, what she knew would be some version of *I felt responsible for what happened,* she drew back and turned away, to greet a group that was hovering to her right. The pleasant nostalgia she'd been feeling was gone.

The years had swiveled the telescope of Genevieve's self-absorption around, shown her to herself as tiny and unimportant; she understood now that events didn't happen because she was a bad mother or a selfish person. Although those things might be true, events occurred for other reasons, confluences of forces both obvious and invisible.

615

Yet, understanding that her guilt was meaningless, she hadn't relinquished it — and it was not divisible. Now that Robert was gone, there was no one to carry it with her. Anyone else who tried to heft the burden, even for a moment, was a charlatan.

She felt Dawson lingering beside her for a while as she chatted with one group and then another; when she eventually turned back, he had gone.

Genevieve always spent a few hours canvassing on foot during each trip, showing the same old photograph as well as the most recent age-progressed image. Maybe someone would remember having seen him, having known or heard of him. She always included the area around Thammasat University, although she never saw that boy again. She chased down every lead as she had always done, the surge of hope each time a little less.

She stopped at a stall selling honey in beautiful jars with glass elephants standing on their tops, and spoke to the farang vendor. *Are you in trouble,* Genevieve asked her, *do you need help*? Force of habit. The woman smiled and shook her head. *I'm happy,* she said, with such sincerity that Genevieve feels tears come into her eyes.

"Keep right beside me," she warns Bea and Philip as they step into the house. Carrying a fretful Laura, she follows the agent through

616

the foyer and into a big empty room with no windows, puts her hand out to a switch on the wall. It clacks upward but brings no light.

The rental agent has scurried ahead into the darkness, is doing something there. A metallic *chunk* and a brilliant line of sunshine falls into the room. It widens as the agent pulls: the wall, it appears, is not solid, but a long series of joined panels that fold *clack-clack-clack* into a box at the far end. Genevieve stands in front of the enlarging oblong of light as Bea and Philip, who have *not* stayed right beside her, shriek from various rooms *Mum, there's animals on the walls* and *Mum, the water comes out brown.*

"Don't drink the water," she calls to them. "Don't touch anything. Come back here."

They crowd next to her, subdued, as the agent leads them around the ground floor. Most of its square footage is dedicated to one very large space behind a door. "For parties," says the agent, demonstrating open, close, with a radiant smile. Genevieve is baffled: What kind of parties is she thinking of, that will benefit from a closed door?

"There must be some mistake," Genevieve says in the kitchen, staring at a monstrous black stove that squats on the tile like a relic from a previous century.

"Don't worry, Madame," sings the rental agent. "Number One will cooking for you. Never come in kitchen again."

She herds them upstairs in a cowed parade through the bedrooms, downstairs again to the side terrace, where she waves an arm, beaming. When they fail to react, she takes Genevieve by the wrist and leads her to the edge of the terrace. "Swimming pool," the agent says, and turns Genevieve to look toward the back garden wall. She points, enunciating carefully, "Soo-wing." Just visible above the jungle of vegetation is the top crosspiece of a swing set, the rest of the structure swallowed by vines.

"We can't possibly live here," says Genevieve, the first words she has spoken in ten minutes.

"This your house, Madame," says the agent, her hand still around Genevieve's wrist, the *M'dumm* a reproachful coo. "Your husband choose it."

Robert had probably selected from a list: *three bedrooms, a big garden, and a swimming pool.* It must have sounded splendid.

"We'll have to choose again," says Genevieve, pulling her wrist from the woman's grasp under the pretext of resettling Laura in her arms. "Where's the list?"

"No list, Madame," says the agent. She holds out a small cluster of keys. Still smiling, but there is a firmness detectable now beneath the sweet, like the stone of a peach or the dark spindle of pip in the translucent fruit they had had at breakfast.

Genevieve realizes suddenly that she doesn't even know where they are in the city. She has no map; in the car she'd been playing pat-a-cake with a fractious Laura, paying no attention to the roads. She has no Thai money yet: *Change money* is on her list of first-day errands. She doesn't even know Robert's office telephone number, nor the telephone number of the hotel. Even if she knew those numbers, she doesn't have any coins to put into a phone box. *Are* there phone boxes? She doesn't recall seeing any.

This is the moment when she begins to understand the enormity of what she has allowed.

"Are you all right?" The honey-selling woman had stood up behind her stall and was leaning forward, her face sharpened with worry. "Ma'am?"

Behind her, a skyline busy with tower cranes. Genevieve felt herself rolling back to the present. Bangkok hadn't been a cozy village for some time. Philip would be thirty-five — no, almost fifty — now, the thread connecting them gone slack somewhere in these streets.

"Yes," said Genevieve. "Thank you."

She bought a jar of the honey and also a cake of the beeswax that bore the same elephant in relief. She would have some of the honey with her breakfast toast in the morning before her flight; she'd give the wax to Noi for her sewing needles. Laura would like the jar for her doll clothes; those little Barbie shoes were always going missing.

She's almost given up wishing that things had gone differently, but she can't help yearning after a few more shining days. That's how that time before appears in her memory: the sun always shining, even through the rain, and all of them together, her husband loving her in that pure, uncomplicated way. Both of them deserving that love, that grace. She looks down into the water, at her children's wet heads slick and dark like bobbing seals. *Come swim,* they say. *Mama, come swim.*

Now she is in the water with them, her body buoyed and light. She bounces on her toes, small bounds up and down, the heavenly coolness swallowing and releasing her, now at her waist, now lapping at her throat. She lifts her face, eyes closed against the sun, and falls softly to earth over and over, with the children invisible but all around her, laughing and near.

The way it might have happened but didn't, but is happening now.

She looks up to see a middle-aged woman with sandy-blond hair, dressed like a teenager in a paint-spattered T-shirt and blue jeans. From behind her, terrifyingly, Genevieve herself steps out. A visual hallucination, it must be. Unless the time slips have somehow become real and she's meeting herself in the past.

"I need to get home," Genevieve tells the nearer woman. Careful not to look at the hallucination beyond. "I've lost something." She doesn't know what it is, but it's something no one should lose.

The woman crouches in front of her. "André says you seem a bit confused."

Genevieve looks down at the carpet. She knows this industrial blue, she's been here many times. She looks up, sees a metal shark fin through a large distant window. So, airport. But which one? She doesn't recognize the logo on the tail — it's not the temple-roof scroll of Thai Airways, nor the Pan Am globe, nor the red phoenix of JAL.

"Mum," says the hallucination. "Do you know where you are?"

Genevieve flicks a brief suspicious glance at her, then looks away. Is this a Jesus-in-the-desert moment, is she being tested? It feels more like a power struggle: *This town isn't big enough for both of us.* Perhaps she should yield, let the younger version of herself go forward in her place. In some ways it would be lovely to succumb.

"Airport," she says.

"That's right," says the crouching woman. "We're at Dulles." She looks up to Genevieve's left and says, "Thank you again."

Genevieve looks up too. A worried-looking young man stands there, in a V-neck sweater; his hairline is an upright swatch, like Tintin's.

"Don't worry," Genevieve tells him. "He'll turn up." He always does, that mischievous Snowy.

"Let's go home, okay?" says the crouching woman.

She puts out her hand; Genevieve takes it.

She accepts the keys, smiles at the rental agent. She understands how it is. She and her children are marooned, at the mercy of this tiny person and a country of people like her, surrounded by streets so foreign that not even the alphabet is intelligible. Genevieve will rise to the challenge. Thank goodness it's only for a year.

PART 6

CHAPTER FORTY-NINE

2019

Laura woke cotton-mouthed under a bright panel of sky, blue with floating clouds. For a moment she didn't know where she was — then she remembered stomping up to the studio the evening before, still stoned from Kelsey's pot gummy, spying on the happy family in the window. The rest cascaded back: *I quit my family* and *paintings no one will buy.* She sat up carefully, experimentally. No dizziness. She got up, drank cold water from the tap, went downstairs. She was in the kitchen poking through the refrigerator when the front doorbell rang.

"You look like hell," said Bea when Laura shot the bolt and opened the door.

"Thanks. Why are you here?"

Her sister just looked at her. A moment of standoff before Laura moved aside to let her in.

Bea put her head back to look at the foyer ceiling as she went through; in the living room, she turned in place. "This is nice," she said. Laura said nothing. "May I see the studio? I've been so curious."

You could have seen it anytime in the last twenty years, Laura didn't say as she led the way up the stairs. It was gratifying to see Bea's expression as she emerged into the glass room.

"This is —" she said. Words failed her; she shook her head.

"I designed it," said Laura. "Well, me and an architect and a very expensive contractor who brought us both down to earth."

"I remember how expensive," said Bea, who'd written the checks. She walked to the window. "What a view."

"It's special glass to bounce the heat off, and there are motorized light-blocking shades, otherwise I'd cook like an egg on hot days. All controlled from there." Laura pointed to the glass control panel. "I wanted clean lines, so everything does double duty. Every interior wall hides a cabinet; that loveseat folds out into a bed."

"It's ingenious," Bea said. She was examining the control panel. "Daddy would have loved this."

A far cry from what she'd said when Laura wanted to build it: *Yes, he left us the money, but not to waste.* Then Laura remembered: *paintings no one will buy.*

"You've been buying my paintings," she said. "Behind my back."

"I was trying to help." Then "It was only

six paintings."

"Beatrice," Laura said, crossing her arms across her chest. "Why are you here?"

"Mum's birthday brunch on Saturday," Bea said. "I don't want you to miss it because —" She broke off before saying *you're sulking.* "You don't have to forgive me, or even talk to me. But it would be wrong not to have you there."

"Why? Mum wouldn't miss me." From Bea's expression, Laura realized she'd interpreted that as a callous reference to the dementia. She clarified, "Not that. I mean — she wouldn't ever have missed me." To her annoyance, she felt her voice tremble in her throat. "I've always been the least important person in this family."

Bea huffed an exhalation, as if Laura had punched her. She walked the few steps to the loveseat, sank down onto it. "I can't believe you think that," she said.

"Of *course* I think that," said Laura.

Bea didn't speak right away; she ran her hand over the rough weave of the loveseat cushion. "The other day you mentioned the Drills," she said finally.

"Yes," said Laura, after a tiny delay of surprise. "I hated those."

"I hated them too," said Bea. Watching her own hand as it moved over the fabric, forward then back.

"Then why?" said Laura, sitting down

627

beside her. "Why did you do them?"

"Philip happened," said Bea. Stilling her hand, but not looking up. "And then we came home, and the Lyon sisters happened. And there you and I were, every day, walking in the early morning, all alone. Two little girls." Laura saw it again, that long empty rise of pavement up Albemarle Street to the first bus stop. "I chose houses that looked friendly. Ones without dogs, that looked like kids or nice older people might live there. Window boxes with flowers, or Big Wheels in the driveways."

"What was the point?" said Laura.

"The Drills were my survival plan," said Bea. She brought her eyes up to Laura's. "I was training you to run to safety, when the inevitable kidnapper came along." A short laugh. "It wasn't much of a plan."

"Why didn't we both run?" said Laura. "Why just me?"

Bea shrugged. "We couldn't both outrun a grown man," she said. "And you were the one who needed to be saved. You were what *could* be saved, of our family."

It was such a new concept — her sister had been trying to protect her, not torment her — that Laura was silent.

"I am sorry we have never talked about any of this," said Bea. "When we came home I planted myself in the present and faced forward. I left the past behind, and put down roots as deep as I could. While you tear up roots as soon as they begin to grow." She put a hand up to forestall whatever Laura was about to say. "Not a criticism, just an observation." Laura nodded. Bea dropped her hand. "And I'm sorry about buying the paintings," she said. "I can see now that it was the wrong thing to do."

"It's humiliating," said Laura.

"You seemed to be in a hole. I wanted to provide invisible assistance while you got yourself out of it."

"I have been in a hole," said Laura. "I don't know if I'll ever get out of it." The admission made her breathless for a moment. "I think I need to be free to paint, and I haven't been free."

"What do you mean, free?" asked Bea. "Edward?"

Laura shook her head. "I think — Mum." She paused for her sister's objection, but it did not come; Bea sat quiet, listening. "Since she was diagnosed it's been like I've been caught in a whirlpool that I can't swim out of."

"A whirlpool of what?" said Bea.

"I don't know. The past? The things I half remember, the things I never understood. I think I always kept a little hope that someday Mum would explain at least some of it." With a scornful laugh at herself, "Of course, I could have asked."

"We were trained not to ask," said Bea.

"And now it's too late. We'll never understand any of it."

"There's the difference between you and me," Bea said. "I don't need to understand." Said without judgment, just a statement of fact: *I am here, and you are there.* "I'm not telling you that you *can't* quit the family," she said. "I'm asking you: please don't quit the family."

"You have to stop buying my paintings," said Laura.

"They're an investment," said Bea. "But I will stop." They smiled at each other, something settled between them. Bea stood, straightening her skirt. "And try to forgive Sullivan," she said. "I talked him into it."

That made sense, thought Laura, following her sister down the stairs; Sullivan would be no match for Beatrice.

At the front door, Bea paused. "For what it's worth," she said. Her eyes a steadier, less unearthly blue than their mother's. "I think all of your paintings are beautiful."

After Beatrice left, Laura made and ate an enormous omelet, stripped the tape from the walls of the most recently painted room, bundled up the drop cloths in there, and repositioned the furniture. She found her phone and turned it on, held it in her hand for a minute, considering. It was Tuesday, one p.m. Edward would be having lunch at his desk. She touched his name in the Contacts list, listened to the rings.

"Hello," said Edward. His voice held a bit of surprise. "Is anything wrong?"

"No," she said. It felt absolutely true. "I was just checking in."

On Wednesday night she wakes, suddenly, as if there's been a shout in her ear. She gets out of bed and climbs up into the dark studio, presses the icon on the control panel to illuminate a set of floodlights over the work area.

When she is done, it's late afternoon. She stands before the canvas, clutching the scraping tool. Five minutes, ten, heart lurching in her body as she looks. Slowly she extends her hand and opens her fingers, lays it down.

"I forgot to tell you to get ice," said Bea when she opened the door of the Tudor. She took the bag of groceries from Laura's arms. "Did you remember the anchovies?"

"I made something good," said Laura. Her smile felt like a cartoon, a half-circle lemon slice of a smile. It had still been good after she had taken a long walk and then a shower; it was still good after she'd napped. She'd left it for two solid days in the studio, almost afraid to look again. Felt it humming up there while she did pre-party prep tasks from the

631

list Bea sent via text, and finally that morning, had sneaked up to the studio for another look.

"That's wonderful," said Beatrice, smiling back. "I look forward to seeing it." She looked behind Laura, where Edward was coming up the path carrying a bag of ice in each hand. "Ah, Edward," she said. "I knew I could count on you."

Edward followed Bea into the kitchen; Laura went into the sitting room, where Philip sat reading a book.

"I'm sorry for what I said to you," Laura told him.

He looked up, blinking, as if emerging from a deep cave into strong light. He'd done that when he was a child, she recalled, exactly that.

"Mai pen rai," he said. He laid the book down. "Waffles," he said, and they both smiled. *Waffles* was Preston family shorthand for: this is mine, don't touch it without permission.

"Where is everyone?" Laura said.

"In the backyard," said Philip, gesturing to the wall of windows. "Clem got Mum a drone for her birthday."

"Oh my God," said Laura. She looked down through the glass at the group of them. Genevieve was holding the controller in both hands, Clem beside her. The twins and Noi and Tom, and all of their daughters, were standing with their heads back, looking up.

632

"Clem is an awesome man."

"He is ridiculous," said Bea fondly, coming to stand with her.

"Hello?" came a call from behind them. They turned to see a white-haired man in the entry hall.

"Uncle Todd!" cried Bea, going to embrace him. She put her arm through his as they came back together, to the doorway of the sitting room.

"It's good to see you," he said, his eyes warm on Bea, taking in Laura, flitting to Philip.

"It's been a long time," said Laura.

"Philip," said Bea. "This is —"

"I remember you," Philip said, in a voice so shocked and deep that it sent a shiver through Laura. His eyes were wide.

Bea's brow furrowed above her smile. "Philip, you remember Uncle Todd from Bangkok?"

"You had red hair," said Philip, still in that same odd, resonant voice.

"I went back," Uncle Todd said. "I went back for you."

"I don't understand," said Bea.

Philip's face was complex, some quiet struggle taking place within.

"There was a dog," he said with effort.

"I remember," said Todd Bardin, his words hasty, tripping over Philip's.

"What," said Bea again.

633

"Shh, both of you," said Laura. "Let Philip tell it."

CHAPTER FIFTY

1972

Philip, walking slowly, was nearly to the corner of the big street. Keeping his eyes front, as if they could pull the Mercedes into view. There was a movement in the corner of his vision; he turned his head to see a yellow dog on the other side of the street.

"Nice doggy," said Philip. It wasn't at all nice-looking. It was a soi dog that didn't belong to anybody, thin with patches of fur missing over its ribs; there was something wrong with one of its eyes. It had stopped walking when Philip had stopped; now it put its head up into the wind, as if it had caught an intriguing scent.

Philip debated. Should he shout, to try to scare the dog away? But that might enrage it. He could turn around and walk back the way he had come, but even if he reached the judo building before the dog reached him, there was no assurance of sanctuary there. He looked ahead at the big street, the noisy blur of cars, tuk-tuks, bicycles. Plenty of people. He began walking again in that direction. The dog kept pace with him, tail down, unwagging, adjusting its path to a diagonal and crossing the street toward Philip, who quickened his pace, telling himself not to run.

The dog reached Philip just before the corner, the pedestrian crowd a short distance away, the rush of traffic beyond that. Philip stood as still as possible as the dog put its muzzle down and sniffed, the leather of its nose making a dry tickle along the tops of his feet.

"Good doggy," Philip said again, trying to keep his voice calm. A woman was approaching on the sidewalk, yoked baskets of pomelo balanced on her shoulders. "Help me," he said quietly. "Help?"

She turned her head to look at him, and collided head-on with a man pushing a cart stacked high with coconuts. Fruit rolled everywhere, the two vendors scrambling to collect it; brakes squealed and passersby stopped, some to heckle, some to help. A yard from the fracas, Philip stood frozen as the dog sniffed along the inside of his ankle, investigated the back of his calf and then higher on his leg, the snout pushing the loose trouser fabric against Philip's skin. Of their own accord, Philip's testicles crowded up tight against his body. He moved his hands upward to get his fingers out of snapping range. He did it slowly, but the dog startled and jumped away with a low growl. The short fur of its neck stood up behind its yellow head, its angry curdled eye. Wrinkling lips back from wet teeth, it splayed its front legs and barked. Philip squeezed his eyes shut and held his breath, waiting for the lunge and the impact.

Through the quarreling commotion of the fruit vendors, he heard a sharp clap and a yell. He opened his eyes to see a man running toward them, clapping his hands together, *Hi, get away.*

The dog, teeth still bared, stared at the approaching man as if reckoning the odds, backed off a bit, then turned to flee. Philip, cold all over with relief, watched the pale narrow hindquarters trotting away.

"Did he bite you?" The man was agitated. "Did he bite you anywhere, even a nip?" Philip shook his head. "Good," said the man. "Close call." He smiled and Philip recognized him. It was the orange-haired man from the party earlier that summer, who'd come with the shiny lady. He was in frayed khaki shorts and a blue short-sleeved shirt, wiry ginger hair peeking out of the V at his neck. Nothing Philip's father would wear; nothing any of the men Philip knew would wear. The man looked at Philip's face. "Looks like something got you, though," he said. He touched his own upper lip.

Philip put his hand up to the swollen throbbing place on his mouth. "I got into a fight."

"With that Thai boxing boy you told me about?" Philip nodded. "I hope you gave him what-for."

"I did, I think," said Philip. "His nose bled a lot."

"Good man. Why are you here alone?" As if only just noticing that this was the case.

"Nobody came," said Philip. To his horror, his voice wavered on the last syllable in a sob. With enormous effort, he sucked in his breath and held it.

"Ah, well," said the man. He looked up the street for a moment, frowning. "I'm very late to an appointment. Otherwise I'd run you home." Philip felt the relief drain out of him. He had not considered that the man might leave him there. "They'll come, yes?" said the man. "They've been late before, haven't they?" With a smile, "Everyone's late for everything in Thailand."

"Never," said Philip, and it came out a squeak. He tried to say *They always come*, but his throat seemed to be shut now. He looked down at his toes, clenched them around the stems of his flip-flops, once, then twice, exactly the same pressure on each side. He watched his dirty toes go white from the pressure, then brown again, then white.

They stood there together for a minute, the long parentless street stretching away in both directions.

Finally, "All right," the man said, with a

note of surrender, as though Philip had been arguing with him. "Let's go."

He turned and walked away, past the coconut vendor and the pomelo woman, who were still collecting their fruit and quarreling, toward a motorbike parked at the edge of the sidewalk. Philip followed, picking his way through sticky pools of coconut water and squashed pomelo, his joints loose and swimmy with relief. The bike was at an angle, parked hastily — the man must have been riding it when he'd spied Philip and the dog.

"Can't very well leave you on the street," said the man, straddling the motorbike, as if he hadn't been about to do just that. He reached down and swung Philip up in front of him. Philip clamped the water-bottle bag between his thighs and held it there with both hands. He'd won a fight, and now a ride on a motorbike. This was turning into the best day of his life.

The red-haired man accelerated into the traffic and immediately stopped short; Philip slid forward, nearly off the seat, the bag sliding from his grasp and falling. The man caught him with a forearm across his chest and pulled him back, kept the arm there as they rode on. He ran the motorbike between the lanes of vehicles, steering one-handed, rarely braking, swooping to dodge the people walking, the other motorbikes that were also dodging and merging, the trucks, bicycles, tuk-tuks, *samlors.* It could have been scary, but with the arm tight across Philip's chest to hold him in place, it wasn't.

The man drove to a hotel, not the pyramid one on the water, nor the one with the good swimming pool, but a small grubby building with an arched doorway and flowering vines hanging down all around. How could *hotel* mean this place as well as the others? But that's what the sign said. HOTEL. The man walked fast and Philip hurried to keep up, his thighs still humming from the ride. Through the archway into a courtyard with a pond in the middle and doors all around, the man already opening one of them with a key.

"Go on in and wait for me," he said, pushing the door inward and standing outside, jerking his head at Philip.

Philip hesitated on the step. The room was stuffy and smelled like hot plastic.

"I told you I was on the way somewhere," said the man. "It's important, I can't be late. I'll go there, and then I'll come back after to get you and take you home. I won't be long." Philip walked into the room. The man added as he closed the door, "Clean yourself up in the bathroom. Your mother will have a fit if she sees you like that."

It wasn't technically a bathroom, as there was no tub in sight. But it did have a sink and a toilet, and a drain in the floor. Philip looked into the mirror. His lip was swollen but not as big as it had felt to his fingers, and there were wide red scratches on his neck, beaded with scab.

Philip used the toilet, then went to the sink and turned the hot tap, standing on his toes to squeak it open as far as it would go. He undressed while it ran from rusty to clear. He kept his underwear on. He lathered up as well as he could with a flat lens of soap he pried from the side of the sink, and cleaned everything he could reach, even rubbing his ears carefully between foamy-slick fingers. He used the small bucket under the sink to splash water over himself, leaning forward to try to keep his underwear dry. He considered, and rejected, the soiled towel on the rack, instead jumping up and down to shake the water off. He dressed again, combed his hair with his fingers, looked at his reflection. His mother would definitely notice his injuries, but he did look better. Then he sat on the bed and waited for the orange-haired man to return.

When the snick of the door finally came, Philip was asleep, curled up on his side with the hard edge of the robe's lapel pressing into his face. He lifted his head and sat up, rubbing the ridge left on his cheek.

The person standing beside the bed wasn't the orange-haired man. It was the shiny lady from the party. He recognized her immediately in the light that buzzed from the ceiling, although her hair was down now and she was wearing a short green dress with a lattice pattern on it, instead of the bright yellow dress.

"Hello, Philip," she said. "Do you remember me?"

"Yes," he said, and added automatically, "How are you?"

"I am well," she said. She smiled but it didn't touch her eyes. He remembered her name: MinWin. "I've come to take you to your parents."

"Thank you," said Philip, sliding off the bed and following her, shoving his feet into the gritty flip-flops that he'd left inside the door. It was dark outside now, cooler than the hotel room. Min held his hand as they walked around the black mouth of the pond and out to the street, to a tuk-tuk standing by the curb. A few soft strokes of Thai between Min and the driver before Min and Philip climbed up and in and were moving.

Philip had rarely been outside in nighttime before, and never in the open air like this. Traffic was light; the wind lifted and riffled his hair. The moon was a flat silver decal in the black sky. They rode between sidewalks dotted sparsely with people. He looked for the Dusit spire to orient him, but didn't see it.

"Nine Soi Nine," Philip reminded Min as

they turned through an intersection.

"I'm taking you to the hospital," said Min. "Your sister's been in an accident."

That explained why his parents hadn't come to get him.

"What kind of accident?" asked Philip.

"I don't know," said Min.

The tuk-tuk turned onto a smaller road, turned again into a narrow passage, bumped to a stop outside a building with a long metal eave. "We're here," said Min. Philip hesitated. This wasn't Fifth Field Hospital, where they got their vaccinations and where Bea had been taken the time she needed stitches. Min pushed against him from behind, and he stepped down from the tuk-tuk onto the street, telling himself that perhaps there was a wider variety of hospitals in the world than he had encountered so far, and this small crude building could be a hospital in the same way that the other place had been a hotel.

"Was it Bea or Laura in the accident?" he asked.

"Mai pen rai," said Min.

Her voice sounded different; her hand was a pincer on the soft place between his shoulder and neck. His heart jumped. "Stop," he said, to the hand gripping him, to the tuk-tuk no longer behind him, that had already driven off. He stared around as he was pushed along, saw eyes scattered in the darkness, people silently squatting and watching. "Please stop it," he said to them. None of them moved.

He felt so stupid. He'd gone along like a lamb, climbed into the tuk-tuk and ridden willingly to this place. Enjoying the breeze, when all that time he could have jumped out, run away, found a policeman. He could have run to a different tuk-tuk — they'd passed so many on the way — could have jumped in and told the driver 9 Soi Nine. Mummy or Daddy or Daeng would have paid when they got there.

Those alternate storylines surfaced in his panicking brain, jumbling his internal horizon briefly like ships of rescue. By the time Min had marched him up to the door of the not-hospital and was knocking hard, all options were capsized and lost.

"I'm sorry," said Min, her hand gripping very tight, holding him in place. "You're a nice boy." Her beautiful face looked broken open, anger in its creases like veins of lava. "So was my brother." She pushed Philip so hard through the opening door that he stumbled. "It's not only little American boys who matter," she said. He never saw her again.

They took his judo outfit. He gave it to them, actually. In his experience, a woman asking for his clothes had always meant she'd take them to the laundry and bring them back clean and folded. When they brought him other clothes he put them on. He didn't think about the judo outfit again until a long while later, when it hardly mattered anymore.

He was given something to drink, which he guzzled gratefully, and then sometime later he awoke in total darkness, his mouth very dry again, a fuzzy collection of memories in his mind — a rumbling of engine beneath him, being carried in someone's arms. *Hello?* He called into the darkness. *Hello?*

A widening slit of gray in the blackness told him there was a door in one of the walls. A door but no windows. Through the door came a girl with half of her face roughened by scar; she was about Bea's age. The thought of his sister and home was so painful that he cried out, an involuntary yip of sorrow. The girl spoke in whispered English as she put down a bowl of food: *If they give you medicine, take.* A fingernail paring of kindness.

The next part will stay in his memory like a dark slurry through all the years to come. A deep-buried river, cutting a rut where light doesn't reach.

He tried to fight them, but it was pointless. After a while he just let them, lay there and let them, the thin sheet under his face salty from crying and his throat hoarse from crying out, until no more tears or sound came, his chest heaving in breaking, empty shudders. When one man said *Take this,* Philip remembered what the girl had said, and opened his mouth to accept the pill fumbled onto his tongue.

Whatever they offered he accepted after that, even putting his arm out when they told him to, the needle under the skin a bright sting but distant, like the memory of a bee, like something happening to someone else. Eventually, he knew to look forward to the bee stings, to the warm flush under his breastbone and then the welcome oblivion.

His body seemed precious to them, even as they allowed it to be torn. They kept him clean and bathed and carefully tended his wounds, the old ones and the new. His swollen lip healed; he could tell by feeling with his fingers.

He managed to escape once, blundering past the scar-faced girl bringing food, down a warren of narrow passages into the open street. After the swelter of the windowless room, the clean hot sunshine and the light breeze carrying the fetid breath of khlong felt ecstatic.

"Help," he said to the loiterers in the street. "Nine Soi Nine."

They laughed while he stood on his toes, turning, trying to see the Sony sign or the

Dusit Thani spire over the roofline. Was he even in Bangkok anymore? He ran up the street, his weak legs making the movement jerky, like falling forward over and over.

"Nine Soi Nine," he cried as he ran. "I'm Philip Preston, I live at Nine Soi Nine."

His voice was frail, a whisper swallowed by the noises of the crowd, music from a radio somewhere. A child looked at him curiously as he stumbled past, but none of the adults looked over.

"Please," he said.

And then he was caught, a clatter of footfalls bursting behind him, a hiss and an onion-smelling hand clapping over his mouth.

He was punished for that.

He went a while without visitors while he was healing from the punishment. His brain had settled on that word for them: *visitors.* In and out of sleep, sometimes turning over in his slumber and coming awake with a cry as his damaged ankle rolled on the mattress. The wall opened sometimes; usually the girl with food or a sour liquid medicine; once in a while it was the older lady with a bee sting. One time he was shaken awake, whimpering at the jostling movement of his ankle, and realized that he had messed the bed and was being scolded. The old woman scolding him held up the pail and knocked on it. *Khi,* she said, over and over. She pinched his thigh.

He yelped and then repeated *Khi*. He understood: she was named Khi and he was to call her if he had to go to the bathroom, and she would come to help.

The room was like a closet, just the bed and a pail on the floor, so dark it was all one color. It was impossible to imagine that this same world included that home he was beginning to think he'd dreamed, with parents and sisters and the trembling blue rectangle of water, the scrambled eggs and chocolate milk, the sparklers and Christmas tree. When those things came into his mind he groaned loudly enough to bring a slat of light into the blackness, the angry sounds that might have meant "bad boy" or possibly "hold still," and sometimes a pill or bee sting. The medicines made a false bright river on top of the dark deep one; he floated along in the current, pushing himself into the middle of it, away from all thought, letting everything sink around him into memory, beyond reclaiming.

The ankle never knitted up properly. That was probably the point, he realized as he was finally allowed to walk a little: he wouldn't be able to run. Once he hobbled down the corridor into a small courtyard and Khi came chattering angrily after him, yanked him back by the arm, making him twist the still-tender injury and shooting a pain up from his ankle to his knee. She pointed at the shade under

648

the eave, slapped her own arm. He understood that he had to keep out of the sun: his pallor was valuable.

He tried to ask some of the visitors for help, particularly those he thought might be American. The first time, it got him a hard slap (*You'll speak when I say*); the next time simply a hand across his mouth, pressing hard to keep the words in, partly covering his nostrils so he had to breathe in snorts. One man, hearing the timid words — *I'm Philip Preston, I've been kidnapped, I live at 9 Soi Nine* — jumped away from him looking terrified, left the room, and did not return. The next visitor assured Philip he would call his mother and father, he would phone the police. After that man left, Philip waited with hope, but no rescue came.

The girl Hong who brought him food told him in English *If you nice, they give present.* She drew with a finger on her wrist until he understood *wristwatch*. She smiled the word *tang* and eventually he knew it meant money. Hong taught him Thai word by word, naming things. She explained, pealing with laughter, that Khi was not the name of the old lady. After some confusing pantomime he understood it meant what he was supposed to do in the bucket — what the Preston children would have called *poo-poo*. He blushed madly during that discussion, although Hong was completely matter-of-fact.

She said *khao*, meaning the rice in the bowl, and he repeated and she burst into laughter. *Khao*, she said again, and again he repeated, and again she laughed, putting both hands over her mouth. He started to become angry, it felt like a teasing game; she saw that and stopped laughing. *Khao*, she said carefully. She put her finger on the rice bowl. *Khaaao*. A long sound, rising and then leaving her mouth, like a balloon swelling and emptying. She put the same finger on his knee, said *Khao*. A shorter, rounder sound, starting and stopping in the hollow of the mouth. *Khao*, he said, tapping his knee. *Khao*, he said, touching the rice bowl, and she beamed.

He understood much later, looking back, that if he'd managed to get outside for more than that one minute in the first year or two he would almost certainly have been rescued, would have been borne like a surfer on a tide of Thai citizenry to the American Embassy or the police or back to the house in the American quarter where the family waited for him. But he wasn't allowed outside alone while there was still any Philip in him, and after the punishment that made it impossible to run, he didn't try to escape again. By then, with the dark river inside him, he didn't want to be found, not by anyone who'd known Philip.

When one of the visitors asked his name, he gave the one he would keep for many years afterward, the name he'd once loathed and rejected. It fit him now. The thing he'd feared so much had happened: the worst part of him was now all of him. To his surprise, he found that something else had changed: his need to even things out was gone, the counting banished from his head.

It was almost a relief, to be Nitnoy.

His first growth spurt came when he was ten, the height he had yearned for and spent his birthday and Loy Krathong wishes on. He shot up just as he'd been promised and was demoted from what he hadn't known was his special treatment. Another, smaller child began living in the private closet behind the hanging carpet with special high-paying visitors ushered in, and Nitnoy slept on the floor in a room with others and lined up with them when a visitor came. He was allowed to wander freely in the courtyard now, no one yanking him back from the sun.

He gleaned from overheard conversations that the war was over, the farang gone home in disgrace, good riddance, but they were also blamed for leaving and taking their money with them. There was a period of few visitors and little food, the old lady he still thought of as Khi particularly irritable. Then business got very good again, even better than before.

Nitnoy learned some words from the new visitors, more Thai and some Korean, some German, some Japanese, but never revealed to any of them any understanding of their language. They preferred it that way, he could tell; they wanted that gulf. They'd traveled far from home so that they could safely take down the masks they wore; they didn't want to be known. Afterward, they hastened away as though leaving it all in that dark room, but Nitnoy knew that they carried an indelible mark, like a secret, vile tattoo.

As Nitnoy continued to grow, he was chosen less often. The visitors looked up into his face and down at his tracked arms, and moved along. *They want fresher boys,* Hong told him in blunt Thai. *Younger. Don't eat so much, stay thin.*

Eventually, he became totally free to wander the streets, although he still limped badly and might not ever be able to run. He attracted no attention — at a glance, tall and tanned, with tangled hair to his shoulders, he looked like any strung-out wayward teenager. The city was filled with those now, backpacked and unwashed and wearing goofy Thai-stick grins. If anyone had looked closely enough, they might have seen that Nitnoy was younger than his height made him seem, but if they'd looked that closely they'd have seen the rest too: that there was nothing left to rescue.

He had few visitors now. He scrounged in the streets, selling the tourists stolen cigarettes or stolen trinkets, leading them to the various heroin rooms or sex clubs or the places they could buy Thai stick, speaking broken French or German, fake-shaking his head when they spoke English to him. Sometimes he robbed them. The first time he did it, seeing the frightened look on a previously trusting face, a muffled compassion stirred deep inside him. Then a voice jumped into his mind — *Your parents would be so ashamed* — and the last bit of Philip winked out. Nitnoy took the money from the sobbing *ngo* hippie, Nitnoy bathed in the khlong Philip had been forbidden to approach. Nitnoy was the one who performed and tolerated acts Philip couldn't name.

He did go back to 9 Soi Nine once, purely by accident, ambling up Sukhumvit into the American quarter and coming upon the address. He was almost surprised to see it, as though he'd been in a different city all along, a different universe. How could it still be there? It was morning; he squatted across the lane and waited. When the gate opened and a light blue automobile drove out, a Thai man at the wheel, Nitnoy couldn't help himself; he got up and ran-limped alongside, looking through the back window. A farang stranger was there in the back seat; he looked up briefly, eyes passing over Nitnoy and then back to the newspaper opened across his knees. The man's lips moved, saying something to himself or to the driver as the car accelerated away down the road.

Hong now urged him, *Eat as much as you can.* He understood her meaning: he'd become too rough, too old and unappealing, and soon they would throw him out.

One morning during the rainy season he was in the market crowd — farang were always distracted and vulnerable in a market — and spotted a good-quality pocketbook being carried on a wrist, handles only, no straps. He trailed the lady as she went from stall to stall, waited for her to wander closer to the mouth of an alley into which he could escape after the snatch. His ankle meant he couldn't outrun a pursuer, but he knew all the shortcuts, had houses he could run through to a rear exit, crevices into which he could fold himself.

The lady was moving awfully slowly. She wasn't pawing the goods the way farang normally did. She hardly even looked at the merchandise. What was she doing? She leaned over to talk to a child and something flashed on her hand. A ring, a large oval opal in a gold setting. Nitnoy felt a deep stab in his chest; he looked up at her face, saw that she was looking at him too. A flame of something like terror jumped inside him, and he ran. He heard a *crack* as though the sky were breaking and he ran faster in his syncopated skip-hobble, the crowd suddenly running with him. He reached the bank of a khlong, dove in, and swam. Gunfire crackled behind him. Was the lady shooting at him? Others were jumping into the water too, all of them swimming for their lives.

He stayed away from that area for weeks, even after the violence had died down. He went back to the place he still thought of as the hospital. He had nowhere else to go: the army was shooting anyone on the street after curfew. He was received with little welcome, allowed to kick a sleeping space for himself among the others. He ate whatever Hong could sneak him and lined up with the others whenever a visitor came, although Khi scolded him and tried to push him out of the room. He was half a meter taller than her now.

The blond visitor who came one day was unexpected. His clothing and shoes, the expensive watch clutching his wrist, the gold chain at his neck — all marked him as wealthy. The rich didn't come to this squalid hole. There were much more beautiful places they could afford. Hong had briefly worked in one of them, palatial with bowls of lotuses and clean soft white beds, before her face got burned. The rich came to the hospital only if they were new to Bangkok or if they had true depravity in mind.

The man walked down the line, all of the eyes following, and stopped in front of Nitnoy.

Sprichst du Deutsch? asked the man. That was also unusual. Usually the negotiation was accomplished without Nitnoy's participation, as if he were an objet d'art or livestock being purchased. *Tu parles français?* said the man, when Nitnoy didn't respond to the German. *Or perhaps English?* said the man, and Nitnoy hesitated, then nodded.

The man's name was Kenneth. He turned out not to be depraved at all. He took Nitnoy to a good hotel, fed him an enormous meal. He was gentle, kept asking *Is this all right?* After Kenneth was asleep, Nitnoy rifled carefully through his possessions, the wallet, the wristwatch, the gold chain, hearing Hong's voice, *Don't be stupid, take it and go* before putting them down and climbing back into the soft white bed.

Kenneth took Nitnoy to Phuket for a week, a private cabin on the beach where they stood waist-deep in the warm salt water, millions of tiny jellyfish swarming and stinging. Back in Bangkok, they spent nights at Kenneth's smart apartment. The consistent feeding began to fill Nitnoy out, his ribs no longer jutting from his skin. While Kenneth was at work, Nitnoy cajoled Hong out for a meal, bought her candy and a lipstick. *Lucky you,* she said, twisting up the tube of scarlet, but her voice didn't sound entirely happy.

Nitnoy made Kenneth describe his home again and again: frosty air, mountain peaks against the sky. An internal flickering reel of memory played while Nitnoy listened, of cold bits falling to his face and melting away, mittens encrusted with cracked white shapes, patting lofty handfuls together to make a ball. *Imagine never having seen snow,* marveled Kenneth. *I never have,* said Nitnoy.

Kenneth needed to go away for business; Nitnoy went back to the hospital and counted the days. When Kenneth returned after a month and walked down the line, Nitnoy was already getting to his feet when he saw that Kenneth had stopped, was resting his hand on the shoulder of another boy. At the door, Kenneth looked back, as if Nitnoy's hurt had called to him. He told the boy to wait and walked back. He and Nitnoy stood eye-to-eye; Nitnoy had had another growth spurt and the nickname was a bit of a joke now, the way that elephants or big men can be called Tiny. Kenneth put a hand out to Nitnoy's jawline, the fingertips reading the bristles there like Braille. *It used to be so smooth,* he said sadly. Nitnoy's eyes glassed with tears and Kenneth took his hand down, said in a voice turned harsh, *You knew this couldn't last.*

Hong had an idea. She had been unwanted ever since the burn to her face; now that Nitnoy was unwanted too, she shared her idea with him. She knew someone with a van they could use to recruit children from the villages. She wanted to start her own house. *Clean,* she said. *Better than this.* She needed Nitnoy for two reasons: first because her own face would frighten off children, and second because Nitnoy was a farang who spoke Thai, enough of a curiosity to overcome wariness. *You can offer them anything,* she said, *and they'll follow you.*

They went in broad daylight, driving into the country, and parked next to a long stretch of brackish water in sight of where some children were playing. Hong set up a stove and began to cook; when the children came toward the smell of food, she went inside the van. But their parents must have warned them, for they didn't come close enough, and in the end only one small boy, maybe four or five years old, climbed inside the van to eat and then fell asleep curled on a blanket. *One is better than none,* said Hong; she closed the van door and Nitnoy jumped into the driver's seat and drove away. The jerking acceleration woke the boy, who began to cry. Hong clamped her hand with a cloth in it over his mouth.

There was a chemical on the cloth; the fumes reached Nitnoy in the driver's seat. His head filled with a buzzing light and he stamped on the brakes.

"What are you doing?" cried Hong, as Nitnoy got out of the van and opened the back door. He pulled the boy out into the fresh air, slapped him on the cheeks and pushed him, staggering, back toward home.

After that, he and Hong were not friends anymore. She would not sneak him food at the hospital. Nitnoy slept wherever he could, climbing into the underpinnings of bridges, tying rags around the metal support bars to baffle snakes. Stealing whatever he could, pickpocketing in the markets.

When the honey seller arrived, Nitnoy noticed him immediately. Farang vendors were generally easy pickings, and this one seemed exceptionally stupid. Young and blond, he kept his eyes closed as he sat in half lotus on a striped cloth on the pavement with a cluster of gold-filled jars and a wide flat bowl beside him. A sign propped up against the bowl read in thick black letters: HAPPY HONEY. A steady stream of tourists flowed by; some stopped and talked with him for a little while. Some of them bought, putting the money into the bowl. Was it a test, how the man sat with eyes closed in between customers, the bowl of money unguarded in front of him? Nitnoy circled around him at a distance, watching and listening.

"The past is a trap," the honey man told two stringy-haired tourists. "Our lives grow crooked, like bent trees. We can't unbend the tree, but if it keeps growing, the top will find the light." The hippies nodded. Nitnoy snorted at their naiveté.

The honey man wasn't a monk, he was just a Thai-stick farang, so Nitnoy stole the bowl without a qualm, nabbing a jar of honey too. He loped down a side street with his irregular stumbling run, and although no outraged calls followed him, kept running all the way to the spot under the bridge where he'd lately been sleeping. There he counted the coins and notes and pocketed them, examined the jar. It had a small glass elephant, trunk raised, standing on the lid. He twisted the lid off, scooped the honey into his mouth with two fingers. It was delicious; under the sweetness, an additional flavor vibrated on his palate that he couldn't identify.

He used the money for a meal and an injection so strong that he slept almost all the next day. The day after that, he went back to the same spot in the market and the man was there again, eyes closed, with the jars of honey, the same sign, a new wide money bowl. Nitnoy squatted in the shade on the pavement across the street. The honey man sat in the broad sun without apparent discomfort, not even fluttering his lashes when flies buzzed around his face. He wore only a pair of shorts. Blond hairs glittered on his deeply tanned chest and abdomen as they rose and fell with his breathing. He didn't move when the rain came, and when the sun returned, it lit his curly head into a halo, jeweled with drops of water. When the sun reached the top of the sky the honey man got up, unhurried and limber, carefully lifted the corners of the cloth, and tied them together, making a tight bundle of honey jars and money bowl, and carried the bundle away.

On the next day it was very hot, few tourists out walking, when Nitnoy settled into the same shady spot across from the honey man, squatted there for no more than five minutes before the man opened his eyes and looked right at Nitnoy, as if he'd seen him through his eyelids. The honey man beckoned.

Telling himself that maybe the man did not recognize him as the thief from three days before, Nitnoy rose and went across the street.

"Smoke room? Thai stick? Boy-girl?" he asked the man, standing a few feet away.

The man smiled.

"What do you want?" said Nitnoy, harshly, in English.

"You," said the man. He stood and tied up

his bundle, walked off without looking behind him.

Nitnoy hesitated, then followed. So the man was another visitor. He felt disappointed, although he wasn't sure what else he'd hoped for. Still, it would mean money, maybe some food, maybe a chance to steal something valuable. They walked a long while, Nitnoy a few feet behind the man, through streets that became greener and less crowded. Finally the honey man opened a gate and went through; Nitnoy followed. Up the long front stairway of a large wooden house, where a line of sandals stretched outside the double-door entrance: a lot of people lived here.

"What do you like?" Nitnoy asked the man as they went down a corridor past a series of closed doors. The man stopped outside one of the doors, opened it to reveal a Western-style bathroom. Nitnoy understood; he stripped off his shirt, kicked off his trousers. Finicky clients sometimes wanted him to bathe beforehand. Sometimes they wanted to bathe with him. Not this man, who stepped out of the room and closed the door.

The room was a luxury of porcelain; Nitnoy took his time. When he emerged, a towel wrapped around his waist, the man was waiting for him in the hallway, as though he had been there the whole time. He led Nitnoy to another door, opened that to reveal a small room with a clean bed. White walls, white bed linens, a white tent of mosquito netting.

"Hungry?" the man asked him. Although he was, Nitnoy shook his head. It had been too long since the previous injection, and he was feeling the claws of craving. He'd finish this, get paid, and run back. No time to steal. He could always return to do that; he'd noticed that there were no locks on the doors.

Nitnoy lay back on the bed. Not relaxing his guard; even the serene, monk-looking outside of a person could hold a violent soul. He had scars to remind him of that. Still, the deep comfort of being so clean, in a room and a bed so perfectly white and clean, reached to him from a lost place in his memory, and he closed his eyes while waiting for the honey man to undress.

He awoke riding the full tossing waves of dopesickness, the sweat pouring from him in a gritty flood and cramping pain seizing his guts. The honey man was there; he held Nitnoy while he sweated and shook and moaned and retched; during intervals of quiet the honey man dribbled water into Nitnoy's mouth, wiped his face with a cool cloth.

Two more days of that, and on the third Nitnoy woke up alone in the white room, with blue sky outside the windows. He stood on shaky pins, saw the pile of clothing beside the bed. It was his, now clean and folded; he pulled it on, then found his way down the corridor to the bathroom. When he returned to the white room the man was there, sitting on the bed, holding a mangosteen.

"How are you feeling?" he asked. He snapped off the cap of the mangosteen and tipped his head back to drop the gout of liquid into his mouth.

Nitnoy sat on the bed.

"I stole from you," he said.

"I know," said the man, smiling, breaking the purple shell of the mangosteen and dividing the cloudy white fruit with a thumb. He held out a section. Nitnoy knelt before him, placed his hands on the man's knees, leaned his body toward him and opened his mouth, indicating that the man should place the fruit there. The man did so, and Nitnoy put a hand higher onto the man's thigh. Still smiling, the man put his hand over Nitnoy's, staying its movement.

"You must be hungry," said the man, standing up. He led Nitnoy down the hall, passing a group of farang meditating in a room, to a large space at the end of the building set about with tables. Tall panels of glass all across the back wall looked out onto the grounds; a long table at the side of the room held fruit, some crocks of congealing porridge, an urn of water, a teapot. Clearly, a communal breakfast had happened already. Nitnoy put his hand against the teapot: still warm.

The food was surrealistically delicious, the

way food always was after pulling free of heroin. Nitnoy ate enormously while the honey man, whose name he still did not know, took only a little bit of *khao tom* rice porridge.

When his belly was full, Nitnoy asked again, "What do you want?"

There wouldn't be a bath and a meal without a price. He'd worked it out while he was eating: probably this was one of those religious groups and the honey man would want to talk to him about Jesus Christ.

"Nothing you don't want to give," the man said.

In the perfect silence, Nitnoy realized that there was no sound of air-conditioning. No breeze of ceiling fans. Yet the room was perfectly temperate.

"What do *you* want?" said the man.

"I'd like to stay here," Nitnoy said, surprising himself.

The man nodded.

"Then you need to meet Gerhard," he said.

Gerhard was an older farang in blue jeans and a wrinkled short-sleeved shirt.

"You've had enough to eat?" asked Gerhard. His accent was Germanic, *youff hat enuff.* Nitnoy nodded. "Come. I'll give you a tour." Vaguely amused, as if the word *tour* were a joke.

There was a set of jointed doors in the

middle of the bank of tall windows, and they walked out of those together. Standing on the terrace, Nitnoy could see how big the compound was, the beautifully kept lawns rolling away. Men and women were everywhere, silently working: sweeping the paths, on their knees in a vegetable garden. Many of them wore beige pajamas, but not all. They looked up and smiled as Nitnoy and Gerhard passed.

Hidden among the flowering hedges were half a dozen clearings, with buildings and open sheds of various sizes. In one of the larger buildings they stood and watched a man blowing into a long pipe, an orange bulb of glass at its end revolving and expanding and becoming a honey pot identical to the one Nitnoy had stolen. Nearby, a slight person with shorn hair was making the glass elephants for the lids, drawing out the glass with a wooden pick into legs and tail and trunk, pressing the thin edge of the pick into the hardening glass to make the wrinkles at the knees.

"Would you like to learn how to do this?" asked Gerhard, after they'd watched for a while.

"It's beautiful," said Nitnoy.

"Trask said you wanted to stay. You must choose the work you want to do," said Gerhard. "We also make pottery and flower garlands. Or you could tend the fishponds or

666

the vegetable garden."

"So that's your game," said Nitnoy, suspicion rising like a bitter acid at the back of his throat, even as the honey man's name *Trask* sang in his mind. "You pull people off the street to staff your factory." He remembered the little boy stumbling out of the van.

"We don't do it for the money," Gerhard said. "We don't need the money. We need the work." He paused. "We all need the work." He saw Nitnoy eyeing the barrel-linked silver chain around his neck, reached up and unclasped it. "Do you want this?" he said, taking Nitnoy's hand and pressing the necklace into it. "Take it. You can take anything here."

"What's the catch?" Nitnoy said it in Thai; he didn't know the English for it.

Gerhard didn't understand the Thai, but he caught the gist.

"We don't want anything from you," he said. "We're here *for* you." Nitnoy couldn't look away from the pale bottomless eyes. "We're a community dedicated to presence. If you want to stay here, we ask only two things," said Gerhard. "First, you will need to work. Second, when you are ready, you will need to tell your story. Just once, to the person you select, and completely. From as far back as you remember up to the very moment you are speaking. And then never again." Gerhard began walking again, down the grassy slope; Nitnoy followed, still clutching the necklace. "If you choose the right time and the right person, and if you are completely honest, your past and all its anguish will run out of you like sand. You will never need to look back again." He gestured to the grounds, humming with industry. "Everyone here has left a life behind."

"Why?" Nitnoy's voice cracked on the syllable. "Why would I do that?"

Gerhard shrugged. "Perhaps you never will," he said.

No one stopped Nitnoy when he left. He sold the silver chain at a poor price — the shopman could see the need in him — but it was enough for three good injections and a few meals. He slept and then woke and slept and woke. Finally he sat under the bridge, watching the water go by, in that short interval of dull consciousness after waking from an injection and before the claws returned.

He went to the hospital, found Hong. Her face darkened when she saw him.

"Listen," he said, and described Gerhard's house. "We can both go."

"I know that place," she said. "Stupid farang Buddha people. You owe me three hundred baht for what I paid for the van and the food that day. All for nothing."

He put all the money he had left into her hand, made a deep wai, and left her staring.

"Would you like to work with the glass?" said Gerhard when he returned. As if their conversation a week before had not been interrupted. "Or perhaps the vegetable garden?"

Nitnoy thought of the elephant being twitched out of a ball of glass, then remembered the honey he'd stolen, the lingering, mysterious flavor.

"Where are the bees?" he said.

He was stung a lot.

"You move too quickly," said Gerhard. "You have to move with awareness. You have to move with love." *Love:* that seemed a ridiculous word to use about insects.

Gerhard himself moved almost in slow motion when managing the hives, placing each frame carefully, allowing the bees to escape, never squashing one. At harvest time, he showed Nitnoy how to fit a harvest insert below what he called the *super,* the top level of the hive that held the frames of honeycomb. The harvest insert had a maze on its underside, a complicated set of channels around a central hole. Gerhard explained that while the hole permitted the bees' easy exit from the super, the maze baffled their return. The harvest insert was left in place for a few days; then they used the smoke to calm the bees and drive them into the lower hive to feed.

They lifted the frames out above the dozing feeding bees, took them one at a time to the honey hut. Gerhard heated a knife blade by running a lighter up and down the metal, then sliced across the honeycomb, removing the caps from the wax cells. He held the frame over the collecting drum, and when the flow of golden honey had stopped, set the frame outside on a table. "For the bees to clean," said Gerhard. They came as if summoned and crawled for hours over the frame in an industrious undulating mat of gold and black, collecting the remaining honey traces and leaving the wax intact. The honeyless frames were put back into the super and the maze insert was removed, so the bees could fill the cells with new honey and seal them with new wax caps, and it all could begin again.

Between harvests there was plenty to do. They inspected the hives regularly, looking for hive beetles or the stringy signs of disease. They also took care of the flowers. To tend to the bees, you must tend to the flowers, said Gerhard. A lot of flowers were needed to entice the bees to stay on the property. Pesticide use was rampant in the rest of the city, and a bee who wandered could bring poison back to the hive.

"All this land is actually for the bees," said

Gerhard, waving his hand to indicate the longan bushes, the trees, the flowering shrubs.

There were other crafts in the compound apart from glassblowing and honey; over time, annoyed at being stung so often, Nitnoy tried all of them. He made flower garlands to sell at the temples, but his fingers couldn't do the fine work as well as the patient women who demonstrated for him. He enjoyed the pottery at first, how the cylinder rose like magic between his circled hands, but one wobble and it went out of shape, the mouth a dented ellipse, the whole thing collapsing sideways. At the end of two days, he scraped the clay back into the slurry and went back to the bees.

At first, he was angry at the bees for stinging him, the pointlessness of their reflex suicides annoying him as much as the painful welts. As he grew more experienced and was stung less he felt superior to them, seeing them as slaves. Then he began to pity them for the futility of their lives, building up stores that were robbed again and again. Finally he began to love them, as their god who cared for them, who took from them for reasons they couldn't comprehend. He strove to be a good deity, to ensure that they didn't suffer unduly, not a leg or a wing crushed. He learned to go slowly, to *walk between heartbeats* as Gerhard said, to focus on just the matter at hand, not looking behind at what had gone before, or ahead to what was to come. Harm to the bees felt like harm to himself. It was love unrequited, love that served no purpose. Which was, after all, love.

"The problem of the bee in the bottle," commented Gerhard with the air of telling a joke, one day when Nitnoy was coaxing a bee out of a jar and back to the hive. He saw that Nitnoy did not understand the reference. "Hm. I shall get you some books." He took the jar from Nitnoy, turned it right side up. "The philosopher Wittgenstein described the human condition as that of a fly in a bottle. The fly bangs against the sides of the bottle why? Because he does not see the bottle. *The world and life are one. I am my world.*" The bee crawled up the glass toward the mouth of the jar. "The bottle walls are transparent, giving the illusion of freedom."

"They don't know they're in our bottle," said Nitnoy.

"Are they?" said Gerhard. "Or are we in theirs?" The bee reached the lip of the jar and flew away.

Nitnoy saw the honey man Trask only from a distance, down the table at breakfast or meditating with a group every morning and evening. Eventually Nitnoy joined them, sitting with eyes closed and pins and needles starting in his bad leg, wondering if he was supposed to be doing something specific. A sudden voice came into his ear: a woman was crouched beside him murmuring instructions, how to find the center of his body by drawing two invisible lines. "Focus on the place where they cross," the woman said, her voice quiet as a breath, "and then I'll tell you what's next." Nitnoy labored to draw the lines and failed, aware of Trask sitting across the room with his own eyes closed.

Sometimes at night, Nitnoy lay alone in his room, the stung places itching and painful, and felt bitter doubt. Was he deluded, a slave like the bees, lured into a hippie factory, trapped and toiling? But then he'd wake alone and safe in the quiet clean room, go out into the common area, and see through the smooth glass of the lockless doors the sun rising over the lockless gate, and think: *I am choosing this.* He'd go back to work.

After one harvest, Nitnoy collected the waste wax that was sliced from the caps of the honeycomb and put it into a pile on the table for the bees to clean.

"I have something in mind," Nitnoy told Gerhard, who was watching.

When the wax was clean and ready, Nitnoy brought out what he'd made in the ceramics building the day before: a tray with a dozen hollow half-elephant depressions in it. He'd made it by pressing one of the glass elephants into a sheet of clay twelve times, then firing that. While Gerhard watched, Nitnoy set the tray into one of the rectangular containers they used to collect the honey, placed the metal filtering screen over the container's top, and crowded the bits of waste wax onto it.

By the afternoon, the wax had melted in the sun and dripped through the filter to fill the oiled clay mold, making a smooth block an inch and a half thick. Nitnoy moved the container into the shade, and after the wax cooled and hardened he shattered the clay and sliced the wax into smaller blocks, turned them over. Twelve cakes of beeswax, each with an elephant in relief on the top, ready for sale.

"Wittgenstein wanted to show the fly the way out of the bottle," Nitnoy told Gerhard one day. "But that's not what you want." He felt daring, telling his teacher this. After two years at the compound, Nitnoy had read the books Gerhard had given him, plowing through the novels and the volumes of history and mathematics, reading more slowly through the philosophy tomes.

"What do I want?" said Gerhard.

"You want the fly to love the bottle," said Nitnoy.

Gerhard smiled.

"I'm ready to tell my story," said Nitnoy. "And I'd like to tell it to you."

■ ■ ■ ■

It took three days. They stopped only for drink; they did not eat. It was hot enough that they rarely had to pause to urinate. Others took care of the bees while Nitnoy told Gerhard everything, from as far back as he could remember, until his voice was hoarse and frayed. Gerhard listened, made no comment. When finally Nitnoy stopped speaking, Gerhard said, "That's not all."

"That's all I remember," said Nitnoy.

Gerhard waited.

Nitnoy rolled onto his back, stared up at the graded pool of light on the ceiling thrown by the candle on the bedside table. Thinking, *No, no I can't tell this part.* Thinking, *I have to.*

"Khi told me." The words stumbling into the quiet. "When she was hurting my ankle." On the ceiling, a monstrous silhouette of an insect: blurred wings, dangling legs. "She told me that she'd tried to return me for money, but my parents wouldn't pay." He felt the shameful truth slip out of him. "They didn't want me back."

He cried for a long time, and then slept, and when he woke, he felt lighter. Not as if the burden he carried had dissolved, but as though it had changed its nature. He remembered it all, he would always remember. Deep within him, the river still flowed, but the liquid between the banks was weightless as mercury.

"You are free now," said Gerhard. "You begin from here. You must live with awareness, choose your life every day. Your first decision: you can stay or you can go."

"I will stay."

Gerhard nodded. "Your second decision: you need a new name."

The answer came to his tongue immediately.

He was Pip now. He continued with meditation — every day, twice a day, trying to draw the lines without thinking about drawing the lines. Most days he spent the whole meditation period fighting urges: to scratch an itch on his arm, to open his eyes. He sat in half lotus — all he could manage with the deformed ankle — morning and evening with his eyes closed, eventually no longer trying to draw the lines but trying instead to accept that perhaps he'd never draw them.

After four years of choosing meditation and the bees every day and reading every book that came into the compound, Pip went to sit as usual on the hard floor, and some unknown time later his eyes opened slowly as if waking from sleep, and when the rest of the group rose and dispersed, he rose too, and went to the instructor.

"I did it," he told her. "I drew the lines."

"What did you see where the lines crossed?"

"A ball," said Pip. It had hovered over the point of intersection, sooty clouds whirling inside it. "Full of darkness." The instructor nodded.

"Clear the darkness," she said. "See what's inside."

That took much longer. That took almost the rest of his life.

One night, Pip went to Trask's room and lay down alongside him. Trask opened his eyes and smiled. It was nothing like Kenneth. It was man to man, it was chosen by both of them every day, it was love.

For the first time since he could remember, Pip could see money and feel no pull toward it. Those bits of metal had no intrinsic value; they were tokens used outside the walls, by people outside the walls. He stayed inside the walls, with the bees and the flowers. There was always someone else to send out for an errand. It might be a kind of bottle he'd crawled into, reflected Pip, or a human version of a harvest maze, easily entered but difficult to leave. But was that a bad thing? Trask, who went outside every day to sell the honey and the cakes of beeswax, described how Bangkok was changing. Pip could see the cranes on the horizon, the buildings rising. There was talk of an elevated train. Some nights Trask stayed out overnight and didn't come back. Sometimes he brought a new person back with him, whom he took to an unoccupied room; that person stayed or didn't stay.

The old habits returned to Pip. He found himself counting, and evening things out. Gerhard noticed.

"It feels — necessary," said Pip. "I don't know why. I'm happy here."

"I am not sure it has to do with happiness," said Gerhard. "I think it has more to do with your relationship to perfection."

Pip considered that. Being Nitnoy had been chaotic, like living with a jangling bodyful of broken glass. No amount of ritual would have had an effect. Pip, by contrast, was happy — but oddly less content. To Pip, good implied the possibility of perfection. The constant teasing nearness of it, the impossibility of achieving it, drove him to self-soothe. *Love my bottle,* Pip told himself. Gradually, over a long time, the habits died away.

One season Trask grew drastically thinner. He was forty-one, only ten years older than Pip, but he began to look elderly. Purple spots bloomed on his skin; he sweated with fevers. He went to the doctor, came back and explained to Pip what the doctor had said. Slowly Pip understood: like a wandering bee, Trask had collected a toxin outside and brought it in with him. There was no cure. Caring for Trask through blindness and hallucinations and a long, speechless, raspy-breathed coma, Pip struggled to practice Gerhard's principles: total presence in the moment, no looking forward or back. *All we have is now.* He didn't completely succeed in stamping out either the longing for the past, for the days when Trask had been the beautiful healthy honey man, or the cringing from the future, waiting to grow sick himself.

Enter this loss, said Gerhard after Trask died. *Feel every part of it, then let it go.*

Selfish thoughts kept breaking through Pip's meditation, *I didn't keep him safe — I let him wander,* and agonized questions, *When will my turn come?* Standing with the bees humming around him in the sunlight, he tried to feel those feelings too, and also let them go.

A new realization came to Pip during that period of acute mourning, as simply as a breeze passing over his skin. Without effort or struggle, with no sense of epiphany, he understood that he was not the bees' deity but their servant. He was part of the cycle of their lives, that endless loop of industry and loss. The realization came to him in a shimmering, clear moment, and Pip was different afterward. He stopped fearing illness and death, stopped festering with regrets. He felt a deep internal balance: from then on, there was no part of that river inside him that was purely light or dark.

Over the years, the group alternately dwindled and grew, breathing in and out like a set of lungs. As Gerhard grew older and more frail, Pip and the others cared for him until the day he closed his eyes forever. Shortly after that Claudette came, with her sharp voice and sharp eyes. She dispatched the whole lot, the weepy Australian girl who'd been there for only a season and the glass-blower who'd been there longer than Pip, and everyone in between.

"You must have family somewhere," Claudette said when only Pip was left.

"I had sisters," he said. He was surprised how easily the girls were called into his mind from that long-ago time tangled up with pain and sadness like bees caught in honey. They'd been there all along, though, for as soon as he looked, he saw them vividly: Laura jumping rope, Bea flutter-kicking across the pool. They'd be women now. If they were still alive, if they had ever existed.

"You're American? Canadian? Australian?" Claudette rapped out. "What's your full name?"

He'd been Pip for decades, but when he opened his mouth to answer, the name slid out easily: Philip Preston.

He gave her the names and facts he remembered. He wanted to tell her not to bother looking for that clean family in 9 Soi Nine, the temple-roofed house with the hibiscus garden and the swimming pool. Trask had described to him how that whole block had been leveled and rebuilt long ago during that time of rapid evolution, when the old Bangkok was being eradicated and replaced by the new. There was no way to find the Prestons now, wherever they'd gone.

He hadn't reckoned with, indeed hadn't known about, Google. Claudette poked her index finger at her phone and after only a couple of minutes, turned it so he could see.

"Here," she said, thrusting the small lit screen toward him. "Is this your sister?"

CHAPTER FIFTY-ONE

2019

He didn't tell all of it, but he told them enough, and when he was done they were hushed. Edward had come in during the narrative and sat beside Laura, putting his arm around her.

Uncle Todd was sitting with his face buried in his hands.

"How could you," Bea said to him. "How could you."

"Why did you leave him at that place?" said Laura.

"I've regretted it all my life," said Bardin, his voice muffled. He lifted his head; his eyes looked hunted. "I was on my way somewhere important when I ran across Philip in the street." He shook his head. "A source I had been cultivating. We used to meet in a heroin room in one of the bars in Patpong. I had an agreement with the girls who prepared the syringes; they'd fill mine with sugar water. I was late to the meeting when I saw" — he looked at Philip — "you, alone."

"You could have taken him home on the

way," said Laura.

"It was the opposite direction from your house. It had been months of work. The source was about to turn. I made a choice." He looked sick with regret. "I took him — you — to the doss house I used as a cover, and went to the bar." To Philip, "I told Min to go and get you and take you home. You'd met Min. She was one of the bar girls I trusted. I didn't know she was angry at me."

"Why was she angry?" said Philip. His voice hushed and high-pitched, sounding almost like a child's.

"I was careless with a photograph," he said. "She'd been trying to get her younger brother out of Vietnam, and I'd promised to try to help. But the photograph of him got into the wrong hands. The VC thought he was an informant. He was tortured and killed."

Whose hands? thought Laura.

"Min blamed me," said Bardin. "I didn't even know yet what had happened to her brother, that night when I trusted her to give me sugar water. Instead, she gave me the full-strength drug. I didn't wake up for two days. I almost didn't wake up at all."

"You never told anyone," said Bea. She sounded as if she were choking.

"I couldn't undo what I'd done," he said. "I tried to make it up in other ways. It wasn't enough, I know."

"It's unforgivable," she said.

"After the driver was arrested, I was going to speak up," Bardin said. "I wouldn't have let an innocent man be punished. But then they let him go."

"He was innocent?" said Noi. They all looked over: no one had seen her come in. She was standing just inside the doorway, her face puckered with confusion. She asked Philip, "Somchit didn't take you?"

"No," said Philip. "Is that what people thought?"

Laura was surprised by the relief on Noi's face. But of course, she and the driver had worked in the same house, they might have been friends.

"I looked for Min, but she disappeared," Bardin told Philip. "I spent weeks looking for you on my own, long after the Bangkok police gave up. I turned the slums upside down, street by street, house by house."

"I was there," said Philip. A tremor passed through his voice: how close rescue had come, just yards away from where he had been in that buried, stifling room.

"I don't think there was a ransom," Laura said. She looked at Bea, who nodded in agreement. "If there had been a ransom, Mum and Dad would have paid it," she told Philip.

"They would have paid anything," said Bea. "That woman lied to you."

684

"I think I realized that after a while," said Philip.

"Then why didn't you ever contact us?" Laura asked Philip. "When they let you out on your own, why didn't you go to a policeman?"

Before Philip could answer, Bea spoke.

"Because you thought it was broken," she said. She was looking intently at Philip, who nodded. "It was already ruined and couldn't be fixed."

"I am desperately sorry," said Bardin. "I *tried* to do something good."

"You did do something good," said Philip. "At first. It just — turned into something else."

"How can you say that?" cried Laura. "Your whole life. You lost your whole life."

"No," said Philip. Firmly. "I've *had* a whole life. Just not the one I would have had."

"I trusted you," Beatrice told Bardin, her voice cracking.

"Hello, Mr. Bardin." The voice cut across the room; everyone turned. Genevieve stood tall in the doorway with Dustin and Dean beside her and Clem behind, holding the drone. "It's very kind of you to visit," she said. With exquisite, firm formality. "But I'm very sorry. It's just family today."

It was a quiet meal at the beginning, everyone separately burdened by what they'd heard, but Genevieve was in high spirits, drawing one person and then another into conversation, and gradually the atmosphere became more celebratory. The boys had made the birthday cake, four layers of white sponge filled with lemon curd and iced with meringue. They brought it into the dining room with great ceremony, holding the plate between them and walking in solemn step like acolytes.

"It's a shame your father isn't here," Genevieve said, after the birthday song and the three rounds of *hip hip hurrah,* and the candles blown out. Laura, who'd been watching Dean cut the cake, looked over, and saw that Genevieve was speaking to Philip. "You're so much like him. But you don't have those funny habits he had."

"I got over those," said Philip.

Bea and Laura shared a startled look — so Mum understood that the man beside her was her son, Philip. She'd forget again, no doubt, but in that moment she did know.

"Mum," said Laura, a thought popping into her mind. "However did you get the chocolate Easter rabbits all the way from Washington without them melting?"

"Diplomatic pouch," said Genevieve immediately, sliding her fork into her slice of cake, and Laura felt one more small mystery dissolve. Leaving hope for the others. Who knows, at some point she might understand the whole of her life, she thought. It seemed something to look forward to.

"The good china doesn't go into the dishwasher," announced Bea as the table was being cleared. "Just scrape and stack, and I'll get to it later."

"I'm tired of being waited on," said Philip. He turned to Laura. "You wash, I'll dry."

When they were alone in the kitchen, Laura asked Philip, "Why aren't you angrier? I would be angry. I *am* angry." She scrubbed a dish in silence for a minute. "They took a lifetime of having a brother from me." Feeling a tear slide along her nose and drop into the stream of rinsing water from the faucet. "We won't get those years back."

"No, we won't," he said. He took the dish from her, turned it round in the drying cloth. "My life hasn't been worthless, just because it wasn't the life I would have had. Longing for things to be different — Gerhard would have said that's the bottle. Not something we can control, or even touch or see." He set the dry plate onto the counter. "Dr. Gomez would call it a stuck point: *What if, what if.*" He smiled. "I like to think of the bees, working the flowers without a thought of past or future, doing the good thing that is right in front of them."

"But aren't you sorry?"

"I'll never not be sorry," he said.

After a sniffly pause, Laura said, "I'm horrible at meditation, by the way." He laughed, and after a moment she joined in. "Seriously. What am I supposed to see in that damned snow globe? If I ever even get that far."

"It's not about supposed to," he said. "You see what you see."

"Don't zen me," she said. "What do *you* see?"

"A Buddha," he said. "A small green Buddha. I've only seen it a few times."

"Did it *do* anything for you when you saw it? I mean, did you reach enlightenment, or Nirvana, or something?"

"It made me realize that it didn't matter what I saw," he said.

"Oh my God," said Laura. Laughter bubbling through her tears. "The Dalai Philip."

But she felt better. Calmer. She'd been living so long with an illusion, that they'd been whole and happy once, a perfect family shattered by tragedy. All her life mourning that loss. When instead they had been more like bits in a kaleidoscope, falling randomly to make small areas of beauty, falling apart again with the next twist, into a new disorder and a new beauty. Perhaps everyone was that way, living their lives out in the clung clump of color in which they found themselves, never seeing the bigger picture and how it all fit.

"So, this is kind of a happy ending," she

said, giving Philip the last dish to dry.

"What's happy?" said Philip. His face grave but his eyes dancing, looking very much like their father. "What's an ending?"

CHAPTER FIFTY-TWO

"My goodness," said the old lady on Laura's doorstep, leaning back. "This is a very tall house."

"Can I help you find someone?" said Laura.

"I think you might be the someone I am looking for," said the lady, bringing her eyes down again and scrutinizing Laura's face. "Laura Preston, yes? I knew your family in Bangkok." She stood with one hand on a walking stick. "You may not remember me. You were very young."

Something about the way she cocked her head, that wide smile as she spoke, ignited a memory.

"You told me not to learn how to make coffee," said Laura slowly. "In Bangkok, at one of my parents' parties."

"That's right," said the woman, her smile broadening further still. "I used to tell all little girls that." She leaned on her cane, put her other hand out; Laura took it. "I'm Marietta Schultz."

"Please come in," Laura said, opening the door wide. Mrs. Schultz crossed the threshold and went into the living room, settled on the sofa and accepted a glass of water.

"You might also remember me as the one with the househusband," she said, as Laura sat on the chair across from her. "In 1972! The ladies were abuzz. No?" A smile. "Oh, well. We always think we are more fascinating to others than we actually are." She sipped the water. "I saw a story in the newspaper about your brother. Is it really him?"

"Yes," said Laura.

"Amazing," said Mrs. Schultz, shaking her head. "I've thought about you all for years. How the time slips away. I meant to write to you after your father died. That was a terrible loss." Laura nodded. With studied care: "I'm not sure how much he told you about his work."

"Not much," said Laura. Something in her tone communicated itself, though, and Mrs. Schultz gave a tiny nod.

"I remember your brother too," said Mrs. Schultz. "A sweet little boy. Very like your father."

"They looked alike," agreed Laura.

"Your father and I only worked together for a short time in Bangkok, but I knew him for years after that. So, I knew him before and after." She drank a little more of the water. "I lost my husband this year."

691

"I'm sorry," said Laura.

"He was eighty-three. I'm eighty myself. I knew it couldn't last forever, but." She stopped herself there, took on a brisk tone. "Well. I've been having an urge to tidy things up." She pinioned Laura with her gaze. "Do you think it's possible for one event — one act — to change a person? I mean, a fundamental change."

"I don't know," said Laura. The old woman hadn't seemed batty at first, but then neither did Genevieve. Maybe she'd wandered off from caregivers. Should Laura call someone?

"Oh dear, I'm being cryptic," Mrs. Schultz said. She smiled. "Occupational hazard. I mean to say that I *don't* think a person can fundamentally change. I think whatever is brought out by trauma was in that person all along." She paused. "I'm talking about your father."

"I don't understand," said Laura.

"I don't think a lot of people knew him well," said Mrs. Schultz. "He was very contained. There weren't a lot of people to speak for him, at his funeral; but there should have been. He did some very important things." Her voice emphatic. Laura nodded. "I used to think he was too soft — too gentle a person — for our work. But as I said, he changed." She paused, then said, "Your father was a good man. I admired him. I wanted to tell you that."

"You wanted to tell me more," said Laura, guessing.

The old lady went still, as if listening to an echo, then put the water glass down.

"Yes," she said. "I did." Her worried eyes on Laura's. "I've gone back and forth about it."

"If you know something about my family, please tell it," Laura said. "We've kept far too many secrets, for far too long."

"It's not actually my story to tell." Mrs. Schultz reached into her pocket, withdrew an index card. "If you really want to know, he can tell you." As Laura's fingers closed on the card, Mrs. Schultz held on to it for a moment. "But be sure you want to know." Then she opened her fingers.

The card bore a name and address, in cursive script. The name was not familiar. "Who is this?" Laura asked.

"Someone from the past," said Mrs. Schultz. "I don't know what state his mind is in now. But he is alive, and that may not be true for long. So if you *do* want to know what he has to tell you, you should go as soon as you can." She put her hand on Laura's. It was nearly weightless, a sparrow settling briefly before alighting again. "And maybe don't go," she said. "It might be better to let things lie." She reached for her cane.

Laura said, "You know, I *was* asked to make coffee once."

Mrs. Schultz, poised to rise, sat back to listen.

"In college," said Laura. "A bunch of us had procrastinated our final projects; we had to work all night." She described it: about a dozen students gathered in the communal studio, bug-eyed on cigarettes and coffee, over the hours one and then another giving up and drifting away to their dorm rooms and sleep, until just five were left. All men except Laura, although she didn't realize that at first. It might have been three a.m. when she heard it: *Laura, can you make some more coffee?* A casual call across the room, from a student a year below her. Deep into her project, hands messy, not anywhere near the coffeepot, Laura had looked up to see a room of male faces turned toward her and felt a shock of surprise. It was 1984, they'd come a long way, baby, wasn't this the postfeminist era? The faces were impatient, their expressions saying *Men need coffee, get over there, woman, and make it.*

"And?" said Mrs. Schultz.

"I told them the truth: I never learned how." Laura shrugged. "They had to make it themselves."

The old woman laughed with delight.

The nursing home was in Mount Vernon, Virginia. A beautiful spot, a green view from every window of the building. Laura wondered how many of the residents were former federal employees; after all of the peregrinations, so many did come back here. No longer at home in their own hometowns and never having accepted *overseas* as more than temporary, they chose to retire near the government buildings that they had served from a distance, coming to final rest in another place they didn't truly belong.

The front-desk woman brightened when Laura read the name from Mrs. Schultz's index card.

"He never gets visitors," she said, rising to show Laura the way.

The old man sat alone in his room, in a chair by the window, gripping a newspaper folded to an acrostic puzzle in one hand, a stub of pencil in the other. How old was he, a hundred? He looked much older than Mrs. Schultz. The skin fell from his jawline in slack papery folds; a few strands of colorless hair struggled across his skull. After Laura introduced herself, his expression became wary.

"You're one of the daughters," he said. Laura nodded. "That was all a very long time ago. You should know better than to come asking about that."

"I don't," said Laura. "That's the point. I don't know anything."

"If you're thinking you'll have me arrested, good luck." He set the newspaper on the rolling tray table beside him, placed the pencil on top. "I'd never live to trial. I'm on palliative care now."

"I'm not seeking justice," said Laura, unsure what they were talking about. "I'm just trying to understand."

"It wasn't wrong," he said.

She looked around the room, spied a hard chair at a desk against the wall, retrieved it, set it in front of him, and sat. "What are we talking about?"

Maxwell Dawson stared at her for a full minute. His cheeks were chased with tiny rosy worms of capillary; above them his eyes were startlingly young-looking, a rich brown, heavily lashed. He tightened his jaw and she had a fleeting impression of lost physical prowess, an ancient panther.

"It wasn't wrong," he said again. "Although I've had cause to regret it."

"Regret what?" asked Laura, trying not to sound impatient.

He looked away from her, out the window, his hands quavering on his lap.

"That driver," he said. And now, as though the spat-out word had been a stopper holding back a fountain, the story flowed. "He was what used to be called a wolf. A playboy. Married, I think, but had a lot of girlfriends." He gave a rattling cough. "He told the police he was fighting with one of those girlfriends while the boy —" he looked at Laura. "Your

696

brother." She nodded. "Was still in his martial-arts class. And then after the fight he'd driven the car away in a drunken tantrum. Not to collect the boy, but out to the country. He said that once he sobered up he was afraid of getting into trouble about the car, so he hid out in a village for a few days. He said he had no idea about the missing boy until he went back to face the music." The long speech had taxed him; his voice was thinned, nearly soundless by the end. He rested, panting.

While he got his breath back, Laura waited politely, looking around the room. It was a spare place to end one's life — no photographs, no pictures on the walls, no personal touches at all, save for a small shelf of knickknacks and a crowd of amber pill bottles at the bedside.

"The girlfriend went to the police and told them almost exactly the same story," said Dawson. He lifted a finger. "*Almost* exactly. Still the drinking, still the fight and the driving off in a huff. The only difference between their stories was the time. He said it happened at three p.m., she said at five." Seeing that Laura didn't understand, he explained. "It was a crucial difference. The boy was taken between four and six. Impossible for the driver to have done it, if he was fighting with his girlfriend at five o'clock."

"If he was drunk," said Laura, amazed at

the man's recall of the details of the long-ago case, "maybe he remembered the time wrong when he was interviewed later."

"Exactly what the police decided," said Mr. Dawson with scorn. "And they let him go. On the strength of his girlfriend's testimony? I don't think so." A half minute for a chest-rattling cough, after which he spat into a tissue, folded it with tremorous hands. "I think they wanted to blame the boy's disappearance on farang parental neglect, and not on a kidnapping by a Thai. They might even have told the girl to lie, and what to say." Another long, wet coughing spell. "I never understood what your mother saw in him."

"Who?" said Laura. "The *driver*?"

"Your father," said Dawson, dabbing his lip with the folded tissue. "She indulged him like a little boy. But the day the police released the driver, she took the kid gloves off." He chuckled. "She dressed him down savagely, told him to *be a man*. He was beside himself."

"How do you know that?" Laura challenged. Irritated by the chuckle, nonplussed by this picture of her parents. Stolid, serious Robert a milquetoast? Dignified Genevieve haranguing him like a fishwife?

"He told me. When he came to me, to ask for my help." He stopped there.

"Your help," said Laura after the silence had stretched out. "What did you do?" Recalling Mrs. Schultz's voice, *It might be bet-*

ter to let things lie.

"I helped him," said Dawson. Darting his eyes at Laura, "Are you sure you want to know this?" Prickles had started along Laura's arms, but she nodded. "We went together and found the driver," he said. "We took him to a place I knew about, and got the truth out of him." He cleared his throat. "I was willing to do it, but your father wanted to," he said. "He was like a man possessed. I'll never forget it. Blow after blow after blow, regularly spaced, like a metronome." With grudging admiration, "He kept going even after his hands broke open and he was bleeding as much as the driver."

Her father had had bandages once in Bangkok, Laura remembered, wound all around his hands like a mummy. They hadn't been remarked upon or explained. She could recall him at the breakfast table, spooning papaya with his mummy hands.

"The driver first tried to change the story back, to the original timeline," said Dawson. He shook his head. "I don't know why he thought that would help." He wasn't looking at Laura anymore; his eyes were on his own hands, where they lay together on his lap. "When he finally confessed, he could barely speak. His tongue was like a wet lump of meat in his mouth, and we were stepping on his teeth, rolling all over the floor." He sounded almost nostalgic.

"The driver confessed?" said Laura. "To what?"

Dawson looked up, as if surprised to see her there. "To taking the boy, of course," he said. "He sold him to a middleman, who sold him to a farang pimp. He wasn't sure where the pimp took him. He couldn't give us names." His lips a bitter line. "When it was clear that he could tell us no more, your father finished it. Even though he'd promised him mercy." A skittering wheeze that was possibly a laugh. "That was a promise no one should have believed. Not from a man who'd just heard that story about his son." He ran his tongue around his dry lips, looked at the glass of water sitting on the rolling tray.

"What do you mean — finished it?" said Laura.

"Your father crushed the driver's windpipe," Dawson said. "It took a very long time." He succumbed to another bout of coughing.

Laura felt hot all over.

"But the driver was innocent," Laura said. Her voice sounded far away in her own head. "He didn't have anything to do with it."

Dawson, still coughing, waved his hand toward the water glass. Laura took it up and held it for him, positioning the straw. He leaned forward and took a long pull, then released the straw, panting. He looked up at Laura. "You're the younger sister?" he said.

She nodded. "The driver planned to take you, originally."

"What?" Laura couldn't process what he was saying.

"He confessed to that part right away." He waved again for the water; she brought the straw to his lips and he suckled and released, then sat back. "He said he drove the two sisters to dance classes every week, and he had a plan. He was waiting for one of you to be sick one day and stay home. He said the older one was prettier, but she was mouthy, and would have put up a fight. So he was waiting to get you alone. He knew it would happen eventually: farang were always getting sick. He said he was *waiting for his luck.*" He cleared his throat. "But it never happened: you were always together."

Laura felt a coldness wash over her. Was it true? She remembered bouncing in the back seat in her leotard, putting her legs out straight to admire her pink tights and pink shoes, beside an irritated Beatrice. Beatrice always there, protecting her little sister without even knowing it.

Laura put the glass back on the tray. "Mr. Dawson," she said. Very slowly, looking into his face. "Philip has come home. He told us what did happen to him. The driver had nothing to do with it."

Dawson's eyebrows rose, lifting the hooding flesh away from his eyes.

"He's come home?" he said. "Impossible."

"He's home," she said. "And the driver *didn't* take him, or sell him to anyone. None of that happened."

For a moment, she could see doubt in his eyes, before his expression hardened into truculence. "Someone has sold you a bill of goods," he said. He stabbed a shaking index finger into his palm for each of the next three words. *"I was there."* His lips a bluish stubborn line. "We did what had to be done."

She realized that nothing she could say would undermine the story he'd told himself for nearly half a century, about honor and vigilante justice. Philip could stand in front of Dawson like the resurrected Jesus and tell him the truth, and Dawson would turn his face away.

"Ask your mother about it," said Dawson.

"What?" said Laura.

"She knew what happened. She knew all of it. Your father told her." With contempt. "He burdened her with that knowledge. And still she chose him. That's the only part I do regret. How I gave him to her like a present." His sigh caught, turned into a cough. He ripped another tissue from the box at his elbow; Laura looked away while he coughed and spat. The knickknacks on the bookshelf were obviously mementos: a small framed pen-and-ink drawing, a glossy conch shell, a light-green ceramic pitcher. The last, she saw, had been broken at some point, and mended with bright gold. It made a beautiful design, actually, forking around the side of the object like lightning.

"Your father never gave up looking," said Dawson when he was done coughing. He folded and smoothed the tissue in his hand. "He believed that your brother had never left Bangkok. When satellite surveillance was in its testing stage, I sent over duplicates of every image. He had the clearance to see them, of course, but it was — outside proto-col." He was looking out the window at the green of lawn cut by white paths, the empty blue sky overhead. "We weren't friends," he said. "It wasn't friendship that bound us."

He didn't speak for a long time, and it seemed to Laura that he had fallen asleep. But as she got up to leave, he turned his ruined-panther face to her.

"Does your mother ever speak of me?" he asked. Sounding almost shy.

"No," said Laura. "She never has." Feeling the cruelty of the next words as she delivered them. "I don't think she remembers you now."

After all this time, here it was: a piece of the deepest truth. Their father was a murderer, their mother a conspirator. The terrible thing he'd done, the thing she'd driven him to do. Had they believed that justice had been meted out? However they had seen it, the act had taken them over a line. They'd never forgiven themselves, or each other. Maxwell Dawson had told at least one person, Mrs. Schultz (had he actually bragged about it to her, Laura wondered?), but Robert and Genevieve had never tried to relieve themselves of the burden of the secret. *The girls must never know.* The parents had carried it, together — and apart.

There was traffic on the return drive; when the car dropped Laura in front of the Tudor, she was late for family dinner. Night was draping indigo shadows beneath the high gutters of the house; crosshatched light came through the diamond-mullioned panel above the front door. That same front door she'd opened and shut a thousand times as a teenager and young adult, coming and going alone from an empty house. It had seemed like a lifeless shell then, around a broken family. She had never stood outside in the gloaming like this, seen it inhabited and alive.

Movement against the gauzy glow of the curtained living room bay window. They would all be in there, scattered between the sitting room and the living room and the kitchen, the twins and Clem and Bea and Genevieve, Noi and maybe one or more of her daughters. The boys had been trying to learn Thai, using apps on their phones, Noi laughingly correcting them. Bea and Philip would most likely be bent over the new garden plan, scrolled out on the coffee table in front of Genevieve. The three of them had been fussing at it for months, tweaking and retweaking the layout in preparation for the beehives that had been ordered. Philip was threatening to do some of the planting himself when the spring came. He had recovered as well as his doctors had predicted; Laura had taken charge of his meds and getting him to his follow-up appointments. To her surprise, Bea hadn't seemed to mind sharing the bossy-sister role. Beatrice had a new fragility about her, still healing from the betrayal of Todd Bardin. Whom she no longer called Uncle, whom she never mentioned at all.

Edward's sedan was at the curb, in front of the crossover. He and Laura had talked more, agreed to kick the marriage question down the road while Laura worked on her new series, slated to show in Sullivan's New York space in the spring. After that, if they both decided to marry, Edward would put his house on the market and move into Laura's. It had been his suggestion. He did have some conditions — a real TV, some comfortable furniture — to which she'd agreed.

Up until that minute, Laura would have argued that secrets always needed to be told, that they brought enlightenment or granted redemption or delivered justice. Keeping secrets had driven her family apart. But the secret Laura carried now was of a different kind. Robert was a murderer, Genevieve guilty of conspiracy and, if Laura had read Maxwell Dawson's intimations correctly, also adultery. Laura remembered what Mrs. Schultz had said. *Your father was a good man.* Was it possible for a person to be truly good, who had done a horrible thing? A question that might be debated forever. There was no possibility of justice for the driver now; Robert was dead already, and Dawson would be dead soon. The knowledge about what they'd done would bring nothing but harm. It was a secret capable only of destruction, one that needed to be kept, to be folded into one generation of a family and not passed down. Standing there on the pavement, Laura decided: she would say nothing about it to anyone.

She walked up the path toward her family. Imperfect and damaged and hopeful. A work in progress, like everything.

That night when Laura meditated, for the first time she succeeded in drawing both lines and saw, at the point of their crossing, a hovering wintry-white globe. She watched as the fog within it settled, revealing a figure: her brother Philip as he was on a long-ago, lost day.

Towheaded and squinting, he stands on the

brink of his complicated future, poised just at the open mouth of the vortex. But not tumbling. Not about to fall inside and take them all with him. Instead, there he is, perfectly in balance, eternally safe.

ACKNOWLEDGMENTS

Every book is a conspiracy; consequently, there are many people to thank (or blame!) for perpetrating this one. First, the wonderful Peter Borland, for loving this story as much as you do, and for your steady kindness and care in helping to bring it forth. Thanks also to publisher Libby McGuire and associate publisher Suzanne Donahue for enthusiastic support, and to Dana Trocker, Kristin Fassler, Gena Lanzi, Maudee Genao, Paige Lytle, Sean Delone, and the rest of the Atria team. I am grateful to Wendy Sheanin at Simon & Schuster for going above and beyond, and I offer profuse, humiliated thanks to my copy editor, Laura Cherkas, and production editor, Liz Byer, for perceptive and meticulous work.

I owe everything to my literary agent, Laura Gross, who is simply the best person on the earth. Thanks for your patience with me while I went off to be a doctor, and thanks for welcoming me back. I am so lucky that our paths crossed thirty-*cough-cough* years ago.

Huge appreciation to early readers Danielle Teller and Emily Scott, who saw the book in its struggling phases and were helpful in deep and multiple ways. Thanks also to Carla Buckley, who did double duty for this book: as an author providing wise and generous counsel on the art of writing, and as a sister understanding how a story can carry a flavor of truth about a family, while not resorting to actual fact.

Thanks to the Murrays, Narisara and Sarawan and Charles, for your gracious and brilliant guidance, and to Rasee Govindani and Sarah Rooney for assistance with translation and transliteration. Also to Suchart Milsted and Jerry Milsted, and Gerald Fauss and Marghi Fauss, and the myriad others who will know what I got wrong, may detect what geographical bits I scrambled slightly in service of story, and who will — I hope! — forgive me. I am also indebted to many, many primary sources, strangers to me, who shared online: their oral histories and memories and video footage refreshed and bolstered my childhood memories of old Bangkok.

I am so grateful to the book community, the independent bookstores and all the delightful, generous people who dedicate themselves to reviewing and promoting books. Your work means more than you know. Shout-outs in particular to Kristy Barrett and

Tonni Callan of A Novel Bee on Facebook, and also to book bloggers Fictionophile and The Librarian in Me; your kind words about my previous book buoyed me up while I wrote this one.

For their relentless encouragement I thank Annalee Harkins, Elizabeth Branch, Pamela Friedman, Mary Huey, Natalie Wolcott Williams, Bilyana Petrova, Kaoru Murata, Spike Lampros, Alyson Denny, Eric Friedland, Ilse Jenouri, Gus Kletzien, Stanley Chin, Sue Cash, Anna Murray, Kate Matthews, Phyllis Sidorsky, Catherine O'Neill Grace, George Chen, Marcy Day, Rick Matthews, Cheryl Graves, Len Seamon, Jocelyn Buckley, Jillian Buckley, Tim Buckley, Jonathon Buckley, Becky Hutchinson, Denise Gerade Schwarz, Richard Bausch, and Bobby Rogers. I also want to thank you who are reading this, for the precious gift of your attention. I do hope you enjoyed the book.

I must note here that my family loved our time in Bangkok; I hope that this work of fiction doesn't suggest otherwise. Any perceived insult to Thailand, the Thai Royal Family, or the people of Thailand would be wholly unintended and a product of my own clumsiness. I offer apologies for any blunders, and deep gratitude for your indulgence.

I am enormously thankful to my sister, Carla, and brother, Harley — for this is a sibling story, no matter how fictional, and I hope they will see what is true here and what is not, and remember with me.

ABOUT THE AUTHOR

Liese O'Halloran Schwarz, a former emergency medicine doctor, published her first novel, *Near Canaan,* while still in medical school. She is also the author of the acclaimed novel *The Possible World* and *What Could Be Saved.* She currently lives in Chapel Hill, North Carolina.